GAMES

Washington, DC, and was formerly the BBC's China Correspondent. He has reported on assignment from Iraq, Afghanistan, Pakistan, North Korea, Mongolia and many other countries. His debut novel, *Night Heron*, was nominated for the 2014 CWA John Creasey Dagger and appeared on best of the year lists in the *TLS*, *Kirkus* and NPR.

Praise for **SPY GAMES**:

'Brookes knows modern China, he seemingly knows the British secret service and, most importantly, he knows how to tell a good story. The splendid result is this rich, can't-put-it-down thriller. A terrific read' Joseph Kanon, author of *The Good German* and *Leaving Berlin*

'This expertly orchestrated novel couldn't be more topical . . . exhilaratingly shows how readily the old-school international spy thriller can be retooled for the era of globalisation, the internet and a superpower's emergence' *Sunday Times*

'A natural storyteller and a thrilling new voice' *Sunday Herald*

'Brookes' second novel is a multipronged spy thriller that fires on all cylinders. A smarter or more exciting mystery likely won't be released this year' *Kirkus* (starred review)

'Brookes has separated himself from the pack: I've read a lot of very good China books by excellent journalists, but I've never before stayed up far too late on a work night to finish one, unwilling to go to sleep until I knew how it ended' *Los Angeles Review of Books*

Also by Adam Brookes

Night Heron

ADAM BROOKES

SPY GAMES

sphere

SPHERE

First published in Great Britain in 2015 by Sphere
This paperback edition published in 2016 by Sphere

1 3 5 7 9 10 8 6 4 2

A CIP catalogue record for this book
is available from the British Library.

ISBN 978-0-7515-5253-9

Typeset in Simoncini Garamond by M Rules
Printed and bound in Great Britain by
Clays Ltd, St Ives plc

Papers used by Sphere are from well-managed forests
and other responsible sources.

MIX
Paper from
responsible sources
FSC® C104740

Sphere
An imprint of
Little, Brown Book Group
Carmelite House
50 Victoria Embankment
London EC4Y 0DZ

An Hachette UK Company
www.hachette.co.uk

www.littlebrown.co.uk

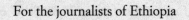
For the journalists of Ethiopia

The British Empire is supposed to have more or less disappeared by the 1960s. This is incorrect. The formal British Empire may have collapsed, but the British-led offshore world is alive and kicking ... Formalities aside, we should treat the City of London, Jersey, Cayman Islands, BVI, Bermuda and the rest of the territories as one integrated global financial centre that serves as the world's largest tax haven and a conduit for money laundering.

Ronen Palan, Richard Murphy and Christian Chavagneux,
Tax Havens: How Globalization Really Works

PROLOGUE

Winter, 1967. Beijing

They had taken a leather belt, bound his wrists behind his back, forced him to kneel.

In the hall, the smell of damp, of unwashed and stale clothing. The muttering of the crowd. Rain drumming on the roof. A cold rain.

They hung a chalkboard on a chain around his neck. On the chalkboard they wrote the character for his surname, Fan. They chalked an X across the character to negate everything he had been. They began to shout and scream slogans. He saw the vapour from their breath billow and rise on the air.

Tell us the names of your conspirators.

Conspirators.

You have conspired. Tell us their names.

He forced his head up, looked out from the stage. How many of them here? A hundred? Two hundred? Some of them screamed their hatred of him. Others seemed bewildered, looked around themselves, mouthed the slogans. He tried to catch the eye of those he knew, but they looked away, all of them.

You conspired to subvert the revolution. You fought in the Nationalist army of the traitor Chiang Kai-shek. You favour the capitalist road. Name your conspirators.

They jerked him to his feet. One of them brought a bucket, overturned it to shower broken glass on the stage, shattered beer bottles, pickle jars. A momentary silence from the crowd. One of them arranged the glass into a pile with his foot, the *chink chink* sound of the fragments. They made him kneel on it.

Who can I give them? he thought.

The man Chen, who fought with you in the traitorous Nationalist army. Is he a conspirator? Name him!

Can I give them Chen? That gentle boy, toting his books in his knapsack, prattling about Lu Xun and Voltaire? We called him Chen Wen, Literary Chen.

He thought of the two of them on a freezing hillside, thirty years earlier, whispering in the dark, siphoning petrol into bottles, the clank and rumble of Japanese armour in the valley. He thought of the boy, blowing on his fingers, tearing the *mantou* into pieces to share, the bread cold and glutinous in his mouth.

The pain, now. The blood leaking through his trousers. They yanked his bound wrists upward behind him, bent him double, forced his weight forward, onto his knees, onto the shards of glass.

He gave them Literary Chen.

They became frenzied. He wondered what they would do to his old friend. He wondered if Chen would ever know, and if he did, whether he'd ever understand.

He wondered how long this sin would endure, imagined future generations scrabbling and clawing at it like dogs at a dry, jagged bone.

One of them tied a blindfold on him, and he saw nothing as he was led away.

PART ONE

The Approach.

1

Hong Kong
The recent past

She moves well, thought the watcher.

She moves so that her size seems to diminish. She conceals her strength. She flits by a wall, a storefront, and she is gone before you give her a second glance. You don't notice her, he thought.

You don't notice how dangerous she is.

The wind was quickening, the sky the colour of slate. The woman was well ahead of him now, making for the park's lurid front gate. The watcher quickened his pace, reeling himself in.

She wore a scarf of beige linen that covered her hair and left her face in shadow. She wore a loose shirt and trousers in dull colours, and sensible shoes. From a distance, her silhouette was that of a woman from the Malay Peninsula or Indonesia, one of Hong Kong's faceless migrants, a domestic, a housekeeper on her day off, perhaps. So, a trip to Ocean Park, for the aquarium, candy floss, a roller-coaster. A treat! Even on this bleak day, with a typhoon churning in from the South China Sea. The woman hid her eyes behind sun-glasses. Her skin was very dark.

3

She made for the ticket booth. The watcher stopped and searched passers-by for an anomaly, the flicker of intention that, to his eye, would betray the presence of hostile surveillance.

Nothing.

He reached into his pocket and clicked Send.

'Amber, amber,' he said. Proceed. You're clean.

Patterson heard the signal, sudden and sharp in her earpiece. She responded with a double click. Understood.

She ran her hand over her headscarf, tugged it forward a little, eased her face further into its recesses. She walked to the window, turned her face down.

'One, please,' she said.

The girl at the ticket counter looked at her, confused.

'Typhoon coming,' she said. She pointed at a sign taped to the glass. It read: 'Typhoon Signal Number 3 Is Hoisted'.

'Yes, I know,' said Patterson.

The girl raised her eyebrows, then looked to her screen and tapped. Patterson paid in cash, turned and walked to the turnstiles.

She took the famous cable car up the headland, hundreds of feet above the rocks and crashing surf, sitting alone in a tiny car that bucked and jittered in the wind. Unnerved, she gripped the bars, looked out at a venomous green sea and watched the freighters fading in the gloom.

Another two hours of this at least, she thought. More. Surveillance detection runs are sent by the intelligence gods to try the soul. Dogging her steps since morning was the wiry little man with the baseball cap and wispy goatee, his speech incised with the clipped sing-song of the Pearl River delta – her street artist, her watcher. They had come together through Kowloon on foot, then taken the Star Ferry across the heaving waters of Hong Kong harbour. She'd walked the deck while he scanned the eyes of the passengers. More footwork, then a bus. He sat near the door, monitoring the comings and goings.

Amber, amber. His voice thin in her ear, distant, yet intimate.

Proceed.

The cable car slowed, deposited her on a platform. The watcher was there ahead of her. How had he managed that? He sat on a bench smoking a cigarette, looking at a map of Ocean Park's recreational delights. She walked on, past the Sea Jelly Spectacular, the Rainforest Exhibit. The watcher inscribed wide arcs around her as the wind hissed in the palm trees. After this there would be another bus to take them through the Aberdeen Tunnel, followed by a taxi, then more pavement work in the rain, hour after dreary hour of it until the watchers pronounced her utterly, definitively, conclusively clean.

For this was China, where the streets were so saturated with surveillance that agent and case officer moved with the caution of divers in some deep sea, silent, swimming slowly towards each other in the dark.

The agent's distress signal had come in to London at 2.47 a.m. on a Tuesday: an email from an innocuous address purporting to be an enquiry concerning the sale of a second-hand book. I am in jeopardy, it said. I request a crash meeting. But the Hong Kong station of the UK Secret Intelligence Service, the officers of which usually handled this particular agent's needs, offered a tepid apology and declined. Too difficult, they said. Too much Chinese surveillance of the consulate building on Supreme Court Road where the station resided. Too few officers. Nothing to be done. Sorry, and good afternoon.

So it fell to Patterson, who was dragged from sleep and isolation in her north London flat by the juddering of her secure handheld. She had dressed quickly in the darkness, opened a small safe in her wardrobe, checked a pre-prepared list of clothing and accoutrements. She crept down the stairs and slipped from the house by the back. It was May and the night air was cool and damp, washed with fragrance from gardens and window-boxes. Two streets away, a car waited for her.

In the SIS headquarters building at Vauxhall Cross, or VX as they called it, Patterson drew documents that underpinned a useful, current and very familiar identity: passport, business cards, pocket litter, a wallet handed to her in a yellow envelope by a nervous, tired boy from the second floor. She was an accountant, one with regular business in Hong Kong, backstopped by an association with a local company long friendly to the Service. Maria Todd. Hello, Maria.

The car drove at speed to Heathrow. In the ladies' lavatory, she checked her pockets one last time. And then again. She consumed a bacon sandwich and a coffee at a loathsome faux pub in Departures, and boarded the long flight to Hong Kong.

'Amber, amber,' said the watcher.

She crossed the street, the traffic sparse now as the typhoon bore down, the rain clattering on the pavement. A stairway led her into an MTR metro station, and on into a damp underground shopping precinct, garishly lit corridors of sunglasses, shoes, magazines, sullen shop girls staring at their phones. And there, a bank of elevators, their steel doors scratched and greasy. Up, to the fifteenth floor of a vast apartment complex above and a preliminary pass of the door to apartment 1527. No cameras here, she'd been assured, but might something have changed? She moved quickly along a claustrophobic corridor of neon and linoleum, passed the flat, walked on.

Around her the background noise of cramped humanity. A television. A crying child. A smell of sesame and cooking fat was cloying on the humid air.

She stopped and walked back. The key turned and she was in. The safe flat appeared to be inhabited, though no one was here now. Patterson closed the door quietly, pulled the scarf from her head and went from room to room. A living room with a sofa in peeling green vinyl, a television, dusty surfaces. Kitchen, the remnants of a breakfast, congee with shredded chicken, tea. A bedroom with a futon, a pink duvet lying askew, blinds down. A bathroom, a woman's underwear hanging limp on a rack, a frosted glass window. Hair in the sink. The flat smelled of sleep, unwashed laundry.

Who lives here? she wondered. An officer? An access agent?

Well, she's a bloody *slob*.

Patterson stopped, took a breath, steadied herself.

In the army there would have been two of them, steadying each other. One to debrief the agent, the other hanging back, listening, maintaining situational awareness.

But the Service sent you in alone.

Two's insecure, said the trainers. Oh, and in the army she would have had enough weaponry concealed about her person to destroy half a city block should the need arise. But weapons are insecure, said the trainers. So she carried a device that looked like a pen, which when activated would administer to an assailant an electric shock, one barely sufficient, Patterson reckoned, to knock out an apathetic hamster. Would she get used to it, this naked feeling, this solitude? The Service valued those who worked well alone. She had yet to show she was among their number.

She put her hand in her trouser pocket and clicked Send.

'Tricycle, tricycle,' she said. I am at the rendezvous.

A double click came back.

She sat and went over the agent's record in her mind. Codename CAMBER. Fifty-eight years of age. Keung, his name. Dr Keung was how he liked it; he had a Ph.D. in econometrics from an Australian university. Patterson had looked up the term econometrics.

For years, under British rule, the doctor had toiled in the colonial government's finance department, but when the colony was blithely handed to China in 1997, Dr Keung had taken his leave of government and joined a bank. A very quiet, very wealthy, very privately owned bank. Dr Keung assisted in managing the bank's government relations. To his surprise, he found himself courted by officials of the Chinese Communist Party. The officials appeared anxious to placate and reassure the inhabitants of their new, wealthy, stroppy possession in the south. Dr Keung found himself on trips to Beijing. He attended private dinners at the State Guest House, held confidential conversations with men whose names were unfamiliar.

Dr Keung came to know the men with unfamiliar names. He came to know their needs. Dr Keung came to know a lot.

And Dr Keung discovered a further, equally surprising side to this new life. He found that, if he were occasionally to assist in some delicate task, as a favour to some senior Beijing official, or their son or daughter – help with an overseas account, say, in London or New York or the Caymans, or the quiet management of some funds, transfers for school fees or a new property abroad – he was rewarded. A nice watch. An expensive restaurant. Dr Keung, you must come to Macau with us! A suite at the Lisboa! We insist! Dr Keung had not previously experienced such things, but he surprised himself by the speed at which he developed a taste for them. He discovered the casino floor, the sauna, the 'little friend' waiting sleek and pouting and perfumed in the air-conditioned blankness of the hotel room.

To Patterson, the rest of the story read like one of the case histories from her Intelligence Officer New Entry Course, a study in execrable choices and male idiocy. The doctor had got in a little deep at the tables. The little friends had become a little too demanding. The requests from Beijing kept coming, and seemed to grow less polite with each passing year. His wife divorced him. His children left for Canada.

And just as Dr Keung sweated at the edge of ruin, the Service stepped in, pulled him back from the brink of disgrace, covered some debts and warned off some little friends. And in return, well, some favours for his erstwhile masters in Her Majesty's Government.

To the Service's surprise, Dr Keung responded with enthusiasm. He began providing regular – if dull – intelligence on Hong Kong's finance and economics. And he provided occasional – and very interesting indeed – intelligence on the quiet doings of China's power elite with regard to their bank accounts, intelligence that provided a view of rifts and points of vulnerability in China's ruling class, the sort of intelligence the Service prided itself on, the sort that satisfied its predatory instincts.

Dr Keung spied for seven years without incident, retaining his position in society, and in the casinos and saunas of Macau. A succession of case officers reported him businesslike, methodical and, very occasionally, brave.

All of which, Patterson reflected as the doctor stood dripping in the doorway of the safe flat, made the expression of near-hysterical panic on his face so surprising.

She reached into her pocket and clicked Send three times, then twice more. The meeting is underway.

'Amber, amber,' came the voice.

She ushered him into the flat, moving to take his coat. He pulled away from her.

'Who are you?' he said. 'Where's ... where is he?'

He stood with his back to the wall. His eyes searched the room behind her.

'It's just me here,' she said.

She gestured for him to sit. Let him settle, she thought. He sat on the green sofa and took off his coat. His hands were trembling.

'I don't know you,' he said.

'Your usual contact was unable to come to this meeting, so I have come. It's safer this way. Much safer.'

His eyes rested on her, uncomprehending.

'Where have you come from?' he said.

'Best I don't tell you that.'

'Why do they send ... you?'

Me, she thought, why not me? She smiled at him, this trembling little man, hair plastered to his scalp, an ageing child with a suit that wrinkled and pooled on his sparse frame, his pouchy cheeks.

'Dr Keung, I know your case very well. I have been a great admirer of your work for a long time.' She paused to look at him in a way she hoped was reassuring. He shrank back slightly on the sofa.

'Now, first let me ask you: do you think you are under surveillance now? Right now?'

'I ... I don't know. That's why I need to meet ... I ...'

'All right. Listen to me, Dr Keung. If this meeting is interrupted, you will leave first. You will turn right out of the front door of the apartment and walk to the elevators on the west side of the building. There's a big sign. It says, "West Elevators". Do you understand?'

He nodded, his mouth slightly open.

'We will be with you, watching your back. You will take the lift down to the second floor, then the staircase down to the MTR station.'

His face was creasing.

'You will board a train to Admiralty.'

He was waving his hand in the air, looking down.

'Stop. Listen . . . please.'

'Dr Keung, I will listen to everything you have to say, and we will resolve this situation. But first we must discuss emergency procedures and fallbacks. Just as normal.' She could feel herself starting to speak fast. She slowed, tried to take the urgency from her voice. 'Let's just—'

'Stop!' he shouted. 'You can't! You don't know!'

Patterson swallowed. This was not supposed to happen – the spindly, diminutive agent yelling at her, the encounter spiralling out of her control. She took a breath. In case of panicking and non-compliant agents, said the trainers, bring a sense of reassurance and calm. Take their fears seriously. Suggest that the full resources of the Service are being brought to bear on their case.

But never lose control of the meeting.

He had his head in his hands.

'Dr Keung, we *will* resolve this situation and ensure you are safe. Is that clear? Now, as long as you understand the emergency procedures, let us move forward.'

Let us *move forward*? For Christ's sake. She licked her lips.

'They know,' he said. He made a chopping motion in the air with his hand. 'They know, they know, they know. Move forward with *that*.'

She waited a beat, heard the wind pounding against the windows.

'Who knows and what do they know?'

'They know. They came.'

'Please start at the beginning. Tell me.'

'They came to my apartment two days ago. In the morning.'

'Did they identify themselves? How many of them? What did they look like?'

'No, no identification. They just expect me to know. Three of them.'

'Mainlanders?'

'Mainlanders. From the north. Beijing, maybe. The one who spoke, anyway.'

'How could you tell?'

'What do you mean, how could I tell?' He looked at her, wild-eyed. 'Because he spoke Mandarin! With that accent they have. And that tone. So polite. So ... threatening.' He put a shaking hand to his forehead.

'And what did they look like? What were they wearing?'

'What were they wearing?' He looked at her with incredulity. He was clenching and unclenching his fists.

Patterson cleared her throat, put her hand in front of her mouth for a moment.

'Well, would you say they looked like military men, for example? Or something else?'

He stood up, raised his hands in a gesture of despair. He leaned towards her, shouted at her.

'I tell you! They know. Why do you just sit there? Fuck!' The obscenity sounded incongruous, unfamiliar, as if he hadn't used it before.

'Tell me exactly what they said.'

He started to pace.

'You get me out of here first. Then I'll tell you everything.'

'I beg your pardon?' said Patterson.

'Get me out.'

'Dr Keung, we may not have much time. Tell me what they said. Now.'

He stopped, pinched his forehead with one hand.

'He said, the northern one, that they wanted me to do a job. That I should use my "contacts". My *guanxi*. He had this smirk.'

Patterson was silent, waited for more.

'He said they had a message.'

'A message? For who?'

'For you, who the fuck do you think!'

'Did he actually say it was for us? Explicitly?'

'No, of course not. He just said it was for my *guanxi*.'

'Well . . .'

'No. No "well".' He jabbed his finger at her. 'You get me the fuck out of here. I am blown, and I am not going back and you owe me, whatever the fuck your name is.' He was warming to his obscenities now, thrusting his despair and anger at her.

'What message?' she said.

'They said I had to go to meet someone, okay? Some big wheel guy. He'd give the message.'

But Patterson wasn't listening.

Because in her earpiece was a voice as close as a lover's, saying, 'Magazine. Magazine. Magazine. Acknowledge.'

She sent nothing, waiting for confirmation.

'Magazine. Magazine. Magazine. Acknowledge.'

Abort. The meeting is compromised. Abort.

2

First, say the trainers, choose your attitude. Choose calm, clear-headedness, optimism. Do not rush your movements. Rushing will make you immediately conspicuous. Move at the pace of those around you, or more slowly. Do not become visibly vigilant. When you are compromised in a denied area, resoluteness and a good cover story are your friends.

All the pabulum of training revolved slowly in her mind like detritus around a plug hole.

Just give it a minute, she thought. In a minute, the instinct will kick in. The rush of cold clarity will come. It will come. It will come to the soldier in me.

Patterson stood up.

'I'm afraid we have to end this meeting,' she said, with a regretful smile.

Dr Keung turned and faced her, panic flaring in his eyes.

'What? Why?'

'Our people tell me it's for the best. Now, you remember the procedures?'

She gestured towards the door. His eyes followed. He looked at the door and then back at her.

'We will be in touch. Try not to worry. We will meet again very soon and we will resolve this situation.'

He didn't move.

'Dr Keung, we need to go now.'

'They're here, aren't they?'

'Follow the procedures. Someone is waiting for you. They will ensure you get away cleanly.'

'Oh, Christ.'

She opened the door and looked quickly both ways down the corridor.

'Dr Keung. Go.' She held his damp coat for him.

The spirit seemed to go out of him. His shoulders slumped, his hands hanging at his sides.

'Dr Keung.'

He walked listlessly to her, took the coat. He walked out of the door. He didn't speak to her or look at her again as he headed down the corridor.

Patterson wrapped the scarf tight around her hair, put the sunglasses back on, clicked Send.

'Sitrep,' she said.

A single click came back. Maintain silence.

Her own egress procedure called for a complicated weave through the apartment block, cutting across the width of the building from stairwell to stairwell, taking a street-level exit through a fire door, where a watcher would pick her up. She walked through a labyrinth of corridors, slowing herself, keeping it natural. She clattered down the concrete stairwells. It took her nearly eight minutes to get to street level – where the fire door she was supposed to use was locked, a padlocked chain linking the crash bars.

A good officer expects such things.

She put her ear to the door, heard the thump of the wind, the rain spattering the concrete.

A good officer anticipates that the door will be chained shut, or the road will be blocked by construction or the electricity will go out at precisely the moment the operation reaches its climax.

She swore.

She checked the time. The watchers should have picked up the doctor by now. They would be on the MTR train with him, seeing him to safety.

Why the panic? she wondered. What had the watchers seen? Who?

She turned and made her way onwards through the dim corridors, looking for another exit to the street, finding none.

A figure was coming towards her. She heard the footsteps on the linoleum. She turned her face down and walked on. A man, carrying something. A phone? He was short, of Chinese appearance, with a wrestler's sloping shoulders, thick fingers. He wore a T-shirt and running shoes. He had stopped, was watching her. She kept walking. He stood to one side, let her pass, said nothing.

Lifts.

The man was standing stock still some twenty feet behind her in the corridor. She could sense more than see him.

Patterson pushed the lift call button.

She waited, every sense strung taut. The lift pinged and the doors slid open. It was empty. She stepped in, pressing the button marked 'Basement 2' – the underground shopping precinct, she hoped. The doors began to close, but a thick hand wedged itself between them and they opened again to reveal the wrestler, looking straight at her.

Was this the opposition? Or an opportunist mugger?

He stepped into the lift, his eyes still on her. The doors closed. She moved carefully onto the balls of her feet.

He was reaching for her.

Choose your attitude. Make your move. Understand that it may hurt, but know that you can win, she thought.

He was reaching for her clothing. What did he want to do? Grapple?

She jogged slightly to the side, waited for him to compensate. His hand was extended, open, searching for a grip on her. She breathed out, then clamped his wrist in her left hand, steadied it, and with her right grasped his index and middle fingers and twisted hard, sinking her elbow and shoulder into the movement, feeling the bone crackle, the tendons go.

He ripped himself away, the flutter of astonishment on his face giving way to pain. He staggered back and leaned against the wall of the lift, looking at his hand, the ruined fingers.

'Give me the phone,' she said.

He looked at her, blinking. She tried in Mandarin.

'*Shouji gei wo.*'

She held out her hand. He didn't move. The lift was approaching Basement 2. She took a step into him and executed a sharp kick to the knee, angled so that the knee buckled and he went straight down, cracking his head on the control panel as he did so. She reached down and took the phone from him. He didn't resist, just lay still, breathing hard.

The doors slid open.

She signalled fallback, and after a decent interval on the street, drenched and chilled by the wind, she was picked up outside a 7-Eleven a mile or so away. The driver – her rail-thin, goateed watcher – had the air conditioning on, and she lay on the back seat and shivered as they ploughed through the typhoon, the windscreen wipers working hard.

'So tell me,' she said.

'They just turned up. Two cars. Two in each. Some guys on foot. I counted three. They covered the main entrance and the MTR station. And, well, there they were.'

He had turned into an underground car park and the car was circling down into its echoing, concrete belly. He parked and checked his mirrors.

'We wait here for a while,' he said. Patterson sat up. His eyes were on her in the rear-view mirror. 'You okay?'

She nodded, giving him a wry look.

'Sorry about the fire door,' he said.

She bit back a response. Frederick Poon was his name, she knew from the file. A watcher, a street artist.

'Who were they?' she said.

He sighed, shifted in his seat.

'I don't know. Clumsy. Not State Security. They could be military maybe. Had the build. The haircuts. But . . . I don't know.'

She waited a moment.

'Private?' she said.

'Could be. I guess.'

'Did they make you?'

He turned in his seat and cocked an eyebrow.

'Not a chance, lady.'

'You're sure?'

'Oh, I'm sure.'

'Did any of them enter the building? A short one, looked like a fighter. T-shirt.'

He frowned, shook his head. 'Not that I saw. But could have come from another entrance.'

'And the agent?'

Frederick Poon was silent. Then:

'Didn't turn up. We were in position. But he didn't come to the platform.'

She waited for more.

'He's tricky, you know, that one. Probably took his own route. Don't worry too much.'

She was hungry. He gave her a bar of chocolate.

The phone was a burner. Nothing on it. No numbers, no calls dialled, no calls received, nothing in the contacts. They'd send it to Cheltenham for a proper going over, but it was, the two of them agreed, of no operational intelligence value. Frederick even had a gizmo for reading the SIM card, and he fiddled with it while they sat there and the car windows fogged up. But, again, nothing.

Which meant, of course, that the wrestler, whoever he was, was practising communications security. In the way a professional might.

'Okay, time now,' said Frederick Poon. 'They'll be here in five.'

And after exactly five minutes, a white SUV swung in next to them. Patterson opened the rear door of the car.

'Bye, Frederick. Next time.' She moved to get out. The SUV was waiting. Frederick turned in his seat.

'Hey,' he said.

She turned.

'Sorry about the fire door.'

'Whatever,' she said.

They drove fast to Chek Lap Kok in the gathering night. Patterson watched Hong Kong recede under the storm, its lights strewn into the darkness, the city tensed on the edge of the sea. Such power in this place, she thought.

She turned to the driver, another Poon. Winston, this one, wiry like his cousin, forty-ish.

'How's your aunt?' said Patterson.

'Eternal,' said Winston. Granny Poon, Eileen, presided over this little jewel of a family network. Eileen Poon, possessed of a will of iron, a taste for the foul Indian cigarillos known as bidi and a gift for operational security, had given the Service more than three decades. In the late seventies, as a guileless factory girl, she had penetrated and laid waste the Communist Party cells that infested the Crown colony. Her Majesty's Government had given her a codename, HAVOC, and, very quietly, a medal she wasn't allowed to keep. Then, with a sniff, it gave Hong Kong to China. Granny Poon carried on regardless.

'I'm sorry not to see her,' said Patterson.

'She's with us in spirit,' said Winston, his eyes flickering to the mirrors. Chase cars, Patterson assumed, watching their rear. Was Eileen behind a wheel back there, weaving through the traffic, reeking bidi clamped in her teeth?

'London wants you,' he said, and passed her a secure handheld.

*

It was Hopko, from London.

'Tell me you're all right.'

'I'm all right.'

'Position?'

'Clear. Heading to the bird.'

'Did he hurt you?'

'No.'

'How badly did you hurt him, out of interest?'

Patterson said nothing.

'And our friend?' said Hopko.

'Gone. No visibility.'

Hopko didn't reply straight away. Patterson pictured her in an operations suite at VX, tight skirt and tawny cleavage, the initial after-action report in her hand, the stillness in her eye as she calculated operational fall-out, cauterisation.

'His concerns?' said Hopko.

'Real, I think.'

'Why?'

'They'd been to his flat. Put the frighteners on and dropped this message thing on him. Whoever they were, they were real.'

'Something gives,' said Hopko.

'Something does.'

Another pause.

'Come home,' said Hopko.

Patterson smiled.

'On my way.'

Winston dropped her at Departures, the wind falling now, the pavements steaming, the glowing terminal rearing into the night. She slipped from the car and into the crowd.

She moves well, thought the watcher.

You don't see how dangerous she is. Or how brittle.

3

Oxford, United Kingdom

The boy, Kai, stood still in his gown at the corner of the High Street and the Turl, his white bow tie hanging loose at the neck. He held a bottle of champagne and swayed slightly. He raised the bottle to his lips, took a long pull, a solitary celebration. The street was thronged with students making their way from the Exam Schools. On impulse, he placed his thumb over the neck of the bottle and shook it, showering champagne over a group of passing girls, leaving foamy flecks on their black gowns. He let out a whoop. One of the girls shot him a look and walked on.

Exams were finished. His were in Engineering Science, specialising in Optoelectronics. He held out little hope that he had done well. His grasp of English, even after three years here, remained tenuous. The lectures were long, the tutorials minefields of misunderstanding and frustration. The subject weighed on him, bored him. He saw his life unfolding before him in swirls of fibre optic cable.

A delegation from the embassy had visited the master of his college. They had spoken quietly, given assurances. Kai would spend the summer at the family apartment in London, cramming, catching up.

He would not see his parents, nor home, nor Beijing. He would achieve his degree at this most ancient and prestigious of universities and he would bring what he had learned back to the family, and to the corporation that sustained the family and guaranteed its position, and he would not disgrace the family. In his stomach, a nub of disappointment, pessimism. Kai walked back towards college, the bottle hanging at his side.

In his room he took off the gown, the ridiculous clothes, and left them lying on the floor. He stood in his underwear and breathed in the stale air, before walking to his desk and turning on his laptop. The email had arrived from the usual, obscure address: the deposit was in his bank account. A carefully calibrated amount, naturally; enough to see him through the summer, not enough to give him any freedom. This was the work of his careful father, carefully winding the bonds of obligation tighter around his son.

The money did not come from China.

The money came, as it always did, from an account in the British Virgin Islands, remitted by a man Kai thought of as Uncle Chequebook. Kai's careful father told Uncle Chequebook how much to remit, and Uncle Chequebook remitted it.

Kai lay on the bed to reflect on the complicated, opaque workings of his family. He had met Uncle Chequebook once, a few years before, in Beijing, a balding Communist Party journeyman with a rutted face, worldly, hard and quiet. He'd worn a grey mackintosh, kept his hands in his pockets, looked at Kai with appraising eyes and flitted silently away. What was Uncle Chequebook's place in the Fan family industrial-political complex? Retainer? Servant? Sage? Kai had no idea.

But the money was there. So tonight he was on a train to London. He had the keys to the Kensington flat and the BMW. He took another long pull at the bottle, then dozed.

4

London

Patterson landed sleepless and wired. She went straight from Heathrow to Vauxhall Cross by Service car, speeding along the M4 in spring sunshine. She showered in the staff changing rooms, pulled on a black business suit, repacked her bag, and ate bacon and eggs in the canteen.

On her way up, she paused to look out over the terrace at the river's shimmer and to recount in her mind the narrative of the previous forty-eight hours, hammering it out through the exhaustion. With Hopko, readiness was key.

Hopko was waiting for her, morning sunlight streaming in her office window, coffee steaming on her desk.

'Trish,' she said, looking over her glasses.

'Val.' She sat heavily on Hopko's couch. Hopko stood and walked round her desk. She wore, to Patterson's disbelief, a leather skirt, boots.

'I want the guts of it now,' said Hopko.

'I'm ready,' said Patterson.

'Keung's state of mind?'

'Panicked. Genuinely fearful.'

'Not ill? Drunk?'

'No. Very alert.'

'And the men who came to his apartment. He was certain they were mainland? Not local thugs trying it on in some way? Debts or something?'

'He said he was certain at least one of them was a mainlander, a northerner, by his accent.'

'But not State Security nasties?'

'Unclear.'

'And it was a message for us.'

'A message for his "contacts", which he interpreted to mean us.'

'Could have meant someone else altogether, silly bugger.'

'Could have. But ... unlikely,' said Patterson.

'Why?'

Patterson shrugged.

'Everything points to professionals.'

'And this mysterious message?'

'He said they wanted him to attend some sort of meeting. The message would be delivered there. But that's all I got. We had to scramble.'

Hopko considered.

Patterson watched this formidable woman, with her Mediterranean looks, her blunt figure, her small hands clad in silver, jade. Valentina Hopko, Controller Western Hemisphere and Far East, lately risen to such grand estate. In her fifties now, but dressed, to Patterson's austere eye, a few years young.

'And this bloke you left mangled in the lift. Who was he?'

'I think he was one of them. But what he wanted with me? No idea.'

'I can't help wondering if you might have asked him.'

Patterson didn't reply.

'I am frankly relieved, Trish Patterson, that we are on the same side,' said Hopko.

23

But you'd never do anything as stupid as getting stuck in a lift with the opposition, thought Patterson.

'Have we heard anything from CAMBER yet?' she said.

Hopko walked back to her desk, sat.

She knows something, thought Patterson.

'Nothing good.'

Patterson waited.

'He fell under a train,' said Hopko. 'After the meeting.'

Patterson felt the adrenalin shock, felt her chest constrict.

'The police say it was suicide.' Hopko's eyes were on her.

Patterson grimaced, said nothing.

Hopko spoke quietly.

'There will have to be an internal inquiry. The board's been convened. They'll see you next week. You are to write the encounter report now. Then you are to go home and stay there.'

'I'm suspended?'

'You could say that.'

Patterson blinked, opened her mouth to speak, closed it again.

Hopko took off her glasses, leaned forward.

'An agent is dead, and they must decide why. Now, write the report and go home.'

Patterson stood, made for the door.

'Trish,' said Hopko. Patterson stopped, turned.

'If someone in Chinese intelligence wants to send us a message, why don't they just use the usual channels? Declared officers in Beijing or Hong Kong? Liaison?'

'Because,' said Patterson slowly, 'someone wants to talk to us outside the usual channels.'

'I must confess, I'm intrigued,' said Hopko.

Patterson took a taxi home to Archway, dragging her carry-on bag, bumping it up the stairs to her flat. The place was as she had left it, the bed hastily made, drawers shoved shut. She checked that the safe in the wardrobe was undisturbed. She opened some windows, let the afternoon air waft in, some late sun, some atmosphere to break the silence and the stillness. Footsteps on pavement, traffic, somewhere a child practising a halting major scale on a piano.

He fell under a train.

She sat heavily on the bed and pulled off her shoes, let the knowledge of it diffuse through her.

He was not the first agent she'd lost.

She thought of the Iraqi boy she'd run in Nasiriyah, a beacon on his moped as he putt-putted between insurgent safe houses. He used to flirt with her, call her my *habashi*, my Ethiopian, my black woman. She thought of the rubbish tip where they found him one smoky dawn, the crows overhead.

And the woman in Helmand who washed the tin plates at a roadside café, spotting licence plates, faces, from behind her burqa, phoning them in to Patterson, Captain Patterson by then. She'd disappeared, and one winter evening they'd found the café shuttered and chained.

All these stories, she thought, the endings that resolve nothing.

She undressed, pulled on shorts and a T-shirt, poured a glass of Cabernet, a big one. She remade the bed, refolded the clothing in a drawer that hadn't shut properly. She vacuumed and ran a damp cloth along the window sills. She scrubbed the kitchen counter.

CAMBER's death isn't an ending, she thought. It's a beginning. Of something.

In the intervening days, she read, fretted and watched Chinese movies on her computer; the vast, blood-soaked epic of war and revolution; the tiny, silent chronicle of love and death in a village of yellow dust. She loved the films and tried to follow the Mandarin without looking at the subtitles. She went running on Hampstead Heath and shopped at a supermarket. In the evenings, she heated up frozen dinners, ate them from the tray as she watched television, a chicken pot pie, enchiladas. She spoke to nobody, apart from Damian, who lived downstairs. He knocked on her door in his skinny jeans and high tops and insisted they go for a drink. They walked to a pub on Highgate Hill in warm sunlight and talked about the football and what was happening in the reality shows. Damian worked in advertising, prided himself on his populist tastes. He bought pints and a packet of crisps and asked her about her administrative job at the Foreign Office, how it was going, where she'd travelled to. He knew her just well enough to tell that something was wrong, and he probed a little, but she answered vaguely, turning the conversation back to him, and after a while they walked back home and said goodnight.

On the Monday, she wore a grey suit and flats, pulled her hair back into a tight bun, as she had worn it under her beret in the army. She got into VX early, sat in her cubicle drinking coffee, composing herself. The board convened at nine-thirty. Patterson was shown in to a fifth-floor conference room and found herself facing Mobbs, the Director, Requirements and Production, his dark suit, a tie of primary colours verging on the frivolous, as if to emphasise by contrast the vulpine features, the aquiline nose, deep-set eyes, the whiff of mercilessness to him. Next to him, Hopko, in a billowing pink silk scarf, silver hoops in her ears, her dark hair full, teased. She looked up, wrinkled her nose and smiled. Next to her, Mika Bastable of Human Resources, known throughout the Service as Bust-your-balls, a tall, sculpted woman, younger, who had come to the Service from a corporation. Fine detailing, thought Patterson: highlights, lip gloss, manicure. She looked expensive, and by comparison Patterson felt dowdy, reduced.

'We have read the encounter report,' said Mobbs, patting a file in front of him. Patterson nodded, sat straighter.

'This was the first time you had encountered CAMBER, correct?'

'Yes, sir.'

'Do you feel you were adequately prepared for the meeting?'

'I was as well prepared as I could be, given the circumstances.'

'That's not the same as adequately prepared, is it?'

'I was adequately prepared.'

'You informed CAMBER of his egress procedures should the meeting be interrupted?'

'Yes.'

'Why didn't he follow them?'

'I can't answer that, sir. I don't know.'

Mobbs opened the file, scanned the page.

'He left the flat all right. He found the lifts, all well and good, down he goes to the MTR station, but then he goes to the wrong platform. Our blokes can't find him. Why the blazes does he do that?'

'I don't know, sir.'

'Perhaps you got it wrong. You told him to go to the wrong platform.'

'Absolutely not, sir. I told him to take a train to Admiralty. Which was correct.'

'And then he's dead. Police say he jumped. Did he?'

'He was panicked, very frightened. He thought he was blown. I could see him deciding to ... do something drastic.'

Mobbs looked at her.

'Then why didn't you calm him down, reassure him, for God's sake? Why'd he leave the meeting worse off than when he went in? That's not what we do, is it? Let our agents run off in a panic.'

Patterson swallowed, took a breath. Stay calm, she thought.

'I was in the process of talking him down. I needed to establish if he was blown. I was questioning him when the signal came through, and we had to go to emergency procedures.'

'I think you lost control. CAMBER didn't listen to you.'

'That is not the case, sir. The meeting was compromised at a crucial moment and I put emergency procedures into effect.'

'Well, there's a corpse says it *is* the case.'

'That's unfair,' said Hopko, bluntly. 'CAMBER had emergency procedures. He elected not to follow them. Agents, on occasion, make idiotic decisions. All on their own.'

A pause, as Mobbs appeared to contemplate being lectured by his subordinate.

Bastable of Human Resources spoke.

'What we are trying to ascertain here . . .'

She turned over a page, slowly, let the silence hang for a beat.

' . . . is whether you mishandled this meeting, and, by extension, whether you are adequately equipped to continue in your present role in operations.'

Equipped?

'One can't help but notice that this is not the first time you have been party to a . . . a what should we call it, I wonder?'

'A flap,' said Hopko.

Patterson stayed silent.

'Quite,' said Bastable. 'Last year. Operation STONE CIRCLE.' She licked a finger, turned another page. She's attempting gravitas, thought Patterson. 'Says here you were responsible for exfiltrating two agents from China by means of an extremely dangerous contingency operation. Rather blotted your copy-book, as I recall.'

'The inquiry found not.'

'All undertaken without the necessary authorisations and permissions.'

'The inquiry found that I acted . . . excusably.'

'Sod the inquiry. What on earth were you doing?'

'I'll tell you, if you like. We were spying. Operation STONE CIRCLE got us inside classified Chinese computer networks. It worked. For once. We used a Chinese asset, and a British journalist as cutout and courier. The two of them did everything we asked of them, and the entire operation bled gold. Then some cretin on the seventh floor of this Service decided to hand over operational control to an external player. To a private company. And the whole thing went belly up. Read the report.' Patterson felt the shock of memory, thought of sitting alone in the P section watching the operation die, watching her agent run. She thought of Mangan's voice on the phone, rigid with fear, and of the ruthless, sharp-eyed bastard around which the whole operation had revolved. They'd called him 'Peanut'. She wondered for a second what had happened to him, where he was.

Hopko was looking at her, a *there-you-go-again* look. Bust-your-balls's face was reddening.

'People died,' she said.

'People do.'

'There was a girl involved, wasn't there. What happened to her?'

'Ting. She was the journalist's assistant in Beijing. They were ... having an affair. She was arrested.'

'Charming.'

Human Resources tucked a stray lock of blonde hair behind her ear, smirked at Patterson.

'You do seem to be a sort of Typhoid Mary of espionage, don't you? People expiring left and right. Getting carted off to the Lubyanka. Or its Chinese equivalent.' She glanced at Mobbs. Looking for approval, thought Patterson. The Director of Requirements and Production was reading the file, doggedly. Hopko was looking at the ceiling.

'I must say,' Bastable went on, 'I sense that the Controllerate has been very accommodating, has allowed you every chance, but from my perspective, I have to ask if your ... your background really has prepared you for operations.'

There it is, thought Patterson. There it is. *Background.*

Hopko was leaning back in her chair, eyes half-closed. Patterson wondered if she was smiling.

'Well?' said Bastable.

'I'm not sure I heard a question,' said Patterson.

Bastable's eyes flickered with irritation.

'Well, let me make it very clear, then. I sense an impulsiveness and a lack of judgement in you, as evidenced by your role in STONE CIRCLE, and in your handling of the lately departed CAMBER. Please tell me why you should retain your operational role.'

Patterson shifted in her chair, but it was the D/RP who spoke.

'Out of interest, what happened to the journalist, the access agent in STONE CIRCLE? What was his name?'

'Philip Mangan,' said Hopko.

'Mangan, that's right. He was a rather clever bloke, as I remember.'

Bastable was regarding him with a frozen expression.

'He's marinading in East Africa,' said Hopko. 'Keeping his mouth shut in this life and the next.'

Mobbs closed the file, placed his hands on the table and spoke directly to Patterson with an air of finality.

'All right. All right. While you retain the confidence of your Head of Controllerate, you will remain in your operational role. I will expect to see performance reviews that reflect that confidence.'

Hopko was nodding, listening to him with a fixed, admiring smile, one which Patterson had long ago learned to read, and which, when correctly decrypted, meant *you swivel-eyed, patronising husk of a man*.

Mobbs turned to Bastable of Human Resources, leaning close to her to whisper, a little too loudly.

'And for pity's sake, less talk of *background*, if you please. You'll get us all sued.'

5

In Kaliti prison, the inmates were not incarcerated in cells. Rather, they were warehoused in vast, corrugated iron structures that rattled under the rain and baked under the sun. Eight zones to the prison, several thousand inmates in each, the whole complex riddled with tuberculosis, it was said.

Mangan sat in the jeep by the side of the main road. He looked out at the prison walls. The late afternoon had turned overcast, the light a smoky purple. There'd be rain later, turning the sidewalks to mud, leaving the city misty and cool.

Kaliti housed criminals for sure, murderers, psychopaths, petty pilferers. But it served also as a political waste disposal, into which the ruling party dropped opposition leaders, judges, journalists, activists, trade unionists and persons of unreliable ethnicity should they prove troublesome.

He'd been waiting two hours. Hallelujah had gone in clutching some clothes and bundles of food, some money to smooth the way. It was delicate. He was to interview an inmate. The inmate was a sallow forty-year-old woman named Habiba Yusuf who had, she said, been distributing alms to destitute Somali Muslims in the east when she was dragged from her car by men in plain clothes. She was in fact smuggling funds to extremist organisations, she learned, and was locked up in Kaliti under Ethiopia's generous anti-terrorism laws. But her case had become something of an international cause célèbre, and the authorities were grudgingly allowing glimpses of her to demonstrate that she was, at least, alive. Mangan, the foreign correspondent, one of the handful based in Addis, hadn't been allowed in, so Hallelujah was doing duty for both of them, would share his notes, and hopefully a photo, and Mangan would file for the paper. Habiba had a lump in her breast. The authorities weren't allowing her to see a doctor.

Mangan checked his watch. What the hell was Hal doing? He stretched, breathed. The evening air smelled of ozone, kerosene, baking *injera*, some subtle sweetness beneath it all.

It was almost dark by the time Hallelujah emerged from the prison gate, shoulders hunched, eyes down. Mangan watched him pick his way along the muddy track in his trainers, his thin, dark frame, his air of anxiety. Hallelujah climbed into the car, put his head back and closed his eyes.

'What took so long?' said Mangan.

Hallelujah lit a cigarette, made a cursory attempt to exhale out of the window.

'I am stupid,' he said.

'Tell me.' Mangan started the car, pulled out onto the road.

'So they take me in. The guards sit there in the room with us. She's terrible, Philip. Crying. So sick, she says. I ask the questions. She answers, but the guards keep interrupting, cutting her off. She keeps saying she needs a doctor, she has this lump. She's terrified. I got a little bit about the conditions. But, really, it was a mess.'

'Any photo?'

'Yes, but ... well, you'll see it.'

'It doesn't sound too bad.'

'It gets worse. After fifteen minutes they say, that's it. Finish. And they take her from the room. They push me out, and as I'm walking back to the gate I snap some pictures of the prison. The courtyard is just ... people everywhere. Filthy. No order. Well, the guards see me and get angry and they take me to the guardroom and yell at me for one hour.'

'Just yell?'

'Yes.' He shook his head, ruefully.

'And the pictures?'

'They took the camera. *Your* camera.'

Mangan swerved to the side of the road as a truck hurtled by, weaving, its horn blaring.

'I'm really sorry,' said Hallelujah.

Mangan sighed.

'Don't worry about it,' he said. 'But the picture of her? Is that gone, too?'

'No, I took that on my phone. We have that.'

'Well, that's something.'

Hallelujah drew on his cigarette and shook his head again. Mangan pulled back onto the road. The traffic had slowed. They passed corrugated iron shanties lit by naked bulbs, alleyways an oblivion of shadow, women roasting corn over charcoal stoves by the side of the road. Rain spattered the windscreen.

They climbed to Mangan's flat, dumped their things, then went downstairs again to the First Choice café. They ordered *tibs* – the spiced, sticky beef – with *injera*, French fries and cold St George's beer. Hallelujah was nervous and fidgety; he lit a cigarette.

'So will you file?' he asked.

'Tomorrow, maybe,' said Mangan, absently.

'Okay. Me too.' Hallelujah reported for an Addis weekly, but moonlighted for Mangan, translating, fixing. Mangan watched him, this lean, earnest boy, his dirty shirt, worry like a stain in his eyes.

'What's eating you, Hal?'

'Oh, nothing. They won't like it, that's all.'

'Who won't? The paper?'

'No, no. The paper will hold its breath and run it. The government, I mean. And NISS.'

'If they're so worried about the coverage, why did they give us access to her?' Mangan said.

Hallelujah looked at him.

'How long have you been in Ethiopia now?'

'A year, a bit less,' said Mangan.

Hallelujah stubbed out his cigarette.

'So you know they like to play with us, lure us out. We interview dissidents, publish their views, write about their situations, we become vulnerable. They can use it against us whenever they choose. Shut us down.'

The *tibs* arrived, and the beer. Mangan took a long, cold pull on the bottle, and ate. The beef was sizzling, the *berbere* – chilli and spice – leaving his throat pulsing with aromatic heat.

'Do you ever see them? Talk to them? NISS?' he asked.

'No. They send messages. Through other people. You have to listen.'

Hallelujah tore the *injera,* moulded it in the stew with his fingers. 'A businessman takes you for lunch. Or an old professor calls you up. Very interesting piece in the paper last week, they say. *Lots* of people talking about it. Have you thought about a vacation? Somewhere far away?'

Mangan smiled.

'Sounds like China,' he said.

'African problems, Philip,' said Hallelujah, rubbing his eyes with the back of his hand. 'African problems.'

Hallelujah took a taxi home. His nervousness and his talk of the National Intelligence and Security Service – Ethiopia's tough, effective intelligence agency, with its vast web of informers modelled on the old East European practice – had put Mangan on edge. He

34

laboured back up the sour concrete stairwell to his flat, four floors above Gotera, his buzzy neighbourhood. He stepped onto his balcony, the night air cool. It was late, but the streets around his block were filled with cafés, tinny music, the smell of grilling meat, coffee. He watched the couples strolling along the weed-strewn pavement, the girls done up in tight jeans, heels, the glint of gold from their necks, their slender wrists.

He went back inside, poured himself a belt of vodka and lay on the sofa in the dark. He thought about Habiba, squatting in the corner of some prison shed, the noise and squalor of it, her fingers probing the lump in her breast hopelessly.

He thought about going home, and where that would be, and how. About how loneliness was not something he was given to – in his years as a foreign correspondent, he had been alone many times. About how when it did find him, it came on as physical sensation, a flood in the veins. He sat up and put his head in his hands. Loneliness came, he knew, from silence, from the inability to speak of what had happened.

Secrecy breeds loneliness.

And after loneliness comes fear.

He thought, as he did every night, when the cafés closed and the darkness thickened and the streets went silent but for the grey dogs in their skittish patrols, that they hadn't talked to him for months.

Surely they must check on me soon.

So when, the very next day, they did finally check on him, it felt like an anticlimax. It came in an email from the Second Secretary, Commercial, Embassy of the United Kingdom. A small dinner, two days hence, very casual, at the house in Jakros village. Do come by.

Mangan filled the time. He prised from Hallelujah the notes of the interview at Kaliti prison, forced himself to write them up and filed a story. 'In Ethiopia, Islamic Charity Worker is Emblem of Anti-Extremist Crackdown'. It ran, cut down, deep in the international section of the website, Habiba's face peering from a tiny, bleary photo.

After some consideration, he roused himself, called the desk and half-heartedly pitched a story on unrest and uncertainty in Ethiopia's south and east. Dogged insurgency in the Ogaden, spillover from the war in Somalia, the bitter traffic in *chat*, guns, humans, zealotry and war that pulsed along Africa's sunbaked Indian Ocean coast. The foreign editor sounded preoccupied: *send me a summary, Philip*.

He bought a new shirt, took a jacket to the cleaners.

On the appointed night, he showered, his lanky body pinkening in the steam, ran a comb through his red hair, dressed and took a taxi to Jakros – the gated community that catered to diplomats, the aid industry and, at the higher end, Ethiopia's wealthy runners. An Olympic gold medallist resided in one of its larger mansions, Mangan knew.

The car pulled up outside the Second Secretary's house, a modest place of brick and concrete walls, creeping plants with orange flowers spilling over them, and an iron gate. Mangan got out of the taxi. The streets were quiet here. No music, no food stalls, no men slumped barefoot on the asphalt, their eyes glassy from *chat*. Expatriate life the world over, he thought. Lived at a hygienic remove.

Hoddinott was the man's name, a pale thirty-something, prematurely bald, a doughy frame in a Marks and Spencer suit. He and his wife, Joanna, were keen to appear stoic and cheerful in their hardship posting.

'We love Addis,' said Joanna. 'We absolutely love it here. How do you find it, Philip?'

She told a long story of squatter families on the edge of the city, kicked out of their shanty and forced from the land by developers, the women gathering up children, plastic buckets, a coffee pot, a blanket, walking away through the muddied building sites.

'Well, we did what we could. I took them clothes and some formula for the babies,' Joanna said. 'But, honestly.'

As it dawned on Mangan that he was the only guest, Joanna stood and announced brightly that she'd better make the salad. Hoddinott gestured that he and Mangan should go out into the garden, where a grill was lit and smoking.

Hoddinott carried a bottle of chilled white wine and two glasses. He set them down on a garden table. Mangan eyed them while Hoddinott put on an apron, opened the top of the grill, peered in through a billow of smoke, then closed it again, sat and rubbed his hands together.

'Right then,' he said. He poured the wine. Mangan watched the glass mist.

'So how are you, Philip?' he said. 'Are you settled? Are you well?'

They are checking, thought Mangan.

'I'm fine, I think,' he replied. 'Who's asking?'

Hoddinott looked concerned.

'Well, I am, for starters,' he said. 'But you're right. Others are interested, of course. They want to know you're in fine fettle, sound of wind and limb, that sort of thing.'

'I'm fine.'

'Getting out much?'

'No. Not really.'

'Got a girl?'

'For fuck's sake.'

'Sorry, sorry, don't mean to pry.'

Hoddinott's expression was very level.

'Heard anything from China?' he said.

'Who would I hear from?'

'Old friends. Associates. Anything?'

'Sometimes.'

'How do they contact you?'

'Email. Social media.'

'What do they say?'

'Normal stuff, they ... you know.'

'Philip, don't be coy, now. What do they say?'

Mangan sighed.

'For a while they asked me what had happened, why I left Beijing so abruptly, where I'd gone. I gave the right answers, what was agreed. That happens less these days. They ask how I am, what I'm up to. They see stuff I've written, they comment on it.'

'No one being more persistent? Asking about the girl? What was her name, Ting?'

'One or two. But I asked them to stop.'

'I'll need names.'

Mangan said nothing. Hoddinott sat, arms folded, and spoke very quietly.

'Does anybody, in your view, harbour any suspicion of your involvement in the operation?'

Mangan shook his head.

'You are sure, now?'

'As sure as I can be. If any of the crowd in Beijing had caught a whiff of it they wouldn't have let go. They're serious journalists.'

'Would you say you're still friendly with any of them?'

'Not really. Many of the old crowd resent me. They blame me for Ting's arrest.'

'I don't have to tell you to keep your distance, I know that,' said Hoddinott. 'And have you had any contact at all from the Chinese state?'

'Nothing,' said Mangan.

'Really? No visits? Messages? Chaps on a street corner watching you go by? You're sure.'

'Nothing I've seen.'

Hoddinott paused as if considering.

'What?' said Mangan.

'Nothing. That's good news, of course. And I know you've been told before, but I will tell you again. There is a great deal of respect and gratitude for what you did. A great deal.'

'Even though it ended the way it did,' said Mangan.

'Even though.'

Mangan drained his wine, slid the glass across the table for more. Hoddinott refilled it, the wine gold in the twilight, its murmur in the glass.

'And financially, Philip? Not bankrupt? Not about to sell your story to the Sundays out of desperation?'

'Not quite that bad.'

'Paper paying the bills?'

'Just.'

'Well, all right then.'

And at that awkward moment, Joanna skipped from the kitchen. She carried a bowl of clever-looking salad.

'Now that's enough shop, you two. Let's eat,' she chirped.

She knows.

'Anything out of the ordinary, Philip,' said Hoddinott. 'Anything at all. You let me know, yes?'

Hoddinott grilled steaks and shrimp, doused them in butter and garlic. They ate in the gathering dark, a candle on the table, and Joanna propelled the conversation with self-deprecating anecdotes of life as a diplomatic spouse in Addis Ababa, the functions she attended, the committees, her exasperating book club. 'Really, Philip, there we are, all these embassy ladies, earnest Americans, clever Germans, and we plough through all this worthy literary fiction, when all we secretly want is a jolly good bodice-ripper!' Mangan listened, did his best to be appreciative. Joanna's ingenuousness was, he suspected, merely part of her cover. They were a Service couple, he was sure.

They saw him out afterwards to a waiting taxi, waved from the doorstep in the darkness, Hoddinott's arm around his wife.

The taxi ground back across Addis, windows open, letting in a breeze cluttered with the smells and sounds of the city's late night, the crowds thronging the pavements, the boys hawking single cigarettes and bushels of *chat*.

So he'd been 'topped up'. A watchful Service, keeping an eye on an old, blown agent. He wasn't ungrateful.

6

London

Kai thought the Park Lane restaurant must be one of the most effete and pointless places he'd ever been in. Charlie Feng was there, straight from the bank, in a suit, waiting for him, and two others were down from Cambridge. Kai walked across the bar to them, mumbled a greeting.

'Well, hello, Fan Kaikai,' said Charlie. 'I wasn't sure we'd see you.' He was speaking Mandarin.

'Well, here I am.'

They all looked at him, then at each other.

'So how are you?' said Charlie.

Kai looked around for a drink.

'I needed a break.'

'From what?'

'Everything.'

'So here you are with us.' Charlie Feng nodded a fake nod of satisfaction. 'It's a thrill to have you.'

The Cambridge boys smirked.

They went to the table, sat surrounded by faux chinoiserie in fancy low light and watched as the pretty little waitress flown in from Guangzhou tottered over with duck and glistening belly pork and lobster in a black bean sauce at forty pounds a plate. Charlie was sneering, spoke in Mandarin.

'What the fuck is this?'

The waitress froze.

'It's your lobster, *xiansheng.*'

'What moron puts lobster in a black bean sauce?'

'If you are not pleased, *xiansheng,* I can take it back.' She gestured towards the plate, her voice quavering a little now.

'I thought we were buying real food, not Hong Kong faggot food.'

'Charlie, just for once . . . ' said Kai.

'Please, *xiansheng,* let me fetch you the menu and you can order whatever you please, and the chef can make it in whatever way you choose.' She backed away from the table, fright on her face.

Charlie looked around the table, grinning. The others were stifling their laughter. The manager approached, a starchy Brit in a suit, looking concerned.

'Good evening, gentlemen, and welcome. I hope everything is all right?'

Charlie spoke in crisp English now, Harrow and Oxford-inflected, ripe with self-assurance.

'Everything's marvellous. Thanks so much.' And then, as the manager nodded and walked away, in Beijing slang, 'Prick.'

They all laughed except Kai, and Charlie picked up an entire lobster tail in his chopsticks and held it over his face, letting the black bean sauce drip into his open mouth. He wiped his face with a napkin, then gestured with his chin to Kai.

'So. Where's your girlfriend?'

Kai looked back at him, startled.

'What girlfriend?'

'The Chen girl.'

'Oh. Her.'

'Still there, is she? Wobbling about Oxford on her little bicycle, in her precious college scarf, sitting in the library, keeping her little legs crossed.'

'She's still there. I don't have much to do with her.'

'You heard the news? About her daddy? General Balls-of-steel?'

Kai blinked, feeling a pinch of alarm.

'No. What news?'

Charlie Feng leaned forward.

'Christ, Fan Kaikai, you really do not pay attention, do you?'

He sat back, picked up his wineglass.

'He was appointed to the General Staff Department.'

Kai thought for a moment, failing to make the connections.

'And?' he said.

Charlie adopted an exaggerated expression of astonishment, held his hands up, looked about the table.

'And? *And?*' he said, then dropped the pretense. 'Kai, listen to me. You need to start attending to matters of self-preservation. The Chen girl's father now resides at the very top of military intelligence. Do you hear me, Kai? Are you with me?'

Kai nodded. Though he wasn't really with him and was afraid to ask. He picked at the lobster.

Charlie stared at him.

'Old man Chen has stepped up, Kai. His people ...' He gestured with his chopsticks. 'They're busy. My old man says they're busy. General Chen and his army eunuchs.'

Kai looked at his plate.

'*Mang shenme ne?*' Busy doing what?

'Doing what? Who the fuck knows what? Scuttling around Beijing. Taking a lot of trips to the south-west, where they have friends. Whispering in ears. Watching. Figuring shit out. Doing nothing that is any good for you, or your family or the company, that's what. They loathe you, Kai. In the Chen girl's pristine little bosom beats a hateful little heart. Do not give her anything she can use.'

One of the Cambridge boys spoke.

'I think he understands, Charlie. No need to torture him.'

'Does he, though?'

'Don't talk about me as if I'm not here,' said Kai. He was aware that he was mumbling.

They ate in silence for a while. Charlie ordered more wine, though he was not drinking.

'So you're not going back to Beijing for the summer,' he said.

Kai shrugged.

'I have to stay here. Study. Catch up.'

Charlie looked to be considering.

'What?' said Kai.

'They've got some sort of minder coming, I hear,' said Charlie. 'To take care of you.'

Kai stared at him. 'What?'

Charlie shrugged.

'What do you mean, a minder?' Kai persisted.

'Well, I can't be there all the time, can I? Looking out for you.'

'A nanny for Kai,' said one of the Cambridge boys, and they all laughed again. 'To protect him from the Chen girl.'

Charlie signalled they should leave it. Kai sat silent, humiliated. Charlie spoke again.

'Uncle Chequebook been in touch? Done his thing?'

'Is there anything you don't know about my life?' said Kai.

'Thought so. Good. The Fan family business can pick up the tab tonight, then. Thank you, China National Century Corporation. We bask in your greatness. *Wan sui*. Long may you prosper.' He made a *please-go-right-ahead* gesture.

Kai sighed, took out a credit card, waved it at the waitress.

The four of them clambered into the BMW, and drove to Hackney, where an Asian events company had hired out some dark basement club and filled it with students and bankers from back home and models and Filipina nurses and a DJ, and got a champagne company to sponsor it. They sat on sofas under ultraviolet light, the music pounding, thumbing their phones. A few of the sharper girls present, recognising Fan Kaikai, the heir to the vast fortune, the scion of political and business greatness, sought to join the group and sat long-legged, pouting, next to him. By three, Kai was unsteady due to the ingestion of substances, so Charlie Feng, sober and vigilant, drove the BMW carefully back to Kensington.

7

Baltimore, Maryland, USA

They walked slowly across the Inner Harbor holding hands, the champagne doing its work, softening the sea breeze, softening their words, their feelings. She wore a blue silk blouse, a light cashmere shawl, Chanel. He seemed to like her in this classic look. A sign of his age? Or some fantasy of privilege? She went along, of course, wearing the Hermes scarves he bought her duty free, the Cartier bracelet, even though it made her feel like a country club hag.

Later, there was dinner at Mancuso's, sea bass for her, crab cakes for him, a bottle of Napa Chardonnay. He was a man of predictable tastes, she thought. And predictable appetites, as when, later still, he undressed in the motel room off I-95 and folded his spindly, sixty-year-old body against hers and told her, predictably, of her beauty and her youth and her litheness and the delicacy of her Asian face, breasts, fingers. And when she jabbed her fingernails in his back to remind him of what lay beneath, of her unpredictability, she felt him pull back and look at her, momentarily bewildered.

'Nicole!' he exclaimed, breathing heavily.

She leaned in to him and bit him on the lip.

45

'Yes?' she said.

'You are like a bad-tempered cat.'

Her legs were wrapped around his waist.

'I will be much more bad-tempered if you don't give me what you've got,' she said.

He smiled, his pompous ownership smile, she thought.

'Oh, really?' he said. He made to pull away from her, get up from the bed, but she kept her legs locked tight about him. He affected an injured look.

'How ... how can I give you what I've got, if you don't let me go?' he said, enjoying it.

She waited a beat, then released him. He stood and walked across the room to his briefcase, bent to pick it up. She watched him from the bed, his smooth hairless back, the hollows in his buttocks.

'Nobody saw you on the way here?' she said.

He had opened the briefcase and was feeling inside.

'Of course not.'

'You're sure?'

He didn't respond, just held up a memory stick, raised his eyebrows, dangled it at her, tantalising. She didn't react.

'Just for you?' Their little ritual.

'Just for me.'

'You are being careful, aren't you, Nicole?'

She smiled, narrowed her eyes at him, and held out her hand.

'What's on it?' she asked.

'Some policy papers. Some estimates. Things you should know.'

'Policy papers. Estimates. Jonathan, how you excite me.'

'Trust me.'

He shot her a mock warning look. Did he know what he was doing? His capacity for self-delusion appeared bottomless. Their charade – that he was 'helping' her with her post-doctoral research – had lasted for more than a year already. She lay back on the bed and stretched.

'Time for me to go,' he said, looking at his watch. 'Are you going back to Boston tonight?'

'Yes.'

'I'll drop you at the airport.'

She waited a moment. He turned to look at her, expectantly. She lay back, showed him her nakedness for an instant.

Now.

'No.'

He hesitated, not understanding.

'But how will you get back, then?' he said.

'I'm going away, Jonathan,' she said.

He looked blankly at her.

'Going away?'

And then there came, from the door, a mechanical hiss and click as someone inserted a key card from the outside, and the door opened, and Jonathan Monroe craned his neck to see who was entering uninvited, and then he turned back to look at Nicole Yang, his lover, his brilliant Taiwanese protégé whom he had mentored and advised and helped towards her Harvard doctorate, and the first poisonous seeds of understanding began to germinate, a tendril of fear curling through him.

She had risen from the bed and put on a robe.

'Nicole?' he said.

She walked across the room to him, looked at him very dispassionately.

He said, 'Where . . . are you going?' As if she could protect him.

'Britain. Oxford. For a year. A post-doctoral fellowship.' She reached out and gave his arm a squeeze. 'Goodbye, Jonathan.'

Three men were standing behind him now – two were Chinese, one of Western appearance. They parted to let her through. She picked up her clothes and her purse from a chair, and left the room, closing the door behind her.

'Mr Monroe,' said one of the Chinese men. 'Please sit.'

He swallowed.

'I demand you leave immediately. I will report this to the proper agencies. Your behaviour is absolutely unacceptable,' he managed.

The Chinese man was nodding. He was elderly, had a kindly demeanour, a dampness to the eye above soft cheeks, a weary old hound in a trench coat. He didn't look unsympathetic.

'Mr Monroe. You have been seeing Nicole Yang for more than a year now, and you have been supplying her with information, much of it classified.'

'That is outrageous. We have been conducting an academic partnership. Who are you anyway? Identify yourselves.' He was reaching for trousers, underpants, anything.

The man sighed, made a placatory gesture with his hand.

'Mr Monroe, I think it is best you sit down.' He spoke as if he bore bad news, a crime, a death. The man with Western features reached into the bathroom and brought out a bathrobe, which he handed to Monroe.

'Mr Monroe, you are a senior intelligence analyst at the Bureau of Intelligence and Research at the US State Department. For the last year, you have been engaged in an ... an intimate affair with Nicole Yang. And you have supplied classified information to her.' He held out his hands. 'We know this is fact. It is very clear. And, if I may say, very understandable. Please. Let us not deceive ourselves.'

'Identify yourselves. If you are law enforcement, I demand to see identification, and I demand a lawyer.'

The man looked sad, shook his head.

'No lawyers, Mr Monroe.'

Monroe sat, unmoving.

'What is this?' he said.

'Mr Monroe, have you reported your meetings with Nicole Yang through the appropriate channels? As a foreign contact? As required under the terms of your security clearance?'

'What is this?'

'No. We thought not.' The man looked troubled. The other two had faded into the background. Monroe pulled the robe tight about him, as if it could armour him. He was aware of the man's watery

48

eyes, the tangled sheets, the whiteness of his own legs and feet. Someone had turned on the overhead light and the room's intimacy and cosiness had vanished.

'Have you disclosed to the appropriate security organs the interest that Nicole Yang, a foreign national, has displayed in certain matters of national security policy? During your conversations?'

Monroe looked at the man, tried to quell the surge of warm, paralysing nausea in his gut.

'No. Well. Fortunately, Mr Monroe, we are not law enforcement. We are friends of Miss Yang's. Good friends.'

'You are from Taiwan,' said Monroe.

The man looked regretful.

'No. No, I am afraid not.' He held out his hands in a plea for acceptance. 'We are from Beijing. From China.'

Monroe jolted backwards as if he had been struck, an involuntary spasm of shock. He felt his mouth open and work soundlessly.

'And we simply wish to continue the relationship you had with Miss Yang,' said the man.

For an absurd moment, Monroe envisaged walks along the harbour with these three men, intimate dinners with them, crab cakes, Chardonnay, and afterwards . . .

'What?'

'I mean, we wish to continue the informational transactions. And we are prepared, of course, to compensate you very generously.'

But the man's reassuring words were lost, because Monroe was up and running. He tried for the door, but the two others were there, the one with Western features blocking him. His robe had come open. He changed direction, bare feet stuttering on the carpet, made a rush for the French window which led onto the balcony, batting away the drapes, but they were there too and, one to each arm, they took him and led him to the bed and sat him down gently.

'I'm sorry. I know this is a bit of a shock. But I assure you, we are professionals. Everything will be very well managed.'

Monroe was spluttering, wild-eyed.

'It is absolutely impossible. I will not cooperate with representatives of the Chinese state under any circumstances.'

There was an awkward pause.

'Mr Monroe. Please. Consider your position. You have been co-operating with us for a year already.'

Monroe shook his head, aghast.

'Nicole is . . .'

The man just nodded.

Nicole, in a bathrobe, was guided quickly down the corridor to another room by one of the team, a lean young woman who looked at her with a hungry admiration. She went into the bathroom, dressed in jeans and a shirt of green silk, picked up her bag and checked her phone.

A car was waiting, a wordless driver in the darkness. So. The airport. Back to Boston, pack, clean out the apartment. Then, next week, Britain, damp little island of self-regard in a sea of change.

She looked out at the headlights on I-95, wondering what would happen to Monroe, the man she had run for a year. Her case officers believed that he was conscious, that he knew what he was doing from the start, but she wasn't sure. Men lie to themselves so completely, so deeply, she thought.

At least she wouldn't have to wear those hideous scarves any more.

8

Dire Dawa, Ethiopia

Mangan stood in a graveyard of trains. Rolling stock as far as he could see, weeds sprouting through the bogies, track sinking beneath sandy soil. Here a wagon-lit with crusted windows, there an old Fiat engine that had pulled Italian infantry up and down the line in the 1930s, rusted out now, but the driver's seat still there, reddish and flaking. In the long afternoon shadows, it was cool, chilly even, at this elevation. He walked along the track towards the disused station platform, the elderly guide gesturing and muttering in French.

Le Chemin de Fer Djibouto-Ethiopien had run for a century, then coughed and expired. It had been four years since its last scheduled service and since then the station and marshalling yards had simply been left, a few remaining staff pottering about, goats tethered in the sidings. Mangan had a vague plan to use the scene as colour in a piece about Ethiopia's economic turnaround.

'Why do the trains not run any more?' he said, in strained French.

The elderly guide looked grave.

'*C'est un problème d'argent, monsieur,*' he said. A problem of money. He walked stiffly towards a pullman, the brown paintwork of which was peeling, and indicated that Mangan should climb aboard. Inside were compartments with leather banquettes, resplendent with leaf residue, dust and bird droppings.

'*Entrez dans le premier classe,*' said the guide with a flourish. The banquettes in first class pulled out into beds, the smell of rubber and decay rising off them.

They walked up to the disused station. Along the platform the signage was all still displayed in a beautiful deco font, *Bagages. Facteur-Chef Renseignements.* And above, the Amharic script, its letters unanchored, dancing.

'And now,' said the guide, 'the Chinese are to build a new railway, all the way to Djibouti and the sea.'

'I have heard that,' said Mangan. 'Will you go to work on the new railway?'

'No, *monsieur*. I will remain here,' said the old man.

From inside the station building, Mangan was sure he heard the hiss of static. He walked, footsteps echoing, into an ancient, decrepit office of yellowing walls and fluttering birds. The static came from an old radio receiver jerry-rigged with antenna and rusting microphone, a frequency dial glowing. It sat atop a wooden table, a power cable winding off into the gloom.

'In case we are needed,' said the guide.

History is not curated here, thought Mangan. It is strewn about, waiting for you to happen across it.

At the hotel that night, Mangan ate alone. He ordered steak and St George's and read a book, a blood-soaked memoir of life under Ethiopia's military dictatorship, the Dergue. In the lobby, two Ethiopian men sat quiet and unmoving, their backs to a corner, facing the door. Mangan watched them from the corner of his eye.

After seven or eight minutes, they stirred. Three perspiring Americans had entered the lobby pulling their luggage. The Ethiopians greeted them solemnly, stood by them as they checked in, and escorted them into the lift.

Later, the American men came down to the restaurant and walked past Mangan's table. They smelled of shower gel, toothpaste. Two of them were young, in polo shirts and jeans. An older, ruddy-faced man wore tan cargo pants and a shirt with a corporate logo stitched on the left breast. They sat and ordered Cokes. Mangan listened to their murmured conversation. They talked about software. Just as they were about to order food, a fourth man wearing sunglasses and a gold chain joined them. There were introductions, first names only, Mangan noticed. The new arrival said he was 'in from Bagram'. The older man asked what he'd been up to there.

'Oh, I process stuff,' the man said, smiling.

'Right,' said the older man, 'we fix stuff.' And they all laughed quietly.

What is this? wondered Mangan. Americans, 'contractor' written all over them, flitting in from Afghanistan? Hard-eyed Ethiopian minders? This smelled of something military, or clandestine. A drone base? Some tiny outpost sucking up signals intelligence from Somalia? Or perhaps a link in the vast surveillance net the Americans had cast across the Sahara, the covert flights out of Djibouti, twin-engined Bombardiers crammed with listening equipment tracking chatter and movement from Sudan to Mali. The men were leaning in to each other across the table, talking in low voices. Mangan watched them and experienced a sudden, gnawing sense of loss, of a life closed to him. *Old, blown agent sits in far-flung backwater, enjoys pathetic sense of yearning.*

He turned, looking for the waitress, and realised that the two Ethiopian men were now sitting not far behind him, watching him. He paid his bill quickly and left.

Early the following morning, in darkness, Mangan left the hotel in a hired Land Cruiser with a sullen local driver. They drove east out of Dire Dawa into the Somali regions, Mangan hoping for a glimpse of the insurgency, of the military's vicious response. If nothing else, some descriptive colour, some photos. They drove into flat, rocky terrain studded with acacia trees, baboons staring from the outcrops in the dawn. By ten it was hot, the light flat and hard. They passed Jijiga, turned south. On the plain, Mangan started to see the encampments of Somali nomads, the rounded tents like turtle shells scattered amid the scrub, young blank-eyed boys standing with AKs slung over their shoulders. They drove on. In the early afternoon, on the outskirts of a small town, Mangan told the driver to pull over. He sat watching the compound's metal front gate, some comings and goings, a guard with an AK squatting, waving away flies.

He got out of the car, walked purposefully to the compound and waved cheerily at the guard.

'I am here to see Miss Maja,' he said.

The guard frowned.

'Maja. Danish lady. A nurse.'

The guard got slowly to his feet, gestured for Mangan to stay. He disappeared into the compound. Mangan waited, watched the goats nuzzling the dust, the barefoot boys loping, twirling sticks. The guard waved him in.

Maja stood in a bloodstained smock, arms wide in ironic welcome.

'Philip. Welcome. You just missed the excitement.'

A breech birth, apparently, an extraction. Maja was energised, her eyes bright. She took off the smock and surgical gloves, washed. They went and sat in the courtyard and a young man brought coffee. Maja closed her eyes and turned her face to the sun, basked for a moment. Her hair was travel blonde, lay untidily on the shoulder. She was tanned, broad-boned and strong-shouldered.

'So don't imagine you're going to get much further,' she said, her English lilting.

He'd lit a cigarette, exhaled.

'How bad is it?'

'Pretty bad. Checkpoints about fifteen kilometres from here. They won't let you through.'

'And on the other side?'

'We hear a little from the women. Sweeps, arrests. Some beatings, some shootings.'

'Do you know where?'

She gave him a wry look.

'Yes.'

'Are you going to tell me?'

She sighed.

'That is not why I am here, Philip. I am a midwife, not an informant.'

He smiled.

'I know. Sorry.'

'They watch everything we do. Everyone we see, they know.'

'I won't stay long.'

She raised an eyebrow.

'You never do,' she said. She reached for Mangan's cigarettes, took one. 'I'm getting a break for a few days, though. I'll come up to Addis for a while.'

'I'll buy you dinner.'

She nodded.

'Then we can talk a bit more, maybe,' she said.

They stood and she walked him to the gate, touched him on the arm, left her hand there.

'See you soon, okay?'

'Sure.'

They drove a few more miles south, the driver nervous. They passed military transports, old Russian four-ton trucks next to battered American Humvees.

Then, a checkpoint.

The driver wanted to turn round but Mangan made him continue, slowly, both hands on top of the wheel. Mangan laid his hands on the dashboard. Soldiers were beckoning at them, pointing at a place on the road. The driver made a hissing sound through his teeth, slowed and stopped, wound the window down. The soldiers looked in, demanded papers. They were lean, dark men, moved like professionals, quietly, economically, their battledress faded, weapons clean and oiled, Mangan noted. One of them saw him, murmured to the others, walked around the car, tapped on the window.

'ID,' he said, in English.

Mangan slowly reached into his breast pocket, took out his accreditation, passed it to the soldier.

'What you do here?'

'I am a journalist.'

'No, no. You go back.'

'Can I get out of the car?' He gestured. The soldier stood back a foot or so, and Mangan opened the door, gingerly, got out.

'Cigarette?' he said. He offered the pack. The soldier did not respond.

'I want to go a little further down this road. Can I do that?'

'No, no. You go back.' The soldier gestured down the road the way he had come.

Mangan smiled, nodded.

'What are you guys here for? Is it dangerous down the road?'

'No, no. Not dangerous. No problem. But not permitted. You go back.'

'I just ...' But the soldier was losing patience, stepped towards him, shoved him back towards the car, then leaned down and shouted at the driver in Amharic. The driver, very frightened now, nodded frantically.

Mangan sighed, got back in the car. The driver, without waiting for instructions, turned it round and started heading back up the road, muttering to himself.

Mangan lit a cigarette. Another pointless day, he thought. Another stretching of my reason for being here. *Hardened correspondent Philip Mangan makes insipid attempt to get story, fails.*

He looked out over a plain speckled with thorn bushes, the light lowering, turning to gold.

Feels persistent regret at loss of other, less respectable, line of work.

They headed back to Dire Dawa, Mangan stopping the car only

56

once, in the evening, when he caught sight of a vast construction project, Chinese engineers with theodolites, high-visibility vests and helmets, the yellow dust billowing skyward. The new railway, China inscribing itself into the very ground of Africa.

That night, in the dim hotel bar, he made up his mind to take a run at the Americans. Just to see. They were sitting in a corner, the four of them. One had a laptop open. They seemed to be watching a football game. Mangan walked to the bar and ordered a beer, waited for a moment, then strode over to their table.

'Hi, guys,' he said.

They looked up at him blankly.

'Sorry for interrupting. Just wondered what the game was.'

There was a pause. Then the older man spoke.

'It's recorded. Nothing recent.'

'Oh. Okay,' said Mangan, standing his ground. 'Are you with the embassy?'

The man with the gold chain had taken off his sunglasses and was looking at him hard. He had sun-darkened skin, sunken cheeks, Mangan saw.

'Yes. We're embassy. And you are?' he said.

'I'm a journalist. British. Just wondered what brought you all to town.'

'A little bit of official business,' said the older man, in a tone that said this conversation is ending. The two younger men had looked back down at the laptop and were murmuring to each other, pointing at the screen.

'Only, I'd heard the US military had something going on at the old air base outside town, and I wondered if you were part of it. All off the record and everything.'

'What's your name, sweetheart?' said the man with the gold chain.

'Mangan. Philip Mangan.'

'Well, Philip, I'm sorry to say we have to draw our brief acquaintance to a close. We don't mean to be rude, but we're just not in a position to have that conversation right now. So, ah, goodnight to you.' He smiled and turned away.

Mangan raised his hands in an I'm-just-trying-to-be-friendly gesture, then walked back to the bar, sat on a stool, pulled on his beer, tamped down his annoyance.

'Interesting, aren't they?'

The voice came from Mangan's right, quiet, accented.

He turned. A man of Chinese appearance was sitting three stools away from him, holding a glass of whisky, looking straight ahead.

'You see,' the man went on, 'they come to Africa, and they bring drones and bombs and monitoring bases. But China comes to Africa and brings railways, phones and hospitals. Don't you find that interesting?'

'Have we met?' said Mangan.

The man turned to face him, put his drink down, the *clop* of his glass on the bar. He wore a white shirt and grey slacks. His hair was to the collar. His face had a strange cast to it, wide, high cheekbones, eyes with no whites to them, immobile, lacking affect. A broad, supple mouth. A startling face, shocking almost. Mangan thought of a marionette, of a clown.

'No, we have not met,' said the man. Then he stood and leaned towards Mangan, a fulsome smile, the eyes like coal.

'But perhaps we will,' he said. He walked from the bar. Mangan watched him cross the lobby and leave the hotel.

What was that? he thought.

Though somewhere in an earlier self – a clandestine self – he knew.

9

Oxford, United Kingdom

Fan Kaikai stumbled through the graveyard, as bidden. When he reached the requisite headstone, one which marked the plot of an obscure statistician, he stopped, and as club rules demanded, raised the silver cup to his lips. The concoction it held was of sickly liqueur topped with champagne to form a vile, frothing swill. In a circle around him stood a group of undergraduates, all male, shouting, jeering in the darkness. Some of them wore masks and tailcoats. He could hear the traffic going past on the street. Why am I here? he thought. What am I to them?

He drank, letting some of the liquid run down his chin and spill down his front. His stomach lurched. The club's other members, all well lubricated themselves, yelled encouragement. Kai dropped the silver cup to the ground and walked away, bent over and heaved up a warm, foul gush.

He felt hands on his elbows amid inchoate laughter. They all spilled from the cemetery onto the street, reeled back to college in the darkness.

As they approached the gate, Kai saw her. She was standing under a street lamp in a long silver-blue gown, closing a purse. Waiting for someone? She saw him at the same time, regarded him from across the street.

He stopped and looked back at her. She turned away. He walked through the college gate, and then they were up in someone's rooms, and there was more champagne and a lot of noise, shouting. And he looked up and there she was again in that incongruous gown that showed pale, slender shoulders. He considered for a moment, then went over to her, leaned into her, spoke in Mandarin, but felt the words thick and slurring.

'I'm Fan Kaikai,' he said.

'I know who you are,' she responded.

'And you are Madeline Chen. We should be friends,' he said.

She leaned away from him, as if from a bad smell, her eyes flickering down to his damp gown.

'We could,' he said. 'We could, you know, get past all this stupid stuff.'

'What stupid stuff?' she said.

He gestured in a way that felt slightly wild. Someone had put music on, complicated, sinister-sounding, with a bass like an industrial roar. Kai tried to focus.

'All the . . . history. All the family history, the anger. It's their fight. Not ours.'

'I don't know what you're talking about.'

He blinked.

'What? Of course you know. We should talk about it. Couldn't we do that?'

She was looking around herself, as if searching someone out. Who? he thought. A friend? A minder?

'Why would I want talk to you about my family?' she said.

'I didn't mean . . . I just . . .'

He stopped, took a breath.

'I'm sorry. We're supposed to avoid each other, I know. We are supposed to mistrust each other. I just thought I would like to make my own decision, that we could make our own decisions.'

She was still leaning away from him, lips pursed, eyebrows arched. The music was a distended roar, a thumping in his chest.

He shrugged.

'Sorry,' he said, and made to walk away. She spoke to his back.

'Are you always this earnest?'

He turned back, struggled to find something to say. She was looking at him as if he had just vomited a magnum of champagne. Which, come to think of it, he had.

'Only when I'm drunk,' he said. 'I'm a sober sceptic.'

'Earnest drunks are the worst. What is this ridiculous drinking club you're a member of?'

'It's called "The Amnesiacs". I don't know what it is, really. They just asked me to join. We have to wear these clothes.'

'And drink a lot.'

'And drink a lot.'

'They don't want *you* in the club. They want your money,' she said. He felt as if she were testing him.

'I think you may be right.'

She was still looking at him askance. Neither of them said anything. Kai pondered the notion that she had creamy skin and elegant, wide eyes, and spoke a soft, educated Mandarin, like an actress. She was slight, elfin almost – not the harridan he had been warned about. She was rather beautiful, close up. Now she was speaking quickly.

'If they see me talking to you I'm in the shit.'

'What? Who? If who . . .'

'Do you have any idea *why* we are ordered not to talk to each other? Do you?'

'I know some of it. I think.'

She sighed, shook her head and, with a brief, disbelieving glance at him, was gone.

*

Kai returned unsteadily to his rooms, thinking about her, her self-possession. He walked up the darkened staircase. The door to his rooms was ajar.

He stood on the step, wondering. He pushed the door open. The room was dark.

'Hello?'

Silence.

'*You ren ma?*' Is anybody there?

Nothing, just the creaking of the wooden boards beneath his feet, a burst of drunken chatter from the quadrangle below.

He felt for the light switch, his hand fluttering against the wall.

The room was still. He walked to his desk. His laptop was gone, but they had left the power cord, for some reason. He felt sick, shaky. He looked quickly in the bedroom, which seemed untouched. But on the sink in the corner, his flannel was draped over a tap and his toothpaste tube was empty. He looked more closely, not trusting his senses. His shoes were jumbled up. And a textbook, *Photonics: Principles and Practices*, was closed, when he knew he had left it open at the section on Fresnel equations.

He went back down the staircase and crossed the quad to the porter's lodge.

The police arrived in the form of two uniformed constables and a young, stocky detective constable in jeans and a sports jacket who chewed a piece of gum and looked at him quizzically. He introduced himself as DC Busby. Kai showed him where the laptop had been.

'Anything else missing?' said Busby, walking slowly around the room.

'No. No, but . . .'

The detective turned and looked at him.

'No but what?'

Kai found his English drying up, as it often did when he needed it most.

'I think, maybe, somebody search. Something.'

'Somebody searched the room?'

'Yes.'

'Why do you think that?'

'Just, things maybe have been moved.'

'Hm,' said Busby. 'And why might they do that?'

'I don't know.'

'Because, you see, in your room search usually, the thief, he'll turn the room upside down. Pull out your drawers, turn your mattress over, that sort of thing.' The detective smiled, spoke deliberately. 'He doesn't tidy up.'

Kai nodded, and then one of the uniformed officers was standing in the bedroom doorway and dangling from his hand was a single latex glove.

And when DC Busby, a conscientious man who viewed the travails of drunken students as every bit as worthy of his attention as any other, returned to the station and entered the details of the case – burglary, accompanied by a search conducted to an almost professional standard, as evidenced by the presence of a discarded latex glove – on the Police National Computer, he was intrigued to see Fan Kaikai's name return a ping. He leaned into the screen. The ping came from the intelligence services, who, it seemed, were possessed of an interest in Mr Fan Kaikai, as they required immediate notification should he be in contact with the police.

Intrigued, the detective filled out the brief explainer form and hit Send. He wondered where the message would go, to whom, what strange unseen mechanism he was setting in motion.

10

Addis Ababa, Ethiopia

Mangan took a late evening taxi to Piazza. Hallelujah was at a jazz bar attached to a decrepit hotel, a big group squeezed around a candlelit table littered with beer bottles and plates of French fries. The band played vibraphone, horns and hand drums, a pulsing, melancholy Ethio-jazz. Hallelujah waved him over and pulled out a stool. The group was made up of a couple of researchers, one or two expats, but mostly glum Addis journalists, battered by newspaper closures, arrests. Those without jobs were struggling, here selling the odd piece to a website, there doing some translation work, living with friends, making their beer last. The conversation slipped between English and Amharic.

'Listen, everybody,' said Hallelujah to the table. 'It seems that, in addition to his bold coverage of our many insurrections, Mr Mangan has been stalking the Chinese.' He turned to Mangan. 'So Philip, what did you find? Are we saved? Is China going to finance the African renaissance?'

'I can announce that there will be a railway,' said Mangan. 'A big one.'

'Think of that, ladies and gentlemen,' said Hallelujah. 'We are to enter the age of the locomotive.'

'We are to enter the age of China.' This from tall, bespectacled Abraha, who worked in an agricultural institute. 'They'll run everything here soon.'

'We had colonisers before,' said Hallelujah. 'Didn't turn out well for them.'

'Is that what the Chinese are?' said Mangan. 'Colonisers?'

'I don't know what they are,' said Abraha, 'but they are everywhere. You've seen! Building railways, laying fibre, God knows what else. Next, they'll bake *injera* and sell it to us.'

The club was dim and loud.

'You know, I heard a funny story,' said Abraha. 'When the Chinese companies first turned up a few years ago, all the huge road projects starting up, they hired Ethiopian workers. Of course. Then they trained them in how you dig a ditch, build a wall, the Chinese way.'

'Very quickly, and so it falls down a week later,' said someone, to laughter.

'As opposed to the Ethiopian way,' said Hallelujah, 'where completion of the wall, or ditch, remains a beautiful dream.'

Abraha, chuckling, sought to wrest back control.

'No, no, listen. This is all true. So the Chinese noticed that the Ethiopians used shovels with very long wooden handles. Always this long handle. So they watched a bit and they saw that the Ethiopians would dig for a minute or two, then stop digging. Then the Ethiopians would stand and cross their forearms on the end of the handle and rest their chin on their forearms and talk, or just close their eyes. All over the site, workers leaning on their long shovels, full of bliss. So what do you think the Chinese did?'

Everyone looked at each other.

'They took the shovels away? But then, how would they dig?' said someone.

Abraha looked pleased, wagged a finger. 'No. They went round at night with a saw and cut one foot off every handle! So the next day . . .'

The table was laughing, holding up imaginary shovels, miming the workers' falling over when they tried to rest on them.

Mangan looked up to the door. Maja was there, walking towards the table. She wore a white cotton dress, her hair unruly on bare shoulders. He waved.

Hallelujah waved at her, too.

'Oh, yes, Philip, here is Maja. She is a Danish.'

'A Dane,' said Mangan.

'Yes, yes, a Dane,' said Hallelujah. He was animated now, Mangan saw, a bit drunk, happier, but still wound tight. 'Maja, come and sit here.'

Maja picked her way to the table, where Hallelujah made room for her, and she leaned over to give him a brief embrace. As she sat, she laid a hand on Mangan's shoulder, and he felt the touch as if hyper-sensitised to it. He caught her eye, and she broke into a great big grin. She looked like someone who had just emerged from incarceration. Hungry for experience, fun. Hallelujah gestured to the waitress for more beers.

'Maja, Maja, how is the poor Ogaden?' he said.

'It is poor and unhappy, as you know, Hal. Let's talk about something else.'

'Yes, yes, but the babies are safe because you are there.'

'Not really,' she said. 'The babies are dying at an alarming rate. And the mothers.'

'Really?' said Mangan.

She looked at him, adopting a weary tone.

'Yes, really.'

'Why? I mean, more than usual?' he said, genuinely curious.

She shook her head.

'You journalists are truly horrible people. Do you know that?'

'Of course we are,' said Mangan. 'But what's happening with the mortality rates?'

66

She took his beer from him, took a long pull before speaking.

'Well, you name it. Forced marriage, genital cutting, disease. And the women are malnourished, so their pelvises don't develop properly. And all their life they carry weight on their heads, which we think deforms the pelvis. So vaginal birth can be very hard. And they die.'

Mangan took his beer back.

'Sorry,' said Maja, 'but you asked.'

'I did. I'm wondering if there's a story there.'

She gave a tired smile.

'A story.'

'You know what I mean,' he said.

'Do I? Please can we just talk about food, or football or something?'

And as she cocked her head at him, the candlelight on her skin, he thought he saw, over her shoulder, a silhouette he knew: a wide face, eyes of dark pewter – eyes with no whites. And then it was gone.

Mangan half-stood, searched the bar, but the Clown was nowhere to be seen. He felt a nervous ripple in his belly.

'What is it?' said Maja.

'No. Nothing,' he said, smiling, shaking his head.

Abraha leaned over to him, speaking quietly. 'Philip, come and see me. I have something for you.'

11

Hong Kong and London

Dr Keung was to be cremated and interred at Diamond Hill columbarium; a daughter was flying in from Canada to oversee the arrangements and to dispose of her father's effects. The coroner was examining the cause of death before releasing the body. A team in Singapore had been put on standby in case a burglary of the doctor's apartment in Mid-Levels was deemed necessary. What sign of his betrayals had he left on his laptop, his mobile phone? Were there contact numbers, emails? A diary? Or, heaven forbid, a private journal?

The Hong Kong police had found video footage, taken by a surveillance camera on the platform, of the moment Dr Keung tumbled to his death beneath the MTR train. The police had sent the footage to the coroner's court, and Patterson pondered how to get hold of it, what she might see there that others didn't.

But the coroner agreed with the police and ruled the death a suicide, and, to the relief of VX, ordered no inquest. The Singapore team was stood down. The daughter hired an estate service to clear out the apartment. The doctor's electronics went quickly to a recycling centre. No guarantee of oblivion, perhaps, but it was decided at VX that no further action was necessary. The offshore account into which the doctor's earnings had been paid was closed, and a substantial amount of money recouped, its disbursement to the doctor's heirs deemed impractical and insecure.

Patterson went to the cinema by herself on a damp Friday night. She considered asking Damian from downstairs to go with her, but it felt unnatural. She watched a maudlin film about a dying French woman and her loyal husband, and wished she'd chosen something easier. Afterwards, she ate at a little Lebanese restaurant. *Table for one, please.*

She thought of Dr Keung's daughter, cleaning out her father's closets, throwing away his shoes.

When an agent dies, she thought, their truest self dies unknown.

Addis Ababa, Ethiopia

Saturday morning. The connection at Mangan's flat was down, so he walked out to an internet café on Mauritius Street. The place was grimy, smelled of generator fuel, sweat, coffee. He sat at a crusted terminal beneath a poster of Michael Jackson on a peeling yellow wall. The connection was excruciatingly slow, but extant, at least. An email from Abraha, suggesting a time to meet at his favourite pastry shop. A vague query from the paper regarding Mangan's progress on the Ogaden story, which he deleted.

Then, something else.

An address he didn't recognise, with attached files, photographs. He almost deleted it, but the subject line caught his eye. It said simply: 'Mangan'.

He opened the message. No text, just four photographs. The first was of Mangan at the jazz bar, taken from a distance, but recognisably him, Hallelujah at his side, back to the lens. The second was closer and pictured him in conversation with Maja. The third showed him leaving the bar, emerging onto the street, blurry, no flash, but there he was, all six feet of him, his face a bit hollow, his red hair a scrape of colour in the night. The last photograph was of Mangan in Dire Dawa, in the hotel restaurant, the Americans behind him, engrossed in his book. That was it.

He met Abraha at Enrico Pastry, an Addis favourite for its faded Italian grandeur and its cakes, which could be procured only through an impenetrable system of queuing and tokens. Abraha had secured a scarred table, and a plate of millefoglie and cream puffs, no small success this late in the day. They ordered macchiato and Mangan watched the milk swirl like smoke in its black depths.

'We hated the Italians,' said Abraha. 'My grandfather was an *arebegna*, a resister, shot at Italians all the way along the Djibouti railway. He was in an Italian prison in, what, thirty-eight. They beat him on the soles of his feet. And look at us. Today, we remain captive to their pastries.' He licked cream from a thumb.

Mangan waited, sipping his coffee. Abraha was complex and deft. His work – in agricultural policy, of all things – forced him into vicious, rocky terrain: land rights, the grabbing of huge fertile tracts by international investors, corrupt officialdom, abrupt and brutal resettlements, ethnicity, food security, poverty, water. A minefield, all of it.

'So, Philip. I know your vague interests have extended to the China story. So, what about this? And don't you dare quote me, yes?'

'Of course,' said Mangan.

'At the institute, we are installing new computers, all Chinese, of course. A technician comes to set up the routers or something, a Chinese guy. He works for this huge corporation, China National Century, you know them?'

'CNaC. Yes, I know them,' said Mangan, quietly.

'Well, this technician gets a little talkative. And he tells us, very grandly, that he's been doing *security* work here in Addis. We probe and he tells us that he's been doing work at INSA.' The Information Network Security Agency, Ethiopia's own signals intelligence and cyber surveillance outfit. 'And he starts smirking and dropping all these hints. "Ah, yes, social media sites, you want to be careful of those from now on. Oh, your handheld? Well, you might want to leave that at home." And so on.'

Abraha's eyes were wide, the alarm on his face real.

'They've got Chinese engineers in there, and they are building a real surveillance agency, Philip, all hooked into the phone and computer network. All the internet and mobile traffic. All the metadata. Our very own little Ethiopian NSA, courtesy of the Chinese.'

'He said this?'

'Well, no. But that's what he meant.'

'Seriously? What for?'

'Oh, come on, Philip. This is Addis Ababa. We are the political capital of East Africa, maybe of all Africa. Every African country has an embassy here. The African Union is here.'

In a huge, glistening headquarters – newly built by China, Mangan thought.

'Everything flows through Addis. Power, diplomacy, ideas, influence. The African renaissance *does* start here, underwritten by China. They are building, Philip. Not just roads and railways, but the real thing. The future infrastructure. Networks. The arteries of power in the twenty-first century. They flow to and from China, my friend. And Ethiopia is plugging in. That is the story, and you as a journalist might stir yourself to find a way of telling it, no?'

Mangan shifted in his chair, felt a familiar flush of defensiveness.

'I need a bit more than a hearsay conversation with a Chinese technician.'

Abraha shook his head.

'You are useless, you people. You won't commit to anything. Soon the west won't be here any more. You'll have left behind some language, a few aid projects, and embassies with high walls.'

He ran his finger across the plate, searching for the last of the sweet cream.

'Just like the Italians left behind their pastries.'

*

Mangan, on his way back to Gotera in the twilight, pondered the meeting. He had found Abraha's lecture self-important, a touch flaky even. China's ambitions in Africa laid bare! How can you be so blind?

But the INSA tidbit was interesting, if true. Mangan wondered what he should do with it, how he could confirm it.

Could he take it to Hoddinott?

The traffic was stop-go, the mauve dusk suffused with fumes. At every junction the drivers gesticulated, argued, nudged and ground their way through the chaos while knots of boys stood by the road-side, barefoot amid the rubble and the mud, eyes skittering across the city's churning surface.

Whatever will they do, these boys? Mangan wondered. How will they live?

12

His first thought was that the burglar was back, and he sat up in bed, listening. Rain on the window, the hiss of the trees. He put one foot on the floor.

There. A scratching at the door. Kai got up slowly from the bed, tiptoed into the sitting room, stood by his desk, held his breath, listened again. A fingernail against the wooden door.

'*Shi shei ya?*' Who's there?

And then a low voice.

'*Wo.*' Me.

He turned on the desk lamp, went to the door. He could sense the person on the other side, their tension. He opened the door a crack.

Madeline Chen wore a dark blue waterproof with the hood up. She was carrying something in a bag. He had no idea what to do.

'It's two in the morning,' he said.

She looked around herself, peered down the staircase.

'I have to be quick,' she said.

He stood back and opened the door wide for her, and she stepped inside, dripping, and pulled her hood down. She had tied her hair up,

73

wore no make-up. She looked even younger than before, slighter, her expression unreadable.

'What do you want?' he said.

She held out the bag.

'I brought this for you.'

He didn't move, just looked at the proffered gift.

'What is it?'

'It's a book. You should read it.'

'Why should I read it?'

'To understand,' she said.

He took the bag, slid the book out. A paperback, in Chinese. The title: *Reaching in the Sea, Drawing up the Moon: My Life in War, Revolution and Reform.* And staring up at Kai from the cover, a photograph of his own grandfather.

'Have you read it?' asked Madeline.

'It's my grandfather's memoir,' said Kai.

'I know. Have you read it? Really read it?'

'Well, no. Not really.'

'We all have, in my family,' said Madeline. She had taken off her coat and sat, drew her knees up, patted her hair.

'You have? Why?'

'My father, the General. He makes us read it. It reminds us, he says, keeps the anger burning.'

Kai turned the book over in his hand, flicked through it, looked at its self-satisfied title, the shabby little photographs. Grandpa as a boy in uniform. Grandpa in the same room as Deng Xiaoping. Grandpa with some forgotten East European, gesturing at a primitive piece of electronics, a teleprinter, perhaps, or an early computer, Kai couldn't tell.

'Is this some sort of test, or riddle or something?' he said.

'No. You said you wanted to talk. Well, here I am. Talking.' Then she stood up, reached out and touched his arm. 'Read it.'

She picked up her waterproof and, her eyes down, walked from the room, closing the door behind her.

He lay in bed, the wind rattling the window, and read.

I was a child of the yellow earth. My village lay in the northern part of Shaanxi province, to the east of the city of Yulin. The village was known as Five Mile Reach. Only a few families lived there. The soil was poor and the water supply erratic. In winter the land froze. In summer it baked, and in spring the wind came down from the Gobi desert and whipped up the yellow dust so that it got in your mouth, ears and eyes. My father had a smallholding. We grew millet and kept some chickens and a goat. Our house was built of mud bricks and had windows of paper. Outside our wooden door hung great bushels of dried red chilli peppers. Inside, the furniture was made of hewn wood, and the family slept on the kang for warmth. As the youngest, it was often my job to get up in the freezing winter nights and feed the fire that warmed the kang. I remember kneeling there in the fire glow, watching my family sleeping, my grandmother, my mother and father and my two sisters. Keeping them warm was a great responsibility, and I would kneel for hours on the cold floor, feeding sticks into the fire.

This sense of responsibility never left me, and I have always put caring for the Fan family above all else. I have instructed my children and grandchildren to do the same. Family is everything, and not even the most misguided ideas of China's turbulent years can change that reality. Today, China is reclaiming its old, and correct, understanding that family is the most cherished institution of the nation.

My father, as well as farming, worked as a porter for a business distributing grain through the valley. The business was owned by a merchant in a nearby township. My father was illiterate, but he saw that reading and counting were important to the merchant and he made it his business to ensure that I got an education.

There was no school in the village, but there was an itinerant teacher who would wander through the valley, giving lessons for cash. The teacher was a gaunt, pale man who wore a long, shabby gown. He taught us our numbers and our characters, yelling at us in a high, raspy voice. We had no books, or paper, or brushes, or ink. We sat in the forecourt of the little Daoist shrine above the village and scratched out our characters with chalk on a slate. As the years passed, the teacher became thinner and frailer. He wheezed when he talked and his skin turned yellow.

One day, when I was eleven, my father said the teacher would not come any more. The old man had died while smoking opium in a brothel in Yulin city. My father laughed and said at least he had died happy. But I was very troubled, and I wondered how a man of learning could live such a base life and die such a humiliating death. I resolved never to give in to the temptations of opium, the drug foisted on us by imperialists and exploiters, and to live a life of service to my motherland.

In those days, we knew little of the turmoil that engulfed China, of the battles of the warlords and the Nationalists. We heard talk of a strange new movement called Communism that was arriving in our province from far away, but when I asked about it, my father clouted me around the head and told me not to talk of it in front of the village elders.

My father, a hardworking and honest man, gained full-time employment with the merchant. He earned enough money to send me away to school. I enrolled at a small military college in Yulin city. We were taught drill and rudimentary tactics, reading and writing and mathematics, by elderly soldiers. Here, for the first time, I saw a wireless. I listened, transfixed, to the signals from Shanghai and from Japan. I begged to be allowed to unscrew the back and look inside, to see its mysterious workings. I was never allowed to do so, but here began my lifelong interest in communications technology, a passion that would take me to the highest levels of government.

But the road before me was to prove long and full of

bitterness. And nothing I learned at the military academy was to prepare me for what was to come.

Kai stopped reading, rubbed his eyes. The memoir was vile, its sanctimonious half-truths dripping from the page. He knew his grandfather as a venal, calculating man. If there had been a radio at the military academy, he would have stolen it. The part about instructing his children and grandchildren on the centrality of family was true enough, although such instruction consisted largely of threats. As for his 'hardworking and honest' great-grandfather, Kai knew his forbear had been muscle for the local loan shark. He wondered what he should be looking for, what Madeline Chen saw in the tatty little book. He read on.

In the late summer of 1937, the Japanese invaders began their frenzied assault on China's heartland. Japanese divisions pushed west, smashing through the Chinese positions, driving stunned and tearful refugees before them. All patriotic Chinese were united with one voice. Resist Japan! In the military academy, we discussed the situation until late into the night. I declared that our duty was to fight. The other cadets demurred, saying we had no weapons or experience. Only one agreed with me, a close friend who always seemed more of a bookworm than a soldier. He read so much that we called him Chen Wen, Literary Chen. He professed a deep love for the writings of Lu Xun, and for those of Voltaire and Goethe, which he had read in translation. He argued that the true source of China's weakness was its lack of democracy and a modern education system. But now all patriotic Chinese should do their duty.

Literary Chen and I made a plan. We packed knapsacks with bedding and warm clothing, and we stole into the kitchens and appropriated cornbread which we wrapped in paper. Then, late at night, we climbed through a window and ran away to join the war.

13

United Kingdom

Nicole landed at Heathrow, the English summer sullen, damp and cool. She waited in the aisle for the struggles with luggage in the overhead bins to subside. She made her way into the terminal, the interminable walk across the airport to the border control officers who eyed her, asked her business in strange, angular accents she found hard to understand, all the consonants in the wrong places, the weird lack of inflection that made the speech sound so passive-aggressive. She smiled her best smile, asked them to repeat themselves as she looked them right in the eyes, saw them soften a little.

Outside the terminal it smelled of cigarette smoke and cooking fat. She sat on a tiny bus that crawled to the car rental place. She took possession of a red Mini, and then, suitcases on the back seat, she was bowling down the motorway towards Oxford.

They had arranged a flat for her in Jericho. At her last briefing, in a brown airport hotel room in Madrid, her case officer, the one she called Gristle, had thrown the keys on the table, gestured to them with his chin.

'There you are,' he'd said.

She'd named him Gristle for the way the years of secret work were etched on his face, his body sinewy, the skin cured by weather and cigarette smoke and the vile sorghum spirit he liked to drink. He was sixty if he was a day and spoke the Mandarin of a Hunanese peasant and was, in all, a duplicitous shit, but Nicole had come to know him and in an unfathomable way, love him. For beneath the keen insults, the manipulations, she saw constancy to him and a perceptiveness that she admired. That and his ruthlessness. Gristle had sat with his cigarette clutched between the second and third fingers, the hand in a claw, trying to unsettle her.

'Nice place, I hear,' he said. 'There are fancy bakeries and restaurants. Boutiques. Just the sort of places you like.'

'I'm ecstatic.' She sat cross-legged on the bed, distanced from him, denying him the ability to dominate the physical interaction.

'You fucking should be on what we're paying you.'

'Tell the Ministry of State Security they can get someone cheaper. See how it goes,' she said, idly.

'Maybe we will. A proper Chinese girl. One we can trust.'

She gave him a dry smile.

'But you can't, can you? You pay, sweetheart, for me and for my Taiwan passport. So suck it up.'

She looked up suddenly, as if something had occurred to her.

'Where's your little boyfriend, anyway?' she said. 'Why isn't he here, with his little laptop and his questions?' Gristle usually brought a junior case officer with him. This time he was alone. '*Chao jia le ma?*' Had a tiff?

'He's outside in the car.'

She laughed.

'Why?'

'He's not cleared for this.'

What? she thought, keeping her expression level.

'My, how you excite me,' she said.

He exhaled, watched her.

All right, we're getting serious, thought Nicole.

'You know the outlines of what we require from you during the coming year,' he said. 'Your Oxford year.'

She gave him a false pout.

'I am to report on Oxford's student groups and assorted crazies. I am to report on anyone who is Chinese while concurrently Muslim. And I am to babysit the bed-wetting princeling, Fan Kaikai. Don't worry, I was briefed into submission long ago.'

'I said, you know the outlines.'

'Why? Is there more?'

He was lighting another cigarette from the butt of the first, leaning back in his chair.

'Foreign intelligence, you know, no one really gives a shit. I mean, they like it. It makes them feel important. All that stuff you got by screwing that old man in Washington, it was pretty good. It went in the reports, and maybe some powdered prick in the Foreign Ministry got to read it, and everyone's happy.'

She was listening to him, every nerve tight, now.

'But this, Nicole, is different.'

She said nothing, waited.

'This has become somewhat serious.'

'Why? Why is it serious? I don't see how babysitting—'

He cut her off, his voice hard.

'I am about to fucking tell you.'

She raised her eyebrows, made a mock frightened expression which he ignored.

'The Ministry is worried. Or, more accurately, the Ministry is in a quivering fit of paranoia.'

He tapped ash from his cigarette, the *tiptip* sound of index finger against paper, the hiss of the burning tobacco.

'Where this paranoia has come from, from what poisoned well it has arisen, we are not cleared to know.'

He made a dismissive gesture. Speaking seemed to be costing him great effort, and she realised she had never seen him like this. Scared.

'These last few months ... well, you wouldn't believe it. Internal investigations, self-criticisms, sudden retirements. Everyone jumping at shadows. It's like a fucking purge.'

He paused, dragged on the cigarette, inhaled. She waited. He spoke very quietly.

'They've seen something, heard something out there, a noise, a signal. A threat. And now we're scuttling around in the dark, chasing it down. Every lead. Every guess.'

She said nothing, just held her hands out as if to say, *What do you want me to do about it?* He was suddenly furious with her, jerking himself forward in his chair, shouting, the spittle flying.

'Don't fucking play with me! Don't fucking sit there and shrug your little whore shoulders at me. You will get to *work*, you little bitch.'

She shrank back.

'Doing what? What am I looking for?'

'Anything! Everything! Who does Fan Kaikai see? Why? When? Why was his room turned over? What was on that laptop? Something was, because the Ministry's biggest hard-arses are in fainting fits about it. They are swooning in the fucking corridors over the Fan family and its stolen laptop and you, *you,* are hereby appointed Fan Kaikai's chief protector, inquisitor, nanny and shrink, and you come to me with everything. *Everything!* Do you understand?'

She swallowed.

'All right. All right,' she said.

'There's more,' he spat.

'More,' she repeated.

'The Chen girl. Madeline Chen.'

'Am I supposed to know who she is?'

'You know perfectly well who she is.' She did, of course – Madeline was the daughter of General Chen, the dour schemer who'd just ascended the throne of military intelligence.

'You will seek her out. Talk to her. She has minders. Or maybe something more than minders. They're not ours. Who the fuck are they? Where do they stay? What do they do? And why?'

'How do I get her to talk?'

The question seemed to thrust him back into his rage. He was shouting, rising from his seat.

'*How?* Use your fucking *charm*! And when that fails . . .'

'What?'

He looked away from her and flapped a hand in the air.

'You will treat her as a hostile target.'

'Meaning?'

'Meaning . . . do whatever you have to do. If there's a mess, we'll clean up.'

She said nothing, let the thought sink in, felt a cold crackle of anticipation in her stomach. He watched her, then nodded slowly.

'You will do this. And when you have something, you signal and you talk only to me. Only to me.' He was jabbing a finger at her again. 'And, trust me, nothing you have done so far in your *career* remotely compares with the significance of this task.'

He sighed, rubbed his eyes.

'You,' he said, 'are a small part of a large effort. Maybe Madeline Chen knows fuck all. Maybe her minders are just . . . minders. I don't know. But maybe she knows . . . *something*. It's called a lead. So we chase it.'

They talked finance, and then communications, arrangements with the Ministry of State Security's London residency, the need for politesse with the Fan family. And he'd gentled her a little, and threatened her again, and then he'd taken everything that had gone between them and twisted it around her like a rope. Then he dismissed her. And she'd left, bound and plucked and willing, for the plane. As she always did.

She crawled through Oxford, braking for rivers of tourists and erratic cyclists. She parked the Mini. The Jericho flat was nicer than she'd expected. It was on the ground floor of a white terraced house in a narrow, crooked street, a hanging basket of geraniums by the dark green door. Quaint, she thought, on the edge of twee. She stood in the airy living room, which opened onto a tiny garden, enjoying her luck.

That first afternoon, a weighty, perspiring man came from the embassy, hefted a black flight case in through the front door, complained about the traffic, the weather, the country, the food, and then swept the place for microphones. He pronounced it clean. After he left, she unpacked, walked to a mini-market, making a mental note of all the cars on the street, their numbers and colours. She bought pasta and coffee and wine and vegetables, walked home, stocked the fridge. She poured herself a glass of Viognier, stood in the garden in afternoon sunlight and birdsong, the glass cool against her fingers.

This was dangerous.

She had always worked against foreign targets, the dance, the seduction, the careful handling of an agent. But this – this smelled of internal security, the boneyards of Party infighting. This was a place where you knew no one, where you found enemies who didn't forget.

She thought about Madeline Chen, the hostile target, and how to get to her.

14

Kai sat in an upstairs coffee shop, a cosy place of pine and frilled curtains that felt unthreatening to him, comforting. The memoir was on the table in front of him. It had, as yet, yielded few secrets. Grandpa was building his wartime credentials.

We walked for days, into a tide of refugees fleeing the Japanese advance. The refugees were in a sorry state. I saw whole families struggling along the road, pushing their elderly relatives and children in handcarts. Some had brought furniture and suitcases full of clothing and family treasures, but discarded them as the miles passed and the road became more gruelling. The roadside was littered with gowns and photographs and broken crockery. We slept on the ground, wrapped in our bedding.

On the third day, I had my first glimpse of the Japanese invader.

The day dawned clear and cold. So many refugees were moving west that Literary Chen and I, walking east, were forced to leave the road and take to the fields. We cursed as we made our way across the dusty soil and corn husks. But leaving the road may have saved our lives.

In the early afternoon, we heard the whine of an engine, and the refugees on the road began to move quickly, urgently looking up at the sky. And then it was upon us, a Japanese fighter aircraft, a biplane, coming in low from the east. I watched, astonished, as it came lower and lower and levelled off, following the road, and opened fire on the refugees.

What followed was horrifying. People ran from the road and threw themselves flat in the fields. Those encumbered with elderly people and children could not move fast enough. The aircraft's machine guns handed them their death. The bullets sent dust and shrapnel flying, and people writhed and screamed. Bodies were strewn all over the road, and a trail of shoes and clothes and eyeglasses and shattered handcarts traced the guns' path. The aircraft was banking, and seemed to be coming in for another strafing run, but to my astonishment people were running back onto the road and looting. I saw one man gathering up spilled rice in his hands, another trying to open what appeared to be an abandoned jewellery chest. Disgusted, Literary Chen and I ran on, ever more determined to join the fight. We passed families sitting in the fields with the bodies of their loved ones, trying to keep away the packs of filthy, emaciated dogs.

We were soon to find our opportunity to join the war.

15

Addis Ababa, Ethiopia

Mangan, in his pyjamas, regarded his laptop in the darkness, his feet cold on the concrete floor, a glass of vodka in his hand. The four photographs that had turned up in his email glowed on the screen.

What *was* this?

It was someone informing him that he was being watched.

But who was being watched? Philip Mangan, the feckless if occasionally inspired journalist who lives alone in a shabby fourth-floor apartment in Gotera and files copy for a reputable newspaper on the rare occasions he can stir himself to do so? Who claims to be unveiling the machinery of insurgency and repression in East Africa? Who has a petulant curiosity concerning China, its corporations, their workings in Africa?

Or the other Philip Mangan? The one from whom, in the recent past, a hidden, parallel life had sprouted like an unexpected limb. The one who had found in himself an unimagined capacity for deception, for betrayal and for a kind of courage.

And an unimagined capacity for killing.

Was the photographer interested in this Philip Mangan, for whom the ordinary, the quotidien, the mundane business of living, had fissured and would not knit together again, ever?

Can I tell Hoddinott about this? he thought. Yes, I can. And perhaps I can give him the INSA tidbit, the Chinese computers and technicians burrowing into Ethiopia's intelligence agencies. He resolved to call Hoddinott. He felt as if he were leaning over some deep, dark pool, touching its surface, balancing on its edge.

Hallelujah phoned, sounding rushed and wired.

'It's the World Cup qualifier tomorrow, so we'll all watch at Burger House. They have a big screen. You're coming, right?'

'Perhaps, Hal.'

'What do you mean, perhaps? This is a time of national glory, Philip! All Ethiopia wants you there.'

'Perhaps.'

'No, no, Philip, I predict Maja will be there. You must come.'

'Oh. All right.'

He paused.

'Thanks, Hal.'

'No, no. Thanks to you, my friend.'

The photographs on his screen looked like a threat – or a promise.

Burger House was packed and raucous. Girls had daubed red, yellow and green on their cheeks. They draped each other in flags and scarves and some had started dancing while the young men leaned against the bar drinking St George's and watched and whooped. In the centre of the restaurant a huge television screen was showing the pre-game, with commentary in Amharic at blistering volume. Around it, chairs were placed in a semicircle, but all of them were taken and people sprawled on the floor. Where to sit? Hallelujah pursed his lips, looked around and caught the eye of the bartender, who gestured them over and mouthed something in his ear. Hallelujah took Mangan by the arm.

'He's my friend,' he said. 'We go to the garden.' They threaded their way through the restaurant and out of a back door into soft evening light, the smoky, sweet smell. More plastic chairs on a scrubby lawn and another screen beneath a spindly tree. Maja stood in a small group, saw Mangan immediately and made a *cheers* gesture with her beer bottle. He went over to her. Her hair was loose, hung carelessly. She wore a dark blue dress and a wrap. He had an idea she'd been waiting for him, then told himself not to be stupid.

'The elusive journalist,' she said.

'Elusive? Me?' said Mangan.

'I'd been wondering when I might see you.'

He looked at her questioningly.

'I was thinking about how I might, what does one say, give you a story.'

'Are we going to Ogaden?'

'Ogaden is hard going, you know.'

'I can do hard going.'

'Oh, yes? You look like the diplomatic cocktail party type to me,' she said.

Mangan blinked.

'I'm not that. I . . .'

'Ogaden is for tough people. You look like you'll blow over in a strong breeze.'

Wrong-footed now, Mangan found a beer bottle being pushed into his hand. Hallelujah was watching the exchange, smiling.

'I've been tough. In the past. I was tough in China.'

'Yes, and I've been meaning to ask you that. Why did you leave China?' she said, abruptly. 'Who leaves Beijing for Addis Ababa? Can it be considered a promotion?'

Mangan took a breath. She was smiling, laughing at him. It dawned slowly on him that she was flirting.

'Who leaves Copenhagen for Ogaden?' he managed.

'I'm not from Copenhagen, I'm from Løkken. A little seaside

town, where the North Sea meets the Skagerrak. Huge skies, freezing beaches.'

'So, Ogaden makes for a contrast.'

'It does. The climate. And the cuisine. Herring consumption is limited in Ogaden.'

'Herring?' said Hallelujah, frowning. 'What is it?'

Maja and Mangan both laughed.

'A fish,' she said.

'A fine, forceful fish,' said Mangan. 'Pickled or charred.'

And as he looked at the two of them and felt the warmth of her look, her laughter, there started up quite suddenly a metallic ringing in Mangan's bones.

He registered in a tiny, rushing fragment of time a flicker of shock on her face and a reflexive jerking movement of her hands. He felt himself drop his beer bottle, or, more accurately, felt it carried out of his hands. A powerful, piercing shriek in his ears and a *whump* of acrid heat hit him hard in the back and enveloped him.

And then he was looking at packed earth and felt strands of grass against his face and something was happening inside his head at the back of his nose, a sort of ticking, as if the pressure were changing deep inside him.

And then pain, deep in his eyes, his jaw.

And as he reached out for support, for anything, he seemed to roll and he looked up to a storm of silent flying insects, black against the evening sky, the air dark, predatory, full of motion.

After that, stillness, and some sense of a period of time passing, though he couldn't say how long. Movement in his peripheral vision, but otherwise he just looked at an empty sky. And the pain receding somewhat, and deep inside his head the thin metallic ring, though falling away a little now, and an awareness of shards and bits on his skin and lips. He tried to spit, but his mouth was dry.

And then the sky was blotted out and he felt fingers on his throat, and Maja's voice calling him from some distance. He felt able to nod, and she was kneeling over him, telling him to get up. He saw that all of the lights were out. He heard, beyond the ringing, what seemed to be glass shattering and other voices.

'Did the . . . the power . . . ' he said.

'Philip, you can hear me?'

'Yes,' he said.

'It's a bomb. You understand?'

He nodded.

'You are all right. We need to move. *Now*. Stand up,' she said.

Slowly he got to his feet. He was shaking. She held his hands. His eyes and head cleared a little.

'Where's Hal?' he said.

'He's here. He's hurt, but it's not bad, some shrapnel to the arms. He's walking out to the street. Don't worry.'

Some shrapnel.

'And you . . . ?' he asked.

'I'm okay. I'm fine. But inside, they're not fine. I am going in.'

'No,' he said. 'There might be another device. We should go.'

'Philip, I am a nurse. I have to go in.'

'No.' He shook his head. She shrugged. He noticed that she was speckled with dirt, her dress torn at the side.

'I have no choice,' she said.

He saw a bottle of water on the ground. He took an unsteady step and picked it up, undid the cap and poured water over his face, washing out his eyes, rinsing his mouth. He coughed and spat. He felt for his phone.

'All right. I'll come.'

'You'll come?'

'Yes. Together, okay?'

She nodded, and he could see now that she was very frightened, and very determined. They walked hand in hand towards the restaurant's back door. Smoke drifted from it and inside was only darkness.

16

She went first, but a figure blundered out, thrusting her to one side. Mangan could hear shouts coming from inside. They were in a corridor; other figures were walking unsteadily towards them.

'Which way?' said one man, his hands over his eyes, his face grey with dust.

'Just walk straight ahead,' said Mangan, 'and you'll get out.' The man trailed a hand along the wall as he walked. They made their way into the restaurant, where the television had been, and the crowd surrounding it. The smell: searing, meat, shit, chemical acrid burning. Cloying smoke, dust like flour in the air, the floor uneven beneath their feet.

Mangan took out his phone and activated it so the screen lit and cast a muted grey light. Through the dust, he saw undifferentiated shapes, dark mounds, splintered furniture. He ran the light along the floor. Liquid spatter.

He could hear Maja's breathing.

'There,' she said, taking his hand and guiding the light. A face, smothered in dust. Mangan pulled a table and a slab of drywall to one side. Maja knelt. It was a woman. She was unresponsive. Her clothes were in shreds. Mangan saw puncture wounds in her arms and neck. Maja shook her head, stood.

'Look again,' she said.

He stepped forward gingerly, moving the light around. There, a movement. Maja went to it. A boy, teeth clenched, a hissing sound as he breathed through them. His hands were reaching in the air, as if he were falling. More puncture wounds. One leg was gone above the knee, the bone a sharp white nub in the light.

'This one,' said Maja. She looked around. 'See there? That flag? Pass it to me.'

Mangan hauled on the yellow fabric, shook it. They began to tear it into strips.

'And a pen, Philip, or a stick ... anything.' She wrapped the fabric around his thigh, round and round, as the boy watched, gripped her shoulder. The hiss of his breath. As she tied it off, Mangan grubbed around in filth on the floor. A metal fork, food still adhered to the tines. She took it, ran it under the fabric, and began to turn with both hands, ratcheting it tight, bearing down on the femoral artery. The boy said something unintelligible, then gave an urgent, rising moan. Maja turned to him, took him by the shoulders, spoke to him sharply in Amharic. He nodded and blinked. Then she stood.

'What did you say to him?' Mangan said.

'Told him he'll live. Come on, Philip, another.'

They picked their way through the room by the phone's light. Maja put on two more tourniquets, an arm, another leg, Mangan frantically searching for a windlass each time – a shard of wood, a spoon. Maja checked shapeless mounds for signs of life, tried to open airways. There was nothing they could do for the puncture wounds. Mangan became disoriented, wondered where the exit was, and where the emergency services were, when, finally, they heard movement and shouted orders, saw torches.

They walked out into the night air, holding each other, through the flashing lights and men in uniform. No one paid them any attention.

They walked onto the street, where a crowd had gathered. Beneath a street lamp, Mangan saw that Maja was covered in blood, her face smeared, her hair matted. He went over to a man and asked for a cigarette. The man looked at him wide-eyed, gave him the pack and matches, shrank away.

They stood in the street and smoked. Mangan called the desk in London. Late afternoon there. He told the duty editor.

'Christ. Can you file?'

'Yes, just as soon as I—'

'No, now, please, Philip. Just go. I'm recording.'

So Mangan stood in the street, the stench in his nose, Maja leaning against him blowing blue smoke into the dark, the shifting, silent crowd around them, and filed copy. Terrorism, yes. The shrapnel. This was no generator explosion. Possibly fundamentalist payback for Ethiopian military operations in Somalia, yes. Number of dead, Philip?

I don't know. Dozens. Go with dozens. For now. Yes, there'll be foreigners.

When he'd finished, Maja looked at him. He saw the emergency vehicles' flashing lights reflected in her eyes.

'That's amazing,' she said. 'How do you do that?'

He called Hallelujah, who was at Tikur Anbessa Hospital. Mangan and Maja walked a little, found a taxi and went to pick him up. Hallelujah was waiting for them on the pavement, both arms hastily bandaged. They went back to Mangan's flat in Gotera, turned on the television and opened the vodka bottle. Maja stood in the shower for a long time, used up all the hot water, and emerged wearing one of Mangan's shirts.

There had been two blasts, said the BBC – the other across town at an outdoor screen. Many more dead there. The devices had been seeded with nails and ball bearings.

Mangan opened his laptop, started getting impressions and facts down, shaping it for an eyewitness piece, asking the others questions.

Process it, he said. It's good to do that. His mobile was ringing, radio stations wanting him live, but he soon turned it off.

'You went back in,' said Hallelujah, wonderingly.

Maja leaned against Mangan and the tears began to come and she wept and wept, silently.

By two in the morning, the desk frantic, Mangan had finished a two-thousand-word piece that captured some of it at least, caught the lethal black spindrift against the sky, the boy's breathing. He sent it, and then they'd had enough, turned off the television and sat in the silence. Hallelujah stretched out on the couch and closed his eyes, and Mangan and Maja went to his bed, where she slipped the shirt off and lay naked against him and cried more, her whole body heaving.

Mangan did not cry. He took it all and placed it beyond the fissure, in the place where such things resided.

The next day was a blur. On three hours' sleep and a strong coffee he was back to what remained of Burger House, blackened and stinking in the daylight. They were still digging people out. He peered over the tape, into the garden strewn with debris.

How did I survive that?

He took photos. A police officer offered to take him inside, but he said no.

The site of the other blast was open air, so less to see, blood trails on grass, scattered shoes. There were press briefings from police and the Prime Minister's office, little more than holding statements.

He called Hoddinott at the embassy and told him he'd been at the restaurant.

'My God. Are you all right?'

'I think so.'

'Philip, I'm so sorry. That must have been terrible.'

'I'm filing. Look, what can you tell me?'

A pause.

'Attributable to Western officials,' said Hoddinott.

'Sure,' said Mangan.

'A credible claim of responsibility out of Somalia. Tawhid. Small but potent outfit, transnational players, links to South Asia.'

'What makes it credible?'

'Explicit. Timing. Knowledge of the locations. MO.'

'Spoken to anyone? NISS?'

'Not on the phone. Got to go. Try later.'

'I knew you were a gentleman,' said Mangan.

'You mistake me,' said Hoddinott, and hung up.

Mangan filed first on the claim of responsibility, beating the wire services, to jubilation at the paper. His mobile started ringing again with interview requests: Radio Australia, NPR, the BBC. He filed again at four with more detail and furious quotes from an official at the defence ministry promising Ethiopian vengeance. Mangan conducted the interview on a dreadful line as he knelt on a street corner balancing a pad on his knee making notes. He went to two hospitals, but could not get access to any of the injured. He spoke to a doctor who described the wounds. He filed again. Traumatic amputation. Penetrating trauma. Burns. Internal blast injuries that they couldn't see.

He spoke to Hoddinott again, this time during a walk in the embassy gardens.

'The thing is,' said Hoddinott, 'where the hell did it all come from? The operatives? The devices? Is there a cell here in Addis, or was it all run in from Somalia? We're offering all the help we can. So are the Americans, the French. But NISS is saying nothing to us.'

'Any forensics?' said Mangan.

'That's another thing. The crime scene's a bloody mess. There were sweepers in there this morning, clearing stuff up, putting it all in bin bags. There's an American forensics team at the Sheraton having litters of kittens.'

He filed again, timing it to beat the big evening TV news bulletins.

Stunned with exhaustion, Mangan caught a cab home, to find Hallelujah and Maja still there, and Abraha and his wife, Hilina, as well. Maja gave him a long hug. Abraha was in the kitchen making *firfir* – comfort food. Mangan stood in the doorway, watching him fry the onions, spoon in the tomatoes, the ochre *berbere,* spice-infused butter, a handful of green chillies. Abraha looked up at Mangan through his glasses, a long, pained look. Then he put down the spatula he was holding and embraced him.

'I'm all right,' said Mangan.

'Thanks and praise to God,' said Abraha.

Turning back to the stove, he picked up chopped beef in both hands, watery blood dripping through his fingers. Mangan had to turn away.

When the news from Addis broke, Patterson had been clearing her desk at VX for the afternoon, locking her safe. The alerts came up blinking at the top of her screen. She sat down again, started scrolling through the reporting, such as it was. Over in Africa Controllerate and Global Issues/Counter-terrorism, they'd be settling in for a long night. Cheltenham would be humming, mining the databases, looking for traffic spikes, patterns.

The monitors had put up the first media reports – some flashes from the wires. She turned on a television feed, saw early pictures of the restaurant, stills snapped by eyewitnesses. She felt the claws in her chest that came from knowing that scene, that smell.

And then, there was *his* byline.

He'd been there? In the restaurant? She leaned into the screen. It was an eyewitness account and an early stab at some analysis. Competent, measured, but tinged with detail that shocked, drew you in. Some lines on a boy, his leg shattered, labouring to breathe in the sour, clogged darkness, how his hands reached out. Pure Mangan.

But that was always his strength, wasn't it? The gaze, the understanding.

For the next three days Mangan worked incessantly, filing several times each day. Maja went back to the hostel where she was staying, despairing of seeing him, and volunteered at the hospital. Hallelujah went to his parents, so Mangan was alone, rushing around Addis as the story went cold. No leads. Or none anyone was talking about. The city shuffled about its business, its people wide-eyed, ashamed somehow.

On the Friday afternoon, he downed tools, turned off his mobile and went to the bar at the Jupiter Hotel. He sat in a brown armchair beneath the towering wooden pillars, drinking in the calm, the faux afro vibe. He ordered a macchiato, and fell fast asleep.

When he woke, the Clown was sitting opposite him, watching him.

17

Mangan sat up in his chair abruptly, rubbed his eyes. His mouth was thick and he was hot.

'What ... do you want something?' he said

The Clown just sat, the black eyes unmoving, expressionless.

Mangan held his hands open, a questioning gesture.

'A terrible week,' said the Clown, in English.

'Why have you been watching me?' said Mangan. The business with the photographs, the man's appearance at the jazz bar, seemed to lie in the distant past.

'Your reporting has been excellent, we think,' the Clown said. 'And we have something to contribute.'

'Who is we?'

'Please take this,' and he drew an envelope from his jacket, laid it on the table. His manner was businesslike.

'Please tell me what it is,' said Mangan.

The Clown leaned forward in his chair. Mangan noticed that he wore a jade pendant around his neck.

'It is a very good story. Of interest to many different readers. Or many different *kinds* of reader. Perhaps you have some *guanxi* to whom it would be of particular relevance.'

Mangan was shaking his head.

'You're going to have to explain.'

'Take a look at it after I leave. It will explain itself.' The Clown placed both hands on the arms of his chair, as if preparing to stand and leave. 'But perhaps you might consider through which channels you decide to report it.'

He smiled and then stood.

'How do I contact you?' said Mangan quickly.

The Clown nodded approvingly.

'Don't worry. I'll find you,' he said. And he turned and walked from the bar.

Mangan got out of the taxi half a mile short of his apartment block in Gotera. The street was alive this warm Friday evening, the girls out, made up, their hair shining, walking arm-in-arm, the rising, questioning tone of their chatter on the air, the way of it in Amharic. He stopped at First Choice café and ordered takeout, a styrofoam box of *tibs*. While he waited, he drank a beer, back to the wall, watching the street.

Anyone waiting with him? Apparently not.

When his order was ready he left the café, walked straight past the entrance to his block, turned a corner, kept walking, stopped and doubled back.

Nothing. Or nothing he could see.

Except? A car, parked at the opposite corner, sedan, battered, white, two unmoving figures in the front seats, windows shut.

Who might that be?

He took the stairs two at a time, let himself into his flat, and looked from the window. One of the figures appeared to be speaking on a phone. Then the car started up and pulled a short distance down the street before stopping again.

He dropped his bag and walked into the bedroom, let the blinds down, sat on the edge of the bed.

He took the envelope from his jacket pocket.

The line is so fine, he thought. You slit open an envelope and everything changes.

18

It was two sheets. One a printout of a scanned document, all in Chinese, with the header clumsily cut off. No indication of classification to be seen. The other a printed list of phone numbers, with a variety of country codes.

He turned his attention to the scanned document. Even though the header information was gone, someone had handwritten a date and underlined it twice. The date was the previous Tuesday, four days ago, the day after the bombing. Mangan began to feel his way through the characters. *Disposition and movements of Ma Te Na Yi Mu: source reports.*

Who is Ma Te Na Yi Mu? A sinicised name, so a foreigner, not a Chinese. But impossible to tell what the original name was, or where it was from.

And why do we care?

Ma Te Na Yi Mu, whoever he might be, had moved residences. He had travelled by road in a convoy of three vehicles, at night. He was now residing at a farmhouse. A grid reference. Mangan went to the living room, brought back his laptop, went online. The grid reference placed the farmhouse just outside the coastal town of Baraawe, in southern Somalia. A satellite image showed a cluster of walled compounds, two or three low buildings to each, some distance from the road, the terrain flat, scrub-covered, rising to a bluff just off to the east.

Ma Te Na Yi Mu resides here. And are these his phone numbers? Mangan looked up the country codes. Somalia, Malaysia, Indonesia, Kenya, Yemen. Two of them appeared to be satellite phones.

Well, then. A name, a place and, perhaps, a network.

Source reports.

And a spy.

Mangan put the two sheets of paper down. He looked from the window. The white sedan hadn't moved. But now there was a boy leaning over it talking to the driver through the window.

He lit a cigarette.

Christ, you're dumb sometimes, he thought.

He went back to the laptop, set the input language to Chinese and entered Ma Te Na Yi Mu, copying the way it was written in the document, the characters meaningless on their own but used to represent foreign names phonetically. He searched the combination.

A blizzard of hits. Ma Te Na Yi Mu denounces Indonesian government's counter-terror tactics. Ma Te Na Yi Mu suspect in resort bombing. Ma Te Na Yi Mu calls on Malaysian men to join jihad. Ma Te Na Yi Mu placed on FBI's most wanted list.

And there, his name romanised.

Mat Naim. Malaysian citizen, fugitive, whereabouts unknown, wanted by the United States and who knew how many other governments. Explosives expert. Bomb maker. A picture in black and white showed a young man of studious appearance, spectacled, earnest. In another he had grown a beard and wore a *kopiah*. He had studied at agricultural college and married a woman on a remote Indonesian island who bore him a son. His published statements revealed a preoccupation with the Christian and Buddhist Chinese of South-east Asia, as sinister and as repugnant as Jews, he wrote, as degenerate as Europeans.

Mat Naim is in Somalia. *Source reports.*

Mangan opened a blank document on his laptop, began to feel it out, just to see.

'Exclusive from our East Africa Correspondent. Addis Ababa – The notorious Malaysian bomb maker known as Mat Naim may be in southern Somalia, according to sensitive sources. The revelation comes just days after dozens of people died and hundreds were injured by twin blasts in Ethiopia's capital.'

He changed 'may be in' to 'has recently been spotted in'.

He could have it on the website in minutes. *Great story, Philip*. He lit another cigarette.

He walked about the room in darkness, listening to the music drifting up from the street. He thought of Beijing, its winter streets, the smell of grilled lamb in cumin on the cold air. He thought of a slender, smiling figure doing her fake sashay across a room lit with afternoon sun.

He thought of a death, and a night highway streaked with headlights, terror pulsing in his blood.

File the story, he thought. Be who you are. Be a reporter.

But it is not who you are. Not since the world broke open and you saw deep into its maw and you became somebody different.

He picked up the two sheets of paper. For your *guanxi*.

He dialled Hoddinott's number.

PART TWO

The Hook.

19

Addis Ababa, Ethiopia

'Hoddinott.'

   'It's Philip. Mangan.'

   'It's very late.'

   'I know, I'm sorry. It's urgent.'

   'Well?'

   'Something you need to see.'

A pause.

   'Can it wait until tomorrow?'

   'No.'

   'Is this for a story? You're filing?'

   'This is ... something else.'

   'You're sure.'

   'I'm afraid I am, yes.'

Mangan heard a breath at the other end of the phone.

   'I'll come and pick you up at your flat.'

Mangan walked to the window. The white car was still there.

   'No. Come to Mauritius Street, corner of Pushkin Street.'

Another pause. Hoddinott spoke slowly.

   'Are we quite sure?'

'Sure enough.'

A sigh.

'All right.' Hoddinott hung up.

Mangan put the two pages back in their envelope, and then, for some reason, in a polythene bag. He put the bag in a money belt, which he strapped around his waist under his shirt. He put on a dark jacket and a floppy sun hat to cover his hair. Leaving the lights on, he slipped out of the front door and crawled along the landing, below the level of the concrete balustrade, the floor cool and filthy against his hands. Once in the stairwell, covered from view, he ran two steps at a time to the ground floor. It was midnight now; the streets still thronged with people, shadows, snatches of music, cigarette smoke on the air. He walked to the rear of the building, pushed open a peeling wooden door that squealed in objection, stepped out into a filthy courtyard; the rustle of rats amid the rubbish bins, a stench of rot. He walked along the exterior wall in the darkness, slipped into an alleyway and stood, breathing hard. *Philip Mangan once again turns operational. Bravely crawls from apartment for no discernible reason.* He could just see the rear end of the sedan, still static. He waited. No one came. He circled around the block, away from the car, and made for Mauritius Street. *Philip Mangan, secret agent, prepares to meet British Intelligence, make fool of self.* Jesus Christ.

20

Oxford

Kai sat on the grass in the quad under limpid sunlight. Grandpa's memoir was becoming portentous, working up to something.

> The day after the strafing we encountered some deserting soldiers, their uniforms in tatters. I wanted to berate them, but Literary Chen warned me to be quiet. He approached them carefully and offered them the last of our cornbread in exchange for two rifles and ammunition. They parted willingly with the weapons, old Hanyang bolt action rifles in poor condition, and a few rounds of ammunition. We walked on, heartened by the knowledge that at last we had the means to fight. The same day, by great fortune, we came upon a company of warlord troops by the side of the road. They said Chinese forces were making a stand at a place called Xinkou, and they were heading there, for this would be the place that Chinese forces held, and stopped the Japanese advance. We asked if we could join them and they said yes, and applauded our courage and fed us with rice and dried bean curd. We boarded trucks and went to war. We were seventeen.

Xinkou. The name lives in my memory. What happened to me there determined everything that I was to become.

When we arrived at Xinkou, we were taken to the company commander at his headquarters on a rocky hillside. He assigned us to making Molotov cocktails. He told us that the approaching Japanese had several dozen light tanks, and the Molotov cocktails would be used against them. We were taken to a cave where a huge pile of bottles and two drums of petrol awaited us. Hour after hour we funnelled the petrol into the bottles and sealed them with an oil-soaked rag. We had nothing to eat except one piece of steamed bread, which Literary Chen divided equally between us. When it became too dark, we rolled the petrol drums out on the hillside and carried on by moonlight. We could hear the grinding of the Japanese armour in the valley below us as the tanks moved up to their start-line.

The next morning, the tanks advanced, about eighteen of them, and we watched from the hillside as Chinese infantry rushed forward and hurled our Molotov cocktails. Several of the tanks caught fire and we could see the Japanese devils bailing out, and pillars of thick smoke rising to the sky. We were inflamed with pride and patriotism. We took our rifles and five rounds of ammunition each, and ran to the trenches to wait for the Japanese infantry.

Kai stopped reading, a memory billowing upward, breaking the surface.

His grandfather and his father, at a table strewn with the remains of a meal, dirty crockery, chopsticks, chicken bones, the air thick with cigarette smoke. They are looking at photographs, tiny black and whites. They are intent on the pictures, which have something to do with the war. Kai, a boy, walks around the table to them, asks to see the photographs. His grandfather waves him away and says, 'You wouldn't understand.' And in that instant a child's realisation takes hold that these two men have in common lived experience of great profundity. They have seen war and revolution. They have seen their country transform itself from bleak and bitter privation to the glossy prosperity of today. They have in common a shared knowledge that he, with his expensive education, his spoiled ways, will never possess.

He thought for a moment about these distant men, then read on.

We lasted a week. Nearly all of the officers were dead. Our supply lines had been bombed and we were out of food and water. Our ammunition was all but exhausted. Many Chinese soldiers had left their positions. Literary Chen and I were sleepless and starving. From our trenches we had watched the Chinese forces counter-attack, and seen the battle ebb and flow. The closest we got to fighting was firing at Japanese patrols as they came and probed for weaknesses in our sector. Our company commander ordered us to make our way to the rear. I asked him why we should leave. He said, with tears in his eyes, that we were too young to die, and he was ordering us to fall back.

We left at night and wandered sadly south-west towards the provincial capital. We had nothing to eat. The roads were infested with deserters and stragglers and danger was everywhere. After two days, close to exhaustion, I went to forage for food in a deserted farm cottage while Literary Chen watched the road in the twilight. I pushed open the door and knew immediately I had made a mistake. The air was thick with the smell of men sleeping, and out of the darkness a huge hand took me by the lapel and forced me to my knees.

I had stumbled into a patrol of the Communist Eighth Route Army. These were tough, self-sufficient men who spoke the rough, earthy Chinese of the villages. They questioned me and took my rifle. Then they fed me millet soup. When I told them that I had a comrade, Literary Chen, out on the road, two of them went to look for him, but he had gone, fearing, I assumed, that I had been taken by deserters or bandits. I did not see him for many years.

The Communist soldiers took me back to their base area, and, on learning I was literate, set me to work reading reports and newspapers out loud to them. They gave me a new uniform, looked after me well and talked to me about the future …

Pages of suffocating pap about his grandfather's conversion to communism, told in treacly anecdotes of kind-hearted, gravel-voiced cadres correcting his mistakes and enlightening him as to the realities of landlordism. Grandpa was reborn, and in a sort of salvation, sent back to his home province, Shaanxi. He ended up in Yan'an, the redoubt of the Communist movement, Mao's headquarters. There, for the duration of the war, he was assigned to the communications department. He watched as the Party's technicians, advised by an affable, absent-minded Englishman, built China's first international broadcast service. They strung copper wire between two mountain tops for an antenna, and sent out news bulletins in Morse, with no idea if anyone was listening. Crucially, Grandpa tinkered with radios and learned how to lay telephone cable, how to splice it when it was cut.

Kai dropped the book on the grass and dozed.

21

Addis Ababa, Ethiopia

Hoddinott came in a white SUV, bouncing in and out of the potholes beneath the dim street lights. The car slowed. Mangan stepped from a doorway, jogged across cracked, uneven pavement, dodging passers-by. Hoddinott saw him and stopped. He climbed in. Music was playing – thick, heavy, classical music, Mozart or something, music for all frequencies. Joanna was in the back wearing a fleece, stony-faced.

'Phone,' said Hoddinott. Mangan switched off his mobile, took the battery out, stowed it in the glove compartment.

They drove in silence for a few minutes, Hoddinott checking the mirrors, Joanna turning in her seat, craning her neck. They took the ring road, picked up some speed.

'All right. What was at the flat?' said Hoddinott. He wore a T-shirt, looked dishevelled, as if he'd been in bed.

'Look, I'm not sure, but I think I was being watched.'

'Who?'

'I didn't go and fucking ask them.'

Hoddinott shook his head.

'It was a car,' said Mangan. 'I had a weird encounter with a Chinese guy, and then this car turns up and sits outside my block.'

'Is that it? Is that why we're here?'

'No. You need to look at these.' Mangan unzipped the money belt, took out the plastic bag, the two sheets of paper.

'Give them to Joanna,' said Hoddinott.

Mangan turned round and handed them to her. She took them, switched on the overhead light.

'What is this?' she said. 'I don't bloody read Chinese.'

'I think it's an agent report,' said Mangan.

'Oh, an agent report,' said Hoddinott. He raised his voice. 'It's an agent report, Joanna.'

'Well, could you possibly enlighten us as to its contents, Philip?' she said.

He swallowed.

'It says Mat Naim is in Somalia and it gives his exact location. A grid reference.'

Silence.

'Do you know who Mat Naim is?' said Mangan.

'Yes! Yes, I know who Mat fucking Naim is!' Hoddinott shouted. 'What do you mean he's in Somalia?'

Mangan waited a beat. He turned in his seat, spoke to Joanna.

'Your husband's a bit of a drama queen, isn't he?'

Joanna leaned forward, and there was a set to her face, a look, that reminded him of someone: another handler, in a different place, at a different time. A woman who'd held herself like a soldier, who'd sent him into China. She'd had the same obdurate, evaluative look, the look that searched for threat.

'Now listen, Philip,' Joanna said. 'Just what the hell is going on here? Is this real? Where did you get it? And just so we know, are we playing out some little fantasy here, a bit of attention seeking? Missing us, are you? Want to get back in the game?'

'I'll tell you . . .'

'Did we, in fact, just make this whole fucking thing up? What do you think you're doing, actually?'

'Christ, if I knew what I was doing I wouldn't be here talking to you two hysterics.'

Hoddinott thumped the steering wheel.

'Tell us where you got this. Now.'

Mangan took a deep breath, slowed his speech down.

'Over the last few weeks, I've encountered this Chinese man a number of times. He's been watching me, somehow. He's taken photographs and emailed them to me. He's wanted me to know that I'm being watched.'

'Why didn't you tell me this?' Hoddinott snapped. 'Anything out of the ordinary, I said.'

'I was going to, but there was a bloody great bomb blast, if you remember, which led to a moment of preoccupation.'

Hoddinott pursed his lips, squinted into the oncoming headlights, shadow sliding across his face.

'Go on.'

'Earlier this evening, he turns up again in the bar at the Jupiter Hotel and gives me this. Tells me to report it, but through the right channels. He says it's for my *guanxi*, my connections.'

'What does that mean?' said Joanna. 'Why did he say that?'

'It means he knows. He knows that I'm linked ... to you.'

'How?'

'He knows.'

'And did he by any chance offer words of explanation as to why he was peddling this material to you?'

'He said, "we have something to contribute". Those were his words.'

'So you are suggesting that a Chinese operative has chosen you, *you*, as a channel to contact us, because of your ... history?'

'It would be an explanation.'

'I mean rather than going through the proper channels, say, like intelligence agencies usually do when they have crucial, time-sensitive, actionable intelligence to share,' she said.

'I have no idea why he is doing what he's doing.'

'You haven't been tarting yourself about, have you, Philip? Showing a bit of leg?'

'I'm a journalist, not a recluse.'

'Jesus Christ,' said Hoddinott.

'I want to speak to Trish,' said Mangan.

'And who might she be, Philip?'

Mangan looked from the car window, saw the darkened city, its millions of buried lives.

'She was my case officer. Before.'

22

The date. A reference number.

FM CX ADDIS ABABA
TO LONDON
TO TCI/29611
TO TCI/64335
TO P/C/62815
TO P/A/39751
FILE REF C/WFE C/A
FILE REF R/84459
FILE REF SB/38972
LEDGER UK S E C R E T
PRIORITY
/REPORT
1/ ADD 2 received a mobile phone call from Philip MANGAN
P77395. MANGAN requested an immediate meeting.
2/ ADD 2 and ADD 3 met MANGAN immediately by car. MANGAN said
he had possession of documents from an unidentified Chinese
source who had approached him earlier in the bar of the
Jupiter Hotel. The documents are written in Chinese. MANGAN

advises that the documents purport to be an agent report
originating from, and directed to, persons/agencies unknown.
MANGAN maintains the documents describe MAT NAIM as being
recently in southern Somalia and include details of his precise
location. Station cannot confirm that this is what the
documents say.

3/ Scanned copies of documents are attached.

DOCUMENT A

Printout of scanned document written in Chinese, with date.

DOCUMENT B

Printed list of telephone numbers.

4/ Station advises immediate translation and assessment of
DOCUMENT A, traces on numbers contained in DOCUMENT B.

/END

Patterson was eating an egg banjo hurriedly in the staff cafeteria when Hopko leaned over her shoulder.

'It's time,' was all she said.

Patterson wiped tomato ketchup from her mouth.

'When you're ready,' said Hopko.

Patterson stood, still chewing, and followed Hopko from the canteen. Hopko walked quickly, her gait assured, polished, that of a politician, or an executive. In her wake, threads of some expensive perfume Patterson did not recognise.

'So can I know what this is about?' said Patterson, catching up.

'Very soon,' said Hopko.

'Am I in trouble again?'

'Not exactly,' said Hopko. She paused, half-smiled. 'It seems your man has done it again.'

'What? What man?'

Unexpectedly, Hopko grabbed her upper arm, and Patterson for an instant found herself having to suppress the urge to parry and strike. Hopko steered her into a ladies' cloakroom, checked quickly to ensure they were alone, and turned to face her. Hopko spoke quietly.

'Philip Mangan.'

Patterson felt a flash of anticipation. She hid it.

'What's he done?'

'They are going to grill you, Trish. It's a very tricky situation and they need to decide, fast, what the hell to do. So stay on point, yes? I'll be with you.'

Patterson nodded. They left the cloakroom and took the lift to the fourth floor in silence. Hopko walked with her into a conference room. The room had the thick air of an all-night session, the table littered with discarded coffee cups, sheaves of paper, computer cables. Two grey-faced men sat jacketless and silent. Patterson recognised them. Weekes, Controller/Counter-terrorism, and Vezza, one of the Targeting Officers in the Africa Controllerate who had lectured on her New Entry Course, young, dark-haired, a wryness to him, a quickness of eye. Vezza smiled, nodded to her. Weekes spoke.

'Trish. Yup. Thanks for coming, especially on a Saturday. We need to talk to you briefly about Philip Mangan. Please sit.'

She sat. Hopko had taken a place at the table.

'You handled Mangan last year, correct? Tell us a bit about him.'

'Some context would be helpful,' said Patterson.

Weekes looked up at her.

'Just talk to us, please. Tell us what he's like.'

'Well, he's quietly spoken, retiring, sometimes. Though he can get angry, if he summons the energy. He's lanky, sort of rangy, tall. He has red hair, which makes him noticeable. He's disorganised, but he's not unreliable. He's very competent in important ways.'

'How? Be specific, please.'

'He knows how to elicit information. He asks questions like a reporter, because he is one. He finds things out very quickly. There were moments during the operation when he really shone. His first operational contact with the asset was remarkable.'

'Did you have a relationship with him?'

'I was his handler, so, yes, I had a relationship.'

'Answer the question.'

'I . . .'

'What he means is,' said Hopko, her voice tight, 'did you screw him?'

Patterson paused, caught herself. They are just trying to unsettle you, she thought.

'No, I did not,' she said brightly.

Weekes was looking at a file.

'What is it that you really want to know?' she said.

'What I really want to know? What I really want to know is if your Mangan is a faker. A pathetic little wannabe.'

There was a silence.

Patterson cleared her throat.

'I don't know how to respond to that,' she said.

Vezza sighed. He picked up a sheet of paper and slid it across the table to her. It was in Chinese.

'Trish, this came in seven hours ago from Addis station. Mangan passed it to station officers. He fancies it an agent report. A Chinese agent report, if you please. Not that we knew the Chinese had agents like this one, but there you are. And it gives a pinpoint location for Mat Naim, the bomb maker.'

Patterson swallowed.

'What did Mangan say by way of explanation?'

'That he had been targeted,' said Vezza. 'A Chinese man in Addis. We don't know who he is. This man passed him the papers, said to report it to his . . . what, connection? What was the word, Val?'

Hopko was looking directly at Trish. Those unmoving, brown eyes.

'He said it was for Philip's *guanxi*,' Hopko said.

Patterson sat very still.

'We have to decide, right now,' said Vezza, 'whether we send this on to the Americans.'

'Mat Naim could be long gone by now, and Mangan may be a fabricator,' said Weekes.

Vezza's voice was raised.

'And he could still *be there*. We are *not* in a position to withhold this.'

'And Mangan is no fabricator,' said Patterson.

'How the hell do you know what Mangan is?' snarled Weekes.

'He has strong instincts. He is a reporter, as well as an agent.'

'He *was* an agent. And he's not much of a bloody reporter.'

'He is good at gauging these things. If he passed it to station, it means he feels it's for real.'

'Very bloody civilised of him. That's enough. Get out,' said Weekes.

Vezza had raised his hands in exasperation. Hopko rose and followed Patterson out of the room. In the corridor, Patterson turned to her, but Hopko spoke first.

'They don't know what to do, and Weekes seems to have a problem handling stress,' she said, smiling.

'Val,' said Patterson.

'Oh, I know. Sounds familiar, doesn't it? "For his *guanxi*",' said Hopko.

'What is this?'

'Someone wants to talk. And they are bringing gifts. Wouldn't you say?'

Patterson just shook her head.

'Tell you one thing, though,' said Hopko, matter-of-factly. 'Mangan's a bloody natural.'

The two pieces of paper were sent two hours later, festooned with caveats. They went via liaison to the National Counterterrorism Center, just outside Washington DC. There, they created considerable excitement and no small degree of bafflement, given their unusual origins.

But their specificity was very persuasive.

For, it transpired, the Americans had already placed Mat Naim somewhere in the Horn of Africa some twenty-six days previously. Through a hideously expensive and complicated combination of cyber surveillance – a penetrated laptop – and satellite surveillance, they had him in Zanzibar, arriving by boat. And they had him moving up into Somalia. And there, a local asset in Baraawe, a boat captain, flickered providentially into life, using an encrypted phone to relay the gossip surrounding a farmhouse on the edge of town. A known transit point, this farmhouse. *And now*, said the captain, *movement*. Convoys of SUVs going in and out, deliveries. Extra checkpoints on the roads, dead-eyed boys lounging in pickups, sparked up on *chat,* cradling their AKs. *A frisson in town, you could feel it. Someone big is here.*

Finally, the kicker. The captain had heard a fellow sailor refer repeatedly to *al-Malisi* – the Malay.

And now, late in the day, collateral and grid references from a Chinese source via the jolly old Brits. The Chinese appeared to have an asset inside the target's circle, said the Brits, obliquely. Well, who knew? And a long and fascinating list of phone numbers, some of which matched known numbers for Mat Naim's south-east Asian handlers.

The numbers were planted in the servers at Fort Meade to see the gossamer web of contacts and associates breathe and grow.

And from there things began to move very quickly, for Mat Naim's full name already resided in the Disposition Matrix, alongside the contingency plans laid for a moment when he might slip into view. Capture, or kill, said the Matrix.

Within hours, from a small airbase at the edge of a lake in southern Ethiopia, a drone lifted off the tarmac, an MQ-9 Reaper, piloted remotely by an air force officer in Nevada. The officer's commands took one point two seconds to reach the drone. The officer pointed the drone's nose south-east. A little more than two hours later, the drone was over the town of Baraawe. It loitered at thirty thousand feet, listened, then eased down to a lower altitude to paint the target.

23

Oxford

Kai, back in his rooms after a soul-crushingly dull meeting of the Chinese Students' Association at which Madeline had not appeared, picked up the memoir. His grandfather's long ago links to the Chen family were explicit. The source of the Chen family's rage was not. Not yet, at least.

Grandpa was victorious. The Japanese surrendered in 1945. And China was able to get back to the business of its own unfinished civil war. This time Grandpa joined the fighting in earnest. His role – running cable from brigade headquarters out to the field telephones of frontline units. Sometimes he carried a great wheel of cable on his back, staggering across China's burned and blistered landscape. When the cables separated, he went on his knees in the mud, found the break and repaired it. He repaired radios, advised on tactical communications. He moved up in the Communist Party.

In 1949, Communist divisions pushed in from the west and took Beijing. Grandpa was quite the technician by now, and in the days that followed the founding of the People's Republic of China, he burrowed into the nascent Communist bureaucracy, securing a billet at the Ministry of Post and Telecommunications. Not very glamorous, Kai reflected, but the ambitious, grasping old man knew very well what he was doing. For the next sixteen years, Grandpa oversaw the building of China's telephone network. He supervised the running of copper cable all over the country for the first time. He travelled to foreign countries, East Germany, Hungary, divining the mysteries of teletype, microwave, even television. And all of this, *all* of it, was crucial work, vital to socialist modernisation, vital to the Party. Grandpa Fan became an important man, a *gaoji ganbu* – a senior cadre in a powerful ministry. He had a wife and three sons and a daughter, a nice flat. Access to a car, maybe. Pork for supper, white rice, even as they were starving in the villages. A tailored Mao suit with pens in the top pocket – all the subtle signifiers of status.

Kai was enveloped in the narrative now, sensed that something was coming. The memoir had taken on a sketchy, withholding tone.

In 1966, China descended into chaos. The Great Proletarian Cultural Revolution had begun. The Red Guards, filled with revolutionary fervour, taking literally Chairman Mao's instruction to 'Bombard the Headquarters', barged their way into ministries across Beijing. Many cadres were taken away for criticism and struggle. It was a very uncertain time.

Initially, the Ministry of Post and Telecommunications was protected from struggle, but in 1967, it was our turn. Senior cadres were forced to undergo long and terrifying criticism sessions. I was among them. I was bound and forced to kneel on broken glass. I said many things under duress that I later regretted. The bitterest moment came when my service in the war was criticised. The Red Guards alleged that I was a traitor because I had fought alongside Nationalist troops against the Japanese. They demanded I name those I fought with, and I did. It is a great cause of sadness to me that I was placed in this position. My family suffered, too. My children were shunned and beaten, my wife ostracised.

Dawn came as a dullness in the window. Kai put the book down, stood and walked around the room, ran his hand along the window sill. He wondered how many his grandfather had denounced. Was it only Literary Chen? Were there others?

24

Kai leaned against the wall. The evening was damp and warm, the pavements shiny with rain. He watched the street, the churning in his gut part unease, part transgressive thrill.

He had left a handwritten note in her pigeonhole. It said, in cheery English, 'Book Discussion! Memoir To Help Historical Understanding. 8 p.m.! Meet Outside Zoology.' Madeline came at four minutes after the hour. She wore sunglasses, a baseball cap, trainers, as if she expected to run. She didn't stop, walked right past him, then hissed over her shoulder at him.

'Follow me.'

He hurried after her. She crossed the road, took the footpath that led into the Parks. He stumbled along behind her, caught her up. He could smell her, something perfumed and lush and feminine and flecked with citrus.

'Is there anyone behind us?' she said.

'Should there be?'

He could feel the tension in her, in her slight shoulders, the tightness in her neck.

'They follow me sometimes. They are there, and then they're gone. They check up on me.'

'What? Who does?'

'These . . . men. My father sent them. But they frighten me.'

'Are you sure you're not . . . ?'

She turned to him, defensive.

'Not what?'

'Not . . . making a mistake?'

'Imagining them, you mean?'

'Well . . . '

She shook her head, made a hissing noise through her teeth. They walked on, her eyes skimming over the parkland, the trees.

'Did you read it?' she said.

'Yes.'

'And?'

'Literary Chen is your grandfather.'

'Was my grandfather, yes.'

'What happened to him?'

'What happened? Your grandfather denounced him. He was with the Writers' Association by then. The Red Guards came for him. They smashed up the family home, dragged him away. His wife and his little boy watched. They put a dunce's cap on him, made him run all round the neighbourhood.' She stopped, and they walked in silence, just the crunch of their feet on the wet, gravelly path. He prompted her.

'And then?'

'And then? Then they made him write self-criticism, beat him, struggled him. And then they sent him to a 7 May cadre school.'

Kai said nothing.

'And that's where he died.'

'How?' The question quiet, tentative. She ignored it.

'My grandmother was left alone in Beijing to bring up my father. She was thrown out of their apartment, of course. They had nowhere to go. She ended up being taken in by a foreman at Capital Steel, and they lived in his dormitory. A terrible place. I don't know much. But I know he hit her, handed her around among the steelworkers. And my father running wild amid all this filth, seeing it all.'

Kai said nothing.

'Oh, everyone was very sorry later. Literary Chen was rehabilitated, posthumously. My father was given a helping hand into the army to make up for things. But my grandmother was shattered, just this broken fragment of a woman who hardly ever spoke. And ever since, my father has taken all the simmering rage, the sense of waste, the damage, the trauma, all the years of poverty and unbelonging, and we have projected it single-mindedly ... onto you. The Fans. The Chens' humiliation is the Fans' fault. Didn't you know?'

Kai shook his head.

'Your grandfather. At the cadre school. How did he die?'

She had stopped and was looking quizzically at him.

'I don't think I'm ready to tell you that yet.'

He couldn't meet her eye, her cool amber gaze. He heard birdsong hanging in the air, registered the puddles on the path, their film of oily mauve and purple. And then she was taking his hand and laughing a quiet, resigned laugh.

'I almost came and talked to you,' she said. 'I saw you around. I knew exactly who you were.'

'And why didn't you?'

She played with his hand.

'I don't know. I was warned that you were some monster. I was scared. I thought ... you'd just be ... you know, dismissive.'

'Well, I'm not,' he said.

'I see that now.' She paused, looked around. 'Do you like it here?'

He smiled.

'Not really.'

'Me neither.' She nodded. 'Thanks.'

'For what?'

'For ... for talking. And for asking about what happened. And for not arguing with me, or explaining to me.'

For the briefest moment, their fingers interlaced. And then she took her hand back and walked away.

He watched her receding figure, stopped himself from walking after her. Where had he suddenly learned such self-control? He lifted his hand to his face, tried to breathe in the smell of her.

He left the Parks alone, the way they'd come. He turned onto South Parks Road, looked around himself. He felt an unfamiliar need for vigilance.

The street was quiet, the light fading now. An occasional car passed, a bicycle.

He headed for his college. As he walked past the chemistry buildings, he caught sight of another pedestrian walking towards him, a man with Asian features, Chinese perhaps, in his forties, a slight waddle to his walk, lank, thin hair. The man wore a grey padded anorak. Too heavy for a summer evening, Kai thought, he must be hot.

The man had stopped.

Kai continued to walk towards him and it became clear the man was watching him, waiting for him, even. Kai crossed the street. The man stood still, his eyes on Kai as he passed, a look of amused curiosity on his face.

25

Addis Ababa, Ethiopia

Mangan was in the Radisson Hotel, seated in the air-conditioned coffee shop, ordering lunch, when he saw the Associated Press flash.

Urgent

Washington, DC (AP) – A United States drone struck a target in Somalia overnight, administration officials confirmed. The drone fired two missiles at a compound in the town of Baraawe, south of Mogadishu.

A second lead moved a few minutes later. The officials still awaited confirmation that the target, a well-known extremist of Malaysian origin wanted in connection with acts of terrorism, had been killed, but there was a '90 per cent probability' that the strike had been successful.

Mangan wondered how they'd confirm. Was an agent in the rubble, grubbing about for DNA? Or were they just listening to the chatter?

He felt light-headed, placed his hands palm down on the table.

From decision to consequence in less than forty-eight hours.

Mangan decided to skip lunch. He got up and left the hotel. He stood on the pavement, lit a cigarette, then walked. He walked fast in the colour-killing grey light of the early afternoon, low cloud fastening Addis in a tight, thick humidity, trapping the fumes, the dust. He went down Tito Street, turned onto Menelik Avenue, found himself walking shakily into the park. And there he stopped, sat heavily on a concrete bench, tried to gather himself in, process it. He found his hands trembling. He felt hot, clammy, feverish.

He took a taxi back to Gotera, stumbled into his flat, threw his clothes off and got under the covers with a thermometer. He had a temperature of a hundred and two.

Patterson sat in Hopko's sanctum, watching a rolling news channel. At a Pentagon press briefing, a spokesman was deflecting questions about the drone strike. Hopko was straightening a picture on her wall, a gorgeous Ming dynasty landscape, crags in mist, thorn trees, a river, a tiny boat and a fisherman half-seen. She wore a long coat-like garment of a crimson velveteen, a hammered silver cross of Coptic origin around her neck. And those boots. She looks like some mad Spanish prelate, Patterson thought.

'So the Americans went with it, the grid reference,' Hopko said.

Patterson took a breath.

'They did. They trusted the intelligence.'

'Is that the most interesting thing we've learned?' said Hopko.

'And the Chinese are running penetrations of jihadi networks in south-east Asia.'

'There is that. A highly successful penetration, too,' said Hopko, absently. 'I wonder who he is. Or she. A Chinese Muslim? Even a Uighur? Ferreting away down there. Someone's compliant wife?'

She stopped, let her gaze fall on Patterson, who hated these searching looks, these pregnant pauses, and shifted in her seat.

'We need to move,' said Hopko. 'Don't we?'

'Do we?'

'Well, I should say so. Wouldn't you? A botched approach to reach us in Hong Kong. Our poor man tops himself, or so we're told. A second try in Addis, this time sweetened with exotic intelligence, intelligence guaranteed to buy us love in Washington. My, someone knows how to push our buttons. There's a plan here, Trish. Someone's probing.'

She scents opportunity, thought Patterson. She's like a raptor. Or a card shark.

'What do we do?'

'Do? We put Mangan back in play, no?'

26

Mangan lay in his wrecked, damp bed, stunned with fever. He tried to read, but his hands shook, limbs soft as treacle. He managed a fitful sleep as the afternoon wore on and the room darkened. Evening brought distant thunder beneath the rattle of the city and at seven the rain came on, the room turning dank and cold.

He lay, the fever singing in his head, bright, brittle images winding and looping behind his eyes. A hot, toxic plasticity, blast wave, trauma, gelatinous spatter, blood trail. In a restaurant, in a darkening city, in a small town by the sea.

Maja phoned. And now she was here, with soup. She turned on the lights, boiled the kettle. He sat up, wrapped in his duvet.

'God, you look miserable,' she said.

He did not respond.

'Well, whatever it is, I don't want to catch it, so I'll heat you some soup and leave you.'

She went into the kitchen. Mangan heard cupboards opening and closing, the clatter of pans. The flat began to fill with smell. She came back and stood in the doorway, arms folded.

'It's heating up,' she said. 'Bygvandgrød. Danish barley soup. Powerfully medicinal, obviously.'

'I'm sorry I haven't seen you,' he said. 'It's just been . . . '

'I'm sorry, too,' she said. 'I needed people.'

He nodded, coughed.

'How did you do that?' she said. 'After the bomb. You just went away, disappeared into work. Is that how you coped?'

'It was just work.'

'No, it wasn't.'

'I hope your bedside manner is better with the afflicted mothers of Ogaden,' he said. But she didn't smile, just leaned her head against the wall, a slow, considered blink.

'You walled yourself off,' she said. And she turned and went back to the kitchen, reappearing with a bowl of steaming soup. It was thick and a nut-brown colour, made Mangan think of beef, oxtail, childhood.

'If the fever's not gone in twenty-four hours, go to a doctor,' she said, putting on her coat. Then she stopped, went to the table, took a pen that was lying there, slid a piece of paper from Mangan's printer. She bent and wrote, big, vigorous strokes. She turned and held up the paper for him to see. It read, 'CALL MAJA, THE DANISH!!', and then her phone number, each digit four inches high.

'And perhaps you can call me this time?' she said, and then she was gone.

He sat in the silence, spooning the soup, letting it warm him.

The fever broke some time around four in the morning, and Mangan slept. He woke at midday, shaky, and padded around the apartment, feet cold on the concrete floor, making tea, picking up his laptop and carrying it back to bed.

There was an email in his inbox, as he expected. The message cryptic.

Following your great success, we feel a meeting necessary. Please be ready travel next week. Congratulation.

He called Hoddinott.

'I have an invitation I need to run by you,' he said.

27

London

A heavyset man wearing a suit and an earpiece opened the door and Fan Kaikai stepped from the taxi in pallid June sunshine. He gestured and another man in a red porter's uniform took his bag to a service entrance.

'Nice to see you again, sir,' the heavyset man said. 'And how is university treating you?'

'Oh. Fine, thank you,' said Kai. He walked through the marbled foyer to the lift, paused for the retina scan.

In the apartment, they were already preparing dinner. In the kitchen, a chef worked on scallops and eels and some kind of fish while an assistant chopped coriander and peeled ginger. They stopped working as he entered, laid their cleavers on the worktop, made little bowing motions. He took two beers from the fridge, went to the reception room and lay on a sofa. Through the glass walls, he could see across Hyde Park, its horses, tourists, runners, sticky-fingered children, to the Serpentine, the little boats. He'd always wanted to hire such a boat, row around in circles on the still water, just like in Beijing, on the lake. But to do so felt foolish, infantile. The room was airless, silent, smelled of a chemical newness, untouched furniture.

Then the intercom was chiming and the butler was opening the door and guests were being ushered into the dining room. Kai joined them at the dining table. Champagne was poured, and some dreadful, insipid saxophone music played in the background.

Across the table from him sat the sour, disconsolate figure of his Aunt Charlotte. Real name Fan Jinmei, but she went by her English name, Charlotte Fan, as she floated from London to Hong Kong and Macau and the Caribbean, tending the family estates, nurturing the fortune, the money dancing through the darkened offshore labyrinths. A bit of a dancer herself, Aunt Charlotte. Fan had seen her inebriated and swaying to show tunes on glowing yachts, in cavernous ballrooms in Beijing, glittering salons on the Peak in Hong Kong. And she was a gambler, a regular in the choosier Macau VIP rooms, an activity that evaded family censure, which Kai never understood. Now she regarded him from across the linen tablecloth, her eyes still and resting on him, her skin stretched tight, matt and powdery, her eyebrows carefully applied in a testy arch.

Next to her, the woman. Miss Nicole Yang. His new nanny.

Some nanny. He gaped at her. She wore a tight silk shirt of silver blue, a hint of black lace beneath, lace on fair skin, and her hair was shiny, and her eyes were on him with a sort of glittering humour and intensity as if she were really *interested* and as if she were sending him a private message which said: *Don't mind your aunt, the old crab, and I understand you're under pressure and you feel like a fish out of water, and we'll talk later and sort it all out, and it'll be all right.* And while he sensed she meant to reassure, he found himself instantly on his guard.

And next to her, to his consternation, the man he knew as Uncle Chequebook, hunched, jaundiced and unsmiling in a debt collector's suit. He had picked up a plate and was inspecting its underside as if for signs of indiscretion. Or betrayal. *Why is he here?* Kai had the sense of facing a tribunal of some sort, of awaiting judgement, the icy justice of his family.

Aunt Charlotte spoke, in Mandarin.

'So. Tell us about Oxford this year. You father is keen to hear all about it.'

'Oxford is fine, thank you, Aunt Charlotte. Please tell my father that I am working hard and I will ensure I get my degree, and I intend to apply for graduate school in the United States next year.'

An impressed look from Nanny Nicole. From Uncle Chequebook, a watery stare. From Aunt Charlotte, a sigh.

'Really?' intoned his aunt. 'I think your father is still keen for you to return home for a while. He thinks that some experience at China National Century would help you at business school.'

'Perhaps I should discuss it with my father.'

There was a pause.

'Perhaps you should.'

He glanced at Nicole Yang, nanny, interloper and unknown quantity, and caught her eyebrow in an arch, just for him.

They picked at chicken poached in soy and sesame. The scallops came, glistening in snow peas and garlic. Aunt Charlotte frowned and spoke as if deep in thought.

'From what your father has shared with me, I think he envisages some time spent in the telecoms division. Travelling. Seeing what the corporation is doing, what it will do in the future. South-east Asia, maybe. Africa, certainly. So much happening there.'

The boy said nothing.

'It's a very good opportunity ...' said Aunt Charlotte.

'Yes, yes, a good opportunity,' said Kai, trying to sound brisk.

Silence. Nicole piled scallops on Kai's plate, suppressing a smile.

'And now,' said Aunt Charlotte, 'please tell us about this ... this unfortunate incident.'

'It was not an incident.'

'Please tell me.'

He sighed, looked down as he spoke.

'I came back to my rooms in college and my laptop was gone. Stolen. And I thought the room might have been searched.'

'And what did you do?'

'I called the police.'

'You called the police.'

'Yes.'

Aunt Charlotte lifted a scallop from her plate with her chopsticks and with an abrupt, snatching motion of the head, disposed of it. Her lips shone with grease.

'Why did you call the police?' she said.

Kai looked at her.

'When a crime is committed, it is customary to report it.'

From Uncle Chequebook, a sniff and a shake of the head.

'In future,' said Charlotte Fan, 'you will communicate with me, or your father, or one of our representatives in London before involving the authorities.'

'Why?'

Uncle Chequebook was speaking in a slow monotone: 'The laptop. What was on it? What did you use it for?'

'I used it for . . . for everything. My studying. The net, email.'

'Banking?'

'Yes, online banking.'

Uncle Chequebook said nothing.

'It was password protected,' said Kai.

Uncle Chequebook ate a scallop, masticated slowly.

'Did you load a tracker on the laptop?'

'No.'

'So you can't track it.'

'Well . . . no.'

'Did you encrypt any of your files?'

'My password file was encrypted. And most of my email.'

'Family email?'

'All encrypted. As instructed.'

Uncle Chequebook thought for a moment, then pointed a finger at him.

'You should assume that everything on the laptop is compromised.'

Aunt Charlotte was looking alarmed.

'Everything?'

'Everything. Email addresses. Company information. Bank details. Account numbers. Sort codes.'

Aunt Charlotte swore under her breath, glared at Kai.

'But I don't see why this ... I mean, it's just transfers from you to me. What's the big deal?' He knew he sounded whiny.

Neither Aunt Charlotte nor Uncle Chequebook responded. Nicole was half-smiling again. Eels, flash fried in chilli and bean paste, the clink of crockery on the glass tabletop. A huge carp steamed in a soy and ginger broth, loaded with spring onions. Nicole filleted the fish, its flesh falling away from the bone, soft as air.

Finally, Aunt Charlotte spoke.

'Why did you conclude the room was searched?'

'Things looked out of place. And then they found the glove. The latex glove.'

'Was anything else missing?'

'There was nothing else to take. Apart from my underwear and trainers.'

Another pause, the ceramic *chink* of chopsticks on bowl.

'You have been communicating with the Chen girl,' said Uncle Chequebook.

'Well, not really ... I mean, I ...'

'You have spoken to her.'

'I ...'

'What were you saying to her?'

'Nothing. I just suggested that ...'

'That what?'

'That we should try to communicate. Build some trust perhaps.'

Aunt Charlotte's eyes were glittering, her mouth working.

'You will do no such thing.' She was trying to collect herself. 'You understand, don't you, that this girl is dangerous to you? That she will find ways to discredit you, use your actions against you, break your reputation?'

Kai did not reply.

Uncle Chequebook spoke.

'Is that all you said to her? Were there any other meetings?'

Kai was looking down, concentrating on his food.

'No.'

Uncle Chequebook sat very still.

'Your father wishes you to be extremely careful. No, let me rephrase that. He *orders* you to be extremely careful. Your behaviour affects the entire family and all those who depend on the family.'

Silence for a moment.

'Miss Yang will be at Oxford for the remainder of your time there. Since you appear incapable of conducting yourself in a way that is respectful of the needs of your family, she will supervise you and ensure that your decisions do not create more trouble and embarrassment than they already have. You will inform her of all your movements and activities. Is this clear?'

Kai nodded sullenly.

'You will not have any further interaction with the Chen girl. Is that clear?'

Another nod.

'And you will not discuss with anyone, *anyone*, the financial arrangements of the family, including the remittance of funds to you. Is that clear?'

'I do not understand this obsessive need for secrecy . . .'

Uncle Chequebook leaned towards him, reached out and took hold of Kai's wrist, his grip like concrete.

'There is a great deal you do not understand about the arrangements your family has in place to protect its position and its honour, and to fulfil its duty to our country. And you will not understand until we feel that you are trustworthy. Until that time, you will behave exactly as we tell you. Your father wishes me to impress upon you what is at stake. Our position. Everything the family has worked for. All this.' He gestured around himself, at the apartment, the furnishings, the art, the safe room, the chefs, the cars, the retina scanners, the cameras, the quiet, hard men in reception. London, its caverns of wealth and privilege.

The rest of the meal passed mostly in silence. Kai absented himself, went and sat alone looking out at the London night, at the lights of palaces glittering in the darkness across the park.

They conflate everything. They are so drunk on their wealth and status that they confuse their own destiny with that of all China. Theirs is the supreme vanity of the oligarch.

Nicole had barely spoken all evening. But just before she left, she walked up behind him, leaned close to him and touched his arm, and said, 'See you in Oxford.'

He stood, walked to the glass walls. The glass was tempered, laminated with polycarbonates for flex when struck by a bullet. He stared into the city's ochre night glow, watched the torrent of headlights.

What was she really doing here?

28

Addis Ababa, Ethiopia

They met the following day, Mangan still weak, even paler than usual. Was this sickness, or some sort of delayed reaction to the blast?

It was a bare room in the Dessie Hotel. Hoddinott was waiting for him, sitting on the edge of the bed.

'You look terrible,' said Hoddinott.

'I've been ill,' Mangan replied.

Hoddinott drank from a bottle of water, regarded him.

'Quite an outcome, the strike,' said Hoddinott.

Mangan just nodded, looked away.

'Look, you mustn't get maudlin,' said Hoddinott. 'It was a very—'

'Drop it,' said Mangan.

Hoddinott raised both hands, calming, placatory.

'All right,' he said. 'Tell me.'

'No detail. Just "a meeting". I'm to be ready to travel next week, apparently.'

'Where to?'

'Did you hear me? No detail.'

Hoddinott was rubbing the back of his neck.

'I will have to pass this to London. But clearly this is way too much, way too soon. We know nothing about these people. My recommendation will be to ignore this contact. I trust you agree.'

Mangan thought for a moment.

'Why do you trust I agree?'

'Well, I'm frankly a little puzzled, Philip. Your previous experience in this line of work, in China, ended, let us say, in dramatic fashion. Your latest flourish seems to have left you queasy. I am not clear why you are so eager to continue now.'

Mangan didn't answer.

'What is your reason, Philip?' said Hoddinott.

Mangan stood, walked to the window. Since coming to Addis, he realised, he had been living in suspended animation. He looked out over rooftops of tin, corrugated iron, a sea of rust, antennas, wild swirls of cable, black mud, shadowed passageways. How do they live down there, he thought, amid such fragility, such contingency? He had read that satellites were mapping shanty towns, ascribing them boundary and shape, lending them fixedness for the first time. All he saw was change, complexity. He felt a strong desire to move, to surge forward.

'Tell them I'm going to the meeting,' he said.

29

The Clown found him on the Tuesday.

He had been at the Ministry of Internal Affairs, scratching around for a lead on the bomb investigation, sitting in a corridor, waiting for an interview that never materialised. On his way home, he stopped at a coffee shop on Mauritius Street, a place with a high ceiling, tall wooden stools, the smell of baking pastries. A television was mounted on the wall. It showed a theatre, a girl on a stage under the lights and the cameras, reciting poetry. She was seven or eight years old and wore a sequined dress. She was reciting doggedly. Men stepped up from the audience holding banknotes. They licked the banknotes and affixed them to the girl's face and neck with saliva. Some of the notes stuck, others fell away.

And then there he was, standing just to Mangan's right.

He spoke quietly.

'I hope you see that we are serious,' said the Clown.

Mangan collected himself and tried to focus, to manage his position.

'You are clearly serious. I would like to know who you are.'

'I represent someone who wishes to meet you.'

'I need to know who,' said Mangan.

'You will travel to Harer. You fly on Friday. A ticket is booked in your name and must be picked up from the Ethiopian Airlines office. Stay in Harer at the Jamal Guest House, in the old city. A room is booked for you there. You will be contacted.'

'I'm sorry, but you are going to have to tell me more. Why Harer?'

The Clown gave a patient smile.

'It is convenient.'

The Clown was looking around himself, scanning the room with those whiteless, inert eyes. Who for? thought Mangan. Them or us?

Mangan leaned in closer to him.

'For this to work,' he said, 'you will need to be a little more forthcoming with me. Do you understand?'

A gibbous smile.

'Please do not push me too hard with your questions.'

'What does your friend want?'

'Everything will be explained in Harer.'

London

Patterson was late. The whole day had been turned upside down by the telegrams coming in from Addis station. Patterson had hurriedly searched for maps of Harer, appreciations of the city as an operational setting. By late morning plans were afoot for station officers to babysit Mangan as he attended the meeting, but Africa Controllerate was incredulous, Vezza vetoing the idea with a quiet shake of the head and a short disquisition on the potency of local counter-intelligence: NISS, the battle-hardened Tigrayan bloodhounds who'd learned their trade over years of vicious insurgency, who knew every inch of the dusty ground, who'd sniff out an under-resourced, over-exposed station operation in a moment. The plans were dropped. By lunchtime the talk was that Patterson herself would deploy, but Counter-terrorism expostulated that a Far East Officer had neither the business nor the tradecraft to be wandering East Africa on a counter-terror mission, Weekes writhing with anger. Security Branch cited 'inadequate optic on the target' and 'multiple threat vectors', and that was that. The plan was dropped by mid-afternoon. Hopko knew when to choose her battles.

Mangan, it was decided, would proceed alone to Harer. Much the best idea, with deniability built in.

And now Patterson was late for an evening drink that she'd arranged weeks previously and was, she realised, the last thing she needed or wanted. An old army friend, in town, keen to catch up, compare notes on civilian life. She cleared her desk, locked her safe and leaned over to turn off her computer.

At the top of the screen was a small notification. What now? she thought. She peered at it. A ping from the Police National Computer. She clicked on it, brought it up.

A Chinese student, in Oxford, had his laptop stolen.

What? She skimmed the report.

The student, a Mr Fan Kaikai, had been marked as of intelligence interest. All interactions with authority, police, border control and what-have-you to be passed on. And Mr Fan had had his laptop nicked. So Thames Valley Police was dutifully passing it on.

And why is he of interest?

He is the pampered son of a corporate titan and nephew of a Communist Party bruiser of rare seniority.

Oh, *that* Fan family, she thought.

The burglary of Mr Fan's college rooms had been accompanied by a search of said rooms, conducted, in the opinion of Thames Valley Police, in such a way as to suggest the perpetrator was more than a common thief, perhaps having an investigatory motive.

Patterson frowned, then shut down the computer, turned off the screen, did a final check of her desk top and hurried out of the office.

The taxi was slow, the driver swearing in whispers. She got out at the end of New Row in watery evening sunlight, a breeze, and walked up the cobbles to the wine bar. It was packed and loud, voices clattering off exposed brick walls, tourists bellowing at wooden tables. In the corner, frantically waving, Joanie. Joanie Linklater, formerly of the Royal Signals. Patterson girded herself and pushed through the crowd.

'Trish Patterson! As I live and breathe. Trish, Trish, Trish!'

They embraced. She's put on weight, Patterson thought. She'd always been big. She'd been a rower, played women's rugby. They stood back and looked at each other. Joanie was smiling her big, generous smile in a face a little more rounded, a little more lined.

'Well, don't look at me like that. It's parenthood that does it,' Joanie said. Patterson chided herself for her own overdeveloped capacity for observation, for judgement, felt immediately guilty. Joanie was as close a thing as she had to a friend. The two of them had bonded as lieutenants in Iraq. They took long morning runs around Basra air base, Patterson the quicker, Joanie the stronger. Patterson remembered the dust in the dawn light, the smell of aviation fuel, Joanie's hair darkened with sweat, plastered to her scalp as they pounded along. Joanie had left the army and married, working for a telecoms developer in Manchester.

They ordered a bottle of Rioja and Joanie recounted the travails of parenting. Patterson listened dutifully, and when her mind wandered to the question of why the scion of one of the most powerful families in China had had his laptop stolen and his room gone through by a pro, Joanie stopped talking and grinned.

'Sorry,' she said. 'I've become a bore. Turned into Mumzilla.'

'No,' said Trish, chiding herself once again. 'No, no. I must come up and visit. Really.'

Joanie laughed.

'So tell me all. How's the, um, Foreign Office?'

'It's fine,' said Patterson. 'It's, you know, routine.'

'Right. I do still have a security clearance.'

'There's nothing to tell. It's the same as ever. Administration, logistics.'

Joanie picked up her wineglass, considered.

'It's been a while since we've seen each other. I was hoping we might have a real conversation.'

Patterson gave a tight smile. Joanie was leaning forward.

'Why don't I hear from you?' she said. 'I mean I know you're busy and there's the travel, but I miss you and I want ... you know ... I want you to come and see us and see the kid, and spend some time with us. But you're not there.'

Patterson sighed.

'I'm sorry.' She thought of what on earth she could add, what pallid excuses she could bring to bear, came up with nothing, so she just stopped talking.

Joanie smiled.

'Do you remember ...' she said, 'do you remember finding the knickers of mass destruction? You remember that day?'

Patterson nodded, thought of the blistered highway north of Basra, the Merlin they'd put down to block it off, the *whump whump* of the rotors, a platoon of Fusiliers tearing the trucks apart, slitting open boxes with their bayonets. They'd been so sure. The composite and timers, the ammunition, the money, all of it was somewhere in those trucks and on the road to Baghdad. But what they found was reams of Chinese-made underwear, underpants, brassieres, stockings blowing across the highway in the hot wind. She and Joanie had stood and watched the operation descend into farce.

'You were so angry,' said Joanie. 'Bloody incandescent, you were. Clenching your fists. This *has* to be worth it, you said. It *has* to.'

'What's your point?' She sounded curt.

'My point is, Trish, darling, what you're doing now. Is it worth it? I have this awful picture of you getting home after work every night by yourself and saying, "It *has* to be worth it".'

'I don't do that.'

'And then telling half-truths to the people who love you, and saying on your way out the door, "It *has* to be worth it".'

Patterson didn't respond. They talked about other old army friends for a while, some home and settled, some off with the big military contractors, but Joanie had done her reaching out for the evening. They embraced, and Patterson left.

As she walked to the Tube, she thought of Mangan, on his way to eastern Ethiopia, with nothing, no one checking his back. And she found herself hoping it was worth it.

30

Harer, Ethiopia

In Harer, Mangan saw Christian Ethiopia begin to give way to Islam. And in the labyrinthine old city, at night, between the whitewashed walls, spotted hyenas wander. They feed on the city's refuse. The hyenas stand as tall as a man's waist and are possessed of powerful jaws. The hyena's back slopes downward, away from the strong forelegs and shoulders, lending the animal the air of a cringe, of cowardly submission. The eyes are dark lamps, and the hyenas are utterly silent in their movements. They dart and pace.

Mangan sat in the courtyard of the guest house amid flowers in pots, listening to the doves coo-cooing, the call to prayer. A girl, in a crimson headscarf, knelt over a brazier to make tea. Then she stood, walked to him holding a cup with both hands, the scuff of her sandals on the flagstones.

'So do people in Harer mind the hyenas?' he asked her.

She smiled shyly.

'The hyena is good. Harer people like him, they say.'

'Really? Why?'

'When the *jinns* come in the city, the hyena chase them.'

'The hyenas chase away *jinns*?'

The girl giggled. 'Also, people do not want to anger the hyena. The hyena hears everything. So people say nice things about him.'

'What will happen if the hyenas are angry?'

The girl made a mock scary face.

'Oh! He will come, take your children. Very bad.'

She gave him a little wave, went to her room, where her mother was. They sat on a platform bed, reading the Koran together as the darkness came down. Mangan listened to their murmur, the girl's soft, piping voice feeling out the Arabic. A bat swooped and veered, its dark flitter against the blue night. Mangan sipped his tea, thought of the hyenas in the alleyways, and waited.

It was after ten when he came. A soft tap-tapping at the locked metal gate. The girl slipped from her room, swathing herself in her headscarf, walked slowly, loose limbed, across the courtyard, a ferrous scrape as she opened a peephole. Mangan heard a man's low voice, her question, a muffled response. She turned to look at Mangan, indicating he should come. He went to the peephole, tried to make out a face in the darkness. The visitor was a slender Ethiopian man, dark, gaunt in the cheeks, tense, his eyes skittering and bloodshot. He spoke in broken English.

'Mr Mangan. Your friend waiting.'

'Where is he?'

'I take you. Come.'

'How far?'

'Not far. Just walk. You come now.'

The girl was watching him.

'You come now,' said the man.

Mangan stood in the silence, calculated. The two of them, the man and the girl, were looking at him. He felt the adrenalin pulse, the needling of anxiety, the thickening in the mouth. The man shifted and looked behind him, and back, expectant. Reading Mangan's hesitation, he spoke quickly in Amharic to the girl, who frowned.

'What did he say?'

'He say you come back soon, one or two hours maybe. He tell me I can wait for you.'

Mangan swallowed, then nodded to the girl, made an unlocking gesture.

She frowned again, cocked her head questioningly to one side, the key around her neck. He nodded and pointed to the gate. She leaned in and unlocked it.

He stepped out into the darkness. He wanted to stop to allow his eyes to adjust, but the man was already starting off down the alleyway. Mangan followed him, moving uncertainly in the dark.

The night air was cool. The man walked quickly, but Mangan stumbled on the angled, jutting cobbles. Their footsteps echoed off the white walls. The path was taking them down, deeper into the centre of the old city. They passed a woman bent over a charcoal brazier, a tin pot of soup atop it, and a broken-toothed man slumped amid sprigs of *chat*. They passed an open doorway and inside Mangan glimpsed a single bulb above a wooden table, a tiny child, an icon of a saint with an upturned face and a woman in a brown robe who returned his look. The tableau stained his eye as he looked away.

The man turned to the right. They were moving upward now along a long, narrow passage, stone steps disappearing into total darkness. The man stopped, Mangan almost running into his back, breathing hard. The man was knocking softly on an iron door, which let out a metallic sob as it opened. He went in, turned and beckoned to Mangan to enter. Mangan stepped through the doorway.

Another life.

'You wait now,' the man said.

He was in a courtyard. Two red lanterns and strings of white fairy lights gave the place a weirdly festive feel. A stunted, gnarled tree stood at its centre. Three doorways led off, all of them dark. Mangan looked around him. He was alone, suddenly. No sign of his guide, nor of whoever had opened the door. It was very quiet.

He sat on a weathered wooden chair, listening hard, senses heightened. He heard only his own breathing, the ticking of some insect, a dog barking in the distance, the moment taut with possibility. Can I play this? he thought. How will I play it?

He stayed like this for some time. He played through scenarios in his mind, how to get out, how to run. He took a cigarette from a packet in his jacket pocket, lit it, the *snick* of the lighter. He had money and passport in a pouch at the base of his back. More money strapped to his thigh. He realised he had no idea how to get back to the guest house. *Jesus Christ.*

And then, from one of the darkened doorways, a footstep. Mangan didn't move. A figure emerged into the light. A Chinese face, male, middle-aged, a face suggestive, to Mangan, of a capacity for humour, of a wry joke, the eyes anticipatory. The hair neatly parted, dusted with silver. The figure walked across the courtyard. He was of middling height, rounded shoulders, a slight paunch. He wore a blue polo shirt, slacks. The man stood before Mangan now, hands in pockets, smiling. He spoke in good English.

'Mr Mangan.'

'Yes.'

'Thank you for coming. You are alone, yes?'

'Yes.'

'I am a little puzzled by that.'

Puzzle away, thought Mangan. He said nothing.

'I thought that perhaps you have some . . . support.'

'Perhaps you had better tell me who you are.'

The man smiled a generous smile.

'Yes, of course.' He sat down in a chair next to Mangan's, which meant Mangan had to turn awkwardly to face him.

'My surname is Shi. Once, long time ago, I was in an English class. We had an American teacher! Very exotic person, back then. She made us choose English names. So I tried to be clever and find one that means the same as my Chinese surname. You know the meaning of Shi.'

Mangan thought of the word, *shi,* said as something like *shurr,* to rhyme with *purr,* on a rising tone. He thought of the Chinese character.

'Stone,' he said.

The man held his hands out, palms up, in appreciation.

'Exactly. So I tried to think of an English name which means "stone". But I could think of nothing. And then the American teacher thought of "Rocky". And all my classmates laughed and they started to call me Rocky. And so I am Rocky. Rocky Shi.' He shrugged. The gesture seeming to be playing a part, speaking lines of its own. *What can I do with such foolishness?*

'And where are you from?'

'Where I am from. Yes. My father was a soldier, so we lived in different places. But my ancestral home, my *jiaxiang,* is in Hebei. Not so far from Beijing. Perhaps you know it.' Mangan thought of the north China plain, dry, winter grey to the horizon the last time he'd seen it.

'And what are you?' he said.

'Mr Mangan, I am a businessman. A Chinese businessman, in Ethiopia looking for opportunity.'

His face cracked into a grin.

'I represent a small investment fund, based in a southern Chinese city. A few tens of millions of dollars, looking for a profitable purpose.' *Who could believe such a thing?*

Mangan watched him closely, took in the geniality, the practised charm, the well-ironed clothes, the good haircut. He noted the compact physique gone slightly to softness, the wide forearms, the hands that looked as if they had known physical labour. He noted, too, the slight tremor in the man's left leg, a nervous jiggle, the knee up, down, up, down. He noted the fingernails bitten to the quick. And what appeared to be a scar on the jawline, just below the right ear.

'And what purpose is your money finding in Ethiopia?' Mangan said.

Why this dance? he thought.

'Oh, such opportunity in Africa,' said the man, Rocky, his face alight with humour. 'We are considering bold ventures in the leather and garment sectors.'

Mangan waited.

'So when we meet, in the future, Mr Mangan, which I hope we will, that is how we shall meet. You, the curious reporter, and me, the ... the ... what is the word you use? Swishing? Something to do with pirates, I think.'

'Swashbuckling.'

'Yes! Yes! Me, the swashbuckling Chinese businessman.'

'I see.' He has just given me his cover, he thought. 'And do you spend a lot of time in Africa?'

'Oh, yes. My business takes me to many places in Africa. But I am not based here. I am based in China. In Kunming. Down there. You know China very well, of course.' He had raised a finger, as if to emphasise an important and amusing point.

'I was based there, as a journalist.'

The man's face shone with suppressed laughter.

'Yes! A journalist. Of course.'

He stopped and his face settled to a more thoughtful expression. He brought his finger to his lips, considering.

'But it is your, erm, other career I wish to talk about with you.'

He raised his eyebrows, as if expecting reassurance that such a career did indeed exist and was a worthy topic of discussion, reassurance that Mangan did not give. He pushed on.

'I hope that the information my associate passed to you was enough to prove my good intentions.'

'I am sure it was gratefully received, but it said very little about your intentions.'

'It was certainly acted on very quickly. Frighteningly so. Your agencies are very *efficient*. And I hope you recover from your experience. The bombings. Very terrible.'

'Yes, thank you,' said Mangan. 'So what *are* your intentions?'

'Yes, yes. My hope, Mr Mangan, is to build a relationship of trust with you and those you are associated with.'

'To what end?'

'Mutual benefit.'

'What sort of benefit?'

'For you, informational benefit. For me and a small group of associates who assist me, well, financial.' The warmest of smiles. *Such strange places our motives bring us!*

Well, that is a reason, thought Mangan.

'And here,' went on Rocky, 'is something to demonstrate further my good faith and, of course, my access.'

He was holding a memory stick.

'I hope that this can ensure acceptance of my proposal and the satisfactory arrangement of financial considerations.' The lines sounded as if he had learned them by heart.

'What is it?' said Mangan.

Rocky nodded, looked down at the stick, cradled it in his hand, as if pondering how adequately to explain the nature of its contents.

'Things we have found, Mr Mangan. The trails money leaves.'

A grin. *So much to be learned!*

Mangan found himself suddenly bored by the enigmatic nature of the conversation, wanting to be blunt.

'The reason I am here alone, of course, is that they don't know you and they don't trust you. They wouldn't come, so I came alone. You are not a businessman, that we know. What are you? Party? Ministry of State Security?'

Rocky looked exaggeratedly shocked, put a hand to his mouth, at Mangan's callous disregard for his fragile legend. *How could you suggest such things?* The knee was still jiggling, up-down. But behind the theatrics, Mangan sensed implacability.

'Mr Mangan, these things will become clear in time. For now, take the information. Then you can see my credibility, yes?'

He held out the memory stick. Mangan waited a beat, then took it. An enormous smile illuminated Rocky's face.

'I will see you in Addis,' he said. He stood, made to leave but stopped as if he were remembering an elusive detail.

'Mr Mangan, one more thing. Please give them my apologies for Hong Kong. I had no intention of it ending that way.'

'I have no idea what you are talking about,' said Mangan.

'No, maybe not. There were mistakes. Please tell them that it was a suicide. Really. The poor man. Oh, and tell them, too, that our operative was wrong to lay his hands on your case officer. But he paid the price. That, Mr Mangan, is a very aggressive woman.'

'What woman?'

'The case officer. A black woman. Tall. Mandarin speaker. My goodness. Very formidable. Our man must have surgery on his hand. Very expensive. But the injury to his . . . what do you say, his *ego* was greater.' Rocky looked as if he were consumed with concern.

Mangan felt something like a smile creep to the corners of his mouth. It's *her*, he thought. It must be.

'Anyway, please convey my apologies and assure them of our professionalism from now on.'

He gave Mangan a long look.

'How are we to communicate?' Mangan said.

'You are not hard to find, Mr Mangan.'

And with that he turned and disappeared through one of the darkened doorways.

Mangan stood, realising with a sinking heart that he had been played. He had nothing but a surname, a description and a threadbare legend. The man's stated motive – money – felt implausible.

But he had a memory stick.

He was carrying, with no idea where he was going. He waited for a moment, wondering what to do. Well, move, at least.

He had wandered the alleyways for six or seven minutes, before the gaunt-eyed Ethiopian fell silently into step with him. They had been checking his back, he supposed. And back at the guest house, the girl, sleepy-eyed, let him in. He thanked her and she gave him a half-smile. He went to his room, closed and locked the door, drew the curtains, left the light off. He sat on the platform bed that made him think of a Chinese kang, listened.

He held the memory stick in his hand. What the hell to do with it?

He booted up his laptop. He laid the memory stick on the table. He lit a cigarette, stared at its knowing orange ember in the darkness, pondered elementary cyber security. *Do not, in general, when in receipt of a memory stick donated by a largely anonymous representative of the Chinese intelligence services, plug said memory stick into your laptop.* A good rule. Prudent.

He plugged it in.

The *sneck* as it lodged in the port, the electronic two-toned *bong-bong* as the laptop found it and began to read.

Mangan sat in the dark, the smoke from his cigarette winding and curling in the glow from the screen.

Not much, this time. Fifteen documents. He opened the first one.

It was a scan of an original hard copy, the text slightly misaligned on the page, a grainy look, the characters shrunken, hard to read. Clear enough, though, at the top of the page: *juemi*, top secret.

The familiar dryness in the mouth, now, the quickening. Mangan felt his way through the first couple of paragraphs. It was a *neican*, an internal report for the eyes of senior Party leadership, written somewhere in the depths of the Xinhua News Agency, but very definitely not for public consumption.

A trial, somewhere in south-west China. A corruption trial, by the look of it. An unfortunate official of the state-owned petroleum corporation. Something about wells, drilling. He'd declared certain oil wells were empty when they weren't, was that it? Mangan skipped to the end. The official had received a sentence of execution by lethal injection.

And?

He closed the document, moved to the next one.

Central Discipline Inspection Commission. The Party's corruption hunters, half of them bent as a gimlet themselves.

Juemi.

The same case, but a much more detailed report. Dates, times, numbers. Technical vocabulary Mangan couldn't penetrate. The unfortunate official had been responsible for the evaluation of the oil wells' production capacity and he had greatly understated it. Bad decision, for sure, but wherein lay its significance?

The other documents told versions of the same story, as far as Mangan could see, mostly shorter, less granular. One seemed to contain bank account numbers.

There's something in here, he thought. Something to be forged into a weapon. To touch someone, undermine them, blind them, ruin them.

Mangan closed the documents, removed the memory stick. His computer did not seem to have melted down. He ran a virus scan which came up clean but that, he knew, meant little. He felt a tremble in his hands, a ringing in his neck and head, reminiscent somehow of the sensation that followed the explosion. He wondered if he had some new weakness in him, as if his store of strength were finite, each weird episode contributing to its depletion, never to be restored.

Fear is born of loneliness and exhaustion. Someone had said that to him.

Loneliness first, then fear.

And something else, some inexplicable kindling of purpose.

He put the memory stick in the money belt he kept strapped to the base of his back. He closed up his pack and put it by his bed. Fully clothed, shoes on, he pulled the covers over himself and tried to sleep.

The next day, all flights to Addis were overbooked, leaving Mangan with twenty-four hours to kill – to live his cover and check his back.

The girl brought him breakfast, tea and pancakes in honey, which he ate sitting cross-legged on rugs and cushions in a reception room, the doors and windows open, morning light flooding in. He walked through the old city, down the Street of the Tailors, the old men working on Singer sewing machines, pins in their mouths, their bolts of saturated red and gold fabric against the white stone walls. He grinned, took photographs, asked questions, ostentatiously made notes. A small herd of children followed him, and behind them, an older man, in a red shirt and sandals. The man stood, arms folded, a short distance away.

He walked out of the old city at its main gate, stopped at a café up a green iron staircase, ordered macchiato so rich it was like drinking dark velvet.

The man in the red shirt and sandals dawdled on the street below.

He walked to Arthur Rimbaud's house, where the boy poet lived the latter part of his short, wracked life. An expansive courtyard wrapped around with wooden balconies, an odd library, a dusty exhibition of photographs. Rimbaud the precocious schoolboy, the winner of prizes, stared flintily past the camera, tie askew, the boy who wrote 'shit on God' on the walls of starchy Charleville, who wrote the founding verses of modernism before he was twenty.

Rimbaud had fled, renounced his explosive poetry in disgust and come here to Harer, to trade in gems and guns.

I am present at the hatching of my thought, he had written.

Mangan stood on a balcony, looking out over the old city, smelling the breeze coming from the hills, the smell of sun on rock and dust. He thought about escape, about watching himself hatch his own decisions. *I am deciding to spy. Here I am, spying.*

The man in the red shirt and sandals had gone. But his relief was there: a boy in a green T-shirt with a phone, looking up at him from the alleyway.

Ignore it, he thought. Live your cover.

But something was scratching at the back of his skull and he descended to ground level, found a door to a neighbouring courtyard and forced it, slipping through a gate back onto the street, walking slowly away, peering at his guidebook. And as he turned uphill towards the main square and the church, an approach ...

'Yes, please, mister. How are you? I can be your guide. Where do you like to go?'

All delivered in an aggressive monotone by a beefy, grey-bearded individual who stood too close and let his hands dangle at his sides.

'I don't need a guide, thank you,' Mangan said.

'Yes, yes, we can go,' said the man.

'Thank you. I'm going back to my guest house,' said Mangan.

'Yes, we go there. We can talk.' He reached out and took hold of Mangan's arm, tried to steer him off the main drag. People on the street were turning away, Mangan saw. The man was pushing him towards a storefront, no, an alleyway.

'Fuck off,' Mangan shouted. He wrenched his arm away, then gave the man a two-handed shove in the chest. The man barely moved, stepped back a foot, maybe. He was looking at Mangan directly in the eyes, his hands open by his side, fingers curled.

'Who you are meeting today?' said the man. 'Where you go?'

Mangan ignored him, walked away fast, heart thumping. The man was shouting at his back.

'Why you are here? What you have?'

Mangan turned a corner, made for the guest house.

I have been warned. By someone.

That night he took a taxi to a restaurant called Fresh Touch and sat alone at an outside table, ate pizza, tried to keep it normal. He walked in the murmuring dark to the edge of the old city, where an elderly man threw offal down in the dust, and the hyenas emerged from the brush and pawed and scuffed for the meat, their feral reek hanging on the air.

The flight back to Addis the next day was horrible, the plane bucking and yawing on the turbulence, passengers gripping their seats and muttering. They landed in rain, the city concrete grey, flecked with green, dripping vegetation, the streets jammed, heaving, sodden, pooling with water, the dogs crouching still, shivering.

On Ethio-China Street, his taxi crawled, the wipers straining and squeaking. Mangan leaned forward and gave the driver the full fare, but slipped out into the traffic. He ran down a side street of shanties and stalls that narrowed, its surface turning to mud. Women watched him from doorways as he hurried past. Children pointed. One man, sparked and jittery on *chat*, stepped in front of him, made to grab him, but Mangan shoved him out of the way and ran on. The man yelled at his back, something indistinguishable. He came out onto a thoroughfare he didn't recognise, hailed another taxi, sat low in the back. He felt for the pouch at his waist, the smooth bulge of the memory stick. He told the driver to head for Comorros Street and the British embassy.

31

Oxford

Nicole had gone to his musty rooms in college. She wore a strappy dress of duck egg blue that lifted her breasts, a whisper of perfume, her hair down. The clothes made her feel girlish, light. But beneath, she was hard, operational.

Kai sat in a scrofulous armchair in T-shirt and shorts, barefoot, gazing at her.

'So,' she said, 'you'll be here all summer.'

'I have to cram. There'll be a tutor.'

He spoke in a monotone, awkward, mawkish, even. She looked sympathetic.

'Not much of a summer.'

He nodded.

'Well, perhaps we can keep each other company.'

He nodded again.

'And will anyone else be around?' she said.

'No. Everyone is leaving for the summer. They'll all be gone soon.'

She considered.

'And the Chen girl. Is she leaving for the summer, do you know?'

He shifted in his seat. Anxious, weak, she thought.

'I don't know.'

'What's she like?' she said.

'Madeline Chen?'

No, the Empress Wu.

'Yes, Madeline Chen. What sort of person is she?'

He shrugged, raised a hand and let it drop feebly to the arm of the chair.

'I don't know. She's smart.'

'Who does she hang out with?'

'Girls from her college. Some other Asians. I don't know.'

This was a *lead*?

'So, when you've spoken to her ... what did you talk about?'

'Well, like I said, I made the suggestion, which my parents apparently don't appreciate, that she and I could communicate, put aside some of the anger.'

'Perhaps you should trust your parents when they tell you that—'

He cut her off, which surprised her.

'I have heard this, already. Really, I know what you are going to say.'

She just nodded.

'So ...' he said, suddenly. 'You're from Taiwan.'

'That's right,' she said. 'Taiwanese girl.' She held up her bare arms, gestured to herself. *That's me!* His eyes flickered over her. 'But I've been in the States the last few years. For my doctorate.'

'So ... I wondered, why my family ... how they know you.'

She frowned, adopting a thoughtful pose.

'Hmm. Let's see. Well, it's through friends. Friends who trust each other. We have to look out for each other, don't we? Chinese people? Out here in the world.'

The dumb nod again. *No future captain of industry, this one.*

32

Late afternoon at Vauxhall Cross, and Patterson sat at her cubicle, palms flat on the desk before her. She took four deep breaths, exhaling slowly, trying to loosen the tension that had built around her shoulders and deep in her neck. Then she stood, gathered the files from the desk in front of her and made her way to the conference room.

Vezza of Africa Controllerate was there before her and flapped a hand idly as she walked in. A moment later, Requirements appeared, in the form of the straight-backed, grey-haired figure of Chapman-Biggs, his charcoal suit and regimental tie. He flashed a smile at Patterson, the two of them complicit in their army backgrounds. He sat heavily, stretched.

Weekes arrived, resentment inscribed on his pale features, his skin shiny, suit creased. He dropped his files on the table, the *slap* of paper on tabletop designed to signal disapproval, to discomfit. A propensity to act out, thought Patterson, is not a useful trait in a spy.

Weekes gave her a deadpan look. 'So where's the mother ship?' he said.

Patterson returned his look.

'What, or who, might that be?' she said.

He rolled his eyes.

'Your fearsome leader, Valentina Hopko, God bless her and all who sail in her.'

'I'm sure she'll be along.'

Enter Hopko, brusque, all in black, a chunky necklace of coral and lapis, something Afghan or Tibetan, heels.

'Sorry to keep you all,' she said. 'Let's get started, shall we? Trish, please bring us up to date.'

Forward.

'Well, as you know, Mangan delivered the memory stick to Addis station. It went by secure bag straight to Cheltenham. They've disinfected it and downloaded the contents, which you should have in front of you in hard copy, with translation.'

Weekes piled in.

'And please, please, tell me why this obscure Chinese corruption case should be of any interest whatsoever to the rest of us?'

Patterson didn't respond, just waited. Chapman-Biggs of Requirements raised his eyebrows. Vezza spoke.

'Just run us through it, if you wouldn't mind,' he said. Patterson swallowed, pushed on.

'Oil wells, in west China, the concessions all owned and run by the state-owned oil corporation. One official decides he's going to get smart. He rules that certain oil wells are exhausted, used up, pumped dry. Then he sells those wells off at bargain basement prices to his friends. Surprise! The wells are not exhausted after all, but seem to have come back to life. So the friends pump away and generate a small fortune.'

Weekes was sighing, writhing in his seat with impatience, but Vezza was more thoughtful.

'So who gets to buy the supposedly dried-up wells? Is that it?' he said.

'Thank you,' interjected Hopko, appreciatively. 'Trish?'

'Document number seven gives us names. One of the buyers, and she made millions, no doubt, was a woman named Charlotte Fan. And that is *the* Fan family.'

A blank look from Vezza. Patterson cleared her throat.

'The Fans are as close to royalty as you can be in China. They are an old revolutionary family. The patriarch was with Mao in the war years. Charlotte Fan is his daughter. One son is on the Politburo. The other is the boss of China National Century, the telecoms and tech corporation. You know who they are?'

'Yes, thank you. Even those of us marooned in Africa Controllerate are dimly aware of CNaC,' said Vezza.

'Yes. Right. There's a kid over here, at Oxford. Heir to the CNaC fortune. He's a bit weedy, apparently, and not terribly bright.'

'So the Fans are well-connected, and bent,' said Vezza. 'So what?'

Hopko stepped in and for a moment Patterson saw what Hopko saw, felt herself balanced on a fulcrum of understanding.

'Our Rocky Shi, whoever he may be, has made us a gift,' said Hopko. 'He has showed us the system at work. You see, everyone in China suspects that the princeling families have their noses in the trough. But it's hard to figure out quite how. Or how much. The Party *ensures* that nobody knows, doesn't it? And the Party decides who gets busted and who doesn't. And if you're the Fans you're off-limits, aren't you?'

She looked around the room, head tipped forward, peering over the top of her glasses.

'But what we have *here* . . . ' she went on, tapping the document in front of her, 'is a weapon. CNaC is a tool of Chinese power in the world. Our Rocky Shi has given us the means, should we choose to use them, to disrupt it.'

She sat back, grinning her hangman's grin.

Chapman-Biggs ran a hand through his hair, and when he spoke for the first time, it was quietly, deferentially.

'But why, Val? And who the hell *is* Rocky Shi?'

'Time to find out, don't you think?' said Hopko.

*

Patterson, like any self-respecting intelligence officer, held an innate suspicion of coincidence, and believed that a strong memory was a potent operational tool.

So when she finally, belatedly made the association, she wanted to kick herself, or strike something. It was late that same evening and she was at home. Damian from downstairs was sprawled on the couch. He had come thundering up the stairs, thumped on the door.

'I need to watch your TV,' he said. 'I was watching on my computer but the connection's gone down.' He made an imploring gesture, fingers locked together, a mock agonised face.

She sighed, let him in and he bounded to the sofa, picked up the remote. It was some European qualifier game. She went to the kitchen and took two lasagnas in plastic containers from the freezer and put them in the microwave.

'Why is your flat always so flipping tidy?' he shouted from the living room. She went back through, carrying two glasses, a bottle of red.

'I said you could watch, not critique,' she said. 'And take your feet off the coffee table, please.'

He gave her a cheesy grin, patted the sofa next to him. She sat down, tried to concentrate on the game.

'You should get a new TV,' he said.

'You should get a new computer.'

'Got too much stuff on it to get rid of it.'

And the memory burst through to the surface. She sat forward. The Fan family is under attack from persons unknown somewhere deep in Chinese intelligence. The Fan boy's laptop is stolen.

There are no coincidences in intelligence.

She stood up.

'What is it?' said Damian.

What the hell did that mean? she thought. How could I have forgotten that?

'Have I done something wrong?' said Damian.

Her mind was racing. The microwave was pinging.

'What? No . . . I . . .'

He was looking at her strangely.

'Trish, you look like you're about to kill someone.'

She ignored him, went to pick up her secure handheld. She just heard him walk out quietly and close the front door behind him.

With a speed and bureaucratic deftness that only Valentina Hopko could muster, an operation was brought into being. Vezza, in Africa Controllerate, and the hard men of Global Issues/Counter-terrorism could only marvel at how she drew together the disparate strands – the approaches in Hong Kong and Addis Ababa, the extraordinary Mat Naim take, the offer of service from Rocky Shi, the corruption of the Fan family – and wove them into a narrative pregnant with possibility.

There's a new source, nestled somewhere deep inside China's blackest of black boxes.

And he's asking for us.

The contents of the memory stick were scrubbed and sent to the Assessments Staff, and a brief report began threading its way through Whitehall to a very few, very carefully chosen desks. *We have found out the Fan family secrets*, the report said. *We have been handed a stiletto. What else might we find?*

A small team of analysts was set to work searching, more in hope than in anticipation, for any trace of Rocky Shi. Cheltenham began mining stored flight data, searching metadata for calls placed between Harer and Beijing, Harer and the Chinese embassies in Addis, Djibouti, Nairobi, on certain dates. They fired up a useful little program that tracked email traffic into and out of hotel reservation sites in search of bookings made in Ethiopia by Chinese government agencies. They came up empty.

Patterson, astonished, found herself rapidly assembling a cover that would hold in Ethiopia. *Eithiopia!* Maria Todd takes a holiday, perhaps, a break from her onerous accounting duties in London and Hong Kong. A vacation to the churches at Lalibela, or among the colourful tribespeople of the south. Why not? A backpack, a guide-book.

No.

'Tourist' is a surprisingly hard cover to live, with its dawdling and gawping and counting the pennies. Patterson, it was decided, would be a small businesswoman, an aspiring importer of handicrafts and fabrics, venturing to Ethiopia for the first time, harbouring a particular interest in the icons of Ethiopian Christianity, whose full-lipped madonnas, wide-eyed Christ children and dragon-slaying saints, rendered on goatskin in shimmering gold and green and magenta, would find approval among the fickle tastemakers of London.

'Because,' said Hopko, 'the only way we'll get to him is on the ground.'

The sticking point was Mangan.

The notion of putting him back in play was met with splutters of disbelief from Security Branch. *Philip Mangan? Formerly of Beijing? Veteran of an initially thrilling, later terrifying, and ultimately bloody venture in China that scared the living shit out of us? That Mangan?*

But as Hopko pointed out, entirely reasonably in Patterson's mind, Mangan was already in play, wasn't he? Because the Service had no earthly means of getting to Rocky Shi, or whatever this man's true name might be, other than via Mangan. Her logic was accepted grudgingly and on condition that, as soon as feasible, a case officer – either visiting or from Addis station – should assume the handling of the asset, if asset there proved to be. Hopko blithely accepted the condition, with absolutely no intention, Patterson could see, of adhering to it.

But what puzzled Patterson was the speed and voraciousness of Hopko's operational approach, the degree she seemed to be invested in Rocky Shi as a source when so little was known about him.

'We don't even know his full name,' she said quietly, as they sat in Hopko's sanctum looking at maps of Addis Ababa. 'What's the hurry?'

Hopko smiled her venal half-smile, didn't respond, waited, as if she knew Patterson had more to say.

'Val, there's something else. The Fan boy, the one at Oxford. There was a ping on the Police National Computer. He had his laptop stolen.'

'Lorks. When?' said Hopko.

'Recently. I'll get you the exact date. There was a search of his room. The police thought it was done professionally.'

Hopko sat forward, took off her glasses.

'Do we know what was on it?'

'No. There was nothing in the police report. I just thought ...' Patterson's voice trailed off.

Hopko was considering.

'I don't like coincidences, Trish.' She took a sharp intake of breath, put her glasses back on. 'But I do like Ethiopian food. Do you? My old dad loved it, bless him. He had an Ethiopian housekeeper when he worked on the wells in the Emirates, and she cooked for him. He couldn't get enough of it.' She reached across her desk and opened a drawer, brought out a photograph which she held up for Patterson to look at. A beach, boats, or dhows, and in the foreground, a broad-shouldered man in a blue shirt, thick, tanned forearms, an expensive watch, eyes squinting against the sun. In him, Patterson saw the source of Hopko's square figure, her stocky, strong shoulders, her air of implacability.

'There he is,' said Hopko. 'The Ukrainian engineer, sitting in Sharjah, in a hundred and ten degrees, mopping up all those fiery Ethiopian stews.' She looked at the photograph for a minute. 'My Lebanese mother was less enthusiastic. Didn't like being cooked for ...'

She paused, looked up.

'By a black woman,' said Patterson.

'Yes, I suppose so,' said Hopko, offhandedly. 'Anyway, there's a little place off Horseferry Road. Let's go. Consider it training.'

Hopko did not mention the laptop again, and Patterson took away the odd impression that she did not want to talk about it.

*

The little place off Horseferry Road was called the Queen of Sheba. It sat sandwiched between a betting shop and an estate agent. Patterson was early and sat at a round wicker table facing the door. The lights were dim, and the dining room was silent and smelled of damp carpet. She contemplated ordering a beer, but thought better of it on this, her last evening before travelling.

An evening to be endured. Hopko arrived at precisely the appointed time and bustled over to her, sat, smoothed her hair, bracelets jangling. She wore perfume, Patterson noticed, and more than a touch of make-up. For dinner at the Queen of Sheba? Without a greeting, Hopko picked up the menu.

'Now then,' she said, 'shall I order for both of us?'

Obviously, thought Patterson.

'Do you like lamb? It'll come in a delicious sort of aromatic sauce.'

'Lamb is fine.'

Hopko looked up at Patterson, who felt herself tensing.

'Lamb it is, then,' said Hopko, holding her gaze. 'And how about a *doro wat*, lovely chicken hot pot with eggs in it.'

'Sounds delicious,' said Patterson.

Hopko flipped the menu, looked at the wine list.

'Feeling a little nervy, Trish?' she said.

'No.'

'It's allowed. New case, new place.'

'I'm fine, thanks, Val.' *I have been briefed ad nauseam. What are we doing here?*

Hopko gestured for a waitress, and ordered briskly, the dishes, a bottle of wine.

'I wanted to talk a bit of history.'

Patterson sighed inwardly.

'What sort of history?'

'The history of the Fan family. Well, more of a dynasty, really, isn't it?'

Patterson gave up and reached for the wine bottle.

'There's a memoir,' said Hopko. 'Written by the old man, the patriarch.'

Hopko had a gift for narrative, Patterson thought. She had the memory, the facility for drawing out only the telling fact. Patterson listened as the little boy scratched his characters on a slate in the yellow dust of Shaanxi, as he watched the refugees scavenge for scraps of food while the fighters wheeled and banked, as he lay waiting for the Japanese bayonets to come glinting up the hillside. As he knelt, the leather belt on his wrists, the screams in his ears, naming names.

33

The restaurant was empty but for one other table, a silent, elegant Ethiopian family. Hopko tore off a piece of *injera,* worked it neatly into the stew, folding it around the meat, and popped it into her mouth. Patterson's fingers were greasy and her throat burned.

'And what happened to Literary Chen?' she asked.

'The memoir doesn't dwell on it, which is not a surprise. But other accounts have it that he was hounded. Sent to one of the cadre schools. They called them schools – they were punishment camps, really. And he died there, apparently.'

Patterson didn't know how to respond, worked stolidly at the lamb.

'But old man Fan survived the whole thing. He was rehabilitated. He even got his old job back. By the late seventies he's a vice minister, no less, dreaming of fax machines and satellites. The kids have been to university and are doing very nicely. Son number one, Fan Rong, is working his way up the Party Organisation Department. He'll end up royalty, on the Politburo. Son number two, Fan Ping, is getting a Master's in electrical engineering. He'll work in a military research institute on radar. And then in the eighties he'll start up a little company importing switching and routing equipment, taking it apart, figuring out how it works, making a cheaper Chinese version. The company does rather well. Today we know it as China National Century, CNaC. The world's largest telecoms manufacturer, sidelines in satellites, radar, missile components, avionics, processors. He's the one with the son at Oxford. See where this is going, do we, Trish?'

Patterson just nodded.

'The daughter is Charlotte Fan. Goes by her English name. She's based in Hong Kong and London and dabbles in business.'

Hopko was looking at her wineglass.

'So the Fan children have every angle covered, you see. Fan Rong, from his perch in the higher reaches of the Party, manages the politics, patronage networks, protection. Fan Ping generates the colossal wealth through CNaC. Charlotte Fan keeps one foot conveniently out of the country, manages the properties and the offshore accounts. But then ... then she goes and buys oil wells she shouldn't from crooked officials.'

'A thoroughly modern Chinese story,' said Patterson.

'Yes,' said Hopko. She leaned forward, put her fork down, tapped the wicker table with her index finger. 'Yes, it is, as long as you remember where they've come from. The poverty, the war, the struggle sessions. The Fans didn't just pass their exams and learn nice table manners like we did, Trish. They fought, they bled, they despaired. And then they survived. And they carry it all with them, the stories, the memories, the sins, all forged into identity and obligation and loyalty. And Charlotte has put the entire edifice, everything they've bled for, at risk.'

Patterson understood now.

'And someone's using it, gunning for them,' she said.

'I think we've found a fault line, a place where two plates meet.' Hopko made a joining, eliding gesture, bringing her hands together. 'And there's enormous energy and tension stored up there, just waiting for release.'

They sat in silence for a minute or two. Hopko had barely eaten. She laid twenty-pound notes on the table.

'Mangan must do more than just bring us offerings from these people,' she said. 'He must find out who, and why. Why us? What are we to them? What do they want of us?'

'I know.'

'Be careful, Trish,' said Hopko. And then she stood and swept from the restaurant, en route to some distant and obscure obligation, Patterson assumed, in a secret Whitehall corridor, or a clubroom panelled in oak, or a Kensington drawing room.

Patterson took the Tube, the air in the station close and thick and scorched. She waited on the platform, feeling the hot wind from the tunnel against her face.

When she emerged at Archway, the evening was warm, past nine and still light. She walked home through the traffic, past the small Victorian terraced houses, the silent dog walkers.

Her flat was dim, the blinds drawn. She took her clothes off and walked naked to the bathroom. She turned the shower up hot, let the water rush against her scalp, let it soothe her. The adrenalin was starting to flow, nerves kicking in. She tried to think of nothing.

She dried herself and put on a cotton dressing gown. She unpacked her case, repacked it, took her travel documents from the safe in the wardrobe. She took the phone, sat cross-legged on the sofa and dialled.

'Hello?'

'Hello, Mum, it's me.'

'Oh, it's you. Hello, my darling.'

'I didn't wake you, did I?'

'No, no, my darling. I'm just sitting up in bed.'

Patterson heard the lingering fleck of Caribbean to her speech, the television in the background.

'How are you? How's Dad?' she said.

'Oh, we're fine. Dad is, well, you know. His hip is bad.'

'What did the doctor say?'

'What? When?'

'When you went to see him.'

'Oh. Well, ask Maggie. She knows about it.' Maggie, her sister, who had a hair salon in Nottingham.

'All right. I'll ask her. Mum, I'm just calling because I'm going away again for a bit.'

'Again? Where this time?'

'Oh, nowhere very interesting. Just around and about.'

'When will you be back?'

'A week or two.'

'Can you call this time?'

'It's a bit hard, Mum. Like usual. I'll let you know as soon as I'm back.'

'They should let you call. Why won't they let you?'

She closed her eyes, leaned her head back on the sofa.

'It's just a bit hard from some of these places. But don't worry. I'll be back in no time.'

'You're so far away all the time.'

'I'll come up and see you in a few weeks. Promise.'

'Dad would like that.'

'It'll be fun.'

A pause. She could hear her mother's breathing on the line, the laugh track from the television.

'It's getting dark now,' said her mother. 'Getting dark outside.'

'It's late. You get to sleep. Give Dad a hug from me.'

'He's downstairs. Sitting there.'

'All right. Lots of love now.'

'You sound all wound up. Wound tight as a fiddle.'

'I'm fine. I just have a lot to do. Lots of love, Mum.'

'You better get on, then. Be careful, my darling, in those places. Call when you get back.'

'I will.'

She replaced the receiver, its plastic *clack* obtrusive in the silence. Patterson sat still, rubbed her thighs, suddenly chilled.

She thought of the last time she'd seen Mangan, at Changi airport in Singapore after the debrief, more than a year before, his quiet, the anger damped down behind those clear eyes. They had stood on the pavement at drop-off. *China makes exiles of us*, he'd said, and touched her on the arm. Then he'd turned and walked towards the terminal, his rumpled jacket and red hair fading into the crowd.

Her agent.

34

Oxford

Kai sat at his desk watching motes of dust in sunlight on their tiny voyages.

You will have no further contact with the Chen girl.

He reached down and opened a draw. In it, his brushes, ink, some rice paper. He unrolled the rice paper on the desk, weighted it down, ground some ink. He hadn't touched the brushes in months and now he picked them up gingerly, feeling them in his hand.

His first few attempts were clumsy, the characters weak and tentative. But the fifth sheet was better, the strokes taut and moving.

昨夜西风凋碧树。独上高楼，望断天涯路。欲寄彩笺无尺素，山长水阔知何处？

In the night, a west wind ravaged the leaves.
Alone, I climbed the tower, stared down a road that
    crossed the edge of the sky.
I wanted to write to you something extravagant, but I have
    no paper.
The mountains are endless and the rivers vast. How do I
    even know where you are?

*

The poet was Yan Shu, writing in the eleventh century. A quiet prodigy, Yan Shu, studious, liked a drink, wandered in his garden. Kai wondered if he should affix his seal, but thought of the blood red ink on the rice paper. Someone would see it, know who'd written it.

When the calligraphy had dried, he folded it carefully and left it in her pigeonhole.

He sat alone in the cafeteria eating chicken curry with rice. Afterwards, he went to the grimy student bar in the basement and drank two beers, the music thumping in his ears. What would happen, he thought, if I just threw everything off? Gave it all up. If I went home, worked in a store, or a gallery? If I rented a room, learned to make furniture and cook with *ma* peppercorns and cumin and star anise, great bowls of noodles slathered with chilli, a layer of oil keeping the heat in. I'd cook for my friends, if I were to have some of those, at some point.

What if I learned to paint? What would happen? What would my father say, the annihilating tone bleeding through his voice? What part of my anatomy would Uncle Chequebook take hold of?

Kai walked up the creaking staircase and opened the door to his room. A piece of lined paper lay on the floor, folded in two. He picked it up. The strokes were written hurriedly, in blue ballpoint pen.

春心莫共花爭發, 一寸相思一寸灰

The stirrings in your heart, do not seek their bloom.
An inch of desire is an inch of ash.

Li Shangyin, the poet. Dark, impossible, impassioned Li Shangyin, signalling, in her rejection, a whole world of complexity – and possibility.

35

Addis Ababa, Ethiopia

Addis Ababa's airport, Bole, had a gimcrack air, half-finished bits of renovation, a powdery dust on the floor. Confused travellers stood looking around themselves for signs or aid. The tall British woman waiting in the queue for a visa, the importer of art and curios – Juliet Dobson, the name on the passport – was already late, a technical fault associated with the plane's doors having delayed departure for a full two hours, while engineers first fussed and then stood silently awaiting a part.

Patterson shifted from foot to foot as the queue inched forward to a window where a harassed woman took her seventeen euros and, without a word or a look, stamped her passport with a tourist visa, the well-rehearsed cover story proving utterly unnecessary.

When they take a sniff of you, Hopko always warned, *it will be in the hotel.*

She emerged into morning sunlight, her mouth sour, eyes dry and grainy. She felt the altitude immediately. It lent the air, the light, a crispness. She took an airport taxi to the Jupiter Hotel at a vastly inflated price. The driver asked her polite questions about her visit.

She gave vague answers and took in the city, its wide, crumbling avenues redolent of plans discarded, of grand schemes forgotten, the shacks drifting into every available space. At the Jupiter, smiling staff checked her in. She went to her room, waited five minutes, then went back down to reception and requested the room be changed. Something quieter, perhaps. Or on a higher floor. The staff conferred in murmurs, complied.

Never take the first room they offer you.

She undressed, chained the door, laid snares around her secure handheld – a hair, a fragment of tissue paper – and slept.

For the meetings, Hoddinott, through a front company, had sublet a flat in a new block off Tunisia Street, one peopled by a number of young expats whose coming and going at strange hours was to be expected. A countermeasures officer was brought in from Nairobi station to sweep it. The flat was pronounced clean. It had tiled floors and neon overhead lighting and was bleakly furnished with a black sofa covered in its plastic wrapping, a dining table of smoked glass and a vast television.

As to the surveillance Mangan claimed to have seen, well, was it Rocky Shi's own people taking a look at Mangan? Or NISS issuing a routine reminder to a foreign reporter to take care? Its intermittent nature and obvious clumsiness ruled out the worst option – that it was a Chinese State Security team monitoring Mangan. Perhaps it was nothing at all. If it was there, Patterson would see it. All in good time.

She spent the late afternoon living her cover, visiting the teeming Merkato in a light rain, picking her way through the handicrafts stalls, buying samples, asking what she hoped were pertinent questions of the stallholders. What saint is this? Where does one source these paintings, these icons? What kind of paint is used? The answers she received confirmed that every icon was painted with only the most natural of pigments, out of ecstasies of devotion in island monasteries that rose from sparkling lakes, pure and unsullied expressions of an ancient, wise and forgiving religiosity, and all available for export. Patterson twisted and turned, boarded a taxi, got out too soon, hailed another one, paid off the drivers with filthy fifty-birr notes.

Now she stood slightly breathless, damp, in the living room of the safe flat, marvelling at its inhospitable nature. She tried to collect herself, took off her waterproof jacket. She wore jeans, hiking boots, a sensible shirt which had been ironed a little too well, she realised. When she sat on the sofa the plastic wrapping crackled. They would sit at the table, she decided.

A quiet knock.

She went to the door, looked through the peephole.

He looked straight back at her, his features distended by the fish-eye lens. She opened the door and he entered silently and she closed the door, and he stood there. He was thinner, the pale skin she remembered more tanned now, the hair a little longer, unruly. He retained his air of creased indifference to his surroundings, his level look.

And now, she saw, he was smiling a crooked half-smile.

'Hello Trish Whatever-your-name-is,' he said.

'Hello, Philip.'

Mangan half-raised his arms, as if for a hug. She turned away and walked to the dining table, motioning to him to sit. He let his arms fall and joined her, scraping his chair on the tile as he sat.

'First things first,' she said.

'Oh, always,' he replied.

'Do you think you are under surveillance now?'

'I don't know. I don't think so.'

'When was the last time you believe you saw surveillance?'

'Three days ago. The car, outside my flat.'

'If for any reason we are interrupted, you leave first. You leave by the stairwell and you take the rear exit from the building at the base of the stairs. Walk across the courtyard, hop the wall and you are in a park, with multiple paths and exits. Is that clear?'

'Crystal.'

'Are you clear on this?' She was speaking too loudly, she realised, adrenalin flooding through her as she thought of a small damp man in a raincoat tumbling under train wheels.

Mangan spoke calmly.

'Yes. Yes, I'm clear. Stairwell, exit, park. Got it.' He smiled.

'Is there anything you need to tell me straight away? Or anything you need from me?'

'Nope.'

'All right, let's get started.' She took her secure handheld, opened the application that would record and encrypt their conversation.

'Before you turn that on,' he said, 'how have you been?'

You must run him, Trish, Hopko had said. *Do not allow him to frame your relationship in terms of the past.*

'Not bad,' she said. 'You?'

He looked at her, expecting more, waiting. She remembered now, this taut stillness in him, this ability to wait and listen, taking you in, seeing you.

'Philip, we are not here to chew over old times.'

'That's not what I was asking. I was wondering if you were okay. But, fine. Proceed.' He gestured to the handheld. She looked down, turned it on, started recording.

They started on Rocky Shi. His appearance, manner, his tone of speech. His bearing, his accent. Any clue as to his identity, his background, his access, his reliability. Anything at all. *Be a reporter. Give us the lot.*

Mangan talked, sketching the man out in words as he might write it.

'He comes over as confident, a professional. He looks like a hard man gone a bit soft on the surface, a bit thick around the middle. He speaks in a knowing tone, as if he's sharing a joke with me. He aspires to . . . to goodness, I think. Or so he says. He's big on rectitude, as an end, if not as a means. He's so very keen to be my friend, to build a sort of shared recognition of the world. He's ingratiating. But then he shares very little. He turns calculating.'

Mangan stopped and thought.

'And beneath it all is a current of . . . something.' He described the jigging of the leg, the bitten nails, the scar. The sense of his being *directed* in something, some endeavour.

'Anxiety?' she said. 'Is he anxious?'

Mangan shrugged.

'You should have heard what he said about you.'

'What's that mean?' Patterson asked, frowning. It came out too sharp, she realised. Mangan was laughing silently.

'He said you were a very aggressive woman. Formidable, apparently. You did something to someone in Hong Kong that impressed him. I have no idea what he meant. But he's marked you.'

Jesus Christ.

'And motive, Philip? Anything on motive? Any idea why this man seems so keen to dump secrets on us ? No expression of anger? Or grudge?'

'The opposite. He seems deeply patriotic. Proud of China.'

Then, suddenly, noise from the street: a shout, a car accelerating away. They both stopped and looked towards the window. Patterson went over, pulled the blind back an inch, watched for a moment.

'And tell me again, the financial motive?' she said, walking back to her chair.

'That was all he said. Financial compensation, for him and his "associates". Didn't say it like he meant it. Didn't tell me why he needed it.'

She pressed him on the associates. Who does he mean? How many did Mangan know of? The Clown, who else? The gaunt Ethiopian in the alleyway in Harer. Any more?

'No idea. But I assume so.'

'What is this, Philip, do you think? What are we buying here, if we buy? Is this a network? A cabal?'

He didn't answer straight away.

'You want facts or hunch?' he said.

'Facts.'

'Well, I don't have any.'

'All right, hunch.'

'I don't think Rocky is in charge. I think he's following orders,' said Mangan.

'Why?'

'I'm not sure I could say. He seems to be weighing what he says and does against a scheme or an agenda. Or something.'

This is a plan, Trish.

'And,' Mangan went on, 'what access would one man have that could get him material like that, so timely, so accurate?'

She looked at Mangan. He's engaged, she thought. He's already committed himself psychologically.

Now.

'And you, Philip, why are you here?'

He stopped, wrong-footed.

'What do you mean?'

'Why do you want back in, Philip?'

He didn't answer. He's reaching for a response, she thought. She broke the silence, pushed her advantage.

'Because, you see, there's a bit of trepidation, frankly, about using you again.'

She paused, let it sink in.

'And there's a bit of bafflement about why you would want to be used. Given everything that happened.'

'Oh, are we allowed to talk about that now?'

'Answer the question.'

'Rocky Shi chose me, I didn't choose him.'

'Don't be cute, Philip. You bloody well leaped at the chance.'

'No, I didn't,' he said softly.

'Yes, you did. I'll ask you again. Why are you here?'

He stood up and walked the length of the room to where the television hung on the wall.

'I was rebuilding my life,' he said. 'Or trying to. I really was. After China.'

'And?' she said.

He raised a hand, let it fall.

'I've seen now,' he said. 'I've seen you, what you do. I can't un-see you. I have this knowledge. I can't see the world without thinking of you, of everything that's . . . that's below the surface.'

He raised a hand, as if reaching for something.

'I need it,' he said. 'I need to be *in* it.'

They talked for two hours. She felt the tension in her neck and shoulders grow, a stress headache coming on. He leaned forward, elbows on the table, listened.

'Get a name, a photograph, a mobile phone number. Anything. A licence plate, an email address, a credit card receipt. Anything that gives us traction on him,' she said. Then they'll work outwards, she thought. They'll plant him in the databases, watch his network take shape, grow, like feathers of crystal in a solution.

'You'll use this,' she said, pushing a small black plastic flight case across the table to him.

Exhausted, talked out, she went to the fridge. Hoddinott had left roast beef sandwiches in foil and St George's beer. She took two of the bottles, looked in the drawers for an opener, couldn't find one. She took a spoon, rested it against her knuckle and popped the caps off neatly. He motioned applause.

'Tradecraft,' she said, handing him a bottle.

'Are we still recording?' he said.

'Yes.'

He sighed, looked at the ceiling.

'Can you tell me anything at all about . . . you know. China. Everything.'

'Not much,' said Patterson.

'Was there ever any news of her?'

'No,' said Patterson.

He gave a tight nod.

Look at him, playing the good soldier, she thought.

'Get used to it, Philip. Our stories don't end. They just sort of hang there, unresolved.'

She sat.

'When you see him,' she said, 'remember to turn the thing on, won't you?'

'You are even harder than I remember,' he said.

36

Sunday afternoon. Mangan took the jeep, headed south-east out of Addis on a smooth, Chinese-built highway in light traffic, slowing for the herds of goats, donkeys standing in the road, rigid, unmoving even as the boys whipped them. The rainy season was coming on, the dun hills laced with green.

Another meeting, the Clown had said, leaning into him, whispering in his ear as he crossed Mauritius Street. *We want you to see something.*

Twelve miles out of Addis, Mangan pulled over, watched his mirrors. He released his hold on the wheel, realised his palms were damp. The traffic flashed past, a brown sedan, two motorcycles, a red Mitsubishi four-wheel drive, an overladen bus listing to one side, the white Isuzu trucks ploughing down the centre of the highway at speed. He pulled out and executed a fast U-turn, headed back towards Addis for two miles, then stopped again at the roadside, watched. Nothing he could see. He turned around and drove on towards Debre Zeit.

Look for the church, the market set on the hillside. Mangan pulled in behind a gleaming white Toyota SUV, left the engine running.

After a moment, a figure climbed out of the Toyota, walked towards the jeep: Rocky Shi, in sunglasses and wearing a vest festooned with pockets of the sort a photographer might wear. Mangan lowered his window. Rocky pushed his sunglasses up onto his head, beamed, spoke in Mandarin.

'*Lai ba.*' Come.

Mangan craned his head out of the jeep's window, looked around. 'Are you alone?' he said.

'No,' said Rocky, pleasantly. 'One more in the car. *Lai, lai.*'

Mangan checked his mirrors one more time. A blue Mercedes had stopped about two hundred metres behind him.

Could be anything.

He opened the door and stepped from the car.

They walked up the hillside, Rocky first, Mangan following, touching his top pocket, making sure the pen Patterson had given him was in place. Women were unloading donkeys, taking the burlap bags, turning them down and laying them on the ground. Lentils, *teff*, grains Mangan did not recognise. *Gesho* leaves for making beer. Some stringy vegetables, tomatoes. The women squatted in the mud by the burlap bags, watched the two men. Rocky stopped.

'They've come down from the villages,' said Rocky. 'Some of them have walked very far, eight, ten miles.'

He walked over to a woman in a brown T-shirt and a ruffled skirt whose goods were meagre. He stood over her, spoke in halting Amharic. She looked up at him, replied, and made a gesture that seemed to indicate far away.

'She says before she never came here, but now the cost of living is so high, she must farm and sell. Her husband is in Addis, looking for work on the building sites.'

He spoke to her again, and she reached into a bag and brought out a phone, handed it to him.

'But she has a mobile phone,' said Rocky. He turned it over in his hand, showed it to Mangan. On the back cover was the corporate logo of CNaC. Rocky tapped the phone with his index finger, gave Mangan a knowing look.

What is this? thought Mangan. Why are we here? The blue Mercedes was still parked at the roadside, a short distance down the highway.

They walked on, to the top of the hill. Rocky stopped. They looked at the market spread out beneath them, the mud, wood smoke, the silent donkeys with matted fur.

'It's so backward,' said Rocky. 'But that's a Chinese road and a Chinese phone. Do you see America here anywhere? Do you see Europe, Britain?'

Mangan decided that these were rhetorical questions.

Rocky was grinning.

'But now I really want to show you something amazing,' he said. 'Show you what China can do.'

Mangan turned towards him, so that the lens could capture Rocky Shi's visage with sufficient clarity. But Rocky was already making his way down the hill, back towards the vehicles.

They drove another eight miles or so, Mangan following the white Toyota, the road winding through flat, muddied country speckled with villages half-seen in the distance, fields of *chat*. The Toyota drove fast, accelerated past the crawling buses. Mangan struggled to keep up, the jeep rattling as he overtook, swore to himself. *British agent fails to make crucial rendezvous due to weak driving skills.* Then the Toyota slowed and he saw, on the right, set back from the road, a wire security fence, high, sturdy, well-built, of the sort that might surround a military facility. Beyond the fence, a quarter of a mile from the road, enormous warehouses, or hangars, ten or twelve of them, rose out of the fields. The Toyota signalled and pulled over at a gate facility with stadium lights and a watchtower looming over it. Mangan watched Rocky lower his window and talk to two uniformed Ethiopian security guards. One of the guards spoke briefly on a mobile phone.

'One car only,' he said. Mangan parked, and as he did so, he thought he saw a streak of blue across his rear-view mirror. He walked to the Toyota and climbed into the back seat. Rocky looked back at him and gave him a high-wattage, anticipatory smile. The driver was of Chinese appearance and said nothing.

The guards raised the barrier and waved them through.

To enter the compound was to enter a different realm. Here, the asphalt was smooth and flat. The verges were of well-kept grass. No rubble, no mud, no weeds. Hundreds of potted plants, ferns and geraniums, lined the roadway. The hangars were vast and identical, the walls a pale yellow, the roofs blue.

Beside Mangan on the back seat lay a piece of paper. A receipt? *AA Car Services, Djibouti Street, Addis Ababa.* The customer's name, phone number.

They drove to the hangar furthermost to the left, pulled in before steel double doors where a youngish Chinese man in a white shirt awaited them, hands on hips. As they climbed from the car, Mangan lingered for a fraction of a second in the back seat, folded the car rental receipt and pocketed it before getting out.

Effusive introductions followed. Rocky spoke Mandarin, gave the line about his fund, his exploratory visit to Ethiopia. Mangan was introduced as a reporter, eager to witness the fulsome fruit of Chinese investment.

The young man nodded and gestured and led them briskly onto an enormous factory floor. Spread out before them, extending into the recesses of the hangar, a production line, manned by hundreds of Ethiopian workers. The air was warm and smelled of cooking rubber, glue, oil. The clatter and hiss of machinery. To his right, Mangan saw lines of presses of some sort, then row upon row of women at over-sized sewing machines. Their guide was leaning in to them, speaking loudly.

'This line produces footwear for the European and US markets. You can see.' He held up a woman's flat shoe, pointed at the label stitched in the tongue – the brand name of a high street chain. Rocky nodded appreciatively. Mangan looked about him. The workers were all repetitive, directed motion. Some of them gazed up at the visitors, their eyes lingering on the tall red-headed Englishman as they worked. The factory was spotlessly clean and overhead hung red banners with slogans. *Together Lay The Foundation For Sino-Ethiopian Cooperation and Prosperity!* The guide gestured and they walked slowly along the production line. Next, a classroom. A hundred or so Ethiopians faced a Chinese lecturer and a screen. On seeing the visitors, the students immediately stood and began to clap.

'They are welcoming you,' said the guide. Rocky nodded and held up a hand in acknowledgement. At a sharp command from the lecturer, the students sat. On the screen, in English, were the words 'Discipline' and 'Responsibility'.

'Here,' said the guide, 'the workers study our corporate values.'

It was, to Mangan, as if a factory complex had been surgically transplanted from southern China, its ethos and expectations entirely intact.

Rocky whispered into Mangan's ear.

'They'll employ fifty thousand Ethiopian workers here. Automotive production, agricultural processing, all kinds of things.' He beamed.

They walked back across the factory floor and out to the cars. Rocky professed himself astounded, delighted. He assured the guide he would report to his superiors at the earliest opportunity.

Mangan followed the white Toyota in the mauve evening light. They drove further from Addis Ababa, into the quiet town of Debre Zeit. Rocky, it transpired, had booked them rooms at a hotel. Mangan's, yellowed peeling walls, a lightshade filled with desiccated insects, looked out on a courtyard of orchids. The driver disappeared, and Mangan and Rocky ate, the only diners in a dark and cavernous dining room, kebabs, *wot*, beer. The food was lukewarm and sickly. Mangan watched Rocky across the table.

'So,' said Mangan, 'what was all that about?' He was speaking English.

'All what?' said Rocky.

'What was I supposed to learn today? At the market. The factory.'

'Didn't you find it interesting? I find it all very interesting.'

Mangan waited.

'I hoped you would see possibility,' said Rocky. He gestured with his hand, as if grabbing for something in the air. 'I want you see what China can do, what we could be.'

'I don't need to be taken on publicity tours.'

Rocky shook his head, adopted a sad frown.

'But imagine, Philip. Imagine projects like that all over Africa!'

'I'm trying,' said Mangan.

Rocky was silent. Then he wiped his mouth with a napkin, gestured at Mangan, spoke in Mandarin, and for the first time, Mangan thought he felt an undertow in the man, some current of anger running beneath.

'You, you Western people. Your naivety. For you everything must fit in the easiest story, the neatest narrative. And for you China is a monolith, just a big, nasty, authoritarian factory, full of people you don't know, can't know. But you know nothing about our struggles. Nothing of our disappointments. Our successes. China can be a force for good, Philip. No more sitting in the corner, silent, pliable. We can change things. We can create new conditions. It might be a little . . . shocking. But that is the China we want. Really.'

Mangan saw the opportunity, took it.

'Who is we?'

'But . . .'

'Who is we?'

Rocky looked to be considering.

'We, Philip, are a small group of patriotic Chinese.'

'Forgive me, but patriots do not usually engage in the activities you have recently engaged in.'

'We have our reasons.'

'I need to know what they are.'

Rocky grinned, said nothing. Mangan spoke very quietly now.

'Why do you want to discredit CNaC?' he said.

Rocky sipped his beer, ignored the question.

'You saw the surveillance?' he said, quietly.

'A blue Mercedes, with us all day,' said Mangan.

'Is it yours?'

'No.'

Rocky made a wry face.

'I think we may not have very much more time.'

'If that is true, it is all the more urgent that you start speaking openly and clearly with me.'

Rocky gave his best puckish, twinkling grin.

'Did you ever study Confucius, Philip?'

Mangan thought back to college days, a course in classical texts, the hopeless slog through *The Analects*.

'A little.'

'So you know. You know that we Chinese have always valued the humane. *Ren,* we call it. Humaneness. Very important. Not because some god tells us so, but because Confucius understood that society works when we are humane. And the true ruler is humane, like a parent to a child.'

Mangan waited.

Rocky picked at his food, spoke carefully.

'There is a man. A very decent, patriotic man. A soldier. When he speaks you know you are hearing truths. He believes in these virtues, real Chinese virtues. Many of us admire this man very much. He shows us the way. We answer to him.'

'Does he have a name, this virtuous soldier?'

Rocky shook his head, put down his fork, sat back.

'So that is what we are, Philip. *Ren.* Humane. That is our motive. You can tell them this.'

Rocky raised a finger and wagged it.

'And you may tell them one more thing. Tell them that I am a soldier, too. An officer of the People's Liberation Army. Tell them that I served as a military observer in the Sinai Peninsula, in Egypt, in 1998.'

When Mangan awoke in the morning, Rocky had already left. But an envelope had been pushed under the door.

*

At the Jupiter Hotel, Patterson had lain awake much of the night, tried to read, watched some television – a vile movie on a satellite channel featuring mawkish man-children who made their cars skid and spin to no apparent purpose, sumo wrestling, an ancient, saccharine rom-com. For a while she paced the room. From her window, she watched the damp, dim city, the streets mostly silent now, the sprawled and ragged figures by the roadside. She went early to the safe flat, brewed coffee, tested and retested the equipment.

Mangan arrived at eleven, unshaven, unhurried, sat on the crackling sofa, rubbed his eyes.

'The surveillance is there. It's real,' he said. 'And it's not his.'

'Was it with you this morning?' she said.

'I don't know. I didn't see it. I left the car at home, took three different taxis to get here.'

'Mobile phone?'

'At home.'

'My, what a pro,' she said.

He gave her a quizzical look, then reached in his pocket, took out the pen and handed it to her. She unscrewed the barrel to reveal a socket which she cabled to the laptop. A short upload, and they were looking at images of Rocky Shi. Patterson studied the screen, watched the compact figure in its ludicrous photographer's vest walking through the market, listened to the reedy voice, the forced laughter, saw immediately the elusiveness of the man, the outward layers of obfuscation.

'That is very good,' she said.

'There's more,' he said.

He gave her the Toyota's licence plates, the car rental receipt. Patterson felt a flicker of excitement, a half-smile forming. He watched her.

And then – finale! – he laid the envelope on the table with a flourish.

'You managed to restrain yourself from opening it?' she said.

'As ordered.'

Patterson put on a pair of surgical gloves, picked up the envelope, opened it and removed a document of some thirty pages. Together they looked at the title page.

Juemi.

Mangan's Chinese was marginally better than Patterson's.

Instructions to Responsible Military Officers and Cadres Regarding Oversight of Procurement Contracts in the Case of China National Century Corporation.

Patterson worked quickly with a handheld scanner. Once the document and the car receipt were uploaded, she pushed the files through an encryption program. She wrote a short covering telegram and encrypted that, too. The laptop was connected to a handheld satellite phone and the files went in short digital bursts.

Mangan lay on the sofa, closed his eyes. Patterson left him alone, went to the fetid kitchen to make more coffee, came back into the living room to see him sitting bolt upright on the sofa, eyes wide.

'I almost forgot,' he said.

'Forgot what?' she said, alarmed.

'He said I was to tell you that he is an officer of the PLA and that he served in Sinai in 1998. He was an observer. One of the UN observers.'

Patterson stared at him, bit back an angry response.

'That's important,' he said, blankly.

'For Christ's sake, wake up, Philip,' she said. 'He's telling us who he is.'

37

Patterson waited, stunned with boredom in the safe flat. The surveillance had left London nervy and it was deemed risky for her to be out, even to build cover. She read, watched satellite television, tested the equipment, thought up elaborate operational scenarios, and in an act of boldness and rebellion, removed the plastic covering from the sofa, so that it no longer crackled when she sat on it.

Hopko came up on secure video link for housekeeping and to, as she put it, 'keep the engine running'. VX, Hopko informed Patterson, had granted Rocky Shi the cryptonym by which he was to be known. He had become HYPNOTIST. For Mangan, BRAMBLE. And as such would they be known in all traffic henceforth.

'They're breathing very heavily,' she said, through the clutter and pixellation. 'Over at Assessments, at Treasury, even in the Cabinet Office. HYPNOTIST has got their attention. They want everything on CNaC. The lot. Links to the Party, the military. CNaC's presence in Africa, Latin America, projects, contracts. Is every CNaC router a bug? Are there backdoors in CNaC encryption? Little CNaC black boxes in every switching room? Malware on every CNaC smartphone? After all, *we* do these things, so why wouldn't *they*? Is CNaC colonising cyberspace? they ask. Is it poisoning the digital well?'

'And you think HYPNOTIST can answer all that?'

Hopko looked at the camera over the rim of her spectacles.

'Perhaps. If we run him well enough.'

'Are you unsure about him?'

Hopko paused.

'What concerns me, Trish,' she said, 'is that HYPNOTIST is pointing us in a certain direction, forcing us to look a certain way. It's as if he's throwing meat to the dogs, keeping our noses to the ground. Why is he doing that? I wonder.'

After the call, Patterson put away the equipment, locked it in the flight cases. Stir crazy, she disobeyed orders and went for a walk in a headscarf, sunglasses. She mapped several blocks around the safe flat, fixed egress routes in her mind, watched the traffic, the people, looked for the tension, the pulse that might give away the presence of surveillance. But in a city this chaotic how the hell do you ever see it? How do you see it amid the crowds, the shanties, the ragged, stunned beggars, the young men who just seemed to float, directionless, across the city? How would you ever know?

NISS could have sixty people on her, right now.

She turned, walked quickly away from the safe flat, took a taxi back to the hotel, surprised, unnerved by her own disquiet.

Mangan lolled around Addis, waiting for instructions. He filed a desultory piece on the investigation into the bombing, to little effect. He wrote an elaborate celebration of Ethiopian quarterly growth figures. *In the Horn of Africa, a Bullish Economy!*

He called the Danish and she was caustic with him, and then, to his surprise, proposed a trip out of town.

Hallelujah joined them and they drove three hours to Ambo to visit the university. Maja was wondering about nursing programmes there. They wandered around the pitted, muddy campus, chatted to the students outside their crumbling concrete classrooms. They sat in a law class and listened to an Indian lecturer explain the Ethiopian pension system in English that Mangan found hard to fathom. The students sat silent and uncomprehending. Many of them, Hallelujah explained, were Oromo and spoke little Amharic, and only rudimentary English.

'It's our biggest problem,' he said with a hopeless shrug. 'No one in Ethiopia understands anyone else.'

Maja shooed them away and sat at a rusted metal table outside the student services building, talking to a group of girls about their nursing course, what they knew of midwifery, trying to gauge what they were being taught. Hal and Mangan played table football with a knot of raucous boys, and Mangan felt taken out of himself for a moment, laughing and roaring with the rest of them as the tin ball rattled and snapped about the table.

In the late afternoon, they set out on the return journey to Addis, Mangan driving cautiously, concentrating fiercely on the road.

Twenty minutes out of Ambo, he slowed, just to see. A white Isuzu truck roared past him, horn blaring. A Nissan pickup, a bus.

But the blue car – was it a Mercedes? – a quarter of a mile behind, did not overtake. It slowed too.

He turned off the main road and drove for half a mile down a bumpy, cobbled track that wound through fields and into a village of thatch and chickens. Mangan watched his mirrors as the other two looked out of the windows.

They stopped, and stepped out of the car into sudden, deep quiet. They watched boys driving cattle home through the haze. Girls with babies on their backs came shyly from the huts and approached them. Hallelujah knelt and joked with them, asked them slow questions in Oromiffa and they answered in whispers. Maja went and kneeled next to Hallelujah, held out her hand, and one of the girls took it in her tiny, dusty fingers.

She's so gentle, Mangan thought.

The girls touched her hair, wondered at the colour of it, tried to braid it. Maja sat cross-legged in the dust, letting them run their fingers through it, her eyes closed, smiling, listening to the children's breathy giggles, their sing-song chatter.

Mangan walked a little way away, on his own, smelled the wood smoke and vegetation on the air. The fields stretched away for a mile to a jagged escarpment. Children in a village, cooking smells, the tinkle of a cowbell. Such places always felt to him intimate yet unattainable. He watched the thunderheads piling up above the dark rock, silver sunlight angling through the pillars of cloud.

Maja spoke from behind him.

'Are you okay?' she said.

'I think so. Coming to places like this helps.'

She threaded her arm through his.

'Helps what?' she said.

'Oh, you know. Everything.'

'You mean the bombing?'

'That, and ... yes, that.'

'I'm only just starting to feel as if I could ever be normal again, but you seem as if you have already left it far behind,' she said. 'Where are you going? It feels like you are looking over your shoulder at me.'

When they got back on the road, there was no sign of the blue Mercedes.

Mangan called her the next day and they went for an Addis walk together, into the Merkato in a dank sunlight, up the hill at What-Do-You-Have? where the metal beaters knelt in the filthy street amid the potholes, the mud laced with oil and chemicals, reconditioning ancient, battered aluminium pots, kettles, bowls, their hammers tap-tapping out the dents, the women scouring, rendering them new, stacking them in dull, silvered piles. Where the boys sat amid stinking piles of old shoes, stitching, patching, renewing, bringing them back to life. The air was full of clanging and shouting, the toil of machinery, showers of sparks. Mangan saw ashtrays and grinding cups made from old shell cases, mortar rounds, sandals cut from reeking mounds of old tyres, rakes, fences, doors fashioned from scrap iron.

'Why do they call it that?' said Maja.

'The trucks come in from out of town, with all this' – Mangan gestured to the mounds of scrap, refuse. 'And the buyers shout, "What do you have?" And the name stuck.' The air was clotted with smoke, decaying rubber, burning. The men watched them pass, bloodshot-eyed, hard-handed, blistered, lean men, their clothes spattered with oil, rotted with acid.

They walked on, into the spice market, her hand suddenly in his. He took her down a covered alleyway, a narrow maze of stalls, the light tinted yellow from a corrugated plastic roof, porters elbowing past them, shouting, laughter, the women carving great slabs of *kocho*, the white banana root, pounded and fermented, falling off the knife. Maja stopped in front of an elderly woman in a plaid scarf, little white burlap sacks arrayed before her. *Feto* seeds for grinding and mixing with lemon, for purification. Kohl for the eyes. *Ades* leaf for infusing in butter, combing into the hair. Sulphur for wounds and exorcism. The woman put crumbs of incense into a twist of paper and pressed them into Maja's hand, waved her away with a smile.

They stopped somewhere deep in the alleyways, sat on plastic stools, while two women grinned at them and chattered in Amharic, its playful, questioning ring. The women took coffee beans from a sack, shook them onto a skillet atop a clay brazier, moved them around with the tiny rake as they roasted. Mangan watched, smoked. Maja leaned forward, smelled the roasting coffee. The women dropped shards of frankincense into the brazier, wafted the smoke over Mangan and Maja, gestured for them to breathe deeply, breathe it in, this richness. The women ground the beans, brewed the coffee, poured cups and passed it to them. It was sweet and dark, the frankincense lingering on it.

Maja was quiet, regarded Mangan, then spoke.

'I was thinking I might move back up here, to Addis.'

'Really? Leave the clinic?'

'I'm not sure how much more I can take down there. I'm feeling burned out, frightened.'

'Perhaps you should think about a break. Going home.'

'Oh, should I?'

'Well, I mean . . .'

'Yes, perhaps I should.' She looked down, paused. She put her cup down.

'Philip, do you think there is any possibility that you and I might . . . might connect? I mean, really? If I came back to Addis we could, perhaps, try, no? I think of it, sometimes. No, a lot, actually. But you seem so . . . preoccupied. You seem so . . . absent. A bomb goes off, and you are all business.'

Mangan wondered how to respond. She was looking at him intently and he was aware that this was some kind of inflection point.

Could he tell her? Hint at it, maybe? The danger she was in? *Don't worry, Maja, my reticence is explained by the fact that I am the operative of a secret intelligence agency. My true interests lie in providing targets for lethal drone strikes. Oh, and by associating with me, you are exposing yourself to the scrutiny of several intelligence agencies whose good manners are not to be relied upon.*

'It's possible I might not be staying here too much longer myself,' he said.

And as he said it, he felt an imagined life recede, dissipate into the air.

38

The traces on Rocky Shi were through. Patterson sat, head in hands, ploughing through them, watching the man take shape, trying to sense the meaning of his experiences.

From 1998, out of the United Nations mission in the Sinai, an appreciation of the then Major Shi Hang, written in starchy prose by an Australian colleague who was clearly intrigued to encounter the fabled Chinese People's Liberation Army.

Major Shi Hang – 'though he insists on the use of a nickname, Rocky' – was a valued member of the UN mission, apparently, enduring the long, hot patrols into the Sinai with professionalism, reporting punctiliously upon ceasefire violations by Egyptian or Israeli forces, as was his mission. The Australian officer found Major Shi somewhat wanting in military deportment – 'he smokes heavily and does not join in calisthenics', yet he was 'approachable, cheerful and good for morale. An accomplished cook, he has been known to return to base in possession of live poultry, which he will transform into a tasty Chinese soup for the benefit of himself and his brother officers.'

Major Shi, it is ascertained, is an officer of the Second Department of the People's Liberation Army General Staff Headquarters (2PLA).

That is to say, he is an officer of Chinese military intelligence, information that is relayed with a certain frisson.

And from this one fixed point of reference, Rocky Shi's life and career can be found out.

Major Shi Hang, alias Rocky, now to be known as HYPNOTIST, pops up all over the place, as you would expect of a resourceful military intelligence officer.

Special Branch in Hong Kong made him, back in the early nineties, as part of a covert Chinese presence in Hong Kong in advance of the colony's return to Chinese rule. And what was he doing there? 'Specific intelligence on Shi Hang's operational role continues to elude us,' Special Branch conceded wearily.

There he was in Honolulu, a military diplomat on a rare trip to United States Pacific Command in 2006, escorting an anvil-faced major-general named Chen. 'Urbane and attentive,' reads the PACOM report, 'Major Shi was a keen observer, an active questioner and an enthusiastic golfer.' Crucially, the report included a group photograph. Rocky, in uniform, stood at the edge of the group, a generous grin plastered across his face, in contrast to the flinty gaze of General Chen.

And here, a liaison report from a furious CIA station chief in Tashkent, where Rocky, as China's deputy military attaché, has infuriated the Americans with his charming and good-natured subversion of the Pentagon's plans for permanent air bases in Uzbekistan.

A true professional, as Hopko had foreseen.

The car rental had been paid in cash, no useful address. The mobile phone number led nowhere. It had called a grand total of three other numbers in its short life. One was Mangan's, the second was the Chinese embassy in Addis, the third appeared to belong to an expensive Ethiopian lady who frequented a 'closed house' near Bole airport, whose favours a wealthy, visiting Chinese businessman might be expected to enjoy. Hopko strongly suspected that Rocky Shi was, again, teasing them.

Not a whiff of his motive, not a whiff of his objective. Just the lingering sense that Rocky Shi had a pitch, that he had not yet made it, that he was waiting.

In the safe flat, Patterson stood while Mangan lounged on the sofa as she briefed him on what they now knew of Colonel Shi. Mangan responded by turning, she thought, a little pale.

'London feels the need for a stronger "operational footing",' she said.

'What the hell does that mean?'

'It means that at the moment we are all just hanging on dear Colonel Shi's largesse. And they don't like that. It makes them uneasy. They want a clear commitment, an arrangement they understand.'

'And what sort of arrangement would that be?'

'Come on, Philip. One that relies on the tried and the tested motive for the agent: money or ideology or coercion or ego.'

Mangan paused, considered.

'That's pretty unimaginative, isn't it?' he said. 'Aren't people more complex than that?'

'Agents may be. London-based operational planners, not so much.'

'And how am I supposed to ease him into an understanding of his own motives?'

'Well, he talked about money before, didn't he? So you can pursue that with him. But more than that, you're to get him talking,' she said. 'Talk about the future. Get him to envisage his future, with us. Let a plan form.'

'If he is the professional you say he is, he'll know instantly what I am trying to do.'

'There is that.'

'You're not helping.'

'I'm passing on instructions.'

He waited. She felt his eyes on her.

'What does she say, your boss? The clever one with all the jangly jewellery,' he said.

'She sees things differently.'

'How?'

Patterson pondered the wisdom of revealing to him Hopko's unconventional wisdom.

'She thinks that Rocky Shi wants something other than a conventional arrangement. Something more. That there's something larger at work here.'

He was listening carefully.

'And what does that mean for me?'

'She believes that you have the gift. That you can open people up, bring them to a point where they reveal themselves. So go and talk to him. Just see what you find.'

He stood up and pulled on his coat.

'And you? Will you be anywhere in the vicinity?'

'No.'

'Can I ask why?'

'I'm grounded.'

'But it's all right for me to go and get snooped on.' He was trying to be jocular, but she could sense tension coursing through him.

'You're starting to see how this works, then,' she said, realising as she did how cruel it sounded. She opened the front door of the flat for him. He stopped and gave her a searching look, a half-smile, then he was gone. She closed the door quietly, wondering once again why he had chosen as he had.

39

Just before midnight, Mangan took a couch in the corner on the third floor of Sky Club, the dance floor pulsating below, loud enough to obscure a conversation, just distant enough to render conversation possible. He ordered a bottle of Black Label, watched. When girls came over, sat down next to him and crossed their long silky legs, leaned against him, he smiled and said, 'Maybe later.'

Rocky appeared after twenty minutes, a big, anticipatory grin on his face. He wore stone-coloured slacks and a smart blazer. He would be dapper, Mangan thought, but for his slight ungainliness, his splay-footed walk. Rocky sat on the couch, gestured with pleasure to the bottle of Black Label. Mangan poured, added a little water.

'To us, Philip,' said Rocky. He was speaking English.

'For sure,' said Mangan.

'To cooperation.'

'All right, then.'

They drank, sat in silence for a moment.

'Found any more promising investments?' said Mangan.

'You,' said Rocky. 'You are my promising investment.' He laughed.

'Tell me how that works,' said Mangan, smiling.

'Soon.'

Another pause.

'So, got any family, Rocky? Parents, wives? Where are they, then? Back home minding the hearth?'

A flicker of surprise on Rocky's face.

'No, no. Not married. Parents long gone.'

'Why not married? Attractive chap like you.'

Rocky looked to be pondering the question, as if for the first time.

'I don't know. Married to work, maybe.' He sipped his whisky, then gestured with his glass to Mangan, index finger extended along its rim. 'Yes. Married to my work.' He laughed again.

'And what about your father? You said he was a soldier.'

'Did I? Yes. Big soldier. Infantry. Fought the Americans in Korea. Later, he commanded a division.'

'He must have been proud of you.'

Rocky adopted an expression of disbelief. His expressions were contrived, deliberately assembled, thought Mangan. There is no spontaneity in him. *Now I shall appear disbelieving. Mark the extent of my disbelief.*

'Proud? Of me? No. He was, you can say, very tough.'

'Really? How?'

'He thinks that young people don't know how to *chi ku*. You know *chi ku*?'

Chi, to eat. *Ku*, a bitter taste. To eat bitterness. To suffer, endure privation. 'Yes,' said Mangan.

'So he make sure I can *chi ku*. Any bad marks, or trouble at school, he takes his belt and *pshh*, *pshh*.' He made whipping movements in the air with his free hand, his face alight with astonished humour. 'Oh! It hurt so much. My mother tried to stop him, but she could not. She was so weak, useless. No good.'

He drank.

'One time I left the dinner table before I finished my food. There's still some food in my bowl. And he says, why are you leaving your food? And I said, oh, it's not good. It was *hong shao rou*, you know? Red cooked pork. Very fatty. I didn't like it.' His eyes went wide, as if the memory still revolted him. 'And my father, he just exploded. He's shouting! How dare you waste food! How dare you say it's not good! It's the favourite food of Chairman Mao! And he picks up the *hong shao rou* in his hand. And he rubs it all over my face, this fat, in my nose and eyes, everything. Too disgusting. So I start to . . . how do you say, *tu* . . .'

'Throw up.'

'Yes, I start to throw up, and then he takes my collar and drags me outside. It was winter, very cold. And he makes me kneel down on the ice and I have to stay there for a long time. So cold! And this fat all over my face, and the smell. And the other kids come out and start mocking me and throwing ice and snow.'

He started laughing, shaking his head.

'So I had to become a soldier, too, of course. But not an infantry officer. I chose my way. So my father was mad again. Such a bastard. What can I do?'

'Did he ever talk about Korea?'

'Yes. He had stories about it. Lots of *chi ku*, of course. He was in the fighting at Chosin Reservoir. No food, and they wore just canvas shoes in the snow, so their feet all froze. Trumpets sounding the charge, straight into American machine guns. And then, later, he was in the tunnels. Some mountain somewhere they tried to hold. No water, so he sat in the darkness, inside the mountain, holding a cup waiting for drops of water from the rock. And he ordered three men to hold the mouth of the tunnel, and they lasted eight minutes, and then he sent another three, and on.'

He lit a cigarette, held it between his thumb and forefinger. At the sight of the two of them, a Westerner and a Chinese businessman drinking expensive whisky, the girls lingered, cast glances. One caught Mangan's eye and walked slowly towards their table. She was attempting a model's walk, the swing in the hips. She leaned over them, a gorgeous caramel-skinned girl, her dress white, skin-tight.

Mangan smiled at her, was about to gently shoo her away, when Rocky turned on her.

'What the fuck you want?'

The girl's face fell.

'Just, maybe, you like company?' She held her hand out. Rocky batted it away.

'You get lost. Now,' he snarled. And Mangan glimpsed it again, behind the carefully constructed joviality, some flicker of rage.

The girl looked to Mangan, who just shook his head, and she straightened up and walked away. Rocky made a dismissive gesture, muttered under his breath, then turned back and regarded Mangan.

You. You are my investment.

'But it sounds as if the army has given you a great career,' Mangan said, carefully.

'Oh, yes. Yes, it has. I have travelled a lot and I have some great comrades,' said Rocky, equanimity restored.

'You must have seen many changes. In the military. During your career.'

Rocky was looking at him, amusedly, a sharpness to his humour now. He broke into quick, incisive Mandarin.

'What can I tell you, Philip? What do you need?'

'Need?'

'That will satisfy your people.'

'I don't follow.'

'Come on, Philip. You want my motive. Of course you do. That I'll be passed over for promotion? That's true enough. No senior command for me, nothing to match my father's. That I earn a pitiful army salary, while everyone in China gets rich? God knows that's true, too. That I am *resentful*? That I loathe the creeps who run the Party? That I loathe their duplicitous shit about the Three Represents and the Harmonious Society and the China Dream and the Six Bend Overs, while their children and siblings siphon billions into offshore accounts thoughtfully provided for them and administered on their behalf by Great Britain and its dependencies?'

Mangan didn't respond.

'Tell them all that if you want. Tell them. And tell them I want my own little offshore account. With twenty thousand a month. No. Twenty-five thousand. So they'll know my motive. And then we're all happy.'

'Pounds or dollars?' Mangan asked after a beat.

Rocky gave him a wide grin, but his gaze was straight and level. Then he drew on his cigarette deeply and exhaled, a long stream of smoke towards the ceiling, and his eyes flickered to something behind Mangan.

'Oh dear,' he said. 'And we were having such a nice evening.'

40

The first thing Mangan noticed was the way the girls were drawing away, standing up, smoothing their skirts and then moving quickly off, leaving their drinks. In his peripheral vision, he saw one of the club security guards come towards them, then stop and move away again, his look hesitant. Mangan was conscious of the dance music still pounding beneath them. Rocky sat immobile, looking past him, trying to summon a look of injured innocence.

Mangan turned.

Behind him were three Ethiopian men, unmoving, unsmiling. The first of them wore a light blue suit, a brown tie and held a mobile phone. He was balding, with a face seemingly hewn from dark, pitted rock, with hooded eyes. The other two were in open-necked shirts and jackets, one on the cusp of middle age, heavily spectacled. The other was older, lanky, grizzled. All of them were watching Mangan.

Rocky stubbed out his cigarette, sitting primly on the edge of the couch.

Mangan thought furiously. What was he carrying? Nothing. Patterson had done her work: he was clean.

Calm and a good cover story are your friends, Philip.

And this is how it works.

Blue Suit gestured, a barely noticeable twitch of his mobile phone. *You'll come with us now.* The eyes in that face made Mangan think of something ceramic, something scoured. Mangan opened his hands, as if to say, what? I don't understand. Rocky did nothing, looked straight ahead.

Blue Suit gave a tight shake of the head. Spectacles walked slowly over to where they were seated and leaned down.

'We just want to talk. A few minutes. Please.' He stood again, made a concierge's gesture. *This way, gentlemen.*

'We can talk here,' said Mangan. Spectacles just gestured again.

'Please identify yourselves,' said Mangan, playing the irritated journalist. No response. He sensed Rocky giving him a sympathetic look.

Spectacles leaned down to the table and picked up the bottle of whisky. He held it, looked at the label admiringly, hefted the bottle in his hand. He looked about himself. The space around the couch had emptied. Spectacles drew back his arm and with a startling ferocity hurled the bottle to the tiled floor, where it shattered, fragments of glass arcing into the air. Mangan flinched, smelled the stench of the spilled whisky. Spectacles glared at the two of them.

Rocky raised his eyebrows, shook his head and sighed.

Two SUVs waited outside the club. Mangan was escorted to one, Rocky to the other.

Mangan began the standard remonstration.

'Please show me some identification.'

Spectacles said nothing, just gestured to the car. A knot of curious boys watched from beneath a street lamp furred with insects.

'I am an accredited journalist here. You have no right to ... where are you taking me?'

But there were more of them now and Spectacles just nodded with his chin and Mangan found himself held by the arms, given a gratuitous shove into the side of the car and then rammed into the back seat. Spectacles got in with Mangan, sat in the front, gestured silently to the driver. The cars pulled away in the cool night, bumping onto Jomo Kenyatta Street and then on to the north-east, to the outskirts of Addis.

Mangan watched the city lights fall away to darkness, felt the shimmer of fear in his stomach and tried to plan what he'd say. They drove for forty minutes, through a district of new, scattershot construction, lamps burning on the building sites amid the wooden scaffolding, mud as far as he could see.

Occasionally Spectacles muttered to the driver and they sped up, or slowed down. Once they stopped by the side of the road and turned the lights off, waited for three or four minutes, before proceeding. Spectacles murmured into his phone. He wasn't speaking Amharic, Mangan noticed.

The car pulled off the highway at nearly two in the morning, into a gated community of villas, great yellow monstrosities arrayed along broad avenues, home to politicians, businessmen, athletes. The driver craned his neck, searched for the right gate, then turned into a curved driveway and parked. Spectacles climbed from the front seat, walked around and opened Mangan's door, gesturing for him to step out. Mangan smelled rain and eucalyptus. Spectacles took his arm, walked him to the villa's front door, where Blue Suit waited. They went inside.

Mangan was ushered into a brightly lit living room with a faux chandelier, tiled floor, beige leather sofas, glass tables with elaborately carved legs, and ornate heavy curtains, pink, with swags and tails. Rocky was already there, sitting on one of the vast sofas, his fingers tapping lightly on a cushion, composed, alert. Mangan caught his eye and Rocky blinked slowly as if to acknowledge and reassure him.

Mangan felt his mouth thick, pasty; a weakness, featheriness to his hands, legs.

This is how it works.

Silent men in hideous rooms, waiting for it all to start.

Blue Suit made a patting gesture with his hand in the air, indicating Mangan should sit. The four of them, Rocky, Mangan, Spectacles,

Blue Suit, faced each other over the glass coffee tables. The other one, the older grizzled one, stood by the door, still, watchful.

Blue Suit raised his hands then let them fall onto his lap, as if to say, *Well, here we all are then, at last.* He cleared his throat, spoke in English, a mid-range rasp.

'So. Mr Mangan. Mr Shi. We have things to talk about.'

Silence. He spoke again.

'Mr Shi. Perhaps you can tell us what brings you to Ethiopia.'

Rocky was sitting forward on the sofa, eager to oblige, his most ingratiating smile ramped up to high.

'Of course, yes. I can tell all about it. But, please, perhaps you can tell us first who you are and why you bring us here.' He nodded, a vision of expectation. Mangan sat very still.

Blue Suit waited for a moment.

'Mr Shi, we are just old revolutionaries from Tigray. You know Tigray? That is where we are from.'

He made a circle in the air with his forefinger to indicate himself and his comrades. 'All of us from Tigray.'

He stopped, sighed.

'And we fought in our revolution, just like in China. We fought our way down from the mountains of Tigray. Years, it took us. Years. And we took Addis in our sandals and shorts! And we threw out the Dergue, the military dictator. We try to build a new Ethiopia. An open, stable Ethiopia. Maybe an Ethiopia where people don't starve, leave their children by the road for the hyena. Maybe we even try for a slice of prosperity. Who knows, maybe Africans can have a little slice. The right Africans. Maybe we allow ourselves to expect it a little.'

He stopped.

They are NISS, thought Mangan. They are intelligence officers hardened in war and insurrection and feared across East Africa. He tried to steady his breathing, to calm himself.

A door had opened at the far end of the room and a girl entered carrying a tray, glasses, a bottle of something that could be cognac. She walked across to the coffee tables and set the tray down. She was slender, wore tight white jeans, a halter top, dark circles around her eyes. Blue Suit looked at the bottle but his thoughts were elsewhere.

'Dangerous, such expectations, for Africans. Prosperity, stability. But then we look at China and we think, see what these fellows have done!'

Rocky, on cue, nodded appreciatively.

In Mangan's mind, fear gave way to anger for a split second. *What is this fucking charade?* But flickering on the edge of his consciousness was the knowledge that they might kill him.

'Yes!' said Blue Suit. 'You understand, Mr Shi! Your country and mine are so much the same. China was never colonised. Not completely. Nor was Ethiopia. You brought down an emperor. So did we. You had your revolution, your terror. So did we. Now China is prosperous, powerful. And we think . . . well, maybe. So, you understand.'

Blue Suit now turned to Mangan and his look was of utter contempt.

'But you, Mr Mangan. Maybe you do not understand so much.'

He sat back, laced his fingers on his stomach, as if his point had been made.

Now Spectacles spoke, blunt, humourless.

'Please tell us, Mr Shi, what brings you to Ethiopia.'

Rocky held his hand in front of his mouth for a second, then spoke as if from a prospectus.

'I represent a small investment fund, located in the Chinese city of Kunming. We are looking for opportunities. Opportunities that can bring great benefit to our partners. We believe that Ethiopia is a country full of opportunity and that Chinese capital investment, conducted wisely, can help Ethiopia down the path to the prosperity—'

Spectacles, bored, cut him off.

'What sort of opportunities are you pursuing?'

'We look at real estate, and infrastructure, and perhaps ventures in the leather and garment industries.'

'Tell us, please, the extent of the assets at your disposal.'

'I am authorised to consider and submit proposals for investments up to and including twelve million dollars.'

Spectacles did not respond, looked over at Blue Suit.

'And Mr Mangan here,' said Blue Suit, waving idly in Mangan's direction. 'Is he a partner, or adviser in your enterprise? What is he?'

Rocky affected surprise.

'Mr Mangan is a journalist who shows great interest in China's new partnerships in Ethiopia. Very smart reporter.'

'You spend a lot of time together.'

Rocky spoke slowly now, carefully.

'We talk a lot about China's interests in Ethiopia.'

Blue Suit turned to Mangan.

'Is this correct, Mr Mangan? You are reporting on Mr Shi's enterprise here? You are just a reporter.'

'Yes,' said Mangan, but the word caught as it came out, and he had to clear his throat and try again. 'Yes, that's right. I am very interested in the way Mr Shi is going to make his investment decisions, and I intend to write about it.'

Blue Suit regarded him.

'Yes, I see. And is that all you intend? You have never considered going into a partnership of some sort with Mr Shi? The two of you together?'

'No.' Mangan swallowed. 'Though I must admit, sometimes the prospect of leaving journalism and trying something new is tempting.' Rocky was looking at him hard.

Blue Suit raised his hands in acclamation.

'Of course. And you could bring all your expertise to such an enterprise. Have you told Mr Shi how unpredictable Ethiopia can be, Mr Mangan? That we are not a country with a mature, well-developed legal system? That sometimes problems can arise, things can ... go astray, here. People, too.'

Christ. Sack the scriptwriter, thought Mangan, absurdly.

Spectacles was nodding gravely. The door across the room opened again and the girl walked in. She held a small clay brazier, gingerly, by its edges. She stopped and looked questioningly at Blue Suit, who waved her over. They all watched as she laid the brazier down on the floor. Embers glowed within it. She left the room again, and then was back with a coffee jug and coffee beans on a skillet.

'Some coffee,' said Blue Suit.

The girl squatted, awkward in her tight jeans and heels. She placed the skillet on the brazier and let the beans start to roast. She moved them around with the little rake. She reached in a pocket and brought out a twist of paper, opened it and allowed flakes of incense to fall into the brazier. The room filled with the smell of roasting coffee beans and grey flecks of incense that the girl idly wafted towards the watching men.

Blue Suit shifted in his seat, impatient.

'So, do you not feel, Mr Mangan, Mr Shi, that any bold person who seeks opportunity in Ethiopia would benefit from the partnership of local people? A guiding hand, a friend to advise, to warn. Do you not think?'

Rocky appeared to be pondering the question.

'Maybe I can see that. Yes, maybe I can.'

'Yes, why not?' said Blue Suit. He had raised his voice and was looking at Spectacles, who nodded. 'What do you think, Mr Mangan? Do you agree?'

'Well, I am just a journalist and I am not experienced in these matters.'

Blue Suit responded with animation and a rigid smile, which seemed to Mangan to have, churning just below its surface, cold fury. The girl was grinding the coffee beans now, in a mortar and pestle, keeping her eyes down, working with a tension and rigidity to her movement that spoke of fright.

'Certainly not!' yelled Blue Suit. 'Surely there must be a role for you!'

Mangan felt the atmosphere in the room as balanced on the point of a knife, teetering just above violence. Rocky stepped in.

'Perhaps you can suggest who is suitable local partner for investment enterprise such as mine,' he said.

'Well, we know many people,' said Blue Suit. 'Trustworthy people. People we are tied to.'

Spectacles spoke.

'Your wife. Why not?'

Blue Suit feigned astonishment.

'My wife?' He turned to Rocky. 'Very able woman. She does business in Dubai. Buys and sells, currency and gold. She charters aeroplanes to bring in the *chat*. She is there now, doing business. Very capable.'

'I'm sure she can bring much to the table,' said Rocky.

'Oh, yes, she would. Most certainly.'

The girl was standing, pouring coffee into tiny cups. When she offered one to Blue Suit, her hand shook. Blue Suit took the coffee, then sat up suddenly, as if another thought had occurred to him. He spoke fast and Mangan heard nothing but threat.

'And of course, I, we, can guide you as well. Ensure you are properly protected from the problems that can arise in an immature market. We can give you guarantees. Who would not want such guarantees, Mr Shi? Who?'

'Such guarantees sound attractive from risk mitigation standpoint,' said Rocky.

'Yes, yes. Risk mitigation.' Blue Suit turned to Mangan. 'Think of the benefits, Mr Mangan. For everybody. Even you. We can get some benefits for you.'

The girl was offering Mangan a cup of coffee, and Blue Suit leaned forward and put his hand on her flank, ran it up and down the inside of her thigh. She stood still.

'What about her? You have her as a benefit. Yes? Want a taste?'

Mangan tried to appease him, holding up his hands.

'Thank you. Perhaps another time,' he said.

'She doesn't mind.' Blue Suit put his hand on the girl's buttock and shoved her and she staggered towards Mangan, began to topple into his lap, then caught herself, spilling the coffee down his front.

Mangan felt her hair against his face, smelled the sweat from her underarms. Blue Suit began shouting.

'Go. The bedroom is there. Go, go.'

Mangan said nothing, put a hand on the girl's arm to help her stand upright. She looked at him, tried to smile an inviting smile, reached for his hand.

This is how it works. The ambiguous threat, the humiliation. In the vile room, by the men who've done it a thousand times before.

'What is his name, Mr Mangan?' said Spectacles.

Mangan didn't understand, the girl pulling at his hand.

'What is his name?' Spectacles repeated.

'I . . . whose name?'

'His.' Blue Suit was pointing at Rocky.

'Shi. You know his name. You used it.'

'If,' said Blue Suit, his voice raised again, urgent, 'if we are to go into business with someone, we must be confident of their identity. What is his name?'

Rocky sat mute, blinking. Mangan struggled for an answer.

'Shi. Shi is his surname and I know him by his English name, Rocky.'

Spectacles was rubbing his chin.

'It says on his passport that his name is Shi Haining. Is that his real name?'

'I must confess, I don't know his Chinese given name. I just know him as Rocky.'

Spectacles looked surprised. Blue Suit shook his head.

'But you are such good friends.'

The girl had let go of his hand and just stood there, miserable. Mangan started to speak, but Spectacles talked over him.

'You were in China before you came to Ethiopia, Mr Mangan. Is that right? You were a reporter there?'

Mangan swallowed. *I was a reporter, until the world split open and I fell through the fissure.*

'Yes. I was based in Beijing.'

'Did you know Mr Shi when you were in China?'

'No. No, I did not.'

'What other work did you do in China?'

'None. I was a journalist.'

'No collaborations there? No business?'

Mangan thought of a cold, shabby hotel room, the taps in the bathroom turned on to beat the listening devices, a flash drive disguised as a car key, passed from hand to hand. A tingle of alarm. *Jesus Christ, what do they know?*

'No, none.'

'So you met Mr Shi here in Ethiopia, yes? Where did you meet, please?'

Rocky spoke.

'We met in the beautiful city of Harer.'

'In Harer. Is that right, Mr Mangan? Please?'

'Yes, we met in Harer. I was on a trip there.'

'So you were.' Spectacles shrugged. 'But we are puzzled, you see, because we did not ever see you meet with Mr Shi in Harer. So we were wondering when you did so.'

Mangan exhaled quietly, tried for calm.

'You were following my movements in Harer?'

Blue Suit looked at him.

'What of it?'

'Well, I am a reporter. I work openly. There is no need to follow me.'

Blue Suit was bristling.

'Tell us when you met Mr Shi. Please.'

'I went for a walk. Late at night. I left my guest house and walked through the old city, and I met him then. We got talking.' Rocky was nodding in agreement.

'I see. And the girl who works in the guest house. Fatima, her name. She will confirm this, will she? If we ask her?'

Panic, rising, fomenting in the base of his stomach.

'I'm sure she will,' he said.

Blue Suit stared. There was silence in the room. Then he stood, put his hands in his pockets.

'Let us hope so,' he said.

There was movement in the room now. Spectacles stood and gestured to Mangan and Rocky. The girl started clearing away the cups. Blue Suit approached Mangan, stood close to him, studied him. Mangan saw the pores in his face, smelled his breath.

'If you are some sort of amateur, Mr Mangan, this is not the place for you.'

'I don't know what . . .'

But he was turning away, making a dismissive gesture. Mangan glimpsed Rocky's back disappearing into a hallway. Spectacles took Mangan by the arm and walked him from the room, out of the villa, to the car.

In the silver wash of the screen, Patterson watched the pulsing red orb leave the villa complex and turn onto the road back to Addis Ababa, its progress through the grid squares picking up pace. She reflected on the fact that Mangan's handheld had not been turned off, but continued to broadcast his position, suggesting that his unscheduled jaunt out of the city in the dead of night aboard an unknown vehicle was voluntary. Or, if it wasn't, that his unidentified captors were quite happy for the circumstances of his abduction to be visible to whomever might be watching. She had resisted the temptation to call Mangan and ask him what the hell was going on. She had persuaded London to restrain themselves similarly.

Now she watched the red orb float quickly across the map, heading back to the city.

But then the orb slowed, and hesitated. Patterson leaned into the screen. The vehicle appeared to be turning off the highway. The little orb pulsed, motionless.

The car had come to a halt on a building site. Spectacles told Mangan to get out, shoved him in the lower back. He stumbled across clods of earth, through rustling grassy weeds, in a clouded, diffuse moonlight. He was out of breath, panic weakening him, his movements infantile.

This is how it works.

'Stop,' said Spectacles.

He stopped, breathing heavily, his thoughts spiralling out of control. Spectacles was several paces behind him.

'Kneel down.'

'Jesus Christ.'

'Kneel.'

'You cannot do this. You *cannot*.'

Spectacles was silent. Then a snort of laughter. Mangan heard his footsteps approaching from behind, felt him close. Then his voice, quiet in Mangan's ear.

'You seem to think that Ethiopia is a *stage* for you to perform on. A *backdrop*. Do not think that. Do you understand?'

'Yes.'

Mangan's knees were in the mud, cold water soaking through his jeans, his thighs shaking.

'Do you understand?'

'Yes.'

'Many white people are like you. They come and they think Ethiopia, Africa, anywhere, is for them a place to *perform* some story, some script.'

'No.'

'Shut up. Listen to me. Whatever your story is, Mr Mangan, whatever it is, be careful how you tell it now. Because we have *agency*, Mr Mangan. We are players, too.'

He said nothing, just nodded. He was shivering.

'Be very, very careful.'

He nodded.

He heard Spectacles walking away, heard the car door slam, the car bump away towards the road. And he was alone, kneeling, in the darkness and a night breeze that smelled of mud and animal dung, fear and relief knotting his gut, pulsing in his skull.

41

Mangan sat at the table in the safe flat, eating instant noodles. He was shaken, Patterson could see, really shaken, but he was pushing through it. He had slept an hour, and showered, and his red hair stood in damp tufts. He wore a brown T-shirt and jeans.

'Why didn't you come to get me?' he said.

'We could have done,' she replied.

'So why didn't you?'

'Because they were watching.'

He didn't respond, shovelled noodles into his mouth.

'Better to let you tramp along the road, make your own way back.'

He had walked for more than an hour, then flagged down a van and paid the driver to bring him back into the city, then jumped taxis, ducked and dived. He'd done well, she thought.

Patterson had relayed the guts of it to London: NISS, the weird stuff about all of them going into business together, the underlying threat to all of it, Mangan's sense that they were shaking the tree, that Blue Suit knew something was up but he didn't know what.

He had told her in short, clipped sentences as he drew on a cigarette. She noted how coherent he was, how he deployed detail despite the exhaustion and the shock of it. He told her the numbers of the cars, gave her details of the villa, recounted Rocky's composure, the fact of the false name on his passport.

He had done very well.

Oxford

Madeline came to Kai's room in the middle of the night again, the creak of the staircase, a soft knock at the door. She was agitated, her face flushed. He took her hand and she let him, and they sat cross-legged on the bed in darkness, their knees touching. For a moment they said nothing, and when she spoke, it was almost a whisper.

'I shouldn't be here.'

'But you are,' he said.

She nodded slowly, took her hand back and stretched her arms upwards. She was lithe, flexible, the sort of girl who could cartwheel, pirouette.

'Nobody ever sent me poetry before,' she said. 'How very literary of you.'

'Your reply was a masterpiece of ambiguity.'

She interlaced her fingers with his again.

'They won't let us go, you know.'

'Perhaps we shouldn't give them the choice.'

'Do you have that in you?' she said. 'To ignore them? Your father? Your family? All their weird retainers and hangers-on?'

'I don't know if I do. I don't know.'

'What would you do?'

He shrugged.

'I don't know. Leave here. Go home. Find a job. Live.'

'But what would you actually *do*?'

'I'd like to work in one of those art shops. Sell ink and brushes. You know the ones, in Beijing. Everyone's an artist and they sit around and smoke and look haunted. I'd learn to carve characters.' He mimed working a piece of stone. 'That's what I'd do. Live in elegant poverty in some tiny courtyard, with pot plants and cracked flagstones. Crickets chirping in a wicker cage.'

She was smiling, shaking her head.

'When I was a child,' she said, 'my father used to give us these lectures at the dinner table. Very stern. He'd quote bits of Confucius at us, stuff about humaneness and filial piety.' She turned down the corners of her mouth to make a po-face, spoke in a deep masculine tone. 'Moderation! Rectitude! "Yu was frugal, but exhausted his strength in irrigation!"'

They were both laughing. She brought her hand up to cover her mouth.

'Really? He knows Confucius? All that stuff?' said Kai

'Really. He admires the ... austerity of it. The cold honesty of it. It's who he is.'

'And did you learn to be righteous and frugal?'

'Me? I was too busy listening to Korean pop.'

She paused.

'He always argues that the world should be ordered a certain way. That the corruption in China isn't just wrong, it's ... unnatural. That China has this deep, ancient moral system. That we all understand it at some profound level. And there are a lot of people – army people – who believe him. Believe *in* him.'

'What are you trying to tell me?' he said.

She sighed and let herself fall back onto the bed. She lay, looking away from him, twirling a strand of hair.

'What?' he said. She pushed herself up on one elbow, as if to speak, but then changed her mind, just shook her head and lay back on the bed again. She took a breath.

'I don't think I'll ever be able to break the rules,' she said.

'Madeline ... I ...'

'I have to go,' she said, and he felt his heart fall.

'Why?'

'Because it's impossible.'

'Madeline ...'

She held a warning finger up, looked towards the door, made a *hush* gesture.

His stomach turned over, an acrid jolt of fright.

They sat silent, very still. Eventually, he stood and crept to the door, listened. Then to the window. The quad was dark and silent, the night sky tinged orange. He turned back to her, and she was standing, readying herself to leave. She looked frightened, but she walked over to him and stood on tiptoe to kiss him slowly on the lips.

'I'll call you,' he said.

'No! God, no calls. No texts.'

He opened his mouth to remonstrate. She just shook her head urgently.

'They'll *know*.'

As she hurried across the quad, he watched from the window, wondered.

Addis Ababa

Mangan's brush with NISS was more than enough for Hopko. She ordered immediate withdrawal, do not pass go. Patterson to pack and scram, Hoddinotts to clear the flat. 'I mean it, Trish,' she'd said. 'Out of there. Today.' And Mangan? Mangan was to stay put for a polite interval and then he was to scram, too.

'Why the polite interval?' he said.

'Because it must look like your decision to leave,' said Patterson. 'Take two or three days. That's all. Book tickets. Stay low. Say some casual goodbyes, give an account of yourself. You're going back home for a bit. A new opportunity. But get out, and soon.'

He was looking into the cigarette smoke as it curled towards the ceiling.

'Are you okay, Philip?'

He exhaled.

'What about Rocky?' he said.

'He'll have to look after himself for the time being.'

'Is it over?' he said.

Patterson was packing the laptop, the comms equipment.

'Would you be sorry if it was?'

'Oh, bereft.'

'Would you?'

He didn't respond. She carried cases to the door, then came back and sat opposite him at the table.

'They'll want to talk to you back in London. Be careful.'

'Why?'

She paused, wondered about his frame of mind, about her responsibility to him.

'Because they are going to ask you to take a step further,' she said.

He cocked his head at her and she felt his look, his green eyes searching for more. She looked away.

'Think about what happened tonight,' she said, 'before you answer them. Think hard about why you would go on with this.'

'I've probably done that already, thought hard about it. A bit. Isn't that possible?'

She wondered whether to say anything, whether to tell him about the living of a life in secret, about the accumulating burden of silence over time, the closing off of expectations.

'Just think about it,' she said, standing up, making a move of finality.

'Do you think I'm not up to it?' he said. She didn't hear defensiveness, just an earnest question.

'I didn't say that.'

Her back was to him when he spoke suddenly, as if expressing something pent up.

'I find that the relationship I have with you is now the only honest relationship I have.'

'You're starting to see how this works,' she answered. But she said it quietly, so he couldn't hear her.

After Mangan had gone, she mopped and scrubbed, cleaned the cups, vacuumed the sofa, wiped down the surfaces, a token attempt at leaving no DNA. By early afternoon she was done.

She stood in the echoing living room, smelled the chlorine in the air. Mangan's declaration of trust had shaken her somehow, sapped her confidence, and she did not understand why.

She closed the door quietly behind her, walked to the stairwell, made her way quickly, quietly to the ground floor. She took the rear exit, hopped the wall to the park, walked briskly. A man on a bench wearing a tan raincoat said something to her in Amharic. She ignored him. He stood up as she passed, repeated what he'd said, loud, angry. She quickened her pace. He was following her. She came out of the park on a broad boulevard in weak afternoon sun and the acrid roar of Addis. She looked back towards the apartment block and saw a van parked in front of it, a man in a suit leaning idly against the driver's door. She hailed a taxi, the man in the raincoat still gesturing at her, offering her something.

A careful stop at the Jupiter Hotel to pay her bill, pick up her bag. She used the lobby, loitering, checking her back. She told the door-man to get a taxi for an address in Jakros, but then, safely aboard, ordered the driver to turn round and head for the airport.

Cairo was the only ticket she could get. So, Cairo it was. She paid in cash and waited three hours, much of it in the ladies lavatory, to board. The plane lifted off from Addis at dusk and she sat in the compressive hiss of the cabin watching the disordered, promiscuous city below give way to grey-purple mountains, wondered at her own sense of lightness, unbelonging.

But for Mangan, it was a more complicated departure. He put it about that it was time for a break. London for a bit, see some friends. A sniff of a new job. He paid the rent on his flat three months in advance.

Building cover, he realised. Shaky cover.

He met Abraha and Hallelujah at the jazz bar in Piazza and they put away a fair few in the candlelight to a jittery seven-piece ensemble, and Hal looked quite stricken.

'But you will be back, yes?' he said.

'Yes, I'll be back. I'm keeping the flat on. Just some people I need to see in London.'

'Well, are you reachable?'

'Yes, of course.'

Abraha was looking hard at him.

'What has happened, Philip? I thought you were getting settled here.'

'There's the possibility of a job.'

Abraha nodded and Mangan could see that he smelled insincerity. And Mangan wondered if he was giving it off, like some bodily effusion.

'May we know what the job is?'

'Not yet,' said Mangan.

And then, to make it all worse, Maja turned up. She gave him a sad smile.

'So our Ogaden trip will have to wait,' she said.

'It will, I'm afraid,' he said.

She dropped her eyes and he realised she was fighting tears.

'Don't let it wait too long,' she said.

When they parted, standing outside on the cracked pavement, Abraha shook his hand and turned away. Hallelujah hugged him, and Maja leaned against him and kissed him on the neck.

'It might have been nice, I think,' she said.

'But it might still happen . . . ?'

She kissed him again and then looked up at him.

'Everything about you says you have left and the rest of us are not invited. I look at you and I see a closed face.' She ran a hand down her own face as if a shutter were falling. 'Closed for business. Or for things more fun. Where have you gone?'

'I can't answer you.'

She gave him a push, turned away.

'Inauthenticity, you know, in your character, that's an awful thing. Especially for you, someone who looks and thinks and writes.'

He said nothing. She made a waving gesture.

'Bye, Philip.'

This is how it works.

Back at the flat in Gotera an envelope lay by the front door. In it were a web address and a password.

PART THREE

The Blind.

42

London

On a warm Saturday in late June, Mangan was installed in a small grey mews house in Paddington. Upstairs, a studio flat, a kitchen, posters of Impressionist art on the walls. Downstairs, a conference room with a wooden floor, blinds and a coffee machine. A short-term corporate rental, in the name of a company domiciled in Jersey. A safe house, he thought, a rather chic safe house.

He slept most of a day, watched the sun crawl down the wall in the mid-afternoon. Patterson came, bringing a curry in foil containers for the two of them, striding up the stairs. She laid it out on the breakfast bar in the flat, and, he noticed, proceeded to eat her generous portion with speed and concentration, mopping the plate with naan. The way a soldier eats, he observed.

'They'll come in a couple of days,' she said. 'And they, we, will ask you to consider making a commitment.'

'What sort of commitment?'

'They'll explain.'

'Doesn't the fact that I'm here rather suggest that I'm committed?'

'You don't know what they are going to ask of you.'

He was, she said, free to come and go. But he should be discreet and report all – *and that means all, Philip* – contacts to her. He was to stay away from friends and acquaintances for now. He was to use the internet only sparingly and emails needed to be discussed with her first. And no mobile phones.

To the neighbours, to anyone who asked, he was to be a returning reporter, in town for a month, maybe a bit more, discussing a new venture, meeting some editors, web publishers, designers. Earnest discussions. The contours of the new journalism. Disruptive change, the death of branded, legacy media. Reporter as curator in a boundless, ever-shifting digital archive of the now.

To himself, he was insubstantial, skittish. He stood in the studio with the lights off, looked out through the blinds at the houses opposite, their brightly lit windows, watched their inhabitants cook dinner, make a bed. He watched a woman sitting at a table reading. As he watched her, he smoked, thought about Ethiopia, wondered what effect the bomb and the episode at the villa had had on him. He sensed his own need for movement, momentum.

I am present at the hatching of my own dubious future.

And on the Tuesday, four days after he arrived, Hopko, Patterson and Chapman-Biggs came to the mews house and sat across from him at the conference table. The atmosphere was anticipatory. There were introductions, first names. Mangan, still in bare feet, made coffee. Hopko began the business abruptly.

'The web address that was left in your flat in Addis is that of a darknet site. Very deep, very secure, the tech wallahs tell me. The site asks for a key. We assume that the password will allow us access, but we haven't tried yet.'

'Why not? Why haven't you tried?'

Hopko smiled.

'We were waiting for you.'

'Is it him?'

Hopko made a *who-knows* gesture.

'The tech wallahs say they anticipate that inside the site will be some sort of secure communications protocol.'

A silence. Mangan watched her, this short, implacable woman with the teased-up dark hair, the expensive suit, the silver dripping from her like some metallic crop awaiting harvest. Patterson sat very still at her side, tall, aligned, in a severe navy blue suit, her flinty look on.

'It's our belief,' said Hopko, 'that HYPNOTIST is now in China and that he is trying to communicate with us securely. We are going to find HYPNOTIST, Philip. And we are going to run him and we are going to find out what he is about. And you, if you are willing, will help.'

Mangan felt his pulse sharpen.

'How? I'm blown in China. The Ministry of State Security has a file on me two foot thick. What should I do? Wear a wig?'

Hopko smiled.

'Wouldn't help. They'll pick you up with facial recognition software. Or they'll spot you with behavioural tracking. Or they'll lift a hair off the pillow in your hotel room and match your DNA. Or, if my experience is anything to go by, some bugger you once knew will recognise you in an airport or a hotel lobby and shout out your name. If we send you back, they'll know you're back.'

'So? How?'

'We intend you to be one element of, let's say, a broader effort. You will be a friendly face for him when meetings abroad can safely be arranged. You'll be a conduit. You will be an initial eye on his product. You will provide continuity and reassurance. The operation will be larger than you, Philip, but you will be a presence within it.'

Mangan frowned.

'I don't understand. Where will I be? Here?'

Hopko turned to Patterson.

'Trish?'

Patterson shifted in her seat, opened a file.

'We have a proposition,' she said.

At the end of the mews stood a Victorian pub with hanging baskets of geraniums, The Compasses, which Mangan came quickly to love.

But Patterson surprised him by warning him sternly, and prudishly, about engaging in anything more than polite chat with the Hungarian girls behind the bar, an admonition he found at once patronising and verging on prejudiced, he thought.

He bought a pint and sat at a wooden table outside, by himself.

He would, he had learned, leave his job at the paper. No great hardship there.

He would establish himself as an independent journalist. He would have a website, a blog. On it, he would post travel writing, commentary, reviews. He would commission pieces from others. There would be seed money from a generous and open-minded venture capitalist who specialised in media startups. The website would be speckled with ads, and it would flourish in a modest sort of way.

And, crucially, the website would provide Mangan with the journalist's enviable prerogative: to be exactly wherever he wished, whenever he wished, talking to whomever he wished. He would travel light and move quickly.

A grand life fiction. Philip Mangan would hide in plain sight.

And there'd be a salary. A real one. Paid discreetly into a quiet little account in a jurisdiction where not too many questions were asked, one whose flag had distinctly British overtones.

'Journalism is marvellous cover,' Hopko had said. 'But we were ordered hands off journalists, oh, years ago. Couldn't touch them, let alone recruit them. Supposedly we were protecting the reputations of the media companies, keeping the reporters above suspicion. Perhaps it was wise. But, now. Well, things are a little different.'

'As cover goes, Philip, it's cushty,' said Patterson, and there had been laughter. Mangan wondered what un-cushty cover would be.

He drank his pint, felt the gentle bite of it in the warm evening. Londoners were emerging from offices, shops, from the station, clutching bags, children, a woman held a bouquet and looked around herself, puzzling out the streets. Mangan thought for a moment about lives he might live. At some point in the future.

His operational focus would be HYPNOTIST. He might be required to assist with other operations. In Asia, or elsewhere.

He was to undergo a month of intensive indoctrination and training.

This is how.

43

The following day, a beginning. At eight in the morning, Mangan opened the door to Patterson and two tech wallahs holding black flight cases.

In the conference room, they quietly unpacked two laptop computers, set them on the table and connected them to the internet. The men worked quietly, fastidiously. They were both young, had the look of students, postgraduates perhaps.

'So, what we have here,' murmured one, to Mangan, 'is a connection to a darknet.' Mangan looked over his shoulder. 'An ironclad browser, all encrypted, which will take you off to places your everyday white bread browser won't, you see. And all twenty-four-carat anonymous as you do it.'

'What places?' said Mangan.

'Well, that's just it. All sorts of places down there. Some of it's not very nice, is it, Jeff?'

The other man shook his head.

'Shocking, some of it.'

'There's lots of drugs. Big sites where you can order up your crystal or your skag. Pay in Bitcoin. There's crims, looking for jobs. Kiddie fiddlers. Crypto-anarchists. Terrorists. Carders. All sorts.'

'Spend much time down there, do you?' said Patterson.

'Oh, yes,' said the man, mildly. 'Because in the dark no one can see you. No one knows who you are. So the spies like it just as much as all the other low-lifes. Don't we, Jeff?'

'We're right at home, Michael.'

'So, if we're careful, and we set up a nice little encrypted file-sharing site, we can talk to people down here and exchange all sorts of goodies, without any danger of being seen, or overheard.'

'And that,' said Jeff, 'is exactly what your friend seems to have done, bless him.'

On the other laptop, Hopko suddenly filled the screen, peering at her camera with the air of a troubled landlady.

The site, when they found it, was nondescript. Black screen, with a password prompt.

'Everybody agreed?' said Hopko, raspy over the wireless link. The two techs nodded.

'We're happy,' said Patterson.

'Philip?' said Hopko.

'Yes. Sure.'

'Tally-ho, then.'

Michael slowly read out the password, a long jumble of letters and digits, one at a time. Jeff repeated them back and tapped them in, hit Enter.

The cursor blinked for a few seconds. A single line of text appeared.

Please wait for respond>

They waited. Hopko bustled off. Jeff and Michael gazed at the screen, seemed to enter a sort of vegetative state. Mangan went upstairs, made tea and toast. After a while, Patterson joined him and sat, watched him spreading butter, marmalade.

'Have you thought about it?' she said.

'Of course. I haven't thought about anything else.'

'And?'

Mangan took a bite of toast.

'I'm still here.'

'There's something they didn't tell you.'

He stopped chewing.

'You're going to be fluttered.'

There was a noise on the stairs. Jeffrey was standing there, looking awkward.

'Sorry to interrupt, but I think we might have something.'

A brief ribbon of text in the darkness.

Please identify>

'Since you have no recognition code,' said Michael, the tech wallah, slowly, 'I would suggest no name, just a relevant identifier.'

Patterson looked at him, questioningly.

'Well, Philip?'

Mangan considered, rubbed his unshaven chin.

'Try, African friend.'

African friend>

A pause.

Please, where we met?>

'Tell him, hyena town.'

Hyena town>

Very good. Here is peter.>

'What?' said Patterson. 'What the hell does that mean?'

'What does that mean to you, Philip?' said Hopko, over the link.

Mangan swallowed. *What?*

'I've no idea,' he said.

'Think, Philip,' said Patterson. 'Peter? Is it a word code?'

Mangan thought back, saw the market on the smoky hillside, the rattling shoe production line. Peter?

'Nary a Peter comes to mind, I'm afraid.'

'Jesus Christ,' said Patterson.

'Oh. Hang on,' he said.

'*What?*' said Patterson.

He looked at her.

'Just … just keep your knickers on, Trish.'

Patterson looked as if she might deliver a sharp blow to his throat.

'Philip, that is the wrong thing to say to me just now. If we do not reply, he may log off and we'll lose him for ever. So fucking think of something to say to him. Now.'

'If it's him,' said Michael.

'It's him,' said Mangan. 'Ask him, what food do you hate most?'

What food do you hate most?>

The reply was immediate.

Ha ha red cook pork. Very disgusting>

A beat, then more text.

You can tell me why I hate it>

'Write, the fat. Kneeling in the snow.'

The fat. Kneeling in the snow>

So my friend good to hear you. This way we communicate. You check this site everyday for message. I am back in home country. Much to tell you>

Hopko spoke via the link. 'Where is he, precisely?'

Are you in your nation's capital city?>

No>

Where? So we know how to find you if you need help>

Remember my investment fund? That city>

Yes I remember>

'He's in Kunming,' said Mangan, 'the south-west.'
Hopko again. 'I want you to get him to commit to a third country meeting. Soon. Make him plan.'

When can we meet? Somewhere safe. You tell me where. I'll be there>

Ok maybe vacation ha ha thailand maybe>

Thailand would be very good. You make a plan, tell me, I will arrange everything>

Ok. I go now my friend. You use this site for message. Bye>

Good bye my friend. Good to talk to you>

Then just the blinking cursor in the blackness.
'The Peter thing,' said Mangan. 'It's derived from Latin, isn't it?

Or Greek? One of them. It means stone. His surname, Shi, means stone. He's Peter. Rocky.'

Patterson was giving him a you-can't-be-serious look.

'His sense of humour at work,' said Mangan, and Patterson noted the budding empathy of the handler for his agent.

'And that, Philip,' said Hopko up close to the camera, her features rounded, distorted, 'is why we pay you the big bucks.'

44

Oxford

The Chen girl was not hard to find. Nicole attended an event spon-
sored by the Oxford University Chinese Students' Association at the
Business School, a lecture on the future of Anglo-Chinese business
links given by a former British ambassador. The man droned on and
on from a lectern, a face the colour of uncooked pork, a soul-
crushing hour of platitudinous jargon. Then, dear God, questions.
She allowed her mind to drift, thought of New York, Hong Kong.

And then there she was, standing, reaching for the microphone, all
petite and virginal, wearing leggings, a loose beige top that slipped from
one shoulder. Her question, something earnest about the sustainability
of China's growth model, corruption, Western over-optimism.

The ambassador answered carefully, moved on, allowing his eyes
to wander hopefully across the audience. For a second, Madeline
Chen looked bemused, unimpressed, but yielded the microphone
with a shake of her hair, a downward, impatient look.

Afterwards, there was warm white wine under neon strip lights in
the common room. Nicole circled, then approached.

'Hi!' she said, her language English, mannerisms American.

'Hi,' said Madeline Chen, frowning at her.

'I thought your question was the most interesting part of the evening so far. But there's still time, right?' She laughed. 'I'm Nicole.' Held out her hand. The Chen girl took it, let it go quickly.

'I am Madeline.'

'Well, it's a pleasure to meet you. I'm new, just arrived, so I don't know anyone.' She adopted a hopeful look. The Chen girl regarded her, her eyes flickering down and up again, registering the silk shirt, the jeans from Barney's, the Tiffany bracelet.

'So where are you from?' said Nicole.

'Beijing. You are American?'

'No. Taiwanese. I'm from Taipei. But I've been in the States the last few years.'

The Chen girl was paying attention now, looking at her searchingly.

Nicole switched to Mandarin, peppered Madeline with questions about Oxford, about Britain, weather, food. Madeline answered guardedly, tried to turn the conversation around.

'So what's your subject?' she said.

Nicole grinned a does-it-really-matter grin, flapped a hand.

'Oh, Chinese strategic doctrine. Ships, nukes, sea lanes. So tedious.'

Madeline smiled a disbelieving smile.

Nicole stood closer to her.

'So will you show me around a bit? I don't know the first thing about this place except it's old and creepy and damp. Perhaps we could meet up.' She looked expectant.

'Perhaps,' said Madeline.

Nicole said nothing more, just smiled and handed her card to the hostile target and with a meaningful look swept from the room, Madeline Chen watching her go.

45

London

They drove him to an office block in Ealing, early in the morning. Patterson told him: 'Don't drink any coffee, Philip, it makes you jittery and affects the readings.' He was left in an interview room. Two chairs, a table and a mirrored window, through which, he was fairly certain, someone was watching him. The room intimidated by its blankness, its lack of affect.

Minutes passed. Mangan felt alert, hungry.

The door opened and a man entered. He carried a chunky case, which he laid on the table. A faded suit, bony hands, thin, downy hair, a mouth that fell at the corners. The pallor of secrecy, thought Mangan, too many windowless rooms, ingrown lives. *My examiner*. The man fussed with the clasps on the case.

A cuff was attached to his arm, a band around his chest, an oximeter clipped to his finger.

'What's most important,' intoned the examiner, 'is that you tell the truth. Whatever it is. You must not try to deceive us. I hope that is clear.'

The man said that they would chat about the questions a bit and he would calibrate the machine, and they'd chat a bit more. Then he'd administer the test. Simple questions to begin with. Name. Date of birth. Queries related to counter-intelligence, foreign contacts, that sort of thing. And then a bit of lifestyle. The man peered at a screen.

'Is your name Philip Mangan?'

'Yes.'

'Are you thirty-seven years old?'

'Yes.'

'Are you wearing a pink shirt?'

'No.'

'Is your father dead?'

'Yes.'

'Is your mother dead?'

'Yes.'

'Do you have siblings?'

'No. No siblings.'

'Have you lived in China?'

'Yes.'

They talked, the examiner delivering questions in a low monotone, in a manner used to communicate with the gravely ill.

'Drug use, Philip, have you ever used illegal drugs?'

'Umm, yes.'

'Have you used marijuana or cannabis?'

'Yes.'

'When?'

'What? Well, at various times, I'd say.'

'Be as precise as possible. When?'

'When I was at university. And since.'

'Can you pinpoint some dates?'

'Is this strictly relevant?'

'Please don't question me, but answer my question.'

'The last time was about six months ago.'

'And before that?'

'I really don't have any idea.'

'Have you used cocaine?'

'No.'

'Have you used LSD?'

'Possibly.'

'Yes or no. Have you ever used LSD?'

'Someone once gave me something at a party in Bangkok and I knocked it back and an hour later I was watching the walls emit great billows of stars. But I have no idea what it was. Wouldn't mind finding out, actually.'

'Please be as truthful and precise as you can.'

'I'm trying to be bloody truthful.'

A pause. The man stood up and left the room.

Fifteen minutes later, he came back.

'I'd like you to tell me about an experience that you found humiliating,' he said. 'When in your life did you feel most humiliated?'

Mangan cast about hopelessly.

'People often reach back into their childhood to find such experiences,' the examiner said, matter-of-factly.

Mangan shrugged.

'There were some moments at school, I suppose.'

'At your boarding school? Tell me about one of them.'

'Is this really necessary?'

'Please be explicit and truthful.'

Mangan sighed, discomfited now.

'Well, my first night at boarding school ...'

'How old were you?'

'Thirteen.'

'And what happened?' The examiner was watching his screen closely.

'The parents dropped the new boys off. It was a Sunday, a beautiful September day. We all dragged our trunks and cases inside, and upstairs, and then the parents drove away, and we were taken to supper and then back to our houses. And in my house there was this enormous stairwell, four floors, towering windows, with elaborate contraptions of brass poles and levers for opening them.'

Mangan stopped, licked his lips.

'And the new boys were on our way up this huge, echoing stairwell to the dormitory, to bed. But a bat had got in, somehow. This tiny bat. And it was fluttering and swooping up and down the stairwell. I remember noticing how quickly it moved. The minute your eye found it, it was gone. It kept hurling itself against the windows, and falling, and fluttering downward. I thought bats didn't do that. But this one did. Or that's how I remember it, anyway.'

He paused.

'Go on,' said the examiner.

'Some of the older boys, fifth-formers, decided they had to catch it. And they took string gym bags for nets and ran up and down the stairs, roaring, screaming. And the bat flew right to the top of the stairwell, banging against the walls and the ceiling, and they chased it up there and threw whatever they had at it, shoes, pillows, anything. And they killed it. And the house tutor came and wrapped it in a towel and took it away. I was pressed against the wall with all these huge boys hurtling by, and the noise, and I started crying. I was tired and overwrought and missing my parents already, and I sobbed. And the fifth-formers started yelling about the new boy blubbing, and the other new boys joined in, and in the dormitory it was just this feeding frenzy. Is that humiliating enough? Look, have you calibrated your machine yet?'

'Have you ever been contacted by a foreign intelligence organisation?'

'Well, yes.'

'Are you an agent of a foreign intelligence organisation?'

'Not that I'm aware of.'

'Are you in the employ of a foreign intelligence organisation?'

'No.'

'Have you passed information you know to be protected to a foreign intelligence organisation?'

'No.'

'Have you been recruited by a foreign intelligence organisation?'

'I don't think so.'

'Yes or no.'

'No.'

'Do you have a sexual partner?'

'Not sure.'

'Do you have a sexual partner?'

'Maybe. It's not clear to me if she's a partner or not.'

'Do you have a sexual partner?'

'No.'

'Do you have sex with men?'

'Don't make a habit of it.'

'Yes or no.'

'No.'

'Do you engage in deviant forms of sexual activity?'

'Whenever possible.'

'Answer the question seriously, please.'

'What the hell is deviant?'

'Any form of sexual activity that goes beyond the norms of a healthy relationship.'

'I haven't the first clue what you mean.'

'Are you homosexual?'

'Nope. Not for now.'

'Do you look at pornography?'

'Sometimes.'

'Do you like to look at pornographic images of children?'

'Jesus Christ. No.'

'Have you ever had sex with a child?'

Mangan stood. The empty case that had contained the machine lay on the floor by the side of the table. He kicked it hard, sending it flying across the room as the examiner flinched. Then Mangan pulled off the cuff and the chest band and the oximeter and dropped them on the table, and walked out.

*

He ignored the waiting car and took a taxi back to the Paddington house, the day warm, clammy, overcast. He went inside and lay on the bed, turned the television on. Patterson showed up after an hour. A decent interval, he thought.

He opened the door to her. She stood hands in pockets, gave him a sideways look.

'That went well, then,' she said.

'I'm not doing it.'

'Can I come in?'

'Spare me the lecture.'

'No lecture,' she said, and went inside, following him upstairs.

'Who the hell was that ghoul?' he said over his shoulder. 'How can it be remotely relevant what my sexual proclivities are?'

'You showed signs of deception on the sexual partner question.' She was suppressing a grin.

'Bloody intrusive wanker. I didn't sign up for that crap.'

'You can spare *me* the lecture, too, if you like,' she said. 'I get fluttered every two years.'

Mangan just shook his head.

'Anyway,' she said, sitting, 'you're a journalist, so we already know how deviant you are.'

He stopped and let his hands fall to his sides.

'Have I screwed it all up?' he said.

'No,' she replied. 'You passed the counterintel test and that's all anyone was interested in.'

He breathed out, letting his relief show. Why such relief? she wondered.

Because he doesn't know what's coming.

Nicole and Madeline met two days later in a wine bar in Little Clarendon Street. The evening was sunny and still. Nicole wore an airy dress of white cotton, heels, more Tiffany, set herself against the other girl's jeans, lycra top. They sat on stools by the window drinking a slightly-too-expensive white, slightly too fast. Nicole crossed her legs, let the dress fall to reveal her long, smooth thighs, twirled the glass in her fingers. She asked Madeline about the other Chinese students. Who was who? Who belonged where? From which families? Who mattered?

Madeline thought, mentioned some names. Not Kai's.

'But who's *interesting*? There must be some exciting people here!'

Madeline shrugged.

'No one I know,' she said.

Not a hint, not a glimmer, of the fabulously wealthy telecoms heir, Fan Kaikai.

Nicole asked her about home and she answered obliquely. Nicole prodded her to talk about her professors and she was diplomatic. Nicole recounted an entirely fabulist version of her own years in the States, the wonders of Harvard, and the girl listened politely. The wine bottle emptied.

'So,' said Nicole. 'What about men?'

Madeline made a snorting sound.

'Does that mean no?'

Madeline was looking at her nails.

'That means no.'

'Must be somebody interesting.'

'No!'

Nicole laughed.

'*Name hai xiu!*' So coy! She ran a finger down the girl's arm.

'The boys here are just that. Boys,' said Madeline.

'What about all those handsome English boys? Big boys, pale skin, all so charming, so assured.'

'*Pfft*. Not for me. Nothing doing.'

'Why? Are you saving yourself?'

Madeline turned and looked at her, eyebrows raised.

'Aren't you the curious one?'

'What about that other Chinese boy, what's his name? The really rich one.'

'Who?'

Nicole tried to remember.

'Father is head of some big telecoms corporation.'

Madeline said nothing.

'Fan. That's his name,' said Nicole. 'Fan Kaikai. What about him?'

'You know him?'

Nicole shrugged.

'No. What's he like?'

Madeline was looking at the ends of her hair, pulling the strands apart.

'Rich. Kind of awkward.'

'Oh! You've talked to him, then?'

But Madeleine was looking straight at her with a very level, wondering look.

'Not my type,' she said, deliberately.

Nicole calculated. Push on, or pull back?

'Ooh. I see,' she said, playing intrigued, a bit scandalised. 'What don't you like about him?'

'I really don't know him.'

'But, wouldn't your family want you to . . .'

The hostile target was looking hard at her now.

'Who's asking?'

Nicole held her hands wide, a show of innocence.

'Just me, sweetheart.'

Madeline spoke very deliberately.

'And who are you, exactly?'

The mood had changed. And as Madeline got up and reached for her bag, Nicole considered the girl's quiet awareness, her sense of self, and thought that this seduction might not be as simple as others she had effected in the past.

46

London

Chapman-Biggs brought Danish pastries in a paper bag. Mangan made coffee and sat at the conference table feeling like a home-schooled teenager. Lesson time. 'A single-source CX report, Philip, is what we live for.' He took a laptop from his bag, booted it up, opened a file, some sort of template. 'And I'm going to show you how to write one.'

Mangan listened. Chapman-Biggs walked him through the format he would use.

'All times in ZULU, please, Philip. We call it ZULU, not GMT. So 6 p.m. is 1800Z. Classification will be UK S E C R E T. Addressee here. That'll be your case officer.'

Chapman-Biggs spoke primly, making Mangan think of a classics teacher in tweed, the whiff of the common room, rugby pitches and mentholatum.

'We'll not want great scads of analysis or interpretation in the report. We do want just the facts. And attributable to a single asset. Don't go cramming product from multiple sources in one report, please. It gets jolly confusing. And if you must add a gloss to what you have learned, you will put it in an appendix and make it clear that it is you who is speaking, not the source. Is that quite clear?'

Yes, sir.

'I am a Requirements Officer, Philip, so everything that your source or sources supply comes via your case officer to me. And I'm the chap that writes it all up, cross references it and pushes it out of the door to the consumer. With me?'

Mangan, bemused, nodded and sipped his coffee.

'And I want every last shred. Everything.'

Mangan didn't respond.

'Is everything quite all right?' asked Chapman-Biggs.

'I just hadn't imagined spying would mean being evaluated on my report-writing skills.'

Chapman-Biggs looked affronted.

'Oh, yes, 'fraid so. Oh, dear me, yes. It's awfully important.'

Mangan forbore from asking why, but Chapman-Biggs carried on speaking as if he had, the classics teacher explaining the ancient certainties of school to the recalcitrant, tearful new boy.

'Because, Philip, in the end, the purpose of intelligence agencies is to gather intelligence.' He paused, allowing the insight to linger in the air. 'To *find things out*. And while we've been treated to quite the spectacle in the last twelve years and more, what with drones and renditions and valiant chaps on horseback galloping down from the Hindu Kush or wherever, that's not what we are about, in the end. Not at all. We assemble knowledge, Philip. Where no knowledge is readily available, we hunt it. And we steal it.'

He sat back, satisfied.

'And then we put it in a single-source CX report.'

47

A spell of heat, the sun a mild shock, turning London's brown-grey stone to amber and gold in the morning. Mangan left the mews house and took the Tube to Highgate, and walked through Waterlow Park. He found a bench, lit a cigarette, watched the white-skinned girls in shorts and bikini tops and sunglasses lying on the grass, reading, texting. No one acknowledged him or spoke to him.

The park was filled with people, but was so quiet he could hear a dove cooing in a tree, the attenuated roar of the city just beyond. He smelled freshly cut grass and thought suddenly of the garden at Burger House, the nails, shards of iron, the feel of packed earth under his hands. Jarred, he threw his cigarette away, stood, walked quickly.

Addis, lying fraught just beneath the surface of memory.

And just a little deeper, a little darker, China, a cold highway at night, the unexpected heft of a knife in his hand.

Hardened operative Philip Mangan encounters inconvenient recollections, courageously ignores them.

He thought of Rocky Shi, his agent. His *joe*. And now, keeper of his future. For everything, Mangan was coming to understand, depended on Rocky's next moves. Far from running his agent, he was in thrall to this man's decisions, and his nervous tics and chewed nails, his envelopes under the door with their lethal, cryptic messages, the smile stretched fit to burst, the hyperextended personality of the man. His ingenuous, conniving *joe*.

In a café with red awnings, he ordered an omelette and coffee. The waitress, young, east European, lips pink and glossy, served him wordlessly.

Rocky loathed women, Mangan realised. He was foul to the weak, dolled-up girls in the nightclub, wary of the tall woman who had bested his goon in a lift, dismissive of his own mother. And he was fascinated by men with power.

So what fascinating man was he serving? Certainly not himself. What fascinating, powerful man was he in thrall to?

Mangan sat and ate, paid, ran his hands through his hair, then walked more, his long stride devouring the pavement in the warm, windless afternoon. He walked for two hours, meandering southward through silent swathes of Victorian north London, through Holloway and Barnsbury. He had a sense of gathering himself in, of shaping an understanding of what was to come.

In Islington, a poster outside a small cinema caught his eye. He went in, bought a ticket for the matinee. It was a Chinese film, a new retelling of the fall of Nanjing, a huge black-and-white wail of pain and fury, Japanese officers in puttees beheading Chinese soldiers by a river, tiny children screaming in bombed-out streets, the camera eking out their trauma.

He came out in the early evening, crossed the street to a pub and sat outside, putting away three beers fast, one after the other.

Back in Paddington, Patterson was waiting for him, sitting in the darkening studio flat. He hadn't known that she had a key. He stood, swaying slightly.

'There's a message,' she said, quietly.

hello my friend. Thailand chiang mai. next month twentieth for three days. You stay at palm pavilion hotel. You be contacted. You confirm soon>

'Christ. That's only three weeks away,' said Patterson. They were sitting side by side at the conference table, Jeff at the keyboard.

'Why's that a problem?' said Mangan.

Patterson rubbed her eyes, looked at him.

'My, you're keen,' she said. 'Well, we have a lot to do – if we even get the authority to move. Your cover. Your preparation.'

'But now I have been introduced to the correct template for the, what do you call it, the single-source CX report, how can I possibly be considered unprepared?'

Patterson was uncomfortable with the deadpan. Hopko did it, and she didn't like it. She didn't find it funny. She found it aggressive. It was intended to leave her at a loss. She decided to ignore it.

'Tell him yes. To be confirmed,' she said.

Mangan was frowning at her.

'Is there a chance the answer might be no?' he said.

Patterson had been wondering the same.

'There are battles still to fight, Philip.'

Yes. To be confirmed very soon. Goodbye my friend>

That surely could not be considered overstepping her authority, she thought.

But it could.

'What the hell do you mean, you said yes?' This from Drinkwater, of Security Branch, an iron-faced, grey-haired pressure cooker of a man. To Drinkwater, Patterson thought, all operations threatened the security of the Service and should be abandoned forthwith.

'I said yes, to be confirmed.'

They sat in Hopko's sanctum, beneath her Ming dynasty landscapes, gentle birds fluttering on spring branches, Hopko delphic behind her desk, Drinkwater going off like a fire hydrant.

'Thereby *intimating* that we would confirm. This is … outrageous.' He accompanied his speech with a tight, wide-eyed shaking of the head, designed to project exasperation, speechlessness. They act out, Patterson reflected.

'What would you rather I had replied to him?' she said, which brought a direct look from Hopko.

'What I would *rather*,' said Drinkwater, 'is that you had come to a grown-up.'

'It was eight on a Saturday evening,' she said. 'Are grown-ups available and sober at that time?'

'I certainly wasn't,' said Hopko, amiably. Drinkwater's face was puce against his lightweight grey suit, his steel-wire hair.

'I *will* be raising Security Branch's concerns at the ops meeting,' he said, grandly. He stood, regarded Patterson for a moment. She met his look. He turned and left the room.

'It's a mistake to humiliate them, Trish,' Hopko said.

'What, then? Tell me what I should do.'

'Well, my strategy was always to try and sort of smother them with respect. But I can appreciate that you might find that hard.' She smiled over her glasses. *Dismissed.*

Patterson stood, wanting to salute, instead inclining her head in Hopko's direction. She left the sanctum and walked down the corridor to her cubicle. At her desk, she reached into her bag and withdrew a tupperware container. She spread a paper napkin on the desk, opened the container and laid out a bagel, a slice of cheese, a yoghurt and a banana.

As she ate methodically, she reflected on Operation WEAVER, for so it had been dubbed by Hopko from her throne. Hopko appeared intent on managing the enterprise herself.

Why?

Why would an officer as senior as Hopko, a Controller, assert day-to-day management of an op?

What was it in Rocky Shi, the round-shouldered colonel with the unfathomable motives, that Hopko saw?

Oxford
Madeline's house was just off St Clement's, a brick two-up two-down

259

painted pale blue, dustbins in the front yard, a bicycle. Nicole walked the length of the street twice, then stopped and waited at the corner. It was nearly twenty-five minutes until the girl appeared. She wore a jean jacket and earphones, and was carrying a heavy-looking tote bag. Books? Returning them to the library, perhaps. Madeline turned, locked the front door and began walking in the direction of town. Nicole kept her distance until the bridge, then caught the girl up, tapped her on the shoulder. Madeline turned, startled, pulled the earphones out abruptly.

'Hello, stranger,' said Nicole.

Madeline blinked.

'Oh. Hi,' she said.

'Look,' said Nicole, 'I just wanted to apologise. For the other night. I didn't mean to . . . make you uncomfortable. I'm sorry. I just wanted to say that.' She gave her best contrite smile.

'Okay,' said Madeline, evenly.

'I was prying. I shouldn't have. It's just . . . you seem to be such a . . . ' But Madeline was looking past her, and as Nicole turned she cursed herself, her own stupidity, her shitty tradecraft.

The man stood perhaps six feet away from her, holding up a smartphone. Nicole registered his wrinkled shirt, lank hair, then the *click* of the digital shutter. And again. *Click*.

The man lowered the smartphone and stood, unmoving, looking at her.

Nicole turned back to Madeline.

'What's that for, might I ask?' she said.

'Precautions, I think,' said Madeline.

Nicole just smiled. *Enough of this shit, now.*

'I'll see you soon, Madeline.' She turned and walked away.

'I don't think so,' she just heard Madeline say, to her back.

'Have you ever handled a weapon, sir?'

'No,' said Mangan.

The sergeant was barrel-chested, shaven-headed, braced in his movements. A Royal Marine, someone had said. The shooting range had a corrugated iron roof, the rain drumming on it, neon lighting rendering Mangan even paler than usual. Between him and the sergeant, on a table, lay a mournful little pistol. Patterson watched.

'No. Well, all right then.' The sergeant scratched his cheek. 'Well, sir, I'm told that we are going to go over some basics today, give you an idea of how to operate the weapon.'

He picked up the pistol.

'Sig Sauer P938. Subcompact, slender, light, easy to conceal. But, a 9 mm round.'

Patterson saw Mangan's sigh. The sergeant's thick index finger flitted around the weapon's black exterior.

'Here you have the safety, the magazine release, and here, you'll see, sir, useful little night sights.' Mangan leaned in and peered. 'Seven-round magazine, sir, a nice little weapon effective up to, well, far enough for our purposes.' The sergeant cleared his throat.

Mangan held the weapon, then learned to hold it properly, both bony hands wrapped around it, one cupping the other.

'Index finger lying along the trigger guard at all times, please, sir.'

Mangan loaded a magazine, felt the metallic *chenk* of the slide on release, and Patterson wondered if she saw a slight smile appearing.

He fired off twelve magazines, and the targets were messy, peppered irregularly, the rounds tending down and left as he squeezed the grip too hard.

'Well, that'll properly frighten them,' said the sergeant.

Patterson shot a three-inch group.

She drove them back to Paddington from the range in a Service car. Mangan was quiet, watched the bleak motorway slip by. She parked outside the house, and the two of them got out and stood there.

'Oh, sod it,' she said. 'Come on, Philip.'

They walked through the jostling crowds, past the station, down Praed Street, to a tapas place. Mangan ordered a bottle of Albarino which came cold and dewy. He seemed to relax a bit, Patterson thought, noting how the relaxation correlated with proximity to alcohol. The restaurant opened onto the pavement and they sat in the cool, damp evening air, candles on the table. They ordered squid fried in paprika, roasted figs, grilled pigeon, chorizo. Mangan poured the wine, made a mock serious *cheers* gesture, and drank.

'So,' he said.

'So.'

'I now have my licence to kill.'

She laughed.

'You have nothing of the sort.'

'You seemed ... adept.'

'I was a soldier. Before.'

He nodded.

'You went to Iraq, Afghanistan, presumably.'

'Presumably,' she said.

'What were you? Infantry?'

'Intelligence Corps.'

He raised his eyebrows, sat forward.

'And what was that like?'

'It was ... interesting work.'

'Oh, come on Trish, what was it like?'

She sipped her wine, hating the question.

'It was hot and demanding. And it got very brutal at times.'

He made a regretful face.

'Subject off-limits?'

'Somewhat.'

He put his head to one side, considered her. He's looking for another tack, she thought. The restaurant was filling up, the clatter of crockery, the buzz of voices.

'Where are you from?' he said.

'Nottingham,' she said. 'An estate on the outskirts. Dad was on the buses.'

'And Mum?'

'Cooked in a hospital kitchen.'

'Happy family?'

'Yes,' she said. 'Yes, a happy family. They were surprised when I went away to college. Felt like I was breaking everything up.'

'Where did you go to college?'

'Coventry.'

'And that's where the army found you, I'll bet.'

She nodded.

'Credulous black girl. All muscles and no sense. Dead eager,' she said. 'They loved me.'

Steady on, she thought.

Mangan just nodded.

'Then Sandhurst,' he said, prompting.

'Yes. God, Sandhurst. Felt like a fairy tale. A wet, cold one. But I could go beagling. Got invited to balls.'

He smiled.

'I'm trying to see you in a ball gown.'

'I had one. It was a huge green thing. Held a powerful static charge.'

Mangan was laughing now.

'Did you enjoy them? The balls? Did you foxtrot?'

'What do you think? No. I stood and stared furiously at others.'

That's enough now. The food started to arrive on little pink plates, glistening with oil.

'And you, Philip? What of the blue remembered hills around ... Orpington, wasn't it?'

'Yes, it was. Orpington. My father was a doctor there. A GP. Mother was a teacher. But I went away to school, a sort of distressed gentlefolk place in Hampshire.'

Patterson had read the polygraph transcript, thought of Mangan weeping in the stairwell, didn't let on.

'Why did they send you to boarding school? Only child, going away like that, seems strange.'

He shrugged.

'It spoke to their aspirations, I think. Important to be a well-rounded, emotionally stunted chap.'

'Did it make an emotionally stunted man of you?'

'What do you think?'

'You're man enough, Philip,' she said, laughing. 'Just not on the shooting range.' He laughed, too, for a second. But then she thought she saw a shadow cross his face.

They paused, ate, wiped the plates with crusty bread.

'And the freelance journalism, all the travel,' she said. 'Why all that? It seems like a precarious sort of life.'

He considered, nodded.

'I like it. Liked it. The feeling of not being attached, settled. Always sort of falling forward into something, something new.'

She took a breath as if to speak, then checked herself.

'What?' he said.

'No, nothing.' That's not true, she thought. You don't like the not being attached. You want more, said so yourself. You're looking to invest yourself, to commit. You want to feel that there's a single truth you can march towards, just around the bend in the road, through the trees.

You're like me.

They paid. She walked to the Tube. Mangan gave her his slow smile and turned away in the twilight. She watched him go. It was the most intimate conversation she'd had in months.

And Hopko wanted to know all about it.

'How's his morale, would you say, Trish? What's his understanding of what's happening to him?'

'I'd say his morale is high and he understands that he is now an agent of the Service.'

Hopko leaned forward, her hands palm down on her table.

'How very cryptic,' she said, deliberately.

'I mean, he has his eyes open. He's reflective. I think he's psychologically committed.'

'And why is he so committed, in your view?'

Patterson swallowed.

'His own reasons. He has a need, we meet it.'

Hopko sat back. Her fingers played with a bead necklace, tiny nuggets of coral, lapis. 'Please, do me one favour.' Hopko had the look of a hawk. 'Remember that he is not your friend. He is your agent.'

A theme rammed home at the ops meeting.

Patterson was unnerved by the cast of characters in attendance, not having realised how much attention WEAVER was attracting. She loitered in the corridor, her stomach turning somersaults. Mobbs, the Director of Requirements and Production, strode into the windowless, secure room, a minion carrying a black legal briefcase hard behind him. Hopko stood by her chair, sipping coffee from a paper cup, gazing benignly at the assembled group; limbering up, Patterson could tell. Chapman-Biggs of Requirements was there, and the senior P officer for China, dour-browed Claudia Mallory, who, Patterson knew, was snappish about the case, feeling sidelined. And, of course, Drinkwater, simmering at the head of a small phalanx of Security Branch officers. Patterson went in, sat in a chair by the wall. She noted that all the Africa Controllerate and Global Issues/Counter-terrorism people had vanished.

Hopko opened.

'The objectives of Operation WEAVER,' she said, 'are threefold. One, the penetration of China south-western military command. Two, the penetration of 2PLA, military intelligence. Three, the mapping of factional rivalries at high level, with a focus on the complex of political and economic interactions surrounding China National Century Corporation. We have reason to believe that HYPNOTIST and those he refers to as his associates can deliver on all three objectives.'

She paused, looked over the top of her spectacles at the room. No challenges, yet.

'The initial encounters, as you know, took place in Ethiopia, and

HYPNOTIST has already generated for us significant, actionable intelligence. We propose to reestablish and develop HYPNOTIST as an asset in place in China's south-western military command.'

Another look. Silence. They're waiting till they can see the whites of her eyes, thought Patterson.

'To this operational end, HYPNOTIST will be supplied with the means of closed, covert communication. And he will be managed and tasked, where possible, at third country meetings by our access agent, codename BRAMBLE, working in turn to Patterson as case officer.'

Patterson felt the eyes of the room on her, the gaze of Claudia Mallory in particular.

'All with me so far?' said Hopko.

The door opened, abruptly. A grey-suited figure stalked across the room to the table, folded himself into a chair, sat cross-legged, chin in one hand. Through rimless spectacles he regarded Hopko.

'Please carry on,' he said.

'How very nice to see you, sir,' said Hopko. She's masking her surprise, thought Patterson – C, the chief of the Secret Intelligence Service, has just walked unannounced into her ops meeting. Hopko allowed a sliver of a moment to pass before she recommenced, a marking of her territory.

'We anticipate that HYPNOTIST's product will be transmitted through these closed, covert channels, and in third country meetings. The darknet link will be used for operational communication only, and sparingly. The access agent is equipped to manage that link securely.'

Drinkwater leaned forward on the table.

'Yes. I wonder if we might discuss the access agent a little. I'm sure we all have questions.' He ducked his head in the direction of C.

'Please,' said Hopko.

'We are aware of Philip Mangan's operational history, of course,' said Drinkwater. 'And, speaking for Security Branch, and I'm sure for others present' – a motion in the direction of C again – 'I think we would all like to understand the operational rationale for using him again in this case.'

'Trish?' said Hopko.

Patterson jumped. *Christ. How about some warning?*

'Well, he knows the asset,' said Patterson. 'He is mobile, has excellent cover and strong judgement. And he's willing. He's ours. He considerably enhances our capacity in East Asia, to fulfil this and other operational needs.'

'There. Mangan is the face and the voice,' Hopko said. 'He's the reassurance, the humanity. And, crucially, he's the cutout. How's that?'

Drinkwater wore a half-smile and nodded patronisingly at Patterson.

'So you have plans for Mangan?' he said.

'We do,' said Hopko.

C looked bored. The Director of Requirements and Production was starting to look alarmed.

'Yes, I see,' said Drinkwater. 'I am sure we would all be interested to know how and why Mangan has wormed his way quite so firmly into your affections.'

'Sorry,' said C. 'I'm not interested.' He was looking at Hopko.

'Ah. Well—' said Drinkwater. C spoke over him.

'What I'm interested in,' he said, 'is what Valentina Hopko feels is at stake in this operation.'

The room was silent. Patterson sat, rigid. Hopko smiled at the aggression.

'I'm not sure I quite understand.'

C spoke louder now, enunciating in an exaggerated way.

'What do you think he's about, Val? Who are these associates he keeps banging on about?' He leaned forward, a questioning look.

What the hell is this? thought Patterson.

'It does appear,' said Hopko, slowly, 'that HYPNOTIST is not acting alone. This fact, while complicating the case operationally, also brings with it great potential. Many spies are better than one.'

Silence. Which C refused to fill. Hopko let it stretch out.

It was Drinkwater who finally blundered in.

'Well . . .' he was shaking his head, smirking, 'one *does* rather wonder at the logic of employing an access agent and an extended network of resources to service an asset, or assets, who are, in effect, an unknown quantity.'

Mobbs rolled his eyes. C gave a shake of the head. Everyone in the room seemed to know what was coming, except Drinkwater. And Patterson.

Hopko was poker-faced. She addressed Drinkwater slowly.

'My logic *is* that if we are to ascertain HYPNOTIST's true motives, and those of his associates, we must proceed with the operation. That is, after all, how we will find them out.' She gave a quizzical tilt of the head. 'No?'

Yes, obviously, thought Patterson.

C sighed noisily, then spoke deliberately.

'Val, *do* you think you might deign to share with the company your view of what we are dealing with here?'

Hopko sat back, looked at the table for a moment, then spoke carefully.

'My suspicion, sir, and it is as yet just a suspicion, is that HYPNO-TIST may represent some element in a factional conflict among China's elites.'

Well, it would have been nice if you'd shared that particular suspicion, thought Patterson, before realising that Hopko had shared it, over Ethiopian food on the Horseferry Road. *A fault line, Trish.* She forced her resentment in another direction. *Why must you always be so bloody oblique, woman?* Hopko was still talking.

'We know there are factions in the Communist Party, of course we do. But we barely glimpse them. We don't really know of whom they are comprised, or why they coalesce, or around what, do we? We don't know the geography of it. Who stands where, who's loyal to whom, who's ready to cut throats.'

She stopped, allowing a sense of climax to build.

'My suspicion is . . . that HYPNOTIST may be trying to use us to his own advantage in a factional conflict. And by doing so he will reveal to us a great deal.'

C was still, his watery, clinical stare. Hopko went on.

'We have a chance to see right into China – not its institutions, not its structure, but its biology, its guts. We'll see it *working*.'

C was brusque.

'I do not like cabals. I like agents whom we can run. I do not like plots. I do not like fantasies that may disrupt our relationship with China and undermine our interests there.'

Hopko nodded. C wasn't finished.

'You will use Mangan. And you will ensure that we do not become enmeshed in something that we cannot control.'

He stood and left the room.

Oxford

Kai found her sitting on the staircase, waiting for him. He unlocked the door to his rooms and Madeline slipped inside. She was nervous, waited in the middle of the room. He started to make tea, but she stopped him, took his arm.

'I have to tell you something,' she said.

'What do you have to tell me?'

'Something's going to happen.'

'What? What thing?'

'Someone's coming.'

His stomach lurched.

'They're here? Now? Your father's people?' he said.

'No . . . no. I mean, something's going to happen. Not now, but soon.'

She took hold of his hand, began to work it back and forth childishly, as if the movement might impress upon him the importance of what she had to say.

'What?' He leaned down, tried to look her in the eye. 'I don't know what you mean. What's coming?'

'They're getting ready for something.' Her voice was small, thin. 'The men.'

With his free hand he made a questioning gesture.

'Why? What have you seen?'

'There are more of them. They've taken to driving me around, shadowing me. They say it's for my protection. They've rented a house somewhere. I heard them talking in the car. They called it a "safe house". They talked about "the operation".'

He shook his head, baffled.

'What makes you think it has anything to do with me?'

'Everything is to do with you. Everything.'

'What are you saying?'

She was withholding, he could tell.

'You have to go, get somewhere safe. Something's coming,' she said.

She leaned against him, put her arms around him, and he breathed in the smell of her hair.

'Please,' she said. 'Go.'

And then he felt himself falling, or more sort of toppling, onto the bed, and her face was very close to his and the thought occurred to him that it was the danger of what they were doing that so aroused them both, and then the thought fell away, replaced by the startling sensation of her hands in his hair, her mouth on his.

48

London

Communications took up the next few days. Michael and Jeff brought Mangan a new hardened laptop. They showed him the dark-net sites, made him log on again and again, made him learn the passwords and the protocols forwards and backwards. How to encrypt; how to use secure email; the digital dead-letter boxes, planted deep in the tunnels and sewers of the web where he could leave them things he wanted them to find.

'And where you'll find *us*. This is how you talk to us,' said Jeff.

'And security, Philip,' said Michael. 'Security is just as important out there in cyber world as it is on the street. Stay aware. If something looks wrong, get out, stay away. Find another route. Or do nothing at all.'

'What if someone steals the laptop?' Mangan asked.

They showed him. They provided lessons as to how to log on from a public computer, from an internet café. How to use a stolen hand-held. Phone numbers in case of dire emergency only.

'And never on your usual mobile phone. Never. Or a hotel phone, god forbid. Buy a burner. Steal one, use it once, drop it in a river.'

Recognition signals, duress codes, digital keys.

This is how it works.

Patterson watched him as he sat at the conference table in a T-shirt, barefoot, hair a mess. The journalist's lips moved as he memorised, as if he were cramming for an exam. She tested him, caught him out, and he'd go back and memorise all over again.

And, for the pièce de résistance, Jeff and Michael waited till late on a Friday afternoon, then brought out a bottle of sparkling wine from the fridge and made Mangan sit down and close his eyes. Jeff tap-tapped on the keyboard, and told Mangan he could look and there was his brand spanking new website. The front page held plenty of white space and a black-and-white photograph lifted from God knows where of Mangan looking tanned, rugged, squinting towards sun-stippled mountains in some godforsaken place, Xinjiang, maybe, or Qinghai. And in a large serif typeface:

at the border: reporting transition in asia and beyond

philip mangan is a reporter of the borderlands, the spaces
where language, ideology and power intersect; where
transition – border-crossing – is a transgressive yet necessary
act; where journalism inscribes possibility.

'the exile knows that in a secular and contingent world, homes
are always provisional.' edward said.

'Bloody hell,' said Mangan. 'What happened to me?'

'Like it?' said Jeff. 'We were rather chuffed with it.'

'Have they done away with capitalisation, in these borderlands?'

'You have become a progressive writer, Philip. You will tell stories others do not, liberated from the false framing and corrupt discourse of the corporate media.'

'Don't look at me. I don't know what they're talking about,' said Patterson.

Mangan looked at the screen, wondering.

'The trick of it,' said Jeff, 'is that it doesn't tie you to conventional news coverage. It keeps you out of the mainstream, away from other reporters. I mean, with a website like that, you're not going to many press conferences, are you? Or natural disasters. You don't have to explain why you're not running to the big story.'

'But,' said Michael, 'it does allow you to go exactly where you want to go and ask whatever questions you want to ask.'

'And there's a budget,' said Jeff. 'Not a very big one. But it will allow you to commission the odd story from others, to keep things turning over. You'll need to write, but you can do it all on your own terms. And we'll make sure you have a readership, or the appearance of one. And that'll scare up some advertising and funding.'

The two tech wallahs looked expectantly at Mangan.

He could see the virtue of it. But there was no escaping the lie.

They spent hours with him on passive surveillance detection. Look, Philip, look all the time, but seeing is not discerning. Look beyond your expectations. Look for the incongruity, the misplaced gaze, the awkward movement. Look for self-consciousness. But if you see it, do nothing. When you employ counter-surveillance measures, they'll know. So don't duck. Don't dive. No getting in and out of lifts or slipping out of back doors. If you do, they'll know.

And if they know, it's over.

They gave him a surveillance detection route and he trudged through the streets of Paddington, Bayswater and Notting Hill on a humid Saturday afternoon. He thought he spotted some of them. A woman in a launderette who looked straight at him and turned away. A kid on a moped who passed him repeatedly. A telephone engineer kneeling at a junction box, who, at Mangan's approach, seemed implausibly fascinated by his work.

The best cover, they told him, is natural cover. The best cover is to be who you are, the traveller in economy class, the progressive web journalist posting his transgressive copy, living in the cheap hotels, sitting in cafés. Don't duck, don't dive. Be who you are. But be watchful. And when you think you glimpse surveillance, and you will, you come to us.

The kid on the moped was just a kid on a moped. No one knew anything about a woman in a launderette. But he was right about the telephone engineer.

Oxford

Kai wished he hadn't obeyed the summons.

He knocked on the door to Miss Yang's house in Jericho and she opened it, wearing a figure-hugging blue dress, with bare feet, holding a glass of wine.

He followed her into the living room and she stood over him with a smile on her face that could cut marble, speaking her sibilant Mandarin.

'Forgive me, Kai, but I think the instructions were quite specific, weren't they?'

'Yes,' he said, miserably.

'No contact with the Chen girl.'

He looked down.

She glanced away, as if preoccupied.

'Well, this is unfortunate,' she said. 'What do you think we should do?'

He waited.

'Kai?' She was bending over him, trying to make eye contact. 'I mean, what if your father found out? Or that awful lawyer. What do you call him?'

'Uncle Chequebook.'

'Yes, Uncle Chequebook. What if he were to find out?'

He stayed silent.

'How many times have you seen her?'

'Three or four.'

She frowned as if an unpleasant thought had struck her.

'Kai, you're not screwing her, are you?'

He swallowed, shifted in his chair.

'No,' he said.

'Oh, for God's sake,' she said.

She put down her glass of wine and knelt in front of where he sat, placed her forearms in his lap and leaned against him. He could feel the swell of her breasts against his thigh. It was sensual, threatening.

'Well, how about this?' she said. 'We'll endeavour to make sure that your father and his minions do not become aware of your weird little tryst. And you tell me everything that she has said to you.'

He could smell her perfume and see the flecks of amber and hazel in her irises.

'I don't understand why this is—'

She cut him off, leaned in further to him, spoke very quietly.

'You are not required to understand. You are required to tell me what she said.'

'We just talked about, stuff. Our families, a bit.'

'I'm waiting, Kai.'

'She said she's scared.'

'Why?'

'Her father has people here. They drive her around, do stuff.'

'What stuff do they do?'

'I don't know. She just said—'

'Where are they, these men? Are they at her house?'

'No, they've rented some place . . .'

'What place?'

'I . . .'

'What place, Kai? Tell me *exactly* what she said, or so help me.'

'She said it was a safe house. They called it a safe house.'

Nicole paused, knelt back on her heels.

'Go on, Kai.'

Kai just closed his eyes, put his hand to his forehead.

'They talked about an operation.'

'What operation, Kai?'

'I don't know. She said it had to do with me. Look, that's all. That's enough. There's nothing more.'

She had stood up, placed her hands on her hips. 'One more question, Kai. And you need to think very hard before you answer. Do you understand?'

He gave a faint nod.

'Did you say anything to her about . . . Uncle Chequebook? About who he is, what he does?'

'He's just the family lawyer, why would she—'

She shouted at him.

'*Did you?*'

Kai shrank in his chair.

'No! No, honestly.'

'What do you know about him? Do you know where he lives? Where he works?'

'I . . . somewhere in the Caribbean, isn't it? Why is everyone so obsessed about Uncle Chequebook?'

'What do you mean? Has someone else asked about him? Who?'

'Well, Charlie Feng, the Cambridge boys, they all know about him. They asked me at that dinner.'

He thought he saw a flicker of disbelief on her face. And then she was all movement.

Copenhagen, this time. A last-minute flight, rain streaking the windows of the plane.

Gristle met Nicole in a silent airport hotel room, ignoring the No Smoking signs. She stood at the window, he sat on the bed, hunched over.

'So, tell me all about her,' he said, face set like a stone. 'Is she cute? Nubile?'

'What were you hoping for?'

'Oh, anything. My life is devoid of sensuality.' He drew on the cigarette.

'Whose fault is that?' she said.

'My wife's,' he said. 'The Ministry of State Security's. Everybody else's. Stop pussyfooting around and tell me what happened.'

'Not enough happened. But she knows . . . something.'

'Are you sure?'

'Yes.'

'How are you so sure?'

'She's been warned not to talk. She was ready for everything I asked her.'

'You are absolutely sure.'

'Yes.'

'We're out of time.'

'Wait, wait. There's more.'

He took a long pull on the cigarette.

'Go on.'

'She squealed to the Fan boy. She told him to get out. Something's about to happen.'

'She *what*?'

That got his attention, Nicole thought.

'I know. They've been seeing each other, secretly. Now *that's* cute, isn't it?'

'Like what? What the hell's about to happen?'

'That's all. Something's going to happen and the Fan boy is to get out for his own safety.'

'To get out? Get out where? Why? Screw them and all their forebears. And what the hell did he squeal to *her*? I wonder.'

'I don't know. But I think the lawyer may be blown.'

Gristle closed his eyes.

'That settles it. Get back there and . . . find out. What she knows.'

'You really want me to?'

He gave a brief, tired nod.

'I need proper authorisation,' she said. 'I need you to order me to do it.'

'I'm ordering you to do it.' He looked exhausted, the lines deep in his cheeks, under his eyes. A tired, frightened old spy.

'We have to,' he said. And she could feel the revulsion in his tone. 'So do it.'

He looked up at her.

'I'll take responsibility.'

'I believe you, for once,' she said. And she walked across the room, leaned down and kissed him on the forehead. He didn't move.

She ordered vodka at an airport bar, let it numb the thought, to push away what was coming. She was back in England by the late afternoon.

As Mangan's departure date drew closer, Patterson felt his restlessness, the desire to be moving. He'd pace barefoot around the mews house, reciting contact numbers, protocols, procedures for her. He saw a doctor, who made sure his shots were up to date. In the evenings he'd go for walks, pounding the pavement through Hyde Park into the West End. The walks made Patterson nervous, so Hopko approved a watcher to keep an eye, and a thirtysomething Irish woman with mousy hair and a sad, slow smile wandered imperceptibly in his wake and reported on his tramping through Kensington and Knightsbridge, his lingering in coffee shops. What's he doing? they asked her. He's not doing anything, he's just watching, she said. Watching what? Everything, she said, the streets, the cars, the Arab women in hijab outside Harrods, the groups of gangly Chinese kids bouncing around in their BMWs, the pale Russians in sports gear sat outside cafés, their eyes on the middle distance, the men in rows, smoking sheeshah. He went book-browsing on what remained of Charing Cross Road. He stopped outside a 'gentlemen's club' near Euston, then thought better of it and walked on as the dusk gathered. He never met anybody, or spoke to anybody beyond a bartender or a waitress. Did he detect the surveillance? If he did, he didn't say. The Irish woman spoke of an instant when he stopped, in Bond Street, and looked about himself, looked in the windows of the boutiques at the shoes, the handbags, the jewels. 'And for a moment,' she said, 'he just looked completely lost, like he was in some foreign city.'

Patterson observed, also, a compartmentalisation. He didn't refer to the China operation of the previous year, and asked no further questions of her about it. She did not believe that it had ceased to matter to him, quite the opposite. She wondered if WEAVER was to be for him some sort of amends, a second chance. But a second chance for what? And amends to whom?

She sat stiffly in her cubicle at VX, attended the ops meetings, watched Hopko assemble around their Chinese colonel the silent operational structure that would protect and exploit him.

Two days before Mangan was due to leave, he did some shopping at a mall in Shepherd's Bush, a cathedral of a place in ice white neon, air tinged with disinfectant, the groups of silent teenagers, faces down and silvered in phone glow, fingers hovering. He bought clothes in unobtrusive colours, lightweight walking boots, luggage, a padded backpack for the laptop, a sponge bag. He bought some sunglasses. He took it all back to the Paddington mews house.

The night before his flight, Patterson, Hopko, Chapman-Biggs and the tech wallahs all came round. Hopko had ordered in some expensive catering. They ate rack of lamb on a risotto, and Chapman-Biggs declaimed on the wine and insisted on gathering everyone's opinions and Mangan nodded and said he liked it, and so did Patterson, and they gave each other a private look. Hopko had decreed that no one could talk about work, and that made it a stilted affair, the conversation meandering through books, films, London and how no one in the Service could afford to buy a property any more, a point on which Michael the tech wallah became quite animated.

'It's all the Russians. And the Chinese. And Kazakhs and what have you. They come over and buy up all the property as an investment because they don't have to pay tax, and that's sending property prices through the roof. And no one in government seems to give a shit.' He sucked on a lamb bone. 'Property in this city has become a *global currency*. It has. You mark my words.'

The evening was warm and the room hot and stuffy, but they wouldn't open the windows for privacy's sake. Patterson, with a familiar jolt of annoyance, found herself doing the clearing up. But Mangan stood up and helped, slightly ineffectually, in Patterson's stern view.

When it was over, the tech wallahs shook hands with him and Chapman-Biggs gave him a clap on the back. Hopko paused on the doorstep and regarded him, smiled, squeezed his arm and left. He lit a cigarette and smoked on the cobbles in the dusk.

'Nightcap?' said Patterson. But he didn't want to go to the pub, and so she said goodnight, and he took her hand in his, her skin deep and dark against his freckled white.

He looked up at her and nodded, an affirmation. She slowly withdrew her hand and backed away from him with a regretful waving gesture and was gone.

PART FOUR

The Fall.

49

Chiang Mai, Thailand

The Palm Pavilion Hotel stood close to the old city wall, what was left of it, an extrusion of ancient stone above a green and vaporous moat, the traffic racing past in the night, tuk-tuks infusing the air with purple fumes.

Mangan arrived late, bumping up from Bangkok on a budget airline. He wheeled his luggage into the hotel lobby's air-con chill, its gardenia smell. He went to the bar, sat, ordered a cold beer. The laptop was a slender, almost weightless thing encased in white, as if it were coated in pure intention. He signalled, 'Arrived'.

He lay awake for hours, slept late the next morning, ate congealed eggs, drank watery coffee and walked out into a formidable wet heat. The streets were littered with tourist traps, garish, blurred signs offering trips to the mountains, to the Hmong villages, to the 'long-necked Karen', to zip lines in the forest canopy, to crocodile shows, elephant camps, butterfly and orchid farms. A place, a city, can become a simulacrum of itself, Mangan thought, the reconstituted object of a Western, moneyed gaze. There's a piece for the website. *Transgressive journalist lays bare neo-colonialist dynamic of tourist industry, fracturing of post-colonial identities!*

No telephone engineers.

No incongruences, no looks that carried a moment's too much purpose. Just clusters of golden-limbed girls in cut-off jeans, loose cotton shirts slipping from the shoulder, murmuring in Swedish, French or German as they fingered the racks of textiles, or turned pieces of pottery and jewellery slowly in their hands.

Mangan, by contrast, was pasty, red-haired, sweating and over-dressed. He marched on.

Chinese tourists were everywhere, alighting from coaches in front of temples of dazzling white and gold, carrying umbrellas against the sun. There had been a hit movie, star-crossed Chinese lovers careening through sensual Thailand, and the tour companies were capitalising on it, bringing in busloads of fans. Mangan watched the Chinese girls strike coy poses before orchids and buddha images, the back of the hand to the cheek, the upward gaze, as their men drilled at them with cameras.

Nothing.

He took refuge in a crumbling temple, the Wat Mengrai, walked slowly across a silent, weed-strewn courtyard to a bodhi tree. The tree's trunk was vast, ridged, rising from the earth in a gnarled, distended swirl, its limbs smothered with gold leaf and propped up with decorated wooden poles. He sat in the tree's shade on a concrete step and listened to birdsong echoing off the temple walls. The air smelled of jasmine. A monk in saffron robes shuffled along the edge of the courtyard, ignoring Mangan, but stopping briefly to greet another visitor.

The visitor was of Chinese appearance and walked slowly, palms out in greeting towards him. A fungible grin, black eyes, the wide face that Mangan knew.

The Clown stopped in front of him, then sat heavily beside him, mopped his forehead with a handkerchief.

Mangan sat very still, said nothing, looked straight ahead. The Clown turned to look at him, then spoke quietly.

'He wants to thank you. For coming.'

Mangan gave a tight nod.

'Tonight. Go to the boxing at Loi Kroh. Get a VIP ticket.'

Mangan shook his head.

'It's too public.'

'He will join you there.'

'No. Somewhere quiet.'

He felt the Clown's eyes on him.

'It is already decided.'

'Undecide it.'

The Clown grinned, but his look was hard.

'Be there. Nine o'clock. He wants to see you.'

'I'm telling you, it isn't safe.'

The Clown leaned towards him.

'Mr Mangan, we will tell you when you are safe. Or when you are not safe.' He stood up, put a hand on Mangan's bony shoulder, walked away. Mangan felt the sweat on his back.

The boxing ring was at the far end of an arcade. On either side were bars, mostly empty but for the sullen girls in skimpy tops, their eyes following the foreigner as he passed. A crowd was pressing in on the ticket booth, excitable young men waving banknotes, some tourists. Mangan waited and bought a ticket to the VIP area. A girl in a black T-shirt showed him into a roped-off area with dilapidated sofas. The ring was a mesh cage. Cigarette smoke, disinfectant on the air, high-volume rock music of the sort Mangan associated with trashy TV. Young Thai men in the cheap seats were whooping, shouting, jostling each other. The tourists looked awkward. The girl brought a beer.

He sat on one of the sofas, put the backpack – he didn't want to leave the laptop in the hotel, so was taking the damn thing with him everywhere – between his knees and waited. He felt hot, exposed, uncomfortable.

An overweight man all in black with a microphone had begun haranguing the crowd in American English and Thai, previewing the evening's fights, vamping in the manner of a fight announcer. *Thai boxing at Loi Kroooooooh!* Mangan looked around, wondered for an instant if he saw . . . something. Some wrinkle in the crowd. But then it was gone.

The first fighters were led out. A muscled European boy, shaven-headed, glistening with oil, white baggy shorts, red gloves. *Duncan from Englaaaaaaand!* A smaller Thai boy, less well-conditioned, a little roll of fat at the top of his blue shorts. *Somchai from Thailaaaaaand!* No surnames; cyphers, the two of them, puppets for the public. They turned and bowed to the crowd, which shouted and whooped. The Thai boy knelt and began making obeisances, the rock music giving way to the whine and shriek of the Java pipes. The English boy stood in the corner, limbering up. The young men in the crowd were starting to bet, hurling down their banknotes, shouting. The referee brought the two boys together, admonished them. They touched gloves and began to circle, the English boy leading with his left, still, confident, the Thai boy in peek-a-boo, jittery, feinting with his knee. The Thai boy kicked, moved into a combination and then the two of them were in a clinch, their knees working. They broke. The English boy watched, waited. The Thai boy was already breathing hard, letting go pointless kicks that found only air. With each one, the young men in the crowd yelled – insults, Mangan assumed. The noise of the pipes was excruciating. The Thai boy looked sullen, resentful. He jabbed, moved, made to get inside, but Duncan from England saw his moment, a roundhouse to the knee that hurt, broke his opponent's balance, and then a jab that skated the edge of the jaw, sent a string of sweat beads glinting in the lights, and a lethal hook, the whole torso behind it. The Thai boy went down turning, the knees gone, the tension in him, in his limbs, his muscles, vanishing, as if at the flick of a switch, the wet *thunk* as he hit the mat, and then blood all over him, his neck, his shoulders. Mangan shifted in his seat, looked up into the lights, tried to breathe in the stifling air.

A hand on his shoulder.

He turned, and there was the ridiculous pocketed vest, a pair of aviator sunglasses and a smile so wide, so taut, it could not be real.

Mangan made to stand, but Rocky didn't let him, and then brought his fists up and made feinting and jabbing motions.

'You don't like the boxing, Philip?' he said.

'The boxing is fine,' said Mangan.

'They said you don't want to come. I said, *zhen de ma*? Really? Why he not want to come?'

Mangan thought briefly of all the protocols they had taught him. Do not be seen together. Make it hard for surveillance. Establish a cover story, fallbacks, routes of egress. Do the housekeeping. He thought of how utterly useless they seemed at this particular juncture.

'I want to talk, somewhere . . . quiet.' Meaning: secure, for Christ's sake.

'Oh, yes. We do that. But now, just watch.'

He sat heavily, waved at the waitress, pointed at Mangan's beer and held a finger for one more. They were helping the Thai boy out of the ring. He was up, blank-eyed, but his legs kept giving way and blood was running in rivulets down his chest. The English boy was doing his victor's pose and the rock music had started up again. Rocky was clapping. For a split second, Mangan thought he caught Duncan from England's eye, and found himself wondering, Where are you from? And how did you get here, bloodying up little Thai boys in this shithole? He felt himself reaching for the story, but the boy had turned away.

'We should go,' Mangan said.

'Not yet,' said Rocky. He pulled his sunglasses down, looked at Mangan benevolently over the top. 'We are quite secure here.'

Mangan frowned. Rocky gestured with his eyes, meaning look about yourself. Mangan put his hand up to shield his view from the lights, searched the crowd, the bars, the lounging girls. And there, a couple of quiet boys in polo shirts drinking Coke. Over there, two more, and a woman, unsmiling, by the entrance to the VIP area. Suddenly, they were everywhere. Two more strolling up and down the arcade, eyeing the girls.

'Christ,' he said. 'How many?'

'Enough.' Rocky sat back, pushed his sunglasses back onto the bridge of his nose, satisfied. 'You must learn to look, Philip. Really.'

Too many, too big, Mangan thought. He tried to choke off his alarm.

Another bout was beginning, the pipes wailing, two slender Thai boys, wiry, taut, their sinewed arms, biceps sliding like knots beneath the skin as they knelt and bowed.

Mangan stood and picked up the backpack.

'Now,' he said.

Rocky grimaced. He waited a beat, looking at the boys in the ring. Then he suddenly got to his feet and made a gesture with his chin. The woman by the door started moving and the others followed. Mangan strode down the arcade, not knowing where he was going, feeling the sweat on his back, his neck. They made a cordon around him, their eyes skating across the crowd, the young Thai men frowning at them, stepping out of the way reluctantly, the bar girls shrinking back. It was a foul, arrogant performance, and Mangan felt the anger rising in him. Then he was on the street in the hot, thick night, the smell of grilled meat, curry, frangipani on the air, drains, exhaust fumes. Rocky was behind him, and Mangan felt the others forming up around him on the pavement. Rocky laid a restraining hand on his arm, and Mangan could feel the tension in it, the ticking anxiety. Two black SUVs pulled around a corner, moving fast. They came to an abrupt halt in front of him, and then the door was open and Mangan felt himself being manipulated into the back seat, the air conditioning dry and frigid, Rocky beside him, the eyes of the Clown polished granite in the rear-view mirror.

I am forever being pushed into other people's vehicles.

50

They drove in the darkness out of town, to the north-west, Mangan guessed, the road fast, straight, flat, cutting across a plain. He watched the city fall away, the traffic thinning. They passed a vast Thai military base, billboards of the royal family flanking its main gate. A Special Forces Group, said the signs. Mangan glimpsed the boys on the gate, flak-jacketed, M4s across the chest.

Then lesser roads, winding sharply upward into mountain forest. Mangan saw the lights of mansions in the trees, their manicured lawns, orchid beds, the driveways lamplit, tantalising in the night.

Rocky leaned forward and tapped the Clown on the shoulder.

'*Zai zher.*' Here.

'*Zhidao.*' I know.

They turned left onto a poorly paved track into the forest, the SUV jouncing over the pitted surface. Mangan tried to steady his breathing, focus. They were pulling in before a villa, light spilling from the windows, the boys there before them, spread out, watching the treeline. Rocky turned to Mangan, grinned, made a big *come-with-me* gesture. Mangan saw the sheen of sweat on him.

He got out of the car, the night enveloping him like a hot, damp blanket, silence but for the wind in the trees, the *clack clack* of bamboo, footsteps on the driveway.

The villa was done out in faux Lanna style, deep, rich teak floors, delicate dark wood furniture, silken upholstery in pale pastels, pale walls downlit. It smelled of money, of dissociation, the taste of a seat-back magazine. Rocky planted himself on a chaise longue, lit a cigarette, gestured for Mangan to sit. Two of the boys lingered by the door, still, watchful.

'Tell them to leave,' said Mangan, quietly, in Mandarin.

Rocky thought for a minute, then nodded. He gestured, and they left the room reluctantly, closed the door.

'What is this?' said Mangan.

'What's what?' said Rocky, the knee jigging now, Mangan saw.

'Why so many people? Who are they?'

'They are security.'

Mangan swallowed.

Rocky had his head cocked to one side, regarding him. He shrugged. Mangan waited.

'They're here, so we just accept,' said Rocky.

'They're not your idea, is that what you're telling me?' He saw Rocky blink, then cover it with a huge distended grin.

'What do you have for me?' he said.

Mangan sighed.

'Tasking.'

'Ah.' Rocky drew on his cigarette, and was that a tremor in his hand?

'What's wrong?' said Mangan.

'Nothing is wrong.'

'It would be best if you did not keep things from me,' said Mangan.

Rocky gave a snort of laughter.

'Not so unusual, in our game.'

Mangan changed tack.

'Look, they want me to tell you that the account is open and a first payment has been made.'

'That's nice.' Another long draw on the cigarette.

'Well, don't you . . . don't you want the details?'

'The details. Yes, I want the details.'

Mangan forced himself to concentrate, put aside his unease. He reeled off the account number, sort code, address in the Cayman Islands, passwords. Rocky just nodded.

'Tell them, thank you,' he said. 'And now, the tasking. Task me.'

He's going through the motions, thought Mangan. He's waiting till we get to what matters to him. *Get him talking, Philip. See what happens.*

'Really?' said Mangan. 'You want me to go through their dreary lists?'

Rocky picked a piece of tobacco from his tongue with his forefinger, examined it.

'Sure.'

'All right. They want to start with 2PLA, command structure, current operations. Then they'd like you to move on to signals intelligence, capacity along the borders, across south-west military region's area of operations. And then, what was next? Oh yes, Party/military relations, chains of command, doctrine.'

Rocky frowned.

'What are they doing, writing a research paper?'

'I think they're warming up. I'm sure there will be more exacting demands in future.'

Rocky pointed to himself, finger to nose.

'If I had an agent like me . . .'

Mangan affected a patient expression. 'Perhaps you should tell them what they ought to know, rather than what they want to know.'

Rocky brightened, in his deliberate way.

'Exactly. *Exactly.*' He held up an admonishing finger. Now he was fiddling with the pockets on his vest, fumbling, tense. 'We must trust, yes? They should trust me to tell them.' He was digging in the pockets, one after another, looking down, his mouth turned downward at the corners. He suddenly seemed old.

'I mean,' said Rocky, looking up abruptly, rediscovering his obliging self. 'I can give them the signals stuff, sure. All the stuff along the border. They should already know, though, shouldn't they? Since most of it's run by CIA.'

Mangan made a wry face. He'd written a story once, about the mobile signals intelligence units that moved along China's southern border, Americans and Chinese aboard, sniffing the airwaves for drug traffickers. And more.

'I'm sure there's plenty you could tell them,' he said.

'Oh, there is.' Rocky laughed, went back to digging in his pockets, then appeared to find something.

'Here we are,' he said.

He laid on the table what seemed to be a small tile, perhaps two inches square, light grey. Mangan peered at it. Rocky watched him.

'I'm assuming you are going to tell me what that is,' said Mangan.

'I thought you might know.'

'I don't.'

Rocky took another cigarette from the pack, lit it, inhaled with a hiss through his teeth. He pointed at the grey tile.

'That, that is a death sentence. For me. For them.' He gestured out beyond the door. 'So you be careful with it.'

Mangan waited.

'It's the skin of the J-20,' Rocky said, watching Mangan carefully.

The what?

He thought hard, almost panicked. No, the J-20, the new fighter aircraft. Stealthy, canard design, built by Chengdu Aviation, fifth generation, officially graded Extremely Scary. Chinese air power for the twenty-first century, and still mostly a mystery. He'd seen weird digitally altered photos of prototypes on the net. And the skin? The composite covering the fuselage and wings to throw off enemy radar.

'I'd guess,' said Rocky, 'your people would want to look at it.'

Mangan picked the tile up, turned it in his fingers, a fragment, loaded with meaning. A little shard of power.

'I'm sure they would,' he said quietly.

'Mind you,' said Rocky, 'I don't think they learn too much.'

'Why?'

Rocky grinned, gestured to the tile. 'It's an American formula. We stole it.'

Mangan opened his mouth, made to speak, then caught himself. Later, he thought. Rocky's eyes were still on him. He spoke in Mandarin.

'And some more things,' he said. He was holding a memory stick. 'On here, some bits and pieces for J-20. New engine specs. Off bore-sight capability. And the weapons bay doors, tell them to look there. The design is tricky. In testing, they've found that the different material densities create backscatter.'

Mangan looked blank.

'Radar can see it,' Rocky said slowly.

Mangan nodded.

'Also, the onboard sensors. CNaC makes them and they're shit.'

He dropped the memory stick on the table, its *clack* on the table-top.

'Oh, and one other thing.' He pointed at the stick.

'Laser weapons. There's a document. CNaC is making laser weapons. Blinding weapons. They can use them at sea, blind ships and aircraft. Also crowd control. Horrible, really. The laser touches your eye: it makes your eyeball boil, inside. It's all illegal but CNaC doesn't care. It's all there.'

Mangan looked at the memory stick. He was suddenly conscious of heat and closeness in the room, could hear the ticking and chattering of frogs in the forest, the whoop of some night bird. The window must be open, he thought. He reached out and took the memory stick and the tile, unzipped a pocket on the backpack, put them in, carefully. So much for tasking, he thought. We ask him cub scout questions about his bosses, he brings treasure.

Why so eager to please?

Rocky was speaking, the knee jigging, fingers working, picking at a nail, a loose piece of skin on the thumb, the smile wide as a chasm.

'So,' he was saying, jovially, 'that's all for now. Let's have a drink.'

He stood up, walked to a sideboard, took a bottle from a drawer. Blue Label this time, two glasses, an ice bucket.

'You know very well I have to ask,' said Mangan.

Rocky walked back across the room, sat, made a fist around the top of the bottle, cracked it open, poured, dropped in the ice.

'Ask away.'

'How? Where from?'

Rocky rolled the whisky around the ice, took a sip.

'You won't respect me in the morning,' he said.

Mangan picked up his glass, drank, waited.

'No,' said Rocky. 'Maybe later, I tell you.'

'They'll want to know the source.'

Rocky just grinned again, shook his head.

'Why do you have it in for CNaC?' said Mangan.

Rocky looked up, sharply now.

'Why do you say that?'

'This is the third time you've given us information to discredit CNaC. The petroleum contracts, the procurement documents, now this. What has CNaC ever done to you?'

Rocky considered.

'This is not about CNaC,' he said.

'What is it about, then?'

Rocky's look soured.

'It's partly about CNaC,' he said.

Mangan sighed, let their silence hang in the air, the night noises coming in from the window.

'And,' he began, 'you said that the formula for the skin composite was ... stolen.'

'Ha!' shouted Rocky. 'I wondered how long it would take you.'

Mangan looked down.

'Who stole it? How?' Rocky was affecting hilarity. 'Well, now, Philip, you ask the *really* dangerous question.'

He stopped, took a pull on his whisky, then laughed more, breathing heavily.

'How we do it? The stealing? Maybe that comes later, too. Maybe.'

'When later?'

'Maybe soon.'

'Why all the security?'

'To be secure.'

'It's not secure wandering around Chiang Mai with twelve goons.'

Rocky tapped himself on the chest.

'Makes me feel secure.'

'The locals will see you in a heartbeat.'

'I don't care about the locals.'

'Who do you care about?'

'You mean who do *we* care about?'

'All right, we.'

'Didn't someone say that hell is other people? Who said that?'

'Sartre.'

'Well, these other people are hell.'

'Tell me who they are.'

'We do not have a lot of time, Philip.'

'Time for what?'

'Time for what? Time for us. Time for this.' He had stood up and was walking towards the window. He turned, ran his hand through his hair. The smile was gone. Mangan had a feeling of glimpsing the raw man, and he was soaked in fear.

The date. A reference number

CX BRAMBLE

UK S E C R E T

URGENT

REPORT//

1/ BRAMBLE met HYPNOTIST at prearranged public location in central Chiang Mai. HYPNOTIST insisted location was secure. A large number of security personnel were in evidence, acting at HYPNOTIST's command. HYPNOTIST agreed to move to a more secure location. Security personnel escorted BRAMBLE and HYPNOTIST to a villa in the mountains north-west of Chiang Mai.

2/ HYPNOTIST declined to answer questions contained in tasking.

3/ HYPNOTIST provided what he said is a sample of the skin used on the exterior of the J-20 fighter. The sample is in BRAMBLE's possession.

4/ HYPNOTIST provided a memory stick containing further information regarding the J-20, also in BRAMBLE's possession.

5/ HYPNOTIST asserts that the formula used in the J-20 skin sample was 'stolen', by implication through espionage.

6/ HYPNOTIST would reveal no further details as to how the sample and information regarding the J-20 were acquired.

7/ HYPNOTIST asserts that CNaC is manufacturing laser weapons in contravention of international treaty obligations.

8/ HYPNOTIST appeared at times amenable and confident, at others agitated and afraid, and made repeated references to an unidentified group pursuing him. He insisted this unidentified group was not 'local', meaning not identical with THAI72.

9/ HYPNOTIST has returned to base. BRAMBLE remains in place.

10/ Next contact to be within ten days, arranged through secure protocols.

11/ Grateful for immediate/immediate contact re onpassing of sample and memory stick, instructions.

APPENDIX 1

1/ BRAMBLE believes HYPNOTIST is not acting alone, but has considerable resources at his command, as demonstrated by the large and intrusive security operation surrounding his presence in Chiang Mai. HYPNOTIST appears to be participating in a larger operation the objectives of which are unknown. The compromising of China National Century Corporation appears to be one element of those objectives.

2/ HYPNOTIST appears to think that the operation is
compromised in some way, but will not say how. He refers
repeatedly to 'not having much time'. He refuses to give
context.

3/ BRAMBLE assesses that HYPNOTIST is privy to a Chinese
operation that has successfully acquired highly sensitive and
closely protected US defence technology including the formula
for stealth skin used on the J-20 fighter.

ENDS\\

At 4 a.m., Mangan sent, pulled out of darknet, closed the laptop. The
hotel room was dark, just the low hum of the air conditioner, the subdued rattle of traffic from the street. He lit a cigarette, went to the
window, pulled back the net curtain, rested his head against the cool
glass, watched.

Very, very careful, now, he thought.

51

Mangan slept for an hour, fully clothed. By dawn he had packed a run bag. In it, the laptop, some clothes. Cash, credit cards, passports were at the base of his back. The sample and the drive he wrapped in a hand towel and pushed deep into the run bag.

At seven he left the hotel and walked north, out of the old city, carrying the run bag, no phone. He walked for an hour in the hot, overcast morning, stopped at a clattering café that opened to the street, the girls presiding over tin trays of curry, pork with basil, dumplings that they served on plastic plates, or put in plastic bags to be taken away. He sat on a three-legged stool facing the street. He ate rice porridge with shredded pork, ginger, spring onions, drank instant coffee from a sachet.

He walked on, no ducks, no dives. Just a pale girl in sunglasses and a pink polo shirt who wafted by him on a moped once too often, he thought. And a wavy-haired man of Asian appearance who carried a tourist map and a camera in this part of town bereft of attractions or scenery, who ate slices of fruit from a paper tub, and who seemed to be asking for directions on his phone. Rocky, keeping an eye.

Or someone else.

People from hell.

Or his overwrought, sleepless imagination.

He turned abruptly west, walked for three minutes, turned into a *soi,* an alleyway of crumbling asphalt, broken glass glistening in the sun. An elderly monk shuffled past, carrying his bowl carefully, the smell of rice, salt fish, rising from it. The slap of the man's sandals on the roadway made Mangan think of the warm night in Harer, the darting, pacing hyenas.

The Banyan guest house had a rust-red iron gate.

Mangan stopped in the *soi* and listened.

He pushed open the gate. A courtyard, a paint-blistered bench, gladioli spilling from pots, a small greenish pool. Through a curtain of beads, reception, and a sixtyish lady, permed and yawning. He paid for a month in advance.

'Some nights I will be here and others I won't,' he said.

She waved a hand, dismissing his concerns, and she showed him to a dim, stale room at the top of the house, painted in dark blue by an amateur, careless hand, the blinds drawn, a dank bathroom, a fungal air conditioner that moaned and vibrated. He rewrapped the sample and the memory stick in the hand towel and pushed the bundle into the space between the wardrobe and the wall.

He lay down, exhausted.

The wash of loneliness.

Fear, edging up behind.

London

Patterson waited for the signal. VX emptied as the evening wore on, the corridors falling silent. She went out to buy a kebab from Nikolai's, as was her habit, and went to a bench by the river, where she sat in the dark and consumed it looking out over the black water, the tourist boats great, churning rafts of light. She watched a yacht making its way towards Greenwich, a party on its aft deck, the men tanned, languorous, shirts unbuttoned, holding champagne bottles, the women swathed in white and gold. She caught a snatch of its music, a popular tenor singing arias. She imagined perfume on the air, laughter, flirtation. The yacht's lights faded in the night and she walked back to VX.

Later, she repaired to the basement, where a small warren of tiny rooms allowed officers hostage to foreign time zones a place to sleep and shower. She had just lain down when her handheld buzzed, notifying her of an incoming signal. She ran back up to the P section and logged onto the system.

She had argued to be there for the encounter, and had been turned down.

And now this.

A deep breath. She dialled Hopko securely.

'Trish?'

Patterson heard voices raised, laughter.

'Contact, according to protocol. He's carrying,' she said.

'Suggestions?'

'We use GODDESS.'

'Do it. Anything more?' said Hopko.

'Our friend believes he may be compromised.'

A beat.

'We'll discuss tomorrow. Early.'

'Understood.'

Then silence.

Oxford

Nicole had not wanted to be part of it, but the three men who'd come from the London residency insisted. For the identification, they said. So now, at 3.30 in the morning, she sat breathing the fetid air of their van. They were parked just off St Clement's, had been for an hour. The men sat silently. She didn't know what they were waiting for. Nicole thought of Gristle, his loneliness, his bereft sense of honour, his promise to protect her. Dear God. If this went wrong she'd need all the protection she could get.

There was no time to plan. It will be very quick and very dirty, said the men. Probably messy, too.

And it was messy.

The men were suddenly all motion. They slipped from the van, closing the doors silently. They jogged down the side street, hopped the gate, gliding down the passage to the back of the house. The men carried mole grips and a crowbar, but, astonishingly, the bump keys worked on both locks, the lead man kneeling, feeling out the placement, tapping with a rubber mallet. It took him eighteen seconds.

Inside, they moved silently through a kitchen, a dining room, to the staircase, and they must have set off a motion detector because the protection – a bulky figure, half-dressed, hair awry – was on them with a yell and a grunt. They took him down very fast and very hard, Nicole didn't see how, some sort of baton, she thought, but he was prone and convulsing, a foot on his neck, when she stepped over him and ran up the stairs.

Madeline Chen was sitting up in bed, a hand in her hair, eyes flickering to the window, her small, pretty mouth an O of shock. The lead man looked to Nicole for confirmation and she nodded and they were on her, spray in her face, a hypodermic in her arm. Her eyes found Nicole, but the fury in her look quickly dulled and her mouth just opened and closed.

'Madeline?' said Nicole. 'Madeline, can you hear me?'

The girl's eyes were open, but her head was lolling. She didn't respond.

One of the men checked her vital signs. Another was on his handheld, texting.

They put her in a bin bag, carried her down the stairs. The protection was lying quite still now. A white van was waiting in the street. They closed and locked the back door. And that was that. Messy.

52

Yip Lo Exports Inc. of Hong Kong, the small but industrious exporter of plastic flowers and children's novelties to the European retailers, was a hive of activity. Following a lively, if pained discussion around the corporate lunch table, a decision had been taken – imposed was closer to the truth – Eileen Poon herself, as proprietor of Yip Lo, would travel in person to Thailand for exploratory meetings with local producers in the plastics industry. Such an enterprise, argued her sons, Peter and Frederick, named optimistically for the rulers of Imperial Russia, and their cousin, Winston, who recalled other imperial aspirations, might tax her unduly and should be left in their capable hands. But Eileen was insistent.

'I'm going,' she said.

Frederick Poon squirmed in his chair.

'Ma, this might be a . . . a demanding meeting.'

She turned to him.

'That is why I need to go.'

'Ma, we don't know,' said Frederick, unwilling to acknowledge defeat, 'what we might learn in such a meeting, who we might encounter. Ma, really.'

Eileen Poon reached for her cigarette case, withdrew from it a bidi, which she lit deliberately, suffusing the room with blue, acrid smoke.

'Ma ...'

'You will be with me.'

'Ma, of course, but—'

'Signal,' she said. She made a dismissive gesture with her finger-tips.

Frederick sighed, then nodded. Winston got up from the table, wiping his mouth with a napkin, and made his way to the altar in the corner of the room. Atop the altar, the white-robed figure of Guan Yin, Bodhisattva of Compassion, whose serene gaze protected Yip Lo Exports in all its enterprises. Beneath the altar, behind its woven cloth, a safe. And inside the safe, a laptop loaded with a particular sort of software similar to that which resided on Philip Mangan's computer. Winston started the laptop, sent the one-word signal, its origins obscured by layers of encryption, proxy and digital obfus-cation, which would indicate to the right reader: 'Understood. Moving.'

And then Eileen went to her bedroom to pack a bag, and Peter was online booking tickets, and Frederick was calling his wife and telling her in a soothing voice that he would be back soon. Winston ordered a taxi to the airport.

Chiang Mai

After dark Mangan left the guest house, carrying the run bag. He walked back towards the old city. From a streetside stall, he bought grilled, spiced chicken in a banana leaf, ate it as he walked. He found a tourist trap café, some sofas, bookshelves with dog-eared novels, ill-lettered signs advertising hill treks and espresso. He went in, ordered a lime soda, sat in a corner, took out the laptop and logged onto the Wi-Fi, burrowed down into the darknet.

CX LONDON

1/ REMAIN IN PLACE

2/ MEETING 23RD. 21.50 LOCAL

Place: BOOKAZINE BOOKSTORE, NIGHT BAZAAR, CHANG KLAN ROAD;

CHINESE LANGUAGE SECTION

Contact: ELDERLY FEMALE, WEARING PINK SUNHAT, CARRYING GREY

TOTE BAG

Procedure: CONTACT WILL OPEN GREY TOTE BAG. DROP SAMPLES INTO

GREY TOTE BAG. IMMEDIATE EGRESS. SIGNAL

Jesus Christ.

That was in less than one hour.

He wiped his palms on his trousers. He felt chilled, clammy.

Less than one hour to retrieve the materials and make the rendezvous. Why hadn't he checked earlier? *Bloody fucking hell, you amateur.*

He left some money on the table, strode from the café, going abruptly left, then right, headed north, looking for an empty tuk-tuk. He turned, walked backwards, shielding his eyes against the oncoming headlights.

And it was there he thought he saw, for a split second, a figure, some thirty or forty metres behind him, backlit, ducking into a *soi.* A bulky figure, girth on it. Something in the walk, the gait, a rolling movement of solidity, strength, the arms out, fingers curled as if for a fight. Short hair, cut to bristle.

For a second Mangan stood like a statue, the adrenalin streaking through his gut, heart pounding, peering into the headlights. The shock of it, the memory streaming across his inner eye: China, chill night rain, the smell of fuel, rubbish, a loading dock, a bus; cigarette smoke in the cold. The running, the panic. And beside him as he ran, the slope-shouldered, bristle-haired figure with the rolling gait.

He turned and ran up the street.

*

GODDESS 2 AND 3 IN POSITION>

Patterson, leaning over the console in the operations suite, the text messages coming in encrypted, Michael the tech wallah bringing them up on screen. The still air, the quiet, just the tap of fingernail on screen, the plastic clatter and click of the mouse.

GODDESS 1 MOVING TO LOCATION>

They're early, she thought. She pictured leathery Granny Poon, tramping the stifling streets of Chiang Mai, the boys on her back, circling.

Mangan stood waving his arms at the passing traffic. A tuk-tuk pulled up and he climbed in, found himself yelling at the startled driver. The tuk-tuk hurtled along the darkened streets, its engine pop-pop-pop with every gear change. Mangan held on to the seat-back. The tuk-tuk bobbled to a halt outside the guest house and Mangan gestured at the driver to wait. He pushed the gate open, ran across the courtyard, took the stairs two at a time. He left the light off in his room, moved quickly to the wardrobe, reached behind it to find the balled-up towel, memory stick, sample, and found nothing.

Gone.

He went back to the door and turned the light on. He inserted his arm behind the wardrobe. Nothing. He dragged the wardrobe out a few inches from the wall, looked behind it. *British agent effects crisis rearrangement of furniture.* He knelt, looked underneath. Where, obviously, the little bundle had fallen. He reached and pulled it out, unwrapped the towel, found the memory stick and the grey tile. He took a deep breath, tried to still the shaking in his hands. He stuffed the items in his pocket and ran from the room, slamming the door behind him, crashing down the stairs. The tuk-tuk was there, the driver wide-eyed, uncomprehending at first as Mangan barked the address of the bookshop at him. And then they were roaring and juddering down past the moat, turning into the night bazaar, the street jammed with tourists who moved as if through some viscous medium which slowed their movement to a crawl. 21.44. Six minutes until the encounter. Mangan felt himself sweating, his neck rigid with tension. He thrust banknotes at the driver, jumped out and pushed through the crowd towards the bookstore.

GODDESS 4, Peter Poon, saw him first, rattled off a quick text to signal visual contact. He watched the Englishman shove his way through the crowd, too fast, too harried, moist at the temples, the red hair spiked and cowlicked. GODDESS 4 pulled himself in a way, close enough to confirm entry to the bookshop. He saw the Englishman, a head taller than everyone else, push open the double doors, step inside. He signalled. Up to his mother now, the encounter, with GOD-DESS 3 watching her back. He turned, pushed his gaze outwards, ran it over and through the crowd. He shuffled a few paces forward, made to examine a silk stall, but let his eyes wander, seeking the break in the flow, the inconstant.

Amber, amber, he signalled. Proceed.

Eileen, in pink sun hat, grey tote bag on her shoulder, perused Fortress Beseiged, Qian Zhongshu's masterpiece, in a new hardback edition, full form characters. She placed her spectacles on her nose, took them off again. She looked at her mobile phone. The bookshop was busy, tourists sitting cross-legged on the floor, browsing the mystery shelves, the travel section.

All these young people, she thought, these Europeans. Have they nothing to do? They wander through Asia, sit on the beaches, walk in the markets, the temples. What for? So beautiful and directionless and idle. At your age, she thought, I was killing communists. Attending their meetings, mouthing their slogans, penetrating their cells deep in the slum blocks that stank of sewage, cooking oil, cats. The silent mainland cadres in white cotton vests, smoking, eyeing me, trying to feel me up. I ruined them.

Her eyes flickered back to her mobile phone, to the book she was holding.

Amber, amber, came the signal.

GODDESS 3, Frederick, was by the door, holding a magazine.

She put the book back on the shelf. She turned, saw the tall Englishman, his face pale, lined, a sheen of sweat, looking around urgently. Too urgent, too tense. Relax, she thought. Being tired and frightened is permissible, but looking it is not. She moved towards him, slowly, allowing her eyes to roam the room as if for a bookshelf. She felt, rather than saw, his eyes connect with her. He started moving towards her, one hand in his pocket. She glanced over at Frederick. He stood still, holding the magazine. Clear.

She walked slowly behind a freestanding shelf of cookery books, hooked her thumb under one of the two straps of the tote bag, slipped it off her shoulder, opening the bag a little.

Peter Poon had climbed the four steps in front of a shuttered bank, giving himself a better view. The street was still bright, thronged with tourists, but the stallholders were starting to pack up their T-shirts, silks, jewellery. A fruit vendor was pushing his cart through the crowd. Peter lit a cigarette, looked at his phone. Then looked up.

There is a moment, for the watcher, when the world lurches, the polarity flips, when what was thought safe is revealed to be saturated with threat. It was as if Peter Poon could feel them coming. It was a flicker of speed and movement in the crowd. It was a car with darkened windows pulling in abruptly at the end of the street. It was two men standing up at the same time, too fast, from their bowls of *khao soi*, and looking about them, as if for confirmation. Five, six of them now moving through the oblivious tourists, their clothes too dark, their movement too focused, towards the bookshop.

5 3

From the corner of her eye she saw the Englishman picking his way through the tourists sprawled on the floor, one hand still in his pocket. She stood still, looking straight ahead, holding open the tote bag. She breathed deeply, smelling the books, the paper.

Her phone vibrated.

She looked down. One word on the silver screen. A code word, searing itself on her eye.

He was four steps away, three, raising his hand with something in it, a small bundle. She stayed still, held the bag open. She looked beyond him to the door, which had opened, shoppers pushing past each other. She looked left to GODDESS 3. He had replaced the magazine on the shelf and was running his hands through his hair and turning away from the door.

Follow me, he was saying.

The Englishman had followed her gaze, had stopped.

God in heaven. *Move.*

He stayed still, looking around himself, unsure.

A calculation, now. She can break off the encounter, peel away, vanish in the crowd. She knows she can. She knows no one can do this better. She will change her hat, her gait, her silhouette and within a moment she will be gone, just as she has been gone before, in Hong Kong under the noses of MSS, in Jakarta with BAKIN on her, in Manila, in Seoul.

And in Beijing, in the cold. After watching this self-same, flushed, crumpled Englishman with his level look, a year before.

She knows she can vanish. She knows she can leave the Englishman alone, to be swarmed by whatever GODDESS 4 has seen on the street. And he will be carrying.

Or, she forces the encounter. And *she* is left carrying, to be swarmed by, well, whoever is out there, while the Englishman stumbles away clean.

To hell with it.

Eileen Poon took three steps towards him, kept them calm, measured. She came level with him.

GODDESS 3 was moving fast towards them.

The doors had been pushed open hard and four men stood there. They wore polo shirts, dark jackets, jeans. Two of them wore shades. One chewed gum. They were scanning the store, searching, she guessed, for foreign faces. Plenty of them here.

The Englishman was looking at her, as if seeking reassurance. She met him directly in the eye and, almost imperceptibly, nodded. She saw his relief.

Now GODDESS 3 was with them, Frederick, implacable, smiling, but moving in a way that she knew: urgent, controlled, ready.

The Englishman was raising his hand, pushing the bundle into the tote bag, pushing it down. The four men were moving into the store, so visible, so aggressive. They are not even *trying* to conceal themselves, she thought. Why so arrogant?

And in a move she knew would infuriate all her teachers, her sons, all her students in tradecraft, every professional she had encountered in her decades on the streets, she leaned into the Englishman, rested her liver-spotted hand on his sleeve, gestured with her eyes to GODDESS 3, and said, 'Go with him, now. Fast.'

Whoever they were, they would get the footage from the in-store cameras. It wouldn't be long before they saw.

So be it. Now we see this stupid old woman's footwork.

And the best street artist in Asia, carrying now, turned away from the Englishman and from her mute and incredulous son, and made for the ladies' bathroom.

Mangan felt the old woman's hand on his arm, heard her whisper, smelled the reek of tobacco on her. He turned to where a younger Chinese man, wiry, a wispy goatee on him, was affecting interest in a glossy book on furniture design. The man put the book down and began walking slowly across the shop floor, away from the door. Mangan turned from the elderly woman, walked after him, trying to look preoccupied, allowing his eyes to pass over the bookshelves. They went round a corner into a short corridor, out of sight of the shop floor, at its far end a staircase. The man had quickened his pace, was climbing the stairs, looking over his shoulder, making a tight move gesture with his chin.

Up the stairs? thought Mangan. You never go up. Going up traps you.

He followed the man up the stairs.

They came out in a dim stockroom, boxes piled almost to the ceiling, the smell of cardboard and dust. The man closed a door behind them, turned off the lights, leaving only a dull glow from the window. He stopped, listened. Mangan could hear running feet, urgent movement. Where? Beneath them? On the stairs? The man gestured again and they crossed the stockroom, entered an empty office. Again, the man closed the door behind them. He seemed calm, moved with purpose, competence. Mangan was breathing hard. The woman. What had happened to her? Did they have her? Had they found the sample? He looked back, licked his lips, calculated.

'We should go back,' he whispered.

The man had wedged a chair beneath the doorknob. There was no other exit from the office, Mangan realised.

'No, we should not,' he said. Mangan heard the Cantonese clip in his voice.

'But what about—'

'She will get out. She always gets out.'

'Well, we can't stay here,' said Mangan.

The man just looked at him, said nothing. Then pointed to the window.

'You can't be serious,' said Mangan.

But the man was already standing to one side of the window, looking. Then he reached for the latch. The window opened outwards on a hinge. In a single agile movement, the man had one leg through it, was straddling the sill, looking around. Then his other leg was through, and with a quick look to Mangan, he jumped.

Mangan stood alone in the dark office. The night heat was rolling in through the open window, along with the sound of the traffic, the popping of a tuk-tuk.

He looked out of the window.

His escort had jumped some twelve feet to land on a flat concrete rooftop below. Now he was crouched, still, listening. He looked like a cat. But the man's jump had also, Mangan realised with a sickening lurch, traversed a three-foot gap between the two buildings. The gap fell away another two storeys to an alleyway far below and looked to Mangan like a dark chasm.

Three feet across and twelve feet down.

British secret agent plummets to his death fleeing bookshop. Poor egress protocol blamed.

Dear God, he thought, there must be some other way out of this, surely.

He went back across the room to the door, placed his ear to it and listened.

At first, nothing.

Then, a creak. A footstep?

From the other side, the door handle was being worked, quietly. The chair back prevented the handle from being fully depressed. The door stayed closed.

Then again. A slight rattling of the door this time.

Mangan backed away, looked at the door, then at the window.

He went over, slipped one leg through, straddled the sill, looked down. The man was still crouched on the rooftop below, but staring up at him, an imploring look on his face. Mangan wanted to retch, felt the weakness in his hands, his legs. He pulled himself through the window, squatted on the ledge. He could hear the door rattling in the room behind him.

Then he thrust out and away.

5 4

Granny Poon's pink sun hat went in the cistern. Hidden in the toilet cubicle, she took from the tote bag hair clips and a green visor of the sort golfers wear. She pinned her hair back into a bun, put on the visor. She added heavy, black shades. The white shirt she had been wearing she replaced with a blue T-shirt, bearing the legend, 'With a Body Like This Who Needs a Pickup Line?'

She worked surely and with certainty. She felt very calm.

Many times. Many, many times.

The samples and mobile phone went into a pouch she clipped around her waist, the tote bag in the bin. Then she stopped for a moment, breathed deeply, allowed her body to collapse into a stoop. She muttered to herself and felt herself sink into an old woman's hesitancy. Her hands quivered, her steps shortened. She unlocked the door of the ladies' room and shuffled out onto the shop floor.

Two of the men remained by the main entrance, watching the crowd. Where the others had gone, she couldn't tell. She took a cookery book from the shelf, opened it. It was in English. She studied the photographs, perfect salads of banana flowers, glistening shrimp, she ran her wrinkled hand over the glossy pages. She closed the book and walked towards the till.

The girl behind the counter took the book from her with a patronising smile.

'Such a heavy book!' she said, in English.

'What?' said Granny Poon, tilting her head towards the girl.

'I said, a very heavy book,' said the girl.

'Yes, yes, very heavy,' said Granny Poon.

The two by the door had been joined by a third, who was speaking to them quietly. Some of the tourists were looking in their direction, craning their necks, picking up the men's urgency. A manager was hovering, trying to pluck up the courage to ask them what they wanted. Who were they? What were they?

'Do you enjoy cooking Thai food?' said the girl, as she put the book into a carrier bag.

'No,' she said. 'Hate it.'

The girl looked nonplussed. Eileen took the bag from her and walked, stiff, stooped, towards the door, the carrier bag swinging at her side, towards the three men.

Eileen Poon glared at the men blocking the door of the bookshop. The men looked at her, this crabbed old woman in shades and sun visor, the hard little mouth, the thin lips edged with wrinkles, like tributaries of some ancient river.

She made an *I-want-to-get-past* gesture, a crabbed flick of the wrist, bony index finger extended, pointing to the door. She allowed herself to list to one side, the carrier bag with the very heavy book weighing her down. One of the men was still talking quietly, urgently, to the others. She could not hear exactly what he was saying, but he was speaking Mandarin, for sure. She edged closer. Northern Mandarin, the soft retroflex *sh* sound, the rhotic *r*.

So. China is here. A State Security team? Something else? Who?

She muttered to herself in Cantonese and one of the men gave her a hard look, and then shifted to one side, opening a way for her. She shuffled forward, reached for the door.

But the man wasn't finished.

Something about her. He sensed it, she knew.

He reached down, grabbed the carrier bag. She let out a squawk. The manager flinched, put his hand over his mouth. The man opened the bag, took out the cookery book, flicked through its pages, but watched her. She let herself shrink, hid behind her absurd shades, let her mouth fall open. She could see the manager girding himself to intervene. The man thrust the book back at her, then the carrier bag. She allowed herself to be flustered, to fumble the book back into the bag, her old, fragile hands quivering with effort. The man was eyeing the pouch strapped around her waist. He was not having *that*. And if he tried, she'd poke his eyes out. She looked away from him, pushed the door open, shuffled onto the street, faded into the milling tourists.

He was behind her, watching her.

She shuffled forwards, saw Peter Poon across the street, standing on the steps, his eyes locked on her, clocking the man behind her immediately and moving fast now, cutting between the stalls, the tourists parting for him, shrinking away from him. Ha! How had she bred such menacing sons?

Then he was beside her, his arm taking hers, protective, murmuring to her in Cantonese. *Ma, where have you been? I've been waiting.* And she snapped at him, *Oh, stop your fussing.* And they walked down the street through the tinny, blaring music and the litter and the smell of drains and overripe fruit, the whiff of early durian, and the man was still behind them but there was Winston with the moped and she slipped onto the back, snorting with laughter, wrapped her arms around his waist, and Winston was saying *Shhh, Ma* and he revved the engine and as they roared off she raised her shades and looked back and saw the man standing there looking about in frustration, and she fastened his face in her eye, allowed it to sink into the vast archive of her mind, to be remembered.

55

As he fell, tilting forward, his feet flying behind, not beneath him, the rooftop rushing at him, Mangan's world shrunk to the night air on his face, the orange wash of street lamps against the night, the black chasm beneath.

Somehow he forced himself not to extend his arms to break the fall.

He slammed into the rooftop, one shin against a gutter, most of the impact in his knees, then in his elbows and torso. His chin snapped downward onto the concrete. Sickened, he felt his world turn cloudy, and he must have passed out for a second or two. Then Frederick Poon was shaking him and looking into his eyes, and he was conscious of thick billowing pain at his very core, and he couldn't breathe. Frederick was sitting him up, bending him forward, and he managed to inhale a little and retch. He could discern Frederick's words in his ear.

'You must get up. You must get up. We have to go.'

His body wracked itself for air, and he could hear himself uttering a weird shriek each time he tried to breathe in. He made out blood on his shirt, and for an instant he sank deep inside himself, reflecting on how effort was now required and how he hated making effort at the behest of others, and the whole point of his life until now had been to get out from others' authority, and yet he'd gone and allowed himself to get drawn into something, and now he was being ordered to stand up and run because the people from hell were rattling at the door.

Frederick wrenched at his shoulder, pulling him to his feet. Mangan still couldn't breathe properly and his mouth had blood in it. His feet and arms were floppy. He half-staggered across the rooftop with Frederick – wiry, quick, strong – propping him up.

They were at the edge of the roof. Another drop. Frederick sat him down and made him dangle his legs over the edge.

Where were the people from hell? He swayed, went away again, his frame juddering with each breath.

Someone was standing beneath, in the darkness, arms outstretched. A bulky figure waiting to catch him. Someone familiar.

Frederick pushed, and over he went.

Two of them supported him now, his arms around their necks, and they were running. He felt his feet juddering along the road and tried to make them keep up.

A car, again. They tipped him into the back seat. He heard the two of them speaking Mandarin, Frederick's etched with the sibilance of Hong Kong, the familiar figure's northern, Beijing. They were disagreeing vehemently. The car lurched forward. His head lolled on the headrest, his breath coming easier now. The familiar figure was driving, his thick hands on the wheel, pushing the car away from the old city, out onto broader throughways. Mangan looked at the big, sloping shoulders, the fleshiness of him, the bristled hair, and thought of a cold, crisp Beijing autumn, of dancers lifting and turning in a park. Of a man with a knife in his chest in the dark, asking for his little boy as he died.

The car made a sudden turn and clattered into an underground car park, the tyres squealing on the hot concrete as they came to a halt in a corner.

The familiar figure jabbed a finger at Frederick Poon.

'You get out. Go,' he said.

'What? No!'

'Go.' He gestured to Mangan. 'I've got him.'

Frederick looked at Mangan.

'I can't leave him.'

The man was looking at his handheld, Mangan saw him sneer in its glow.

'Why not? We're old friends, me and Mang An. I will look after him.'

He turned and looked at Mangan. 'Aren't we?'

Mangan felt a wave of disorientation. He had last seen the face more than a year before, the face of an agent, his agent, the face that had come to him in China, tapped him on the shoulder and forced secrets on him. A face that ruptured his life, ripped open a fissure that would never knot back together. Mangan blinked, struggled to understand.

'Peanut . . . ?' he stammered.

The man spoke again, to Frederick.

'They are all over you like flies on shit. You need to get far away. Now.'

'You know who they are?' Frederick was saying.

Mangan struggled to lean forward, to hear.

'We think they're private,' said the man he'd known as Peanut. 'Chinese. Corporate. So you're in luck.'

Mangan, mouth thick and dry, spoke in Mandarin.

'Why . . . in luck?'

'Because my lot don't like your lot running around here without asking but they like Chinese corporate even less. So you get a pass.'

The man grinned, raised his hands in a mock *welcome* gesture to the two of them.

'Now be good and fuck off.'

Frederick looked at Mangan, who managed a nod. And Frederick was out of the door and off across the floor of the parking garage at a jog, and gone.

The man reached in his pocket and pulled out a packet of cigarettes, Tiananmen brand, lit two with a hissing gas lighter and passed one to Mangan. He saw his own hand shaking as he took it.

The familiar voice. Its undercurrents of humour, anger, threat, coursing beneath the Mandarin.

'Well, Mang An. That was the worst jump I have ever seen. Quite useless, actually. Perhaps you are too old for this.'

Mangan inhaled, tried to collect his thoughts, think. He stayed in Mandarin.

'What are you doing here, Peanut?' he said.

'I'm not going back into business with you, if that's what you're worried about. One time was enough. Thanks all the same.' He made a tight *no* gesture.

'But what . . .'

The man turned to him, the eyes ticking with calculation.

'This is where I washed up, Mang An. After everything. This is where they put me. And you could say the Thais find me useful. So many Chinese here! Everywhere! Running here and there, spying, stealing things, smuggling, money laundering. So I do a bit of this, bit of that.'

'And what are you doing today?'

'Today? Well, I would say I am trying to ascertain why Chiang Mai is swarming with Chinese goons, even more than usual. Quite brazen, these goons. Barging around, frightening people. Some seem to be military. And the others, the ones we saw tonight, as I say, corporate. And these corporate goons are very jumpy. They want something, or someone. My masters in Bangkok are keen to know what or who. They say to us, get the fuck up there and find out what's going on. So we let them run, a bit of watching, a bit of listening. And suddenly, here you are, too.'

He paused, inhaled.

'So, your turn, Mang An.'

Mangan shifted in his seat. Pain flared on his right side. He wondered if he had cracked some ribs.

'It's just a meeting. Nothing important.'

'Any Thais involved?'

'No.'

'Sure?'

'Yes.'

'Don't screw me around, Mang An. I can help you here, and you need all the help you can get. But you must tell me this. Any Thais?'

'None – really. All foreigners. Nothing to do with Thailand. Third country meeting.'

'China?'

'Yes.'

'You are running a Chinese source and you meet him here.'

Mangan said nothing.

The man considered.

'Is that who they want, Mang An? The source?'

'Couldn't say.'

'Yes. You could.'

'I'm guessing they want the source more than me.'

'So why are they chasing you?'

Mangan laid his head back, closed his eyes.

'I don't have answers for you.'

The man opened the door of the car, spat theatrically.

'If it were up to me, I'd take you in and question you properly. Politely, but firmly. But my masters say I'm to let you run.'

'You'll probably learn more that way.'

The man they'd called Peanut turned in his seat and looked at him.

'Small world, ours, isn't it, Mang An?'

He started the car again, cigarette between his teeth, reversed out of the parking space, the car veering from side to side. He has only just learned to drive, thought Mangan.

320

'I'm to take you to your hotel. You get your stuff. Then, I think, you leave.'

'No,' said Mangan.

They were squealing up the ramps.

'If you stay, they will find you.'

'They'll find me quicker on a plane or a train.'

'Maybe. But I tell you this. My people won't be so charitable next time.'

Mangan thought for a moment.

'I'll leave soon,' he said. 'Just let me out. I'll make my own way.'

'What?'

'Let me out.'

He pulled the car over abruptly. 'Your funeral, Mang An.'

Mangan opened the rear door, forced himself out, his ribs an agony, legs stiffened and shrieking. He leaned down at the driver's window.

'I suppose I should say thank you,' he said.

'I suppose it doesn't matter if you do or you don't.'

Mangan nodded and made to go.

'Mang An.'

He turned back. Peanut was proffering something, something the size of his hand, wrapped in cloth.

'This is strictly unofficial now, understand? Just for old times' sake, yes?'

Mangan nodded, took it.

'You'll need it, Mang An. Before this is over.' Then he pulled away fast into the traffic, oblivious, tuk-tuks swerving, honking at him.

Mangan felt the heft of a pistol in his hand.

Kai used a public phone at Oxford railway station. He fingered the business card of the detective who'd investigated the theft of the laptop. He telephoned the number, got voicemail. He hung up quickly. He felt light-headed, precipitous, as if suspended over some chasm. He was conscious of crowds of commuters around him, but

321

he seemed to hear nothing. He went to the men's lavatory, sat in a cubicle for twenty minutes, hugging himself. He wondered where this would end. He thought of his father, of the ministrations of Uncle Chequebook. He went back to the phones, called again. Detective Constable Busby answered.

'I want to report a missing person,' Kai said.

56

Outside Oxford

The place was only thirty or so minutes north of the city. Nicole turned off the main road, and a mile later she could just make out stands of beech trees and a body of water in the darkness. The road was potholed, barbed wire to either side, and led into woodland.

She pulled in before a silent bungalow in the trees, its pale paintwork streaked with mould, drifts of leaves against its walls. A sign: Holiday Lets. Fishing, Swimming. The minivan was already there. She got out, stood listening. Just wind hissing in the trees. She went to the door, tapped.

Madeline Chen was slumped on a foul, mildewed sofa, her eyes open. The only light was from a table lamp, the curtains drawn. Two of the men were with her. The third, they said, was outside, circling the property. She heard the crackle of a walkie-talkie.

They waited. Two hours, three. The girl began to move, stirring on the sofa, looking at them, her mouth working.

The two men began to undress her, her limbs still limp, unresisting. They left her underwear on, picked her up and sat her on a kitchen chair, taped her hands behind, her ankles to the chair legs. Her look was coming back to life, her eyes drenched in fear now.

Nicole dragged a chair over and sat in front of her.

'Madeline, can you hear me, sweetheart?'

The girl's eyes focused on her.

'Can you speak? Or just nod if you're understanding me.'

The girl nodded.

'You'll be back to normal very soon. I promise.' She raised her eyebrows, gave the girl a questioning look. The girl nodded again.

'I'm going to ask you some questions and it's very, very important that you answer them, okay? It's very important, Madeline. And then when you've answered them, we can all get out of here and get back to normal, and no one will know any of this happened.'

The girl's eyes roamed around the room.

'It's important for you and for your family. Some people are making some stupid mistakes, Madeline, and it's important that you should not be one of them. So you can carry on with your life and we can be friends.'

The girl blinked, her face pallid, a sheen on her forehead.

'I think your father, or someone in your family has told you something about a plan. A plan to attack the Fan family. To ruin them. You've heard about this, haven't you?'

The girl made a barely discernible shake of her head.

Nicole looked down, put her hand to her mouth. *Let's try this again.*

'You need to let us know what this is about, sweetheart. Really, you do. Let's think back.'

She raised her hand and put it to the girl's cheek.

'You father has spoken about this, hasn't he? You've heard him speak about it, haven't you?'

The girl seemed to be making a monumental effort, leaning back in her chair. She jerked forward and spat at Nicole. One of the men handed Nicole a tissue and she wiped her face, waited a beat, smiled.

'I don't doubt your bravery, Madeline. I don't doubt your loyalty to your family. Those are good things. But some mistakes have been made, sweetheart, and we just need to make a readjustment or two.'

Nicole looked meaningfully at the two men in the room.

'And we don't have very long. It's much better you talk to me than to them.'

Madeline was starting to speak, the words coming out half-formed, as if her lips were numb or cold.

'I don't know,' she said.

'But you do,' said Nicole.

'Not . . . anything.'

'But you told the Fan boy, didn't you, that something was going to happen.'

'Don't know what will happen.'

'Well, Madeline, we have to know what you *do* know, sweetheart.'

The girl sat back, shivered.

Nicole sighed, rubbed her eyes.

'Where is your father now?'

The girl shrugged, her eyes down.

'When did you last talk to him?'

Madeline thought.

'Last week.'

'And what did you talk about?'

Another shrug.

'When did he last talk to you about the Fan family?'

She shook her head.

'When you said "something is coming" to Fan Kaikai, what did you mean?'

'Nothing. I just meant . . . that things are changing. China is changing. That's all.'

'I think you meant something a bit more specific than that.'

She shook her head.

'You have to do better than this, Madeline.'

She shook her head again. Nicole leaned in to her.

'You *have* to do better. These men . . . they're waiting. Soon they'll want to take over.'

The girl blinked, fear staining her eyes.

'Why? Who are they?'

'They are from Beijing, sweetheart. They're very, very serious. This whole thing is very serious. You must start talking to us, properly now.'

The girl was shifting, squirming, looking at the men. A tear rolled down her cheek.

'I know,' said Nicole. 'So talk to me. What did your father say about the Fans? About a plan.'

The girl looked away, crying now.

'Nothing. Just . . . just he wanted to get rid of them.'

'Okay, that's good. That's very good. Well done. Now when was this?'

'Spring. March, maybe.'

'Good. And what exactly did he say?'

'Just like what I told you. They had to go. Things would change.'

Nicole was nodding, smiling.

'Good, good. Now what did he say about when, and how?'

The girl looked at her, shook her head, closed her eyes and the tears spilled out.

One of the men spoke.

'All right. Time now.'

Nicole ignored him.

'Come on, Madeline. Quickly now. Tell me. Just tell me anything he said.'

The man walked across the room, gestured at her with his chin. Nicole sighed. The girl was shaking.

The man was holding a plastic bag, a length of elastic. He spoke again.

'We need to move this along.'

Nicole looked up at him. He gestured again with his chin. She looked at Madeline, then got up and walked away. The girl began making a mewling sound, straining against the tape.

Chiang Mai

Mangan found he was all but past caring. Exhausted, dehydrated, sweat and fear in his pores, the pain in his side flaring with each step.

And at exactly that point, Philip, when you are exhausted and lonely and afraid, and you get sloppy, is when they find you.

He remembered Patterson talking, at one of their sessions at the Paddington house.

So when you find yourself there, go to ground, if you can. Lock the door, close the curtains. Do nothing. Sleep. Eat. Wait for daylight. Then make a plan.

He took a taxi, then another, then walked for a while. It was midnight and the streets were quietening. He went into a late night supermarket, wandered up and down the aisles. Up and down. Nobody wandered with him.

He bought a bottle of vodka, antiseptic cream, bandages, sticking plaster, plastic bags. The man behind the counter looked at him, saw the dried blood on his shirt and whatever had happened to his chin and frowned.

He paid, took the carrier bag, walked to the back of the store, slipped through a plastic curtain into a storage area. A woman in a surgical mask and rubber gloves was sweeping the floor. She gestured at him, urging him back the way he had come. Mangan said something, pointed to his watch and smiled, kept walking. A steel door led out to an alleyway, the reek of piss. He didn't know where he was. He kept walking, then took a taxi he found crawling slowly along the street.

Back at the Banyan, he stood in the bathroom, picking pieces of grit from the gash on his chin. His shin was scraped raw and badly bruised. He taped his ribs, poured an inch of vodka, lit a cigarette and sat on the bed.

He unwrapped the pistol. It was a Chinese thing, metallic and heavy, the butt emblazoned with a star, a weird retro look to it, bringing to mind People's Liberation Army propaganda posters, rosy-cheeked soldiers, the glow of a Maoist dawn behind them, brandishing just such a weapon. Two full clips. He unloaded it, worked the slide, found the safety catch.

One of the two passports, the weapon, the two clips and some of the money went in plastic bags and into the cistern in the bathroom.

He logged on to the darknet site.

Transfer effected>

He turned off the light and stood at the window for a while. He watched the insects drifting through the light from street lamps, a dog, watchful, pacing.

No response.

He lowered himself gingerly onto the bed, tried to sleep.

57

Outside Oxford

Nicole left the room, walked down a darkened hallway to a grimy kitchen, battered Formica cabinets, a stove, vinyl floor tiles. The place smelled of damp. She sat at the table. A pack of cigarettes lay there, a lighter. One of the men's, obviously, Zhongshan brand.

Poor tradecraft, she thought. They'll find the butts.

She took one, lit it, exhaled, closed her eyes, ran a hand through her hair, listened. She was part of it, now. The realisation was thick, heavy, tinged with loathing. This filthy place. She had thought of herself as something other than this. To Gristle, she was just ... whatever he needed her to be. She felt a flicker of anger. His protection be damned.

A thump from the front room, muffled voices.

She sat, smoked, waited.

The man came into the kitchen after seven or eight minutes. It doesn't take long, she thought. She stood up and went back to the front room.

The chair had fallen over and Madeline, still taped to it by the hands and ankles, lay on her side. She shook violently, her face white, hair plastered to her forehead, jaw trembling. Her chest was heaving, as if she'd run a long way. The man lifted her and set the chair on its feet. Nicole leaned over her.

'I'm sorry,' she said.

The girl's look was stunned, disbelieving.

'Now you must tell us what your father said, Madeline, or I'm afraid it will happen again.'

She was moaning, shaking her head, her mouth distending, turning down at the corners.

'Tell me, Madeline.'

The man walked back across the room, opening up the plastic bag, and Nicole heard a muffled scream as she left the room.

It took four applications of the bag – whether from the girl's innate toughness or her panic and confusion, it was hard to tell. Nicole looked at her watch. It was nearly four in the morning. She wanted to be gone by daylight.

'Madeline.'

The girl was slumped in the chair, tendrils of snot and saliva dangling from her. She seemed very small and weak.

'Madeline.'

The head moved upwards fractionally.

Nicole leaned over, put her hand under the girl's chin and pushed the head up.

'Did your father talk to you?'

A nod.

'When is he going to move?'

'Soon. This month.'

'Why now?'

'Before Beidaihe.' Beidaihe, the annual retreat of the Communist Party elite to a scruffy beach resort. The place where strategies were planned, deals were done.

'What did he tell you is to happen?'

'Arrests.'

'Who?'

'Fans.'

'All of them?'

A nod.

'Names, Madeline. Who else is involved?'

'The staff.'

'Your father's?'

A nod.

'Who else?'

'There's a colonel. 2PLA. He's in the south. Kunming. Friends down there.'

'His name, Madeline?'

'Don't know.'

'Really?'

A nod, the tears coming again.

'In Kunming? Is that where the friends are?'

'There's a place, somewhere they control. It's ... on the border. There.'

The man was stepping forward with the bag. But Nicole gestured no. There wasn't much more.

What there was, was another hypodermic. And a medevac jet waiting at Kidlington airport twelve miles away. The real interrogation was still to come, somewhere out of the country, somewhere secure. And Nicole pushed the thought to the fringes of her mind, picked up her things, left without a word, gunning the Mini down the track.

Gristle was waiting. He'd come in on a diplomatic passport and was sitting, crumpled, diminished, on the edge of the bed in the Hounslow safe house. The traffic roared past outside, trucks rattling the windows. She leaned against the mantelpiece, exhausted.

He just said, 'And?'

She walked across the room and handed a memory stick to him.

'The recording's on there,' she said.

'Tell me,' he said.

'There wasn't much, but enough, maybe.'

'*Tell me.*'

'It sounds like some kind of factional thing. General Chen wants to take down the Fan family, all their people, networks. He'll use 2PLA to do it. They have some sort of support structure in Kunming, the south-west.'

'When?'

'This month.'

'She said that?'

'Before the Beidaihe meeting.'

Her mouth was like sandpaper. She felt clammy, her clothes clinging to her. She was frightened, she realised, and exhausted. Gristle looked appalled.

'What happens now?' she said.

'Now?' he repeated. 'Now, you go back to Oxford and get ready.'

'Ready? For what?'

'Fan Kaikai's an easy target. He talks too much. He doesn't know how much he knows.'

He looked at her.

'They may come for him,' he said.

She nodded. He was looking past her, into some private nightmare. 'The fucking soldiers, you know. Self-righteous bastards. Always muttering about how special they are. How they're better than the people they serve.' He was holding a cigarette between his second and third fingers, shaking a lighter.

'What happens?' she said.

The *snick* of the lighter.

'What happens? Well, after what we've done to his daughter, General Chen goes berserk, I imagine.'

It was getting light. Nicole went downstairs, found a couch, slept.

58

For a spy, Patterson reflected, there truly are no coincidences.

She had been putting her jacket on, clearing her desk of every last scrap of paper, logging off for the day, when the ping from the Police National Computer ticked up on her screen.

Another one?

She sat down.

A Thames Valley Police report.

MADELINE CHEN, PRC NATIONAL, STUDENT, CURRENTLY RESIDING OXFORD, REPORTED MISSING.

Today's date.

REPORT FILED BY FAN KAIKAI, PRC NATIONAL, STUDENT, CURRENTLY RESIDING OXFORD.

She called the detective, a DC Busby, on his mobile phone. Hubbub in the background.

'Give me a minute,' he said. The hubbub receded.

'Very distraught, he was,' said Busby. 'Said he'd been round to her house, no answer, didn't answer her phone. Didn't reply to messages he left in her pigeonhole, whatever that means.'

'How long?' she asked.

'Well, that's just it. Twenty-four hours, less. I told him, not much we can do. She's an adult. Give it some time, she'll turn up. But he was screeching down the phone. "No, no, you don't understand, something's happened, she's been taken away by . . ." well, I couldn't understand much to be honest. He was becoming rather emotional.'

'I need to talk to him.'

'Talk to Five. Get a warrant.'

'I've got one.'

'Really?'

'No.'

There was a pause.

'That's a problem.'

'No, it's not.'

Another, longer pause.

'Well, I might be going to check up on young Mr Fan in about two hours' time.'

'I'll be there.'

'No, you won't be. And if you were, you wouldn't say anything.'

'Not a thing.'

She wouldn't – couldn't – take a Service car. Instead, she booked one online, jogged to Horseferry Road to pick it up. She pulled out into the traffic, pushed and nosed her way across the West End. The way out of town was slow but it cleared on the M40 and she drove into blinding evening sunlight, into a green-gold middle England.

As she drove, she tried to lay the pieces out, place them in order.

A new source brings gifts, but we do not know from where, or why.

Someone is probing. There is a plan.

Among the gifts, weapons to hurt the Fans, their corporation. Weapons to pierce the political-corporate heart of power in China.

We have found a place where two plates meet.

The Fan boy's laptop is stolen.

334

The Chen girl disappears.

There are no coincidences.

By eight she was parking in St Giles. Detective Constable Busby was leaning against his car. He looked pointedly at his watch.

'What did he say to you, on the phone? Exactly, what did he say?'

'Good evening to you, too. Can I see some ID?'

She pulled her badge from her pocket and he fingered it, intrigued.

'Please,' she said. 'This could be very, very important.'

He gave her a lingering look, then folded his arms, speaking in a way meant to signify disbelief.

'He said there was some sort of plot. In China. That this missing girl, Madeline Chen, had said, no, hinted, to him that there was a plot in China, and "people" were coming to take him. Fan Kaikai. Here, in Oxford. But then she's the one who disappears. Can you imagine? Not often we get global intrigue here. Not often I get to talk to people like you.'

'Who was coming to take him?'

'Just these "people". They're already here, apparently, wandering our sylvan streets. None of it made any sense. To me at least. Maybe it does to you.' He looked down at her badge again, then handed it back to her.

'I need to ask him—'

'You don't ask him anything. You have no jurisdiction, you have no warrant. You lot may not operate on UK soil without authorisation. *I* will ask him.'

She held her hands up.

'Ask him, please, for whatever he can tell us about these "people". Who they are, who they represent. Why they are doing what they are doing.'

'What *are* they doing?' said Busby.

'I don't know, and even if I did, I couldn't tell you.'

He grimaced.

'You can assure me that this is ... important, can you?'

She just nodded. He looked her up and down, then pushed himself off the car and started along the street.

Kai answered their knock, wide-eyed in a T-shirt, shorts, flip-flops. They went into his rooms. Patterson noted the bare walls, the lack of possessions, clothing strewn on the floor, the smell of bedding, sleep. The room of a child, she thought.

They sat. DC Busby cleared his throat.

'Mr Fan, these people you referred to. The ones who are coming for you, who are they, please?'

'They are, maybe, from the Chen family.'

The detective frowned.

'They are family members?'

'No, no. They are like bodyguards, or security. Probably they are military.'

'Military? Well, now. You are suggesting we have Chinese soldiers on the streets of Oxford.'

'The Chens, they are military. They have many supporters.'

'And why would they want to harm you?'

'They . . . they hate my family, yes. But there is more, I think.'

'What more?' said Patterson. The detective turned and glared at her. 'Is there something happening in China? Is someone attacking your family, your father, your uncle, maybe?'

The boy looked alarmed.

'I . . . I don't know . . .'

'What my colleague means,' Busby began, 'is—'

The door flew open. Kai jumped almost out of his chair. A woman strode in, dropped a bag on the floor. She stopped and looked at them: first the detective, then at Patterson. Very calm, very controlled. Of East Asian appearance, slender, striking, even in jeans and fleece and no make-up, and her hair up in a casual knot. Holds herself well, athletic, fit. Without saying a word the woman turned and regarded Kai, and Patterson saw the cold fury in her. The boy shrank. He's terrified, she thought. The woman's eyes flickered past the boy, to the other room, then to the detective, his shoulders, torso, then to Patterson, running over her waist.

She's looking for weapons.

Busby spoke, held out his business card.

'We were just having a short conversation with Mr Fan here. We'll be done soon.'

The woman looked at his card.

'Well, I think Mr Fan has probably answered enough questions for now,' she said.

American accent, intonation, layered over the clip of south China. Taiwan, maybe? *Who the hell is she?*

Patterson spoke.

'We were asking Mr Fan about the disappearance of a . . . a fellow student of his, Madeline Chen. Were you aware of—'

DC Busby was speaking over her.

'Yes, might we ask if you are aware of Miss Chen's whereabouts?'

The woman was staring at Patterson. *She's wondering why I don't get to ask the questions. Why I don't give her a business card.*

The woman had turned to the detective.

'I am not aware of Madeline Chen, or of her disappearance. Mr Fan has no information either.' She turned to the boy. 'Do you?' He said nothing, looked down, his fingers clenched tight in his lap.

She's cool as a bloody cucumber, thought Patterson. Busby could see it too.

'Might I ask your name and the nature of your relationship with Mr Fan?'

'You may not ask my name and I am a family friend. That is all. And I think it is time for you to leave. Mr Fan has nothing else to say.'

Patterson stood.

'I'm not sure we are ready to leave quite yet,' she said with a smile.

The woman held out her hand.

'Identification,' she snapped.

'That won't be necessary,' said the detective.

'Why won't she show me identification? Who is she?' said the woman, her voice rising. She bent down suddenly, reaching for her bag on the floor. She pulled a phone from it, pointed it directly at Patterson and snapped three pictures, the *snick* sound of the simulated shutter.

I have just been made, thought Patterson.

This woman is a professional.

DC Busby had his hands out in a calming gesture and was burbling about how sorry he was, and how we'd be going now. But Patterson raised an index finger, pointed at the woman and spoke in Mandarin. 'I think you and I can help each other,' she said.

The woman cocked her head to one side. She had beautiful, hard eyes, eyes that a certain kind of man would submit to.

'*Zhen de ma?*' Really? she said.

Busby was hopping from one foot to another with anxiety.

I will just hazard this one, thought Patterson.

'We need to know what the Chens are doing. Here, and in China,' she said.

The woman considered, measuring her response.

She knows.

'Whatever they thought they were doing,' the woman said, 'it is no longer relevant.'

Patterson opened her mouth to speak again, but she felt the detective's hand on her arm.

'That's *enough*,' he hissed.

'You should listen to him,' said the woman, with a dismissive flick of her wrist.

Patterson felt a surge of anger, the urge to act: to take the step forward, put heel to knee, knuckle to throat. The woman sensed it and moved a step away from her, her eyes dropping to Patterson's hands.

'We are leaving. *Now*,' said the detective.

Patterson looked at the woman as Busby tugged at her sleeve. She spoke in Mandarin again.

'I will be seeing you again. Soon.'

The woman actually smiled.

'Don't wish for things you can't have,' she said.

As he closed the door behind them, Patterson, furious, lingered on the staircase and listened, and heard from inside the room the beginning of her tirade against the boy, delivered in controlled, rapid Taiwan-inflected Mandarin: *just what in the name of god were you doing talking to the police, you fucking imbecile.* But DC Busby was pulling her away down the creaking staircase.

Patterson pulled onto the motorway in twilight, Busby's raging admonishments to silence ringing in her ears. She pushed him out of her mind, tried to let the thoughts come by themselves, to let the pieces float and move and cohere.

Over here, the establishment: Chinese royalty, cloaked in wealth, dripping with corporate and Party power.

And over there, an insurgency.

They are circling each other, sniffing the air, readying for the fight.

And where will Mangan be when it all starts? she wondered.

Where is my agent?

59

London

Patterson, red-eyed, caffeine-jangled, stood at the door to Hopko's sanctum. Hopko was standing behind her desk, gathering papers, a notepad, her handheld. She spoke quietly, without looking at Patterson.

'Where were you yesterday evening?'

Patterson did not reply.

'Did you take the evening off? You probably deserved it, I should say.' She looked up and smiled.

'Val ... they're here. On UK soil,' said Patterson.

'Who is?'

'The Chen people. Military. I think something might ... might have happened. In Oxford.'

Hopko nodded, non-committal.

'I see,' she said.

She peered at what seemed to be an encounter report. Then she straightened as if a thought had struck her. The movement injected a streak of menace into the air.

'Good communication is awfully important, isn't it?' Hopko said. 'I mean, for a business that's all about betrayal, trust is vital. Don't you think?'

Patterson, confused, nodded. Hopko spoke again.

'The trouble with going off the reservation, Trish, is that it corrupts the intelligence, doesn't it? Makes it unusable, don't you see?'

Hopko gave her a lingering look, then was suddenly all motion, sweeping past her.

'Come with me,' she said.

Patterson followed, clenching her fist to generate self-recriminatory pain, jabbing her fingernails into the palm of her hand.

They were in the secure conference room, Hopko herself presiding, wearing her battle face, expensively suited in black, at once austere and lavish.

'The sample,' she told the room, 'will soon be under the microscopes in the Defence Intelligence labs at Gosport. The memory stick is on its way to Cheltenham to be disinfected.'

Hopko leaned over the table.

'Early indications,' she said, 'are that HYPNOTIST's latest offerings are of prodigious importance. He appears to have spilled the beans on the J-20 stealth fighter. For which we are truly grateful. We anticipate starred CX. We intend to grade the product A1.'

The highest grade of intelligence, from a proven source. Prodigious indeed, thought Patterson.

'Amen,' said Chapman-Biggs.

C was unfolding, mantis-like.

'My,' he said.

Hopko waited to see if anything more was forthcoming. Security Branch was silent. She went on.

'Our attention must now turn to the complex operational exigencies of the case.' She looked over her glasses, fingered the Coptic cross around her neck. 'Everybody's thoughts, please.'

It's a triumph, Val. We've stumbled across the best-placed, most loose-lipped China source in years. He's deep in 2PLA and he's got dirt on the leadership. And never mind if he's also got ulterior motives and a band of groupies. Wring him dry.

It's a bust, Val. HYPNOTIST is just a player. Someone else is leading us a dance. We're dating a psychopath and soon he's going to want to screw us. Get out while we can.

It's all academic, Val. The opposition is sniffing us like we're on heat. Nice while it lasted. Rain stops play and everybody goes home.

'Trish?' said Hopko.

Oh, Christ.

'Our immediate concern must be the welfare of BRAMBLE.' She licked her lips and tried not to bark out the words. 'He is highly exposed. He is the object of aggressive surveillance. We must extract him. Only then should we make decisions about the future of the operation, when we have his read on it.'

C spoke.

'BRAMBLE remains in place.'

He stood, stalked from the room.

Hopko picked it up.

'It has been decided,' she said, 'that you will deploy as soon as possible, Trish. You will establish a safe house. You'll debrief BRAMBLE. You and he will reestablish contact with HYPNOTIST as soon as is feasible. You'll be joined by E Squadron personnel who will take over responsibility for his security.'

Her years in the army and in the Service had lent Patterson the ability to decrypt orders given her, to strip them down and reduce them to their essence.

This one: Go, with heavies. Force Mangan back into the breach.

A pause.

'Do you have any questions?' said Hopko.

Plenty.

'None,' she said.

Chiang Mai

Mangan woke mid-afternoon, wrenching himself from some place of panic, from images of a cold highway in sleet, of a bulbous little knife with a rubber handle in his palm, blood-sheened.

He tried to move, but his ribs screamed. In the course of sleep, his injuries seemed to have multiplied. His wrists and forearms throbbed, his neck felt stiff and jarred. He lay, tried to flex each limb, feeling ridiculous.

He forced himself from the bed, went to the shower, stood in the cool water, thinking about the previous night, the fall from the roof, the visitation from the big, brush-cut figure that, were he to dwell on it, would preoccupy him entirely. *How the hell?* He put on a T-shirt and jeans, limped downstairs to the reception desk, where he pressed two hundred baht into the hands of the permed lady and asked for someone to send out for food. Anything, he said. Anything will do. And some water. He went back upstairs.

He logged onto the darknet site.

Remain in place. Personnel en route. Instructions to follow>

A tap at the door. He wondered why he had put the sidearm in the cistern.

'Food, mister.'

'Just leave it outside.'

'Food.'

'Yes, just leave it.'

A scuffing at the door, footsteps receding down the stairs.

It was a big bowl of *khao soi*, the noodles in a coconut curry, loaded with glistening, crispy belly pork and pickles and scattered with fresh coriander. Mangan looked at it and his hands began to shake and hunger hit him like a train. He sat on the bed, squeezed lime juice into the bowl, started to eat, then to wolf it, the sweet, mellow heat of it blazing in him, strength surging back.

Remain in place.

This is how it works.

He stayed in the room for two days. He slept, sent the boy out for more food and waited.

60

Chiang Mai

To Patterson's considerable relief, Bangkok station made the arrangements for the safe house. It was a villa to the north of Chiang Mai in the hills, a tourist rental, barely visible behind high walls and a creaking steel gate. She pulled up in a rented Toyota. The gate opened for her. She got out of the car, smelling the evening perfume in the air: champak, water jasmine.

The E Squadron types, two of them, were already there. One beckoned her inside. He was fortyish, sandy, trim, sharp-featured in a way that looked accusatory. To her he reeked of army, the sergeant's mess. She felt all her old snobbery surging back.

'No names,' he said. 'So I'm Mac.'

Oh, God, she thought, I've landed in an airport thriller.

'And this is Cliff.' He gestured behind him. Cliff was tall, dark hair past the collar, a jaw you could sharpen your bayonet on, but a posture that said calm. Cool, grey eyes that caught Patterson's attention immediately, to her annoyance.

'And what do we call you?' said Cliff, with a half-smile. He sounded Antipodean. New Zealand, perhaps?

'How about "Boss"?' she said.

Mac raised his eyebrows, turned and glanced at Cliff, who didn't respond.

'Boss it is,' said Mac.

'How do,' said Cliff, and picked up her bags for her, led her upstairs to an echoing bedroom, laid the bags down.

'Whenever you're ready, Boss,' he said, and left her.

She unpacked, made sure her run bag was together and took out the laptop. She cabled it to the sat phone and signalled her arrival.

Downstairs, someone had brewed coffee. She poured a cup, went looking for the two of them. The villa was bigger than it seemed. A long wallpapered corridor took her to a gloomy annexe. She walked in on Cliff unpacking equipment. On a camp bed were laid out light-weight body armour, boxes of ammunition, two sidearms and two MP7s, the quiet, vicious, compact submachine guns.

'Christ, we're not here to start a war,' she said. He turned quickly, looked startled.

'No. But we like to be prepared, you know?' he said. He began putting the weapons into a duffel bag.

'Whose idea was it to bring all this?' she said.

'Normal operating procedure.'

'Not for me, it's not. Whose idea?'

'We were just told to be ... prepared for contingencies.'

'What bloody contingencies?'

'Nothing specific.' He held his hands out, conciliatory. 'Look, we really don't expect to be using any of it.'

'Bloody right,' she said. 'Kitchen. And bring Mac.'

She pointed to the screen.

'His phone signal puts him about a mile north of the old city, on this street, probably in this building. It appears to be a guest house called the Banyan.'

'Well, what's he doing there? He's supposed to be at the Palm Pavilion,' said Mac.

'Using his initiative, I expect,' she said.

Mac rubbed his chin, doing a very-concerned act.

'Think you can manage?' she said.

Now he looked affronted, made to speak, but Cliff cut in.

'I'm sure we can,' he said. 'When do we go?'

'Later. When he says he's ready. You'll bring him back here. We let him rest for a bit and then begin the debrief.'

Cliff nodded.

'And no weapons,' she said.

Mac was leaning forward.

'Hang on. What are we supposed to bloody do if the entire bloody Chinese State Security lands on us?'

'Use your charming personality,' she said. She loathed his type, aggressive, insecure men, always second-guessing the female officer, the black woman. Loathed them because, like a cracked mirror, they showed her some version of herself.

She signalled Mangan on the darknet.

Be ready to move>

Now, Cliff, on the other hand – she could get used to him.

Mangan lay on the bed, smoking.

Another tap at the door.

'What is it?' said Mangan.

'Mister,' said the boy.

He walked to the door, listened.

'*Kai men.*' Open the door, said the Clown, quietly.

In the villa Patterson waited. No response came from Mangan. Mac paced and sighed, shook his head. Cliff lounged on a sofa reading a book.

At one in the morning, Patterson stood up.

'All right, let's go. Let's just go and see.'

They took the Toyota, Cliff driving. Less than fifteen minutes and they were approaching the *soi*. Cliff stayed with the car. Patterson and Mac tapped at the gate of the Banyan guest house. No response. She rapped. The slap of footsteps on paving, the scrape of the bolt. The gate opened a few inches to reveal a sleepy-eyed boy in a T-shirt.

Patterson smiled winningly.

'Hello there. So sorry to wake you up. One of your guests. Tall man. Red hair. We need to see him. It's rather urgent. Sorry.'

She could feel Mac straining at her shoulder, wanting, she guessed, to kick the gate open and put the boy in a stress position.

The boy frowned.

'English? Guest?'

'Yes. Very tall.' Patterson put her hand above her head, moved it up and down to indicate height.

The boy nodded.

'Yes. He go.' He gestured leaving, gone.

'Gone? When was that?'

'Maybe . . . eight. Nine. He go.'

From Mac a whispered *Jesus Christ*.

'And where did he go?' she said.

'He say go away, maybe come back two . . . three day.'

'Did he say where?' Patterson's face a rictus now, Mac shifting on his feet.

The boy shook his head.

'Was there anyone with him?'

The boy nodded. 'One man, with him. Chinese man.' The boy made to close the gate.

'Wait,' said Patterson. 'How did he look? Did he want to go with this man?'

The boy looked confused.

'Did he . . . did he look angry? Like it was a problem?' She gestured to her face.

The boy shook his head.

'No. No. He look okay. No problem.' He closed the door.

Mac looked at her, made a contemptuous snorting sound. She turned and walked quickly back to the car. She sat in the front seat, took out the laptop and activated the satellite link. The pulsing red orb on the map showed Mangan, or his phone at least, three hours or so north of Chiang Mai, heading towards the Mekong River.

I'm to force him back into the breach, and he's already gone charging off by himself.

The Clown had begun to hustle him out of the room.

'We have to go now, Mr Mangan.'

Mangan attempted to stand his ground.

'Tell me why, and where.'

'He needs to see you. We have to go fast.'

'Why the urgency?'

The Clown went to the window, looked out. Mangan shook his head.

'How about we drop the drama. Why do we have to move fast?'

The Clown looked at him, the rubber face, eyes like lead.

'You saw. They are here. Looking for us. Events, Mr Mangan. Events have caused us to speed up our plans. So we move. And so do you, now.'

'Who is they?'

'He will explain everything. We have to go.'

'Where?'

'A safe place. Our place.'

'I cannot. Do you understand? I have orders to stay here.'

The Clown sighed. Made a regretful face.

'Mr Mangan. You know a lot. You know my meaning? Too much maybe. You here ... it is dangerous for us. If they find you.'

He held out his hands, supplicatory.

'So. Really. You are coming now. He will explain everything. He has very much to tell you. Lots of valuable things. So come.' The Clown's expression had hardened. 'Now.'

'Let me signal my ... people.'

'No time. Now. You bring your computer, phone. Later you talk to them.'

Mangan considered. He picked up his run bag, went to the bathroom, closed and locked the door. He stood on the toilet seat and reached into the cistern, pulled out the dripping bags. He took one passport, some of the money. The pistol he stuck in his waistband, the spare clip went in the bag.

When he emerged, the Clown was standing, impatient, by the door. Mangan packed the computer in the run bag. Phone on? Or off? He thought for a moment. Phone on.

'How long are we going for?' he said

'Not long. A day, maybe two days,' said the Clown.

They went down the stairs. The boy was in reception watching television, K-pop music videos.

'I'll be back in a couple of days,' said Mangan. The boy nodded.

They roared out of the city, heading north, the Clown apparently caring nothing for their silhouette, not even a glimpse over his shoulder. There'd be chase cars, Mangan assumed. They were silent and he watched the deepening night over the forests, the glistening lights through the trees, the insects in the headlights. After two hours they stopped. The Clown got out and made a phone call, spoke fast and urgently. Mangan stood by the car, stiff, his ribs aching. He tried to stretch, and lit a cigarette, felt the moist heat on his skin. Later, as they skirted Chiang Rai, Mangan broke the silence in Mandarin.

'Will you tell me where we are going?'

'Somewhere we control. To be safe.'

'You need to tell me where the threat is coming from.'

The Clown said nothing for a moment.

'They are people who want to stop us. To stop change. Kill us, maybe.'

'Why? Why do they want to stop you?'

'Because they ... they fear we will take everything from them.'

'Are they right?'

'Probably.'

'Who are they? What do they want?'

The Clown smiled.

'Everything. They want everything. They want to buy everything. Own everything. Eat everything. Fuck everything.'

Mangan shook his head.

'I don't understand. This is who? Is it the Communist Party? People in the Party? A faction? Who do you mean?'

'We tend to think,' said the Clown, 'we tend to think these words – *Party*, *faction* – don't mean much any more. These are just ... empty shells. What we see are systems, structures, networks.'

'So we're talking about a network. In China.'

'Oh, it goes far beyond China.' He lifted a hand from the steering wheel, waved away Mangan's naivety. 'Far beyond.'

The Clown sighed, shifted in his seat.

'That's why you're here,' he said.

They turned off the highway, onto an unmarked road snaking through fields, silent villages under a pale moon.

61

Cliff drove them back to the safe house, Mac in the back seat pointedly silent, arms folded. Patterson sat in the front, composing a telegram on the handheld.

The date. A reference number.

CX WEAVER

TO LONDON

TO C/WFE

TO TCI/64335

TO P/C/62815

FILE REF R/84459

FILE REF SB/38972

LEDGER UK S E C R E T

PRIORITY

/REPORT

1/ WEAVER personnel went to BRAMBLE's last known location, a guest house. BRAMBLE was not there. The staff said he had left at approximately 20.00 local/14.00 ZULU, and would be gone two to three days. BRAMBLE's destination was unknown.

2/ Trace revealed that BRAMBLE's mobile phone was approximately 130 miles to the north-east, and was continuing to move in that direction.

3/ Staff at the guest house said that BRAMBLE left in the company of a Chinese man, and indicated BRAMBLE left the guest house willingly.

4/ Grateful for confirmatory traces on BRAMBLE's position, instructions.

//END

She sat in silence, furious with herself.

'We can go after him,' said Cliff. 'We're still in contact with him. It's okay.'

From the back seat, another snort.

'Something to say there, Mac?' said Cliff.

'Just that, next time, maybe, we should get the agent's location—' Cliff cut him off.

'Yes, I think we all realise that, thanks. We'll do better next time, eh?'

Silence from the back seat.

'We could just call him,' said Cliff.

'Don't be ridiculous,' she said.

She glanced across at him, but he was looking straight ahead into the darkness.

They arrived at the Mekong River. Mangan stood on the bank. A quarter of a mile away, across the sluggish, black water was Laos. He tried to let his eyes adjust to the darkness, shielded them from the lights of the town with one hand. Chiang Saen had been an opium town, but now the money was in tourists lumbering along on elephants, stewing in spas, while the heroin and the little pills came down the river from Myanmar. He put his hand beneath his shirt and ran it over the sidearm.

The Clown was standing at the water's edge on a wooden jetty, looking both ways, as if about to cross. Then he held up what looked to be a torch, but no light came from it. Across the water, from the north, the low grumble of an engine. The Clown was tilting the lightless torch up and down.

The boat was low and fast, a shallow draft to it. It was painted some dun colour, had the look of a patrol boat, but Mangan could see no markings. The boat, its bow wave a white flicker in the dark, came scudding in, suddenly slowed and slid onto the jetty.

Mangan took a deep breath, smelled the diesel over the river's oily, mulchy stink. The Clown was gesturing to him, and, from the side of the craft, a crewman was holding out a hand.

Another step. Into what?

He looked around, heard the sound of the car they'd come in being driven away.

The Clown was aboard already, hissing at him.

'Come on, Mr Mangan, we must go now.'

He hefted the run bag, touched the sidearm one more time, put one foot over the side and felt himself pulled aboard, chivvied below. The crewman showed him into a cabin with beds recessed into the sides. Mangan dropped his bag, lay down, tried to slow his mind down, collect himself. He thought of Patterson, thought of the flinty look she'd give him, the starchy admonishment coming his way. Should he call her? Too much of a risk? Probably, in this hyper-surveilled environment. Steal a phone? Now, *there's* a thought.

The pitch of the engines rose and the boat leaned away from the jetty, into the current.

Towards China.

He slept for hours, to his surprise. When he woke it was light. He put his head out of the cabin. The boat was ploughing forward in a fine rain, pitching in the river's chop. On the right bank, distant through the damp mist, Laos. On the left, closer, Myanmar. Ahead, China. He climbed to the cabin above, where the Clown stood next to a helmsman and another man who was looking through binoculars, the captain, Mangan assumed. The Clown turned, saw Mangan and, irritated, brought him quickly inside the cabin.

'You must stay out of sight. Please,' he said.

The captain lowered the binoculars, studied Mangan, then returned to scanning the river.

'Now, please, you can tell me where we're headed,' said Mangan, trying to sound brisk, businesslike.

'Another twelve hours or so,' said the Clown. 'By evening we'll be there.'

'You're taking me back into China.'

'Not exactly.'

'What do you mean, not exactly?' Mangan allowed his voice to rise a little. 'It's either China or Myanmar. There are no other bloody countries I'm aware of up this river. So which one is it?'

'Well, as I said to you, we tend not to think too much in those terms. So we are going to a place which is sort of ... between places.' He faced Mangan. 'I understand this is frustrating for you. But please be patient. You are quite safe. I give you my word.'

His eyes flickered down to Mangan's waist.

'And you are armed for your own protection. And that's fine. Just please do not use the weapon, Mr Mangan. This would be a very unfortunate outcome.'

He smiled.

'*Hao ma?*' Okay?

Mangan said nothing.

'Now, please, Mr Mangan, how about some breakfast?'

They fed him the thick, rich rice porridge with shredded pork and spring onions, instant coffee. He ate it seated in a tiny galley, a crewman looking on. When he'd finished, the crewman offered him a cigarette, which he took. The crewman lit it for him and he inhaled deeply, felt the hot bite of it in his chest.

'So,' said Mangan, 'spend a lot of time smuggling people up and down the Mekong, do we?'

But the crewman just smiled.

The rain slackened off in the afternoon, then stopped, and with a tremulous sun the temperature rose sharply. Through the porthole, Mangan saw steam rising off the forest on the bank. Visibility had improved and they were moving much faster now, the boat's bow up. He lay in the cabin, teetering between boredom and anxiety. They were, he realised, trying hard to make him feel as if he were not a captive. And in the Clown's tone of voice, beneath the obliqueness, Mangan discerned anticipation, the sense of a plan progressing. He was, quite clearly, part of an operation now. Someone else's.

At around six in the evening, the boat suddenly reduced speed, then hove to. The engine noise lessened to a low rumble and Mangan heard a loudspeaker across the water. They were being hailed. A crewman appeared in the cabin, gesturing urgently. Mangan picked up his run bag and followed the crewman forward through the galley into a dark storage compartment. Another engine, now, this one higher-pitched, pulling alongside. The crewman was running his hands along the bulkhead, looking for something. Then a *snick*, and the bulkhead came away to reveal a narrow space, eighteen inches or so deep, insulated with rubber matting. The crewman pushed Mangan in, gestured for him to lie down, on his side. Mangan eased himself down, and then the bulkhead was back in place and he was in a sweltering, stinking darkness. The rubber matting was saturated. He felt the water soaking into his clothes.

Footsteps on the deck above. Muffled shouts.

He could barely breathe, the air thick with rubber, mould, the stench of the river.

Footsteps closer, now. In the galley, perhaps. Entering the storage compartment. Rapid-fire Mandarin, an officious tone. And a second quieter voice, explanatory. A patrol? Customs? Then more movement, and silence.

Minutes passed. Mangan felt sick. The roll of the boat, the stench, the heat. His ribs pulsed with pain. He tried to breathe, but the nausea grew and he felt the prickle of sweat. He tried not to but he threw up, soiled his shirt, retched.

Interminable, there, in the dark and the filth. He closed his eyes, let his mind wander. He thought about Maja, standing in the mauve evening light, looking over the thatched huts, the wood smoke. He thought of her questioning of him, her immediate knowledge of the lie in him, its carving away of the truth like the current carves a riverbank, leaving only warped fragments, oxbows on a plain.

And he thought of Maja's dismissal of him. Of her turning away. *Why do I allow this to go on? What need in me does it fulfil?*

And then the panel was unlatched and pulled away and the crewmen pulled him out, recoiling at him, the stench of him.

He stripped and washed from a bucket, and they loaned him some coveralls. He rinsed out his foul shirt, laid it on the deck to dry. He lay in the cabin, trembling. They brought him food, a bowl of rice loaded with *mapo* bean curd. Mangan felt his senses strangely heightened, watched the startling reds and ambers of the sauce bleed into the white rice, smelled the oil and peppercorns rising from it.

Darkness came on, and the boat moved upriver, towards China.

Not long, now.

They docked at midnight. Mangan changed out of the coveralls, emerged from the cabin with the run bag, the sidearm at the base of his back, loaded. The weapon gave him comfort, a sense that he retained some measure of autonomy.

The night was close and hot, filled with the hiss and chatter of insects. The Clown stood on the dock with two heavies in polo shirts and khakis. One of the heavies held a machine pistol, covering the boat, his eyes following Mangan as he clambered over the side.

Beyond the dock, Mangan saw palm trees, lawns crisscrossed by torch-lit, gravelled paths leading to a sprawling complex of buildings in pale brick. The buildings were lit, blindingly bright, rearing up into the night out of the trees. Atop them, a faux temple roof, fringed with neon. Some sort of resort?

The Clown motioned to him and they walked, one heavy in front, one behind, their footsteps crunching on the gravel. The path wound across the lawn, up some steps, to a reception area of teak and marble, flickering candles, frangipani spilling down the walls. The staff were suited in impeccable cream uniforms with high collars in the manner of hotel porters. They smiled, made little bowing motions. Mangan saw the cameras, high up in corners, heard the crackle of a walkie-talkie. The two heavies handed him off to three more, all in their cream suits, buttoned to the collar. Nothing was said. They walked a corridor, glassed on one side to provide a view of ornamental gardens, pools. The Clown followed.

Situational awareness, Philip, at all times.

Mangan, every sense strung taut, tried to map the place in his mind, retaining the position of the dock relative to where he was, where the river was.

If I have to run, I run this way.

They took a lift. One of the suited staff held the door open, murmured, '*Qing.*' Please. So – Chinese.

The lift doors opened and Mangan was led out into a dim, cavernous space.

A casino floor.

A vast, murmuring, low-lit casino floor.

Two of the cream-suited minders, compact, controlled men, moved in close to him, almost crowding him as they walked, as if ready for him to make a move. Mangan slowed deliberately, trying to take the scene in.

The casino was suffused with blue light. Prominent at its centre was a roulette table of rich polished wood. Mangan heard the *clack clack* as the wheel span. To one side, a row of perhaps fifty or sixty screens for digital poker, the players washed in their glow. Mangan saw blackjack and baccarat tables. The players were young women dressed in black, with numbers fixed to their uniforms. The women wore headsets, earphones, little tubular cameras. They swivelled their heads robotically, fixing their cameras on the cards, on the croupier or another player, laid their cards down slowly, carefully. And all, Mangan realised, at the remote command of some distant player in Beijing or Changsha or Wuhan.

And the visible clientele? Mangan made out Chinese kids, Shanghai hip, in quiet, nervous groups. Older Chinese men in poor suits, the maker's label still on the left cuff, cadres from central China haemorrhaging someone else's cash. Here, some Russians in sportswear and gold, sour-faced, dismissive, their Italian girls in couture frocks hanging on their arms, sullen. Willowy girls in cream *cheongsam* split to the thigh toted trays of martinis, iced bottles of vodka. And at the far end of the floor, on a low stage, to a subdued beat, two naked European girls performed a sex show, writhing and quivering in the half-light. As he walked past them, Mangan saw the gooseflesh on their thighs from the air conditioning's chill.

They walked on, left the casino floor, entered a cavernous split-level marble lobby, a hissing, bubbling fountain at its centre – to beat the listening devices, Mangan thought. He smelled cigar smoke. Men lounged on sofas of cream leather, staring at tablets, laptops, whispering into mobile phones.

Another lift. One of the cream-suited minders punched in a security code. They went up three floors and the doors opened into a suite.

'Here we are,' said the Clown.

And there he was, standing by the window, arms wide in welcome. He wore a grey suit and a white shirt open at the collar.

'Philip,' Rocky said, walking across the room to greet him. 'Sorry for all this, this trouble for you.'

'Rocky,' he said.

'Come. Come and sit down.'

He took Mangan by the arm and walked him to a sofa. His grip was hard, pulsing with tension. Mangan looked at him. His eyes were bright, feverish, his face moist, shiny. Two of the cream suits were by the lift door. The Clown stood behind him, slightly off to the side.

'Come,' he said. 'Oh, and sorry for this also, but ...' and he gestured to the Clown, who came at Mangan quickly as Rocky gripped his arm, reached behind him and took the weapon from his waistband.

Mangan felt panic seeding in his gut.

'I'm sorry,' said Rocky, again. The Clown took the clip from the weapon and worked the slide. He walked across the room and disappeared through a door.

'You need to tell me what is happening, now, Rocky,' Mangan said.

'Yes. Yes, absolutely.' He walked to a veneered drinks cabinet, opened it, ran his finger across the bottles, chose Black Label. He poured two shots, dropped ice into the glasses, walked back to the sofa. He took out a packet of cigarettes, dropped them in front of Mangan.

'You like our place?' he said.

'This place? Do I like it? Well, no, not really. Where are we, Rocky? I mean, what fucking country are we in?'

Rocky grinned his over-extended grin, his eyes skittish, febrile.

'This is our safe place. We call it a special economic zone!' *Hilarious!*

'Are we in China?'

'Physically, no. We are in a different place. We have many guests. You see them? They come here, they stay awhile. Nice rooms, nice food, girls. There's a golf course. They get some privacy, do some business. It's a place where our people can meet and be secure. And we'd like you to stay for a time.'

'I'm not staying a minute longer than I have to.'

'There is something you need to do. For us. And when it is done, then you can go.'

'I suppose I have to ask what.'

'That would be best.'

359

'Well?'

Rocky sipped his whisky, the left knee jigging, the tremor in the hand.

They're all here tonight, aren't they? All the symptoms. It's crunch time.

'We have,' Rocky said, 'certain requirements.'

'And what requirements would those be?'

'Intelligence requirements. And you must help us satisfy them.'

Mangan wondered, again, if he was in the presence of madness.

'And how am I going to do that?'

'You will contact your Service, you will talk to them, reasonably, and they will supply us with what we need. And all this will happen very fast.'

The tongue flicked across the lips.

You leak fear like a weeping faucet.

Mangan swallowed.

'What are you doing, Rocky? Am I a captive here?'

The Clown came back into the room and leaned against the window sill.

'No, Philip, no! We just need you here while this business is finished.' Rocky was breathing hard, the leg going up-down, hands clutching at the sofa's upholstery.

Mangan stood. Tried to breathe, felt his knees shaky. He picked up the run bag.

'No!' Rocky yelled. He rushed across the room and planted himself in front of Mangan, grabbing a fistful of Mangan's shirt and shaking it as if to bring the journalist to his senses. And then he was reaching under his jacket and pulling out a black pistol, and some part of Mangan's brain was recognising it as a PPK, and Rocky was shouting in Mangan's face in Mandarin, *Sit, sit, now, Philip, please*, and Mangan smelled his foul breath, its load of alcohol and cigarettes and fear, and the black pistol was being rammed into his forehead and he felt the cold metal against his clammy skin and was teetering backwards and falling onto the sofa, where he lay, still, rigid, ribs flaring with pain, Rocky leaning over him grinding the pistol down into his head.

'You do not leave,' Rocky hissed. Mangan saw the flecks of white spittle at the corners of his mouth. He lay still and didn't resist. Out of the corner of his eye, he saw the Clown pick up the run bag and leave the room again, and the two cream-suited heavies standing close by.

Silence for a moment.

Then Rocky stood back, levelled the pistol at Mangan's face. Mangan felt his limbs rising involuntarily, pawing the air as if to stop what was coming. He tried to speak but couldn't. Rocky was shouting again, gesturing with the weapon, raising it and flicking it downward like a wand, as if he were casting a spell. One of the cream suits was standing over Mangan now, and was rolling him onto his front, and Mangan felt his hands grabbed and forced against his back and a thin plastic cuff slipped over them and a crisp *zip* sound, and then he was rolled onto his back again and he lay there, looking up at Rocky, his hysteria, the sweat pouring off him, the weapon still now, dangling at his side.

'Now,' Rocky said, breathing heavily, 'now you listen. I am running out of time. So you *listen* to me.'

Mangan, petrified, said nothing.

Rocky put the pistol down on a table, rubbed his face.

'We are a group of patriots. We are patriotic Chinese soldiers. And we are . . . we are bringing about changes. Are you listening?'

Mangan gave a tight nod. He needed to piss, he realised.

'Some parts of the Communist Party have become . . . become diseased. And we are going to cut them out. We will clean the wound.' The words came out hesitantly.

This is it, thought Mangan. Now. This is the unblinding.

'Who's in charge?' he said.

'A very great man. A general. His name is Chen. He is head of military intelligence now, and he has friends, supporters, all through the army. Really, a wonderful man. A leader! A leader who does not seek power for its own sake. He sees a future for us, for China. He knows. And right now, as we speak, he is moving. He is moving against those who have insulted us, have insulted and degraded China.'

Script's deteriorating, thought Mangan.

'You are launching a military coup,' he said.

Rocky's face creased, and Mangan, for a split second, thought he might cry.

'*No!* This is *not* a coup.'

He closed his eyes for a second. 'This is a purge. This is a purge of a few, to warn the many.'

Mangan swallowed, spoke slowly, feeling the tremor in his voice.

'If you launch a coup – no, sorry, *a purge*, in China, Rocky, do you . . . do you understand what the consequences will be?'

'*Yes!* The consequences will be *good*! We will rectify China. No more corruption. No more disease.' Mangan shifted on the sofa, tried to loosen the cuff, let the words tumble out.

'You . . . you'll screw everything up. No one does coups. You'll be ridiculous. China will look like some unstable basket case. Remember Moscow? Nineteen ninety-one? Whenever it was? The coup? Those frightened old men, sweating under the lights, trying to explain, while the entire world howled with laughter at them. That'll be you. For fuck's sake, Rocky.'

Rocky turned and walked to the window.

'You have no idea what he is, what he can do.'

Not the faintest, Rocky. Not a clue.

And then the Clown had taken him by the arm, was hauling him to his feet, walking him across the room, shoving him towards a door, pushing him down a corridor. Mangan glimpsed vast bedrooms, a bathroom suite with a hot tub. At the end of the corridor, a door marked 'Fire Exit'. The Clown opened it and pushed him into a concrete stairwell.

'*Shangqu*,' he said. Go up.

Mangan climbed.

Two floors up, the Clown shoved him out onto a landing. No bedrooms here, no silk upholstery, just grey breeze-blocks, naked light bulbs surrounded by mesh of the sort used on a building site, their drooping cables.

The entire floor had been crudely divided, Mangan realised, into cells.

62

Patterson, tense as a steel wire, hunched over her laptop in the villa in the darkness, waiting for orders. Only caustic queries from Hopko:

```
CX LONDON
TO: CX WEAVER
REPORT\
1/ RELAY ALL INFORMATION REGARDING POSITION/CIRCUMSTANCES
BRAMBLE/HYPNOTIST IMMEDIATELY
2/ AWAIT INSTRUCTION
END/
```

Nothing from Mangan. She had left him five messages on the dark-net site, ordering him to check in.

The little red orb on the screen had progressed north following the Mekong, dropping out at times, then rested for a matter of hours at a point exactly on the China-Myanmar border, then disappeared. The battery in his handheld was dead, she assumed. Hoped.

Her alarm had not yet spread to London. But it wouldn't be long now.

Mac prowled around downstairs, muttering. Cliff was asleep.

The Clown propelled Mangan across the concrete floor, the cells on either side.

'I need a bathroom,' he said.

'What?'

'A bathroom.'

The Clown turned him round and looked at him, his face entirely blank, then clapped one tensile hand on Mangan's throat, propelled him backwards into a wall, ramming Mangan's head against the breeze-block. Pulled him away from the wall, rammed him into it again, then leaned in, pressing on Mangan's throat. Mangan could feel the pressure deep in his head, in his eyes, imagined capillaries bursting, leaking.

Then, without a word, the Clown let go, pulled Mangan away from the wall, thrust him into one of the cells, slammed the plywood door, bolted it from the outside.

Mangan stood there, hands cuffed behind him, shaking, head pulsing. He looked around. The cell was empty, the floor filthy with construction debris, dust. High up, a sliver of a window.

After loneliness, fear. And, layered on top, for good measure, searing self-recrimination.

Am I this stupid? Did I see none of this coming? Did Patterson? The lure. The blind. And here I am.

He leaned his back against the wall and allowed himself to slide to the floor, sat there, tendrils of self-pity creeping upwards. *British secret agent unexpectedly acquires self-knowledge. Profoundly unsuited to line of work.*

Stop.

He took a breath, struggled to clear his mind.

He made himself stand, shaky, blood sugar low, mouth like leather, bladder distended and painful.

I will not piss myself, he thought.

He walked to the door, kicked it. It vibrated in the frame, but didn't give.

He sat again on the floor of the cell, then lay on his back, brought his cuffed hands around his feet, so they were in front of him. He reached up, felt the back of his head. The hair was matted. Blood?

He bit at the plastic cuff, gnawed on it. Nothing. Far too hard.

They need me, he thought. Or they think they need me. I am a part of their mission. What leverage is in there?

He lay on his side, pillowed his head on his arms, tried to think.

The bolt on the door was being worked. He jerked upright. The door opened. The Clown walked in, carrying two plastic chairs, Rocky just behind him. Rocky looked exhausted, his face sallow and drawn, the grin long gone. The Clown put the chairs down, went and stood by the door. He had the run bag on his back, Mangan noticed.

'Sit, Philip,' said Rocky.

'I'm not bloody doing anything until you take me to a lavatory,' he managed.

Rocky turned, looked at the Clown, shook his head in disgust. He gestured *Go.*

Mangan stood, and the Clown took him roughly by the arms again and walked him past the cells to a squat lavatory, no door. Mangan pissed as the Clown watched. They went back to the cell.

A small piece of territory regained, thought Mangan.

Rocky was smoking a cigarette, gave one to him and lit it.

'So now, Philip, you will help us.' He was speaking Mandarin.

'I am to help you launch your coup.'

Rocky just shook his head.

'Not a coup. Please understand. General Chen will, what do you say, make an *example.*'

'Of who?' said Mangan.

'To start with, a member of the Politburo, and his family. His network. His protégés. His power.'

'Which one?

Rocky sighed.

'Fan Rong. The Fan family. The corporation that they control, that they run like their ... their personal whorehouse. China National Century. Come on, Philip, you know what I am talking about.'

'What sort of example?'

'We will expose them and ruin them. They will be arrested, tried and punished.'

'A trial? Whose court are you planning on using, I wonder?'

Rocky ignored the question. He looked at Mangan.

'When this happens, Philip, foreign governments will think, like you, that it is a coup, some terrible upheaval. They will go pale, get upset. Oh no, China's unstable, they will scream. And, like you say, everybody gets frightened, and that has consequences for us. Big consequences. Business men will all run away, pull their investments. Cost of borrowing goes up. Consumption drops. People pull their money from the banks. Markets fall. Everything goes to shit.'

He put his hand to his mouth, swallowed.

'We wish to prevent this. So you will warn them, Philip. You will tell them, no. This is not a coup. This is a correction. We have had big corrections before. Remember? Gang of Four? And 1989? But we are always okay. We survive. You will tell them they must understand it, welcome it, even. Nothing to fear.'

He leaned forward, put his elbows on his knees, his weird earnestness returning.

'That way, the West, Japan, Korea, everyone will understand. China is correcting itself, cutting out the corruption, cleaning the wound, so it can heal. Yes?'

He raised his hands, palms up, trembling. *You see?* 'That is the first thing. You will tell your Service that this is nothing to worry about. And your Service will tell everybody, the Americans, the Germans. And everybody will listen, and there will be no panic.'

Mangan said nothing.

Inexplicably, Rocky had broken into English.

'The second thing, Philip, the second thing is more complicated.

But you will help us. The second thing is about evidence. We need evidence.'

'No evidence? You have no evidence? You are looking for evidence *now*?'

Again, Rocky ignored him.

'You know what is a "junket", Philip? The real meaning? In China?'

Mangan frowned.

'A junket, Philip, is a company. A gambling company. The junket company say to you, you like gambling? Like casinos? Okay, let's go to Macau. The junket will buy the plane ticket, make the reservation, everything. Lots of casinos in Macau. Much bigger than Vegas, even. You can gamble there till you are broke or dead.'

He raised a warning finger.

'But there's a problem. For Chinese, you can only take a few thousand dollars out of mainland China. Any more, not allowed. Not enough to gamble in Macau! So, the junket says, no problem. You deposit your money with us, in China, maybe a hundred thousand, maybe a million, ten million. Then you go to Macau and you can draw on your account. Like a bank. You deposit one million in China, we'll give you one million to gamble with in Macau, less commission. All very legal. So legal you are surprised, yes? That is one way to move money out of China. A good way.

'So, the Fan family. Number one daughter Charlotte Fan. You know? The oil-well woman? I told you about her, yes? She likes Macau, goes all the time. She gambles *a lot*! Plays VIP baccarat.'

Rocky frowned now, looked disapproving.

'That is a very dangerous game. You play against the house. Big stakes. Private room. Only the cameras can see how much you bet. Charlotte Fan, she goes to one casino. Always the same. Drives up in her pink Porsche, tips the valet a hundred dollar. A really disgusting car, believe me. Then she goes to the VIP room for baccarat.'

He was lighting a cigarette.

'And she loses! Always, she loses. We are told this. She loses maybe two hundred thousand, three hundred thousand sometimes. But she comes out, gets in her whore car and drives away. Next night, still she goes back, plays more, loses. The casino just take her money, like candy from a baby.'

'Now, and you must listen here, Philip. The casino has need of certain services. It needs consulting services. Consulting on what, do you think?'

He had his wide-eyed look on. *What could it be? Mark my innocence.*

'The casino needs advising on its information systems, yes. And on security. And on forecasting. And finance, yes, lots of finance consulting. So, the casino hires a consulting company. Several consulting companies, in fact. Pay a lot of money for this confidential consulting. A lot! This is what the General has found out. And the consulting companies, they are based mainly in Hong Kong. And who owns them, do you think?'

He looked expectantly at Mangan.

'Hm?'

Mangan shook his head.

'Well, these consulting companies, they are owned by other companies, shell companies. Not real, just one address, some phony director. These shell companies, well, some are based in Jersey. You know Jersey? Yes, of course. And one is based in the British Virgin Islands. And one is based in Cayman Islands. And one is based . . . in London! Yes. London!'

He dragged on the cigarette, exhaled.

'Now, we try very hard to find out who owns these shell companies. Really we try. But, you know, your country makes it very hard to find out. We go to Jersey, we try to look up who owns this company. Well, it's just another company! Maybe in Gibraltar, or in Cook Islands. Or some place. We go to the British Virgin Islands. We send good people. They ask, who own this company? No answer. Nothing. Really, British are very secret. More secret than Chinese.

'But the one in London, we find out something. We find out that

Charlotte Fan is listed as Director. Charlotte Fan. Yes. Charlotte Fan is director of the company which owns the company which owns the company which consults for casino where Charlotte Fan loses all her money. How about that?'

Mangan shook his head. Rocky looked exasperated.

'She is moving money out of China. Millions. Money they steal from China National Century. Or money they get in corrupt deals, like the oil wells. It's China's money. *It's not her money*. You understand this? She washes it in the casino. The casino take a cut. Then gives the money back to Charlotte Fan by hiring her phony consulting companies. The money is all clean now, so clean. All sparkly. So she puts it in these shell companies, a bit here, a bit there. All offshore, no tax. Very secret. And suddenly the Fans are living in a big apartment in London. Very fancy. Servants, everything. And all that money . . .'

He made a strange effeminate gesture, wiggling his fingertips in the air.

'*Pfff*. It just disappeared. Gone. So many companies, so many secret places. Turks and Caicos. Isle of Man. You never find it. But the Fans know where it is. Only them.'

He thought for a moment.

'Well, one other man, in Hong Kong. We try to talk to him, but he killed himself.'

He put his index finger to his lips, an overwrought parody of thoughtfulness. Spying as performance art, thought Mangan. Agent as artiste of camp.

'Funny thing. All these secret places, well, nearly all – they are British! Yes! They belong to Britain. What are they called? *Crown Dependencies*. Yes. *UK Overseas Territories*. Such glorious names, like full of tradition or something. Very ancient. Imperial flags and uniforms and the Queen, everything. To an ignorant Chinese soldier like me, they sound very important, very . . . intimidating.' He got up, came and stood over Mangan, smiling, ingratiating.

'Britain . . .'

He looked up, as if searching for the words.

'Britain is like ... what do you say ... an *accomplice*.'

He blinked and looked Mangan in the eye.

'So we thought, Philip, you can say to your Service: find out for us, please, where all this money has gone. Just tell us. We need *evidence*. We need to show the Chinese people. We need to show the court. Just tell us. UK Secret Intelligence Service! Of course they can find out fast. Then they tell us. Bank accounts, amounts. Where it is. How much.'

He turned away.

'Then once they tell us, you can go.'

Mangan closed his eyes.

'Sound good?'

Sounds deranged, Rocky. Sounds twenty-four-carat bloody barking.

'So you are holding me hostage,' he said, letting his voice rise. 'You little shit.'

Rocky held his hands up in a feeble protest, but the Clown was moving across the cell fast. He walked around behind Mangan's chair. Rocky's expression turned sorrowful. And then Mangan's head exploded in pain, white particles spinning in his eyes, his neck jarred and wracked.

Then a voice in his ear, the Clown's.

'Let us concentrate on the issue at hand, shall we? Or I will hit you again. And again.'

Rocky was wearing his best distraught expression.

'We just need you to stay for a while. We find out this very important information, where the Fan money is, evidence of all their corruptness, and we can show all China the evidence. Then we shoot them. Then we all go home.'

The Clown dropped the run bag at his feet, felt in his pocket, pulled out a clasp knife. He leaned over Mangan, opened the blade, brought it down just a shade closer to Mangan's face than it needed to be, cut the cuff off him. Mangan's hands were swollen, a dark, unhealthy colour. He reached into the run bag, pulled out the laptop.

'There's a wireless connection. Very good, very fast,' said Rocky.

Mangan opened the computer, balancing it on his knees, his eyes streaming, nose running, and booted it up.

Rocky reached inside his jacket, brought out three sheets of paper, which he unfolded and handed to Mangan. On them, a list of corporate titles and addresses.

PLBC Holdings Ltd
    Purlaw Legal Services, PO Box 7710
    Georgetown, Grand Cayman

Yung Chee Lucky Yield Investment Associates Ltd
    PO Box 7940, Bermuda

Thirty or forty such addresses. And names. Lawyers, accountants, nominee directors.

'You let me see before you push Send,' said Rocky absently. 'Oh, and tell them one more thing. To show we are serious, they should watch Charlotte Fan. In London. Today. And the boy. In Oxford. Fan Kaikai.'

The date. A reference number.

CX BRAMBLE

TO: CX WEAVER

TO: C/WFE

LEDGER UK T O P S E C R E T

URGENT

/REPORT

1/ BRAMBLE is being held at an unidentified location. HYPNOTIST and associates have insisted he remain until certain requirements are satisfied.

2/ HYPNOTIST relayed to BRAMBLE the outline of a plan to move against corrupt members of the Chinese Communist Party leadership. HYPNOTIST says the plan will be implemented by a group based in the People's Liberation Army, led by 'General CHEN, head of military intelligence'. Politburo member FAN RONG will be arrested, tried and executed. FAN RONG's family, including the leadership of China National Century Corporation, will also be brought down. Implementation of the plan is imminent, starting with the arrest of FAN RONG.

3/ HYPNOTIST demands UK agencies provide advance warning to 'Western governments' of the plan in order to reassure them of China's underlying stability. HYPNOTIST insists that the plan does not constitute 'a military coup', and should be thought of as 'a purge'. He insists the aim of the plan is not to replace the Party. He maintains that the plan will serve to reduce the culture of impunity among China's elites and draw them closer to normative behaviour, thus underpinning Chinese stability, not undermining it.

'Yes. All correct. Good,' said Rocky.

4/ HYPNOTIST has further demands. He requires UK agencies to furnish him with information regarding the disposition of funds secreted out of China by the FAN family and distributed among holding companies and trusts in UK-administered jurisdictions, including Jersey, the Cayman Islands, the British Virgin Islands and the UK itself. HYPNOTIST believes this information constitutes evidence against the FAN family and will justify their arrest in the eyes of the Chinese public. HYPNOTIST accuses the UK of complicity in the crimes of China's corrupt elites through its administration of jurisdictions designed for secrecy, tax avoidance and money laundering.

'Yes! Philip, that is very good. That is exactly what I mean.'

5/ HYPNOTIST says that proof of the seriousness of his endeavour will come 'today'. He insists that we should 'watch

373

CHARLOTTE FAN' at her address in London, and FAN KAIKAI at his residence in Oxford.

'Good, good,' said Rocky.

6/ Attached as appendix is a list of names and business addresses, supplied by HYPNOTIST, thought to be associated with the FANS and their financial concerns.
7/ HYPNOTIST insists that only when this information is made available will BRAMBLE be free to leave.
END\\

Laboriously, he copied out the list of names and addresses, put them in the appendix. Rocky nodded. Mangan dropped the document, encrypted, on the darknet site.

They cuffed him again, and left.

The Clown came back with a plate of food which looked as if it had been arbitrarily assembled from a hotel buffet. Slices of prime rib, sickly salad, grilled shrimp, some cold dumplings, slices of cheese. He dropped the plate on the floor, spilling the food into the dust and grit.

63

Patterson saw Mangan's message almost as soon as it dropped, the computer alert waking her from a subterranean sleep just after 4 a.m.

She had seen many versions of the crazed midnight telegram, an agent in a bad place, imagining footsteps outside, terror dictating their demands. She'd watched operations sink, and the Service's deft pulling away, scattering plausible denials in its wake while the *joe* drifted into the dark.

But never had she seen anything quite like this.

A *purge*?

She read it again, trying to break it down into its component parts, to prioritise. An agent held hostage. A demand for intelligence. A rupture in the delicate skein of power that held China together.

Military units, moving against the Fan family and its interests, and against the Communist Party, too.

Patterson imagined soldiers rattling along the grey brick *hutongs* of Beijing, smashing down the big red steel doors to beautiful court-yard mansions, dragging out the Fans, their retainers, allies, bankers, nieces, nephews, fixers, goons. Squirrelling them off to God knows where. Some military base? Safe houses? Barrelling through the offices of China National Century up there on the Third Ring Road in the ghastly silvered tumescence that was its corporate headquarters, breaking into the safes, the networks.

How on earth did they think they were going to do this?

Who did they have in Beijing, General Chen, Colonel Shi and their feverish little band of plotters? Did they have military? Elements of 2PLA? How the hell did they think they would get around the Ministry of State Security? The People's Armed Police? The Capital Garrison, its two divisions right outside town?

And watch Charlotte Fan in London and Fan Kaikai in Oxford? Why? What were they going to do on UK soil?

Why on earth did they think Britain would help?

Because if we don't, they will kill our agent.

She sat still for a moment, tried to rein in her thoughts, but nothing occurred to her that matched the enormity of what she saw.

What is my part in this? What are my lines now?

She began to pack, then abruptly stopped and sat back down to look at the telegram again. The only other addressee was Hopko. Mangan was keeping it close. It was 10 p.m. in London.

It was light by the time her secure handheld buzzed, birdsong coming in through the window. It was Hopko.

'You've seen it?' she said.

'Yes,' Patterson said.

'Secure video conference, twenty minutes.'

She spun up the sat phone, logged in to London on a scratchy secure feed, the signal squelching and pixellating. Arrayed across the screen were the sleep-slapped faces of Chapman-Biggs and Mobbs, the Director, Requirements and Production. Hopko looked calm and serious, dressed as if she had arrived straight from the opera, her hair teased up, a dress of midnight blue silk, her tanned, stocky shoulders, a necklace of silver in beautiful, beaten ingots.

'So sorry to have dragged you all here,' she said. 'But we do seem to be at a rather significant moment.' She looked straight at the camera, went on. 'If HYPNOTIST is to be believed, and his reassurances notwithstanding, we find ourselves in a place one could best describe as perilous, and I submit we *should* send this intelligence up to Cabinet and we *should* alert our partners.'

'Do we believe him?' This from Mobbs, a sour tone to it.

'We find him credible,' said Hopko.

A pause. The Director spoke, deadpan.

'What are you telling me?'

'I am telling you,' said Hopko, 'that the deal between the soldiers and the Party which has kept the world's largest country afloat for sixty years and more appears to be coming apart.'

She left a beat for effect.

'Chairman Mao decreed that power grows out of the barrel of a gun, and the Party commands the gun, and the gun must never command the Party. Well, these clever chaps at 2PLA appear to envisage a new arrangement.'

Chapman-Biggs cleared his throat, spoke.

'And there is the matter of the UK's role as a repository of certain funds which may prove problematic in the way it is perceived, were this information to become public.'

Now, thought Patterson.

'And there is the matter of our agent,' she said, 'who is being held hostage in an impossible situation.' It sounded weak, childish, she knew as soon as she said it.

The Director turned his wolfish features straight to the camera.

'That,' he said, 'I'm rather afraid, is the least of our concerns at this juncture.'

It was a sparkling July mid-morning by the time they got the authorisations, flash messages to the Home Secretary, the Met, Thames Valley Police, Hopko and the Director working the secure phones. Two squad cars to the Fans' flat in Kensington and two more to the house in Regent's Park they were known to own. Two more to the Fan boy's college in Oxford. The detective inspector in charge spoke to Hopko by secure video link, and, accustomed to her foibles, reported as much detail as he could.

At Kensington the hard-eyed men in the lobby didn't want to let them in and there was some squaring off until the inspector stalked in and pulled rank. With ill-will, the hard-eyed men opened the lift, tailed them up to the apartment.

Nobody there but the housekeeper, reported the inspector. She was cowering in the kitchen and didn't appear to speak English. Nobody else. They had taken a look around and decided it was quite a place, marvelled at the huge windows of bulletproof glass, the surveillance systems everywhere, motion sensors. Panic room with its own egress system, apparently. That was locked, though, so they couldn't get in. And all this bloody awful furniture, all cream and gold and twirly, like something out of Versailles but cheap-looking.

But Regent's Park, that was different, said the inspector. One of those bloody great white Georgian places, a palace, surveillance everywhere. A Bentley in the driveway. On buzzing, a croaky voice didn't want to let them in, told them to go away at first, so a translator told it about warrants issued under Section 42 of the Regulation of Investigatory Powers Act, and after a short interval, the gate slid open and the big black front door was opened by this little old lady in chef's whites, face like a collapsed paper bag, all red-eyed, weepy. She'd been cleaning up, smashed crockery all over the floor. The house had been turned over. The old lady said she was the cook and had worked for Madame Charlotte Fan for thirteen years, and loved her for the way she looked out for the cook's family in Lewisham, and the cook made her pork and coriander dumplings and *dandan* noodles and onion pancakes and proper *rou jia bing* with tender minced pork and sesame and pickles all wrapped up in the pancake and Madame Fan always told her how much she loved it because you couldn't find proper food in London anywhere. And when gently pressed she said men had come in the early morning, and she didn't know how they'd got in, and Madame Fan had got out of bed and there'd been a big row and the men had started searching the house and smashing things up, and then they'd said they were taking Madame Fan with them and the cook was told if she said anything to anyone or talked to the police that would be the end of her and her family down in Lewisham, so she wasn't to say anything. So, really, she was afraid she couldn't tell them anything at all.

The inspector looked up, smiled. But Hopko had her eyes closed. He pushed on.

The translator was sitting with her arm around the cook, and one of the constables had brought her a glass of water, and the Service liaison officer had knelt down beside her and said she shouldn't worry, the police would make sure her family were kept safe and what, please, had happened to Madame Charlotte Fan. And the cook, face creasing and puckering, said that Madame Fan had grown very pale and then given her, the cook, a nod as if to say it's all right do what they say. And they all went out of the front door, and a big grey car drew up and they all got in and drove away. And, no, she had not seen the licence plate, even though as the car turned out of sight she realised that she should have and now was cursing herself for being so thoughtless and disloyal and stupid. And the translator said not to worry, we'll find it, and what time was it roughly and the cook said they left at about four-thirty in the morning. And a police guard was put on the house and the cook was left, weeping over the shards of early Qing vases which had been hurled to the floor as General Chen's men moved against those who had corrupted and degraded China.

'Though I must say, I wonder,' said Hopko, in her sanctum, to Chapman-Biggs, paper cups of coffee on the desk, 'if we are right to frame this as a move by the military against a Communist Party elite. Or whether we ought to see it as a sort of family feud. Is that what it is? Two bloodied old revolutionary families and their retainers duking it out?' She brought up her fists in a Queensberry rules gesture. 'They loathe each other, you know. The Fans are all metro-politan and modern and entrenched in the Party, rich as Croesus and principled as cooked spaghetti. And the Chens, all austere and nationalist and martial and convinced they're the true repository of Confucian virtue.'

She stopped and Chapman-Biggs knew better than to say anything. This was pure Hopko, the careening analytical zigzag at the last minute.

'Or is it a combination of the two?' she said. 'Are they reverting to something? To an older way of doing things, of being. Perhaps Communism *was* just a blip, after all, and clans, warlords, dynasties are reawakening, remembering how to function.

'But whatever it is,' she said, 'it's here. In the UK. And it's begun.'

The car, a silver Pajero, showed up on the cameras at 4.22 a.m. leaving Regent's Park and heading west on the Marylebone Road. Later, it turned north and entered the underground parking facility of a large residential block. Multiple vehicles left the block, rendering further tracking of the abducted Charlotte Fan difficult.

The squad cars that roared through Oxford's early morning streets and came to an overly dramatic halt outside the gates of Fan Kaikai's college were disappointed. The boy was not there.

Kai had walked as the evening turned and the dark came on. He needed movement. Movement served to calm the gnawing, impotent fury in him. He walked around the city centre, avoiding the knots of late night drinkers. He walked over the bridge and down St Clement's. At her street, he stopped, looked around. He walked quickly to the small wrought iron gate in front of her house. The windows were dark.

He opened the gate, went to the front door and listened.

He bent over and pushed open the mail slot to peer through it. He could just make make out the tiled floor in the hallway. He smelled something rich and pungent, a chemical overlay to it.

And then, from inside, a muffled movement. Someone standing, perhaps, a footfall on a carpeted floor.

He stood upright, let the mail slot snap shut, its metallic *snack* startling in the darkness. He backed away, towards the front gate.

And there, in the downstairs window, a flicker of movement, a face to the glass. Then, gone.

Kai turned and ran.

He ran back to the main road, panic driving him. The road was empty now, open and silent, the traffic lights at green. He ran up a long hill with parkland to one side, his breath roaring in his ears. He stopped, chest aching, rested against iron railings, his hand on the cold black metal. He looked back towards her street, listened to the city's low frequency night hum, and over it, the sound of a motorbike starting up, revving.

He straightened up, another bilious jolt of fear.

From her street, a bike pulled out, fast, came in his direction, accelerating hard into the turn, the back wheel giving slightly, then righting and racing through the gears.

He ran blindly on, up the hill. The bike's roar was growing in his ears. I have seconds, he thought.

He turned to the railings. They were six feet or so high, the spikes atop them blunted by layers of black paint. He hurled himself at them, grabbing hold of the spikes, dragging himself upward, feet scrabbling furiously against the railing for traction. He got one knee up, wedged between the spikes. He hauled his torso up, balanced precariously, felt the fence wobbling beneath his weight.

The bike was hurtling up the hill towards him.

Nothing for it. He toppled to the side, the spikes jabbing him in the stomach and groin, one catching his shirt. For a second he hung there, half over, stuck, and wondered if this would be how they caught him, absurd, dangling. And then the shirt ripped and he fell, hitting the grass hard with his shoulder and the side of his head. And then he was up and running into the park, into darkness, shrubs, trees. He glanced over his shoulder.

The bike had stopped by the side of the road, its engine idling. Its rider seemed to be holding a phone. And just as the thought registered, he felt his own phone vibrate in his pocket.

What?

He rounded a corner, ducked behind an oak and pressed himself against its trunk. He answered the phone.

'Where the hell are you?' It was Nicole. He struggled to comprehend what was happening.

'Is that you?' he said.

'Yes, it's me. Where are you?'

'I mean ... you're on the bike? Calling me?'

'What? What bike?'

He shook his head, tried to focus.

'I'm ... that's not you?'

'What the fuck are you talking about? Why are you not in your rooms?'

'I ... someone's chasing me, on a motorbike.'

'What? Where?'

'I ... I don't know ... I'm in a park. It's dark.'

'Oh god, what park, Kai? Tell me. I will come to you. *What park?*'

Kai took the phone away from his ear for a second, heard the motorbike revving its engine.

'It's ... it's near her house ... on the hill.'

'Listen to me. I am coming. By car. I will call you again when I am near, and I will find you.'

'What should I do?'

'Run, or hide. Do not let them take you, Kai.'

'No ... I ...'

'Kai, do *not* let them take you.'

The line went dead.

He crept out from behind the tree, looked back towards the road. The bike was still there, its headlamp on, its engine idling. But there was no one on it.

He felt as if he were reduced to childhood, to a blind, uncontrollable, infant fear. He ran, arms flailing, aware of a mewling noise escaping his mouth. Suddenly he was in open parkland, the shelter offered by the trees far behind him. He stopped, crouched in the dark. Another engine, a headlight streaking up the far side of the park.

Two of them, now? More? A new flood of panic, and he was off and running again.

To his left, more trees, and beyond them street lamps. A way out? He turned and ran for them. The darkness seemed to be full of engine noise, flickering headlamps nosing along the edges of the park, closing on him.

He made the trees. A gateway led out of the park and onto a narrow, dimly lit street, the park's vegetation spilling over into it, lending it a wooded, overgrown feel. He stopped and crouched, looking in both directions. He was breathing heavily and in his mouth the saliva had turned thick, pasty. Then, a weird moment of clarity. He took out his phone and, with a trembling finger, opened the maps application. Cheney Lane. He was on Cheney Lane.

He dialled her number.

'Where are you?'

'Cheney Lane. There. I'm . . . in the bushes.'

'Where are they?'

'They're . . . oh god . . . they're all around. They're on motorbikes. I can hear them.'

'Three minutes,' she said.

He looked up: at the far end of the wooded street was a headlamp, moving slowly towards him. He backed into the bushes, crouched, then lay flat, smelling the cool earth, the night damp. The bike was zigzagging down the street, letting the beam from its headlamp play along the verges.

He dug his fingers into the earth, held his breath.

The bike came closer. Opposite the gateway to the park, it stopped, the engine slowing. Kai could see the feet of the rider resting on the tarmac, clad in black boots. He imagined the rider sniffing the air, like some scenting animal. He forced himself down into the leaves.

His phone vibrated.

He dared not move, so let it buzz. And now – *shit* – the ring-tone, a stupid train whistle sound. Could the rider hear over the bike's engine? He watched the booted feet on the tarmac, unmoving.

And then the rider gave a flick of the wrist and the engine growled briefly and the booted feet lifted and the bike nosed slowly, warily, away.

He lifted one hand and pulled aside the leaves. More headlamps, but a car this time. Was that her? It was a red Mini, coming on fast. No time to dial her now. He eased himself up onto one knee and looked the other way. The bike's red tail light seemed to be receding. As the Mini got closer he readied himself, and then, when it was almost on him, he launched himself up and out into the road, arms up, waving. The tyres screamed against the asphalt and the car turned slightly in the skid and lurched to a halt. She was gesturing at him from behind the wheel, her eyes wide. He ran for the passenger side door, jerked at the handle. It was locked and he thumped on the window, bent down, mouthing at her *open the fucking door, please open it*. She was staring straight ahead through the windscreen. He followed her line of sight.

The motorbike was turning back.

The door unlocked with a *chunk* sound, and he wrenched it open, got in, slammed it shut and the Mini accelerated, Nicole's hands white on the wheel. The bike had turned and was heading towards them. He looked over at her, saw light sliding across her face, light from the rear-view mirror. He turned. Behind them, another bike, very close. She shifted slightly in her seat.

'Put your belt on,' she said, quietly.

The bike in front of them was veering crazily across the road and came to a stop, side on, thirty metres ahead.

'You're going to hit . . .' he said. But she had already clipped the front wheel, the *thunk* from the driver's side. He turned to see the bike spiralling away. He couldn't see the rider. He wanted to shout, scream at her, but nothing would come. He was grasping the safety belt in one hand, his seat with the other, his feet rigid against the floormat. The bike behind them was swerving, staying with them. Nicole accelerated suddenly, pulled away from it.

'Hold on to something,' she said. She stamped on the brakes, threw the car into reverse, turned in her seat leaving one hand on the wheel, and gunned the Mini backwards down the street, its engine whining. The bike behind them slowed and veered to the side. Nicole wrenched the wheel around and hit the accelerator. The Mini lurched at the bike. They shuddered to a halt in bushes, tree branches scraping the roof of the car. Kai saw a gloved hand against the rear window, then nothing.

Nicole, calm, jaw set, jammed the car back into drive and they took off down the street, Kai rigid and gasping with fright. They turned back on to the main road into the city centre. Nicole brought her speed down, took a deep breath.

From the villa outside Chiang Mai, Patterson watched it begin with a fascinated horror, piecing it together from the net. She sat in her room staring at her laptop, Cliff looking over her shoulder, Mac on the sofa, silent and hostile.

There would be no troops crashing down the alleyways of Beijing, because Fan Ping, the poorly tailored chairman of the high-tech behemoth and whorehouse, China National Century, she saw, was on tour in China's far south-west, Yunnan Province, dangerously close to the plotters' stronghold. He was due to tour a new manufacturing facility some eighty miles from the provincial capital, Kunming. The facility manufactured cellular repeaters, which, CNaC hoped, would speckle the buildings of all South-east Asia as the corporation's networks spread across the continent. The factory's managers stood, nervous and fidgety, in rows beside a red carpet.

But a Hong Kong journalist, representing an impudent web-based business publication and hoping for a fleeting moment with Mr Fan, remarked indecorously on social media that CNaC's chairman had not arrived, that the managers were perplexed and milled about, and a planned luncheon had been abandoned.

Fan Ping, chairman of all CNaC, progenitor of China's digital future was, in some fashion, indisposed.

His elder brother, Fan Rong, whose presence on the Politburo guaranteed the political fortunes of the clan, was also out of the capital, according to the papers. The previous day, said the *Chengdu Daily*, he had addressed the Party School there and had undertaken a tour of the factory at which the J-20 fighter was built, and was due to address a conference on organisational work in the national defence industry.

So where was he now? And the boy, Fan Kaikai?

She stood, pushed past Cliff, went to the window, reaching for anything, any course of action. But her sense of agency had left her, and the feeling of redundancy was overwhelming.

64

Oxford

Fan Kaikai was in Nicole's bedroom, the curtains drawn.

He had wanted to resist, but he had not known how. Her manner made him powerless. She was very cold, very calm as she drove them back through the city. He had tried to protest and she had spoken to him very quietly.

'What do you wish to do, Kai? Do you want to call the police again? Do you hope that the British police will come to help you? To protect you? The little detective? That black woman? Whoever the hell she was. Do you know who she was, Kai?'

He just shook his head.

She had forced him into the house, a hand in his back, in through the front door, the lock snapping into place behind them, two dead bolts which looked to be newly installed, he noticed. Then, up the stairs to the bedroom.

'You will stay here, without speaking, or moving, until I say you can come out.'

'What happened to Madeline?' he said.

She was looking at a handheld.

387

'Madeline went away,' she said absently. 'Anyway, she was too smart for you.'

'What did you do to her?'

'Me? I didn't do anything, Kai.' She gave him a smile of such intensity, such beauty, that he was rattled, and she turned away, making to close the door.

'Is she dead?'

She stopped, gave him a long look, as if she were making some sort of concession.

'No, Kai, she's not dead.'

It was dark. There were locks on the windows. He lay and shivered under a blanket, dozed a little. Sometime before dawn, he tiptoed to the door and opened it a crack, and she was sitting on the top stair, wrapped in a blanket, unmoving. Next to her, on the wooden floor, lay her handheld.

'Shut the door,' she said. 'It won't be long now.'

By the middle of the afternoon, Chapman-Biggs had composed a brief, pungent CX report. The report was reviewed, edited and cleared by Hopko and the Director, Requirements and Production, and C, the head of the Service himself. It was titled 'Indicators of Imminent Political Crisis in the People's Republic of China'.

It was, Chapman Biggs remarked to Hopko, one of the most important CX reports that the Service had produced in years, and Hopko did not disagree.

The report was read immediately in the Cabinet Office by the National Security Adviser and several members of the Joint Intelligence Committee. A crash meeting of the Current Intelligence Group for China set about drafting an assessment which expanded upon and contextualised its content. At the Foreign Office, the Director for China readied herself to interrupt the Foreign Secretary's evening. A Cabinet-level meeting was called for first thing in the morning. The report was sent to Langley, Ottawa, Sydney and

Auckland. A stripped-down version, scrubbed almost into invisibility, went to the European Union Situation Centre in Brussels.

Patterson lay awake in the hills outside Chiang Mai, her mind racing.

She threw the sheet off, padded in her underwear to the bathroom, splashed her face with water, drank from a plastic bottle. The ghastly limbo of the operational officer awaiting a decision, an order, an outcome.

She checked the website for further communications from Mangan. Nothing. From London, just:

standby>

She lay down again.

She listened to the hum and hiss of insects in the night.

The sudden import and complexity of the operation terrified her, sapped her will, even as her role in it shrank. She could feel the grinding of the machinery of national power, the abrupt gaze of powerful men, who, she was certain, would examine her and find her wanting, in her youth and amateurishness, her outsiderness, her *background*. The thought sent her stomach writhing. She sat up, hugged her knees.

Why was she so frightened of these people?

She hated herself anew for the self-doubt.

65

The Cabinet meeting was unusually short. The running was made by the Foreign Secretary, whose doughty certainties reassured the others at the table.

'It is clear to us,' said the Foreign Secretary, elbows on table, leaning forward, 'that any move by a group of military officers against prominent Chinese political and corporate leaders constitutes a serious threat to Chinese stability.' He paused. 'It is concomitantly clear that the interests of the United Kingdom, as well as those of UK corporate entities, will *not* be served by such instability. Nor will those of the global financial system as a whole.'

He took a sip of water.

'I have, by the by, spoken to my colleagues in the Treasury, in the financial regulatory apparatus and in the Corporation of the City of London, and they have made it *abundantly* clear that revealing the disposition of the Fan family jewels is neither possible nor desirable, nor legal, probably.'

The Foreign Secretary looked around the table.

'It *is* however, my view, that we should avail ourselves of this opportunity to relay to the Chinese leadership what we know of this impending political crisis.'

A short document was drafted.

Within the hour, the National Security Adviser and C made their way to a secure communications facility in the Cabinet Office building, where they oversaw the encryption of the document and its transmission as an email to China. The email went by way of a dedicated, secure line which led directly to the Communist Party Headquarters in Zhongnanhai. The Chinese account was managed by senior staff of the Ministry of State Security, who, by common agreement with the British, possessed an encryption key.

It has been brought to the attention of the government of the United Kingdom.

Her Majesty's Government takes the view.

The document named General Chen and Colonel Shi, both of 2PLA, as suspected conspirators.

It suggested a possible location for Colonel Shi, supplying GPS coordinates, lifted from the last known location of Mangan's phone.

The Service and cabinet office fully expected, and were prepared for, a barrage of questions and demands from the Chinese in response to their message. They were utterly unprepared for what came back.

It read:

Your message received and passed to responsible
departments>

And that was all.

Perhaps, someone suggested, they already knew.

It was about two hours later – barely any time at all – that Patterson saw the monitoring report from Hong Kong.

On a Hong Kong website, a blurred photograph snapped in the business class lounge at Beijing airport. An elderly man in a business suit held his hands out for the cuffs and glowered at the camera. A Chinese general, gushed the copy. Detained! In full view! A General Chen, along with several members of his retinue, were led away by paramilitary police and operatives of the Ministry of State Security, just before they boarded a flight to south-west China. On what charge, no one knew.

Minutes later Reuters came through with a two-line flash.

Patterson felt the entire operation lurch and stagger, felt the chill of failure creeping into her stomach.

She dialled Hopko on the secure handheld, knowing full well she hadn't thought it through, a voice in the back of her head whispering, *Don't do this*.

'Hopko.'

'Val? Trish. The General's arrest. Is it confirmed? How did they find out? Did we—'

'Calm down.'

'*Did we . . . ?*'

'Did you expect otherwise?'

'I expected—' but she caught herself. 'I'll go and get him, Val. I'll go. I'll get both of them.'

Hopko sounded distant.

'Mangan is a cutout, Trish.'

'Meaning?'

'I mean that he is on his own. For now.'

Mangan, exhausted, lay in a foul and roiled sleep as the day wore on, the mosquitoes whining in his ears. He had been bitten on his eyelids and they had swollen. The cell was fetid and sweltering. His hands beneath the cuff had regained their ugly, dark colour.

Earlier, they had come, Rocky and the Clown, and made him log on to the darknet site to check for messages.

standby>

Mangan, astonished, disheartened, looked at them, unspeaking. Rocky rubbed his chin, and the Clown shook his head and looked accusingly at Mangan. They snapped the laptop shut and left.

Later, the Clown had come with a bottle of water and plate of sandwiches that contained a vile pulpy meat paste.

Mangan tried to engage him.

'Tell me what the situation is,' he said. 'Let me message them again.'

The Clown said nothing, went to close the door.

'We should message them again,' called Mangan after him, and he could hear the pleading tone in his own voice. They took him to the bathroom, and he had diarrhoea. He walked unsteadily back to the cell, weak, depleted.

66

The rapping on the steel gate made Patterson jump. She leaped from the bed and hurtled down the stairs.

Cliff was there before her. He held his hands up to her.

'I'll deal with it,' she said.

'Let me,' said Cliff.

Irritated, she snapped at him.

'I will deal with it.'

'Boss, let me. I look the part.'

He was fresh from a shower in baggy shorts, flip-flops, a vest which showed his shoulders and arms, thought Patterson, to alarmingly good advantage. A prominent clavicle, smooth chest.

She breathed out.

'All right. Go.'

He nodded, as if accepting an order. Deftly done, she thought.

More rapping, loud, urgent.

He ambled across the courtyard, dragging his feet, slowing everything down. From outside, a voice in broken English, the accent Thai.

'Open, please. Police here.'

'Coming, coming,' said Cliff. Patterson watched from the doorway.

He worked the bolt on the door, creaked the gate open about a foot. Patterson could see a Thai police officer on the other side, the tight brown uniform, the cap. Cliff spoke, a tone of languid Kiwi surprise.

'Well, hello, officer.'

'Sorry to disturb.'

'Not a problem. What can I do to help?'

'We receive report that you are staying here, this house, but not registered with police.'

'Not registered with police,' said Cliff, blankly.

'Yes. All aliens must register with police. Local police station. You rent this big villa, so you must register with police.'

'Oh,' said Cliff. The police officer had one hand on the gate, was pushing it open. He was plump, bull-necked. He looked straight at Patterson, then scanned the courtyard. Behind him, Patterson saw a squad car and another, unmarked car. At its wheel, a man in plainclothes, craning his neck to see into the courtyard.

'Well,' said Cliff. 'I do apologise. I had no idea. We will come and register at the police station tomorrow. What time should we come?'

'OK, so we come in please.' The policeman gestured.

Cliff waited a beat. The man was getting out of the unmarked car. And another. Both in jeans, polo shirts. One chewed gum.

'Would you like us to come now, to register?'

The policeman just gestured with his chin. Cliff opened the gate. The policeman walked into the courtyard and the two in plainclothes moved to come in behind him, but Cliff had taken a chance and shut the gate on them. The police officer glanced over his shoulder for them, but he was alone. He frowned, looked at Cliff, but something in Cliff's movement, his face, dissuaded the officer from complaining.

'How long you stay?' he said.

'Six days,' said Cliff, with a smile, making it up.

'Passport.' Patterson handed him her passport. Cliff walked into the house, took his from a table, came back out. The officer gave them both a cursory glance.

'I look inside.'

'Be my guest,' said Cliff, a look to Patterson. Nothing to be done. The policeman walked into the villa, through the living room, stuck his head in the kitchen, then looked down the gloomy passage towards the annexe. Where a small arsenal, lovingly cleaned and oiled, was laid out on the bed.

They came back once more as the evening progressed and the cell darkened, kicking the door open, the Clown barking at him. The Clown hauled him to a sitting position, didn't take the cuff off this time. They made him kneel and tap in the passwords one finger at a time. Rocky stood over him smoking, trembling. Nothing from London. Nothing from Patterson. Rocky turned and paced, one hand in the air gesturing his fury. He spun and shouted at Mangan.

'Why?'

'Why what?'

'Why they not answer?'

'I don't fucking know. Let me message them again.'

'What will you say?'

'I'll . . . I'll ask for clarification. Something.'

'Tell them they must respond.'

'I will tell them.'

Rocky was looking straight at him, exhaling smoke through his nose. He pointed at Mangan.

'I am disappointed,' he said.

'Not as disappointed as I am. But what did you think they were going to do?'

'I think they should cooperate.'

'Why? Why would they cooperate with you?'

Rocky's eyes were widening. He leaned over as he spoke, as if forcing the words from his body.

'Because we are the future. We can be. *We* can be the face of China.'

He was breathing heavily.

'A *humane* future. You know that word, humane? In Chinese we say *ren*.'

He had steadied himself, lifted a finger.

'From Confucius.'

He was rubbing his eyes, mumbling.

'Very important, this *ren*. It is how the ruler must rule. With *humaneness*. Just like the parent with the child. Like that.'

You are repeating yourself, thought Mangan. You are falling back on what you think you know. You, the attacker, the insurgent, are now on the defensive. He shifted on the concrete floor.

'Let me message them.'

Rocky's head had fallen, he was staring at his feet.

'Nothing to say.'

'When's the General coming?'

'He's not coming.'

Mangan swallowed.

'Why not? Why is he not coming?'

'Because he is too good. He gives himself for this. And we have failed here.'

'How have we failed?'

'Because of your people!' Rocky was screaming now, the muscles in his neck taut as cable. Mangan could smell him, saw his spittle flecking the air. 'Your people. They betray us, maybe. Did they?'

Mangan turned his head away.

'What are you going to do?'

'What should we do?' Rocky spat. 'What we do with you? Shoot you maybe?'

And as he spoke the Clown gestured for them to be quiet. And they found themselves listening to the *whump whump* of rotor blades pulsing on the air.

The Thai police officer walked purposefully down the passageway, the light failing now. Cliff was behind him, moving easily in a way

Patterson knew well, the shoulders dropped, arms loose, hands open, ready to move very fast, very hard.

The police officer slowed before he reached the back room, put his hand on the butt of his sidearm. Patterson saw him, silhouetted against the light, poke his head around the doorway, then enter the room. Cliff stayed close to him, Patterson followed.

The police officer had stopped in the middle of the room, hand still on his weapon. Mac lay on one of the beds, reading a magazine.

No sign of the weapons, the ammunition, the body armour, the duffel bags. A faint smell of oil on the air, windows open.

Mac lowered the magazine, glanced up at the police officer, a surly expression.

'What's this?' he said.

Cliff cleared his throat.

'The officer says we need to register. Which of course we shall. At the station. He is just checking up on the house.'

Mac looked the officer up and down, nodded, went back to his magazine.

'You stand up,' said the officer.

Mac lowered the magazine again, slowly swung his legs off the bed, stood. His every gesture exuded knowingness, one-upmanship. Why do they do this, these men? thought Patterson. Why do they act out these little scripts?

'Passport.'

Mac walked to the end of the bed, a half-smile, reached into a jacket pocket, gave him the passport. The policeman took it, barely glanced at it, threw it on the bed.

'What you are all here for?'

'Vacation,' said Patterson. 'We are going to do some trekking, in the hills.'

The policeman looked at her, then walked towards her.

'You are going on trek,' he said.

'Yes,' she said.

He turned to Cliff.

398

'You married to her?' he said. 'This woman?'

'No,' said Cliff. 'Just friends.'

'Girlfriend, yes? You have a nice black girlfriend?'

Cliff gave the warmest of smiles, said nothing.

'What are you doing here?' said the policeman. Cliff shrugged.

'Like she said, officer. Holiday. Some trekking.'

The officer walked to a sideboard, ran his finger along its surface, lifted the finger to his nose, sniffed. He walked to the bathroom, looked inside. Then, without a word, he left the room, walked quickly back to the living room, out into the courtyard, to the gate. He opened it. The two other men were waiting for him. They spoke Thai. One of the two men, the gum-chewer, was insistent, snappish, tried to pressure the policeman to do something. But the officer shrugged, pushed past them and walked back to his car. Patterson, mouth dry, walked over to close the gate, and the gum-chewer gave her a look of pure hatred.

'*Huanying lai Taiguo,*' she said, quietly. Welcome to Thailand. The man, hearing Mandarin, looked at her sharply, shook his head and went back to his car. She closed the gate.

'Who were they? The other two?' said Cliff.

'China,' she said. Cliff arched his eyebrows.

Inside, Mac stood waiting for them, a triumphant look on his face. He made a magician's *ta-da!* gesture.

'Where are they?' she said.

'In the duffel bags and over the back wall, sharpish,' he said, pleased with himself.

She forced herself to give him a nod of acknowledgement.

'We leave. As soon as it's dark. Start loading,' she said, too curt, too quick.

They went to the back of the house. The bags had fallen into a thicket of some ferocious gorse-like plant, and Cliff picked his way through the thorns, swearing. They loaded the weapons into the SUV. Mac insisted on having one of the MP7s under the driver's seat. The darkness was coming on. Patterson jogged the road outside their house, half a mile in both directions, looking for surveillance. She couldn't see it, though she was sure it was there. She stopped in the road, listened to the whirr of the insects, the jabbering of some night bird in the trees, felt the warm movement of air against the sweat on her face.

A Chinese team was in bed with Thai law enforcement.

So *move*, now. Be a hard target.

Mangan, if he is to get out, will come by the river, or by road through Myanmar. If he sets foot in China, it is over for him.

She bent double, breathed deep, tried to still the quaking in her chest. What was this? Fear? She'd never been frightened before a fight. Fear of failure? Perhaps. Fear of inadequacy. That's the fatal kind. She'd seen it in soldiers, in Iraq. Wild-eyed second lieutenants way out of their depth as the smoke cleared and some boy bled out by the side of the road. They'd make absurd decisions, demand their orders be followed.

She jogged back to the villa.

They sat in the kitchen, ate instant noodles and drank coffee in silence. Just before midnight, they drove slowly out of the gate, lights off, Mac at the wheel, Patterson with a satnav in the front seat, Cliff in the back with a pair of night-vision goggles. They bumped onto the road and made their way north-east, towards the Mekong.

67

Rocky and the Clown moved for the cell door, ran out into the corridor. The Clown turned and slammed the door shut. The noise of rotors had grown louder. Mangan estimated them to be a mile away. Had they landed? He sat, his back against the wall, listening. He raised his swollen hands, the cuff biting, placed them against his lips. They pulsed with heat. He wondered if they were infected. The skin on his fingers felt distended and tight. It hurt to move them. He wondered at his own deterioration. They had done so little to him, but his strength was fading astoundingly quickly, replaced by something timorous and shaky. He forced himself to stand, tried to get ahold of himself. He jumped up and down, rolled his head on his shoulders, shook out his legs, breathed.

He listened again. The rotors were still chattering. He walked to the door and kicked it, kicked it again, put his shoulder into it. The door juddered but did not give.

And then the door was flying open and there was Rocky. He wore a golfing jacket, a backpack slung over his shoulder, his sunglasses on, failing to mask the panic. He ran to Mangan, an old man's splay-footed run. He took Mangan's arm, spoke in Mandarin, and Mangan smelled the alcohol on him.

'Listen. We leave now. And we go to your people. Yes.'

'Tell me what is happening.'

'We leave. I have a way.'

'You need to tell me.'

'Two helicopters. I don't know. They are coming. Someone is coming.'

'Who?'

Rocky's face creased in an agony of frustration.

'I don't *know*. How they find us?'

'You're not making sense. For God's sake. Who has come?'

'Listen to me. This will make sense. We go now, back to the river. I have a way. We go to your Service. I come with you. I have so much to give. So much. *Networks*, Philip. I give them to you, to your Service. Whatever they want. You remember? The J-20? How we stole the skin from the Americans? Yes? I can tell you. I can tell them. The agents, everything. Protocols, finance. *Everything!* But if we stay here, I think the next ten, fifteen minutes become quite ... unpredictable.' He gave a ghost of a grin, but the look in his eyes, behind the shades, was imploring. Mangan saw the pulse in his neck, the sweat on his lip.

'Get me out of these.' He put his hands out.

Rocky looked confused, pulled at the plastic cuff, then fumbled in his backpack, brought out a sponge bag, a pair of nail clippers, and worked at it until it snapped. Mangan tried to flex his fingers, but they were bloated, tight.

Rocky looked like an expectant child.

'You do not get out without me, Philip, you know this. So, now we go, yes. Together.'

'You're a shit.'

'Together. To your people.'

'I'm not making you any guarantees.'

'My guarantee is what I know. *That* is my guarantee. Very valuable. Your Service will want everything. Everything.'

Mangan swayed slightly. He felt suddenly dazed, sick. Rocky took his arm again, began pulling him towards the door.

'Come, I have a way. You come, and then we go to your people.'

Mangan lurched out of the cell, struggled to think clearly.

'We need the laptop. My bag. We need them.'

'No time.'

'We need my passport. Handheld. Laptop. To contact the others.'

Rocky swore, yanked Mangan to the lift, then changed his mind. They took a dark emergency staircase, emerging four floors lower, in a hotel corridor. Rocky stopped, looked both ways, moved quickly to a door, waved an entry card.

In the room, the Clown stood at a window, watching the lawns, the illuminated fountains, the black river. The rotors were loud – close. The Clown turned and glanced at them, seemed unconcerned.

'*Qu nar?*' he said. Where are you going?

Rocky didn't reply, tried to assert himself, walked across the room to where the laptop and Mangan's bag lay on a bed.

'What is happening out there?' said Mangan.

'They are coming for us,' said the Clown. 'That is what is happening.'

Rocky was putting the laptop in the bag. Mangan saw his own retro pistol lying on the bedside table, the star on the butt.

'What has *happened*? Will somebody bloody explain?'

'We thought we were coming for *them*. We thought we were coming for the Fans, for all their whores and cronies and bastards. But it turns out, in an unexpected irony, that they are coming for *us*,' the Clown said. He gestured out across the grounds. 'However the fuck they found us. Two helicopters. About twenty of them, twenty-five maybe. Maybe more coming by road.'

'Where's your ... your general?' said Mangan. Rocky stopped, looked up.

The Clown shrugged.

'Somewhere outside Beijing. They picked him up at the airport. Took him to some facility, a villa, maybe. State Security has plenty of those places. Interrogation places. Very quiet. They took him yesterday, it turns out.'

He turned and looked at Mangan.

'Oh, and his daughter disappeared, too. In England, of all places. Just gone. That's why we had to move, to set everything in motion.'

He had cocked his head to one side.

'Madeline. No sign of her anywhere. Did you have anything to do with that?'

'Don't be bloody ridiculous.'

The Clown stood very still.

'We have Fan Ping of course, emperor of CNaC. And the bitch of a sister, Charlotte. That might buy us something, some time, maybe.'

Rocky had his hand over his eyes.

'But I wonder,' said the Clown to Mangan, 'if you are still worth anything? What you might buy us. I suppose we'll have to see.' His eyes flickered across the room, to the door.

Mangan lunged for the bedside table, the weapon, brought it up. Its weight told him it was loaded, the butt cool against his reddened, swollen hands. He levelled it at the Clown, whose expression remained unchanged.

'We are leaving,' said Mangan.

From behind him, Rocky spoke.

'Shoot him.'

The Clown's gaze shifted to Rocky.

'You fucking whore,' he said.

'Shoot him!'

Mangan sighted on the Clown, saw the foresight wavering across the man's face and neck, felt the trigger tensile beneath his forefinger. The Clown didn't move, just stared, his eyes black as carbon.

Mangan brought the trembling foresight to the Clown's neck, his chin.

I have murdered before.

'Do it, Philip.'

I murdered a man by a highway, at night, as the cars roared past.

'Do it.'

I didn't even know his name.

The Clown's eyes, the contempt in them.

The foresight was sliding down the Clown's chest, stomach, groin, pulling away to the side when Mangan squeezed the trigger. The weapon barked, tried to kick free of his hand and the report clanged around the room. The Clown lurched sideways, his feet stuttering, but the round smacked harmlessly into the wall. Mangan brought the weapon up again, and the Clown was shouting something at him.

Rocky had slung the backpack and was going for the door. The Clown turned and spat at him. Rocky didn't stop, wiped the saliva from his face with his cuff. Mangan followed him, keeping the pistol levelled at the Clown.

'You little fucking whore,' the Clown shouted. And then they were running down the corridor, Rocky leading. Another emergency staircase, down six floors. Mangan was nauseated, out of breath, knees weak.

'We need to stop. To signal.'

Rocky calculated, then pushed open a fire door. They knelt in a corridor, Mangan fumbling with the laptop, opening it, booting it, barely any charge to it. He searched for a power socket, tried to plug it in, realised he didn't have an adapter.

'For God's sake, faster,' said Rocky.

He found the wireless signal, went to the darknet site. His hands were shaking.

'So where? Where will we be? What do I tell them?' he said.

'Tell them I am bringing treasure.'

'Where?'

'You tell them. I have so much. They must take me. Please tell them, Philip.' His voice had taken on a wheedling tone. Mangan was repulsed by it, angered even.

'Jesus Christ. Where?'

'Tell them the same place we left from. By the river, the dock. Chiang Saen. Tomorrow.'

Mangan paused. Did he have it in him? He did, apparently.

'What treasure?'

Rocky stared at him.

'Forgive me, Philip, but perhaps we do not have time for this right now.'

'What treasure?'

Rocky shook his head, adopted a flabbergasted look.

As artificial as every other face you show to me.

'Networks, Philip, I will give them *networks*. I told you before.'

'What do you have, Rocky?'

Rocky leaned into him, close. Mangan could smell his breath, see the panic behind his eyes. Rocky was starting to gabble.

'I will give them the threads, and then they pull on those threads. They pull on them. And ... and they watch the networks unravel. Europe, Japan, even America, Philip! Military, State Security operations, things I know, things I've heard about. Leads. Threads. I will give them this.'

Mangan looked at his colonel, this man coated in betrayal, then typed, dropped it on the site.

They crashed through a pair of double doors and were back on the casino floor, in the blue light, the golden glimmer of the tables, the air thick with perfume, cigars.

The clients were streaming for the exits, the girls in black at the poker tables were unplugging their headsets. Someone was shouting, on the very edge of panic. One of the sex show girls stood on the stage, naked, her hand up to shield her vision from the spotlight, trying to make out what was happening.

Rocky began to run across the floor, Mangan behind, the weapon stuck in his waistband. Rocky was elbowing people out of the way, and some were starting to get angry. He pushed a woman in a white silk sheath, and her ankle, perched atop absurdly high heels, suddenly gave, and she went down onto her knees with a shriek, dropping a sequined purse. Mangan felt a hand on his arm, which he flung off. People were becoming disoriented. A Russian was shouting, waving his phone in the air. A Chinese man in a grey suit was scooping up chips in great handfuls from a table. And then they were out into the atrium lobby, and Rocky was running ahead, making for huge glass doors. The heavies in cream suits were jittery, looking for direction, murmuring into their walkie-talkies.

Mangan felt it first, rather than heard it, a wave passing through the air, the panic rising, a surge of voices, a scream, and behind it a clatter, a crackle. Breaking glass. He turned. On the other side of the atrium, just leaving the casino floor, six or seven men in black fatigues, body armour, ski masks, were moving along the walls. They were loose-limbed, fit, Mangan could see. They carried machine pistols and moved easily. One was down on a knee, giving orders with hand signals. The clientele were backing away from them, some raising their hands, but the men in black ignored them.

Rocky gave a kind of squeal of fear, and they were crashing through the doors, out into the night.

68

The crowd spilled from the floodlit building. Mangan heard rotors and engines. Limousines and black SUVs were speeding away into the darkness. A group of women in evening gowns clutching purses were attempting to board a small bus. Men in suits were riding mopeds, bumping across the lawns.

They ran away from the building, past fountains, beds of orchids, out of the light. Sweat was running into Mangan's eyes, stinging. He looked over to where he thought the river was, saw a helicopter hovering, a searchlight trained on the dock, the *thunk thunk* of its rotors. Rocky was ahead of him, running doggedly, splay-footed, the backpack bouncing up and down. They ran deeper into darkness, towards the trees, and then they were forcing their way into undergrowth, out of sight. They pushed on, following the tree line, moving parallel to the river, the ground rising. Mangan was slowing, his chest pounding, ribs hurting badly now, specks dancing in his eyes.

'I have to stop,' he said.

Rocky slowed, turned.

'What? Are you mad? No stopping.'

'Just for a minute.' Mangan bent double, retched, spat. 'How much further?'

'Two kilometres. Maybe three. Something. We must go.'

'Just wait, for Christ's sake.'

Mangan looked out from the tree line. They had gained some height. He saw that the vehicles speeding away from the complex had been stopped by a roadblock. A queue had built up, drivers leaning on their horns. The helicopter was still over the dock. He saw its searchlight, the river's glitter. He could just make out shadowy black figures moving about outside the complex, a scattering of the clientele still on the steps, the lawns, some pulling suitcases on wheels. And then, to the edge of his vision, a flicker of movement. A man had come out of the building by a side door and was running across the lawn in the same direction Mangan and Rocky had come. Mangan touched Rocky's arm and pointed.

'It's him,' he said.

Behind the Clown, three of the black-clothed figures were moving fast, effortlessly. They were catching him. The Clown half-turned, saw them just yards behind him and ran for the tree line. But the three of them were with him in seconds, and one did something with a foot and the Clown was down, rolling on the grass. One of the men had him covered with a weapon. Another grabbed him by his jacket, hauled him to a sitting position. The Clown had his hands up as if trying to fend them off. They seemed to be talking. One of the men delivered a hard kick to the Clown's midriff, but the Clown carried on talking, gesturing to the tree line. The three men in black all looked in unison towards the trees.

'Shit,' said Rocky.

'What?' said Mangan.

'He's told them.'

'What? Told them what?'

'Where we're going.'

Two of the men had shouldered their machine pistols and stepped away from the Clown, who sat on the grass, leaning on one hand. The third man, the one covering him, moved in closer. A fraction of a second later there was a mild *tap tap* sound on the air and the Clown slumped quickly to the side. The man repositioned himself. *Tap tap*.

Mangan felt the falling sensation engulf him, as if something deep and heavy inside him were yawling through space, drawing his stomach and heart down, and for an instant he was quite lost; he felt himself going over, caught himself with one hand in the cool damp earth, leaf litter. He held himself there, a prickling rising up his back, a flushing in the face, the feeling that his bowel would open, that he'd shit. Rocky was whispering something, the same thing over and over. Mangan couldn't make out what it was.

More people were running now, women in gowns and mini-dresses, men in tuxedos, the croupiers, scattering across the lawn. Someone was screaming. A moped was describing a wide circle across the grounds, looking for a way out. The three men had left the body crumpled on the lawn and were loping towards the tree line. One was using a walkie-talkie. They moved with a powerful, unhurried grace. Rocky was pawing at him. He stood, stumbled on into the wet dark. Rocky had them on some sort of path, beaten earth, patches of mud, puddles, the surge and ebb of insects. Mangan felt himself retreating inward. *This is how it works*, an inner voice was telling him. This is how fear works, when you are here rushing through the heat and the night and the new appalling knowledge of it all.

I am present at the hatching of my terror.

They ran, upward, in the darkness, Rocky keeping a punishing pace towards the top of the rise. Mangan thought of the men coming through the trees. Rocky took them off the path, into undergrowth. It slowed them, and made their progress noisy, so they went back onto the path. After eight or ten minutes, Mangan thought he heard footfalls some distance below. He stopped, his chest a furnace, hissed at Rocky. They listened. Not so far behind now. Rocky, bathed in sweat, was clenching his fists. He gestured urgently, making a sign to go right. They cut off the path again, quietly. A downward slope, then a wrecked wire fence. Mangan saw a darkened building silhouetted against the night sky, Rocky running for it, up steps, through a splintered and rotting wooden doorway. A long corridor, something soft and squelching beneath their feet, and a stench of mould, disrepair.

'Where the fuck are we?'

'Quiet! Just follow.'

Mangan could see almost nothing; he blundered behind Rocky, a crunching of broken glass underfoot, up more stairs, the banister damp, slimy. A frenzied flutter of wings above him scared him. Bats? Then rotors, *thunk-thunking* in from the direction of the river, and everything was glowing. He looked up at shafts of light boring in through holes in the roof. He looked around himself. Rocky had dropped to one knee, staying very still, head down, one hand over his eyes to protect his night vision.

They were in a wreck of a place, wooden panelling splitting from the walls, vile, sodden carpet scattered with filth. In the sudden light Mangan saw abandoned gaming tables, a vast *fu* character on the wall, spilling golden chips into a red, glittering ether, streaked with slime. The rotors deafening now, the beams playing around the room.

Still. Stay still. They see movement.

The helo repositioned, the beams stalking away, playing along the outside wall now, hunting. Rocky was up and moving, through two more reeking gaming rooms of mouldering baize and rusting slot machines, to a window, crouching. Mangan came up beside him. The searchlight was scanning the front of the building. And there, briefly illuminated, as the beam painted them, the three men, standing on the cracked concrete forecourt, one pointing, another checking his weapon. What were they waiting for?

Mangan forced the words out, his voice someone else's.

'Do you have a plan? Are you going to tell me what it is?'

'There's a boat. A fast boat. Driver is waiting. I keep him there, in case. We go there.'

Mangan closed his eyes, shook his head.

'We can't go back on the river.'

'Yes, fast boat.' Rocky patted the air, a *calm-down* gesture.

'We can't.'

Rocky rounded on him.

'Where do we go, then? How else? You want to drive? Hundred and twenty miles through Myanmar to the Thai border? You want that? Or walk maybe? Or maybe we follow those cars, the mopeds back into China. You want that? What do you want?'

The men had started to move towards the building. Rocky swore, reached in one of the pockets on his vest, brought out his handheld. He poked at the touchscreen.

'Come,' he said.

They ran towards the back of the building, down a long dark corridor lined with what appeared to be hotel rooms, the doors splitting, the jambs warped, holes in the drywall, a smell of fouled drains. Rocky laid the handheld down on the carpet. He took Mangan by the arm and they went further down the corridor. Rocky motioned him to lie down. As his eyes adjusted to the darkness, Mangan made out at the far end of the corridor a window to the night sky. Rocky was rummaging in the backpack, had pulled out something, but Mangan could not make out what it was. Mangan pulled the sidearm from his waist, but Rocky hissed at him.

'*No!* No shooting, Philip. Let me do this.'

They lay there, three minutes, four. The alarm went off on the handheld, a gritty, metallic whine. The handheld pulsed silver, forty feet from where they lay, casting a glow on the walls and ceiling. The whine grew louder. Another minute passed. Still, the alarm whined.

Silhouetted against the window, now, shapes flitting, very slow, very silent. Two, or three?

They were coming.

Mangan felt Rocky shift, very slowly, bring up whatever it was he was holding.

The first of them approached the shrieking handheld, weapon to his shoulder, scanning, the muzzle stroking the air. The man knelt, reached very slowly to pick up the device, and as he did so he looked up.

From Rocky's hands shot a silent, flickering, green beam.

The beam played down the corridor, scudding over the walls, ceiling, running over the bodies and the weapons and the faces of the three men. Mangan saw the eyes of the men as tiny points of light in the darkness as the beam touched them, watched the men jerking away. A thud, a weapon dropping to the floor? A shout. *Zenme?* 'How?' Then a wail, turning to a scream. And one of them was trying to run, hitting the wall, thudding away down the corridor, Mangan could see his lurching silhouette. Another got some rounds off, silenced, their *thop thop* in the darkness over the screaming of the alarm, but Mangan couldn't tell where they were going. He forced himself downward into the carpet, felt specks of plaster falling on his hair. The green beam was still playing down the corridor, the handheld's alarm screeching now, distorting. The first of the men, the one who had gone to pick up the handheld, was on all fours, one hand over his eyes, blind, gasping, his breath catching, chest heaving. His cheeks were wet, liquid dripping through his fingers. And the thought skittered across Mangan's mind that he had never seen anything so brutal.

They ran, took another stairway down, and fled through a fire door into the night, over an expanse of shattered concrete and rubble, making once again for the trees. The helicopter loitered over the building, didn't see them go.

69

Mangan was close to collapse when they came on the boathouse. Rocky, pulling him along, soaked in sweat, bright-eyed, maddened, hammered on the door, Mangan falling to his knees. An old man in faded blue denim beckoned them in. Mangan couldn't stand, crawled into the boathouse, which was lit by a single bulb, the river slapping and shimmering against a tiny concrete dock. The boatman regarded him, spoke in broken Mandarin.

'Who is he?' he said.

'Never fucking mind. Get him on board,' said Rocky.

The boat was a wooden thing with a flat bottom, twenty foot or so, two powerful outboards on the stern. But the boatman was pulling up panels.

Christ, no.

'How long will it take?' Rocky was saying.

The boatman shrugged.

'Go fast, no stop, maybe ten hours.'

And then Rocky and the boatman were pulling him onboard and forcing him down. He tried to struggle, pushed against the boatman's arms of corded muscle, felt the man's hands like clamps on his shoulders. He thought of the weapon for an instant but couldn't reach it. They made him lie down on the same foul, sodden rubber mats, and Rocky was lying next to him, and the boatman dropped in a bottle of water, then the panels came down and the light was gone, and the boatman seemed to be hammering them back in place.

Mangan heard himself emit a scream, battered his fists against the planking, thrashed with his legs, but the engines started, drowned everything out. The wood felt slippery, soapy, against his fingers. He could see nothing. The boat started to move, the water bubbling beneath the hull. His breath was coming shallow and fast, panicky, the air hot and soaked with the stench of the river.

'Are you there?' he said.

'Yes.' Rocky's voice was tight, straining over the engines.

The boat was starting to pitch and jerk with the river's chop.

'This is our coffin.'

'No, no.'

'I cannot do this.'

Rocky was speaking, but he could hear nothing over the engines, the vibrating hull, the slosh and slap of the water. The boat pitched mercilessly, Mangan scrabbling for purchase against the wet wood. He was sodden, deafened, weak with panic, when his mind suddenly flooded with a childhood memory.

At a fairground, he had been urged onto a ride, a drum that started to spin, flattened you against the wall and held you there as the floor fell away. He was terrified, loathed it and cried and wet himself, and his mother had pulled him away and taken him home and his father had not said anything, smoked his pipe. Damp with piss, he had sat and watched television, an animation, singing animals in a herb garden, his mother telling him not to be babyish. The animals' songs looped in his head – *I'm Dill the dog, I'm a dog called Dill* – as the boat crashed down on the water and the engines screamed. He tried to shout to Rocky. *Should have told the polygraph man about that. So he could calibrate me.* But the words came out blurred, knotted, half-formed.

He was retching, choking, drifting, receding.

By three, Mac had them hard by the river, just outside Chiang Khong. They stopped by the bridge, looked across the water. Mac turned off the car, and the night was silent, no traffic, just the effervescent insects.

'Now what?' he said.

Patterson ignored him. She had the laptop out, was cabling it to the sat phone, searching for a signal.

CX BRAMBLE

PLAN ARRIVE CHIANG SAEN BY RIVER WITHIN EIGHTEEN HOURS.

COORDS 20.261048, 100.094416. EXPECT TWO FOR EXFIL. EXPECT CX>

She said nothing, showed Mac the message, then Cliff, who nodded. 'So we park up and wait,' he said.

Mac started the car and they nosed up the road. Chiang Saen, she calculated, was about thirty miles. They settled on a rutted track behind a temple, a stand of bamboo and palm trees hiding them from the road. Mac put his chair back, tried to sleep. The heat was oppressive, even in the pre-dawn. Cliff got out of the car and ambled a way off, stretched, shook out the stiffness. Patterson watched him go, then got out and followed him. He turned a corner in the track, slipped from view.

When she caught up with him, he was murmuring into a secure handheld.

She walked back to the car, the disappointment aching in her.

At the beginning, she thought, we are in control. And then control slips from us. Who is in control now? Who are we serving?

Late evening at VX. Hopko, her left wrist wrapped in a beaten silver spiral, glasses poised in mid-air for emphasis. Tonight, thought

Chapman-Biggs, she is embattled. She demands the attention of the crowd with her smoky charisma, her knowingness, but she has choices to make.

She had a screen set up in her office. Chapman-Biggs, Mobbs, C, and a cluster of other Service worthies studied it.

'The reports,' she was saying, 'are filtering out from the Hong Kong press and are as yet, unconfirmed.'

She looked around the table.

'They report odd troop movements in Beijing. Social media is showing images of a cordon around Party Headquarters at Zhongnanhai.'

Click.

On the screen, a photograph of Chang'an Avenue, shot at night from a moving vehicle, the image soaked in orange, the street lamps streaked across it. Before the vermilion walls of Zhongnanhai, security barriers lining the street. A column of *wujing*, the paramilitary police, snaked away past five or six armoured crowd control vehicles.

'The embassy is being roused from its stupor. Foreign reporters are trying to get down there, but they're being stopped before they can get close.'

She turned and studied the image.

'And we're seeing messages on social media saying roads in and out of Beijing monitored, checkpoints and what have you. They're deleted as soon as they appear.'

Click. Beijing airport, more armoured vehicles on the approach road, *wujing* lining the shoulder.

'And we have Chinese bloggers, God bless them, declaring that troops of the Capital Garrison and all Beijing Military Region have been ordered to stay put in barracks. Normally something we'd discount, but Cheltenham say they're seeing something strange. A big military exercise in Inner Mongolia has gone silent. Airwaves should be crackling with signals, but they're not. Everyone's stopped work. Or gone home. Reduced Air Force activity, too. The People's Liberation Army seems to be on hiatus.'

She smoothed her hair.

'So this is what it looks like.'

'What what looks like?' said the Director.

Hopko sighed.

'China coming undone.'

C, arms folded, his head cocked at her, spoke.

'I don't think that's going to happen though, do you?'

Hopko waited a moment.

'I wasn't aware it was up to us.'

C laughed, a harsh little bark, spread his arms wide.

'But, Valentina, we have exercised extraordinary leverage, wouldn't you say? We've been able to warn, to advise, even provided them with first-rate operational intelligence, the pinpoint location of key plotters.'

He paused, watched her through his rimless spectacles, and then rammed it home.

'And all due to your superb tradecraft, Val, your peerless operational planning.'

And it was there, for a sliver of a moment, that Chapman-Biggs saw Hopko reel.

'I hope they are grateful,' she said.

'Oh, they are. They contacted us twenty minutes ago.'

'And?'

'The Chinese Communist Party thanks us and welcomes our intervention on behalf of security and stability in the face of criminal plots.'

No one said anything. Then C spoke again.

'Oh, everyone is grateful, Val, everyone. They're, well, relieved, frankly, not to have to think about all those Chinese accounts in Jersey and Cayman.'

She had put her glasses on the table in front of her and sat looking at them, with her hands in her lap.

'Foreign Office is thrilled,' C went on, 'to be basking in Beijing's approval. Anticipating all sorts of goodies, they are.' He nodded, but she had had enough.

'Did they say anything else?'

'Oh, if you mean did they say anything about Mangan, yes. Yes, they did. Said they had no knowledge of his whereabouts. Which I took to mean that if he can skedaddle, they won't go out of their way to find him, wring him dry and shoot him. Rather generous of them, I thought. Given his history.'

A long, awkward silence. Chapman-Biggs felt himself on the very edge of saying something, anything to fill it. Until C finally broke it.

'They do, however, want HYPNOTIST, of course.'

Hopko put one hand on the table, palm down.

70

He came and went over interminable hours. He heard Rocky talking, shouting at him, once felt Rocky's hand on his shoulder, understood nothing over the engine roar. The boat lurched upward, crashed down onto the water relentlessly, over and over and over, hurling the two of them about the sodden compartment. Mangan writhed in the filth, sometimes present, sometimes deep inside himself, in chaotic whorls of thought and memory, teetering on the edge of hallucination, entangled in semi-conscious dreams of punishment, of a beating he'd had as a child looping in his mind, the voice of the master as he bent, *I'm going to give you twelve and I don't want to do it but I will*, and the thwack of the shoe echoing away into his mother's voice, scolding him for something intangible, something forgotten in everything but her tone of voice, his awareness of it, standing in the kitchen, the back door open, the smell of mown grass from the garden. *I am present at the hatching of my doubt. I am present as it lives in me and grows old with me.*

Sometimes he was just gone, oblivious.

Once, he was aware of the engines cutting out, orders shouted through a megaphone. The boat wobbled and tipped as they were boarded. And then the grumble as the outboards restarted, and it began again.

Then, hours, weeks later, a slowing, a calming. The engines idled, the movement lessened. He heard the boatman's feet, the creaking and straining of the wooden panels.

The sunlight was blinding. He felt the boatman pull him from the compartment, lay him down, pull a canvas tarpaulin over him.

'Thailand water now. You can lie here.' He imagined Rocky was there beside him but he couldn't tell. He slept.

Cliff pulled the vehicle off the road just to the south of the jetty, shielded from the road. He and Patterson clambered down to the water's edge. The river was brown and sullen. They sat in silence amid thorn bushes. They took it in turns watching through binoculars, swigging water from a bottle. She had one of the sidearms under her shirt. Cliff had another. The MP7s were with Mac in the car.

At around nine-thirty in the morning, a fishing boat, its orange paint flaking, pulled onto the jetty, and a dark, spindly man in shorts tied it up and stepped out, but it was too early, she thought.

Later, a launch, peopled by portly men with clutch bags and sunglasses who struggled to clamber ashore, fussing and offering each other a hand, their purposes on the river entirely unclear.

Water birds skimmed the river. Midges floated around her. They sat in silence watching the water.

And then, at nearly midday, hugging the Thai side of the river, there crawled towards them a flat bottomed boat of the sort used to transport desirable items from place to place along this stretch of the Mekong. A single boatman aboard, but as Patterson refocused, she could see a green tarpaulin in the bottom of the boat, covering something.

Bodies?

The boat was moving slowly, cautiously, towards the jetty, the boatman craning his neck, searching the shoreline.

'That's him. Agreed?' she said.

'Agreed,' said Cliff.

'We do it quickly. Get them to the car and go.'

'After he touches the jetty, should be two minutes, tops,' said Cliff. His voice was calm, supportive. For a moment, she felt reassured.

'So we go.'

She stood, exposing herself to view, and started to walk along the bank. Cliff was right behind her. The boat was a hundred metres away. She climbed onto the jetty. Cliff stayed down on the bank, watching her back. She could see Mac getting out of the car, scanning the road. The boatman saw her, and the engines came alive and the boat sped up its approach, the prow lifting, flecking the brown water white. The boatman brought it up to the jetty, turning it deftly at the last second, so it glided in side on, the engines cutting out.

And there he lay, covered by a tarpaulin, filthy, pale, hollow-eyed, accusing her with his look.

And next to him, kneeling, HYPNOTIST, the look anticipatory, a gesture, something of a wave, or the offering of a hand.

They were moving fast now, Cliff bounding up onto the jetty, into the boat, lifting Mangan to his feet, helping him onto the dock, where he stood, sodden and shaky, silent. Then HYPNOTIST, Cliff handing him out of the boat. The Chinese man was in better shape, went immediately to Patterson and began to speak.

'I am Colonel Shi Hang of the Chinese People's Liberation Army—'

Patterson cut him off, spoke fast, in military.

'We know who you are, Colonel—'

'And I wish to defect.'

'We must move now, talk later.' Cliff was behind him taking an arm. Mac was waiting, the car doors open. Mangan just stood like a drowned dog. Cliff began marching HYPNOTIST up the jetty to the car.

She went to Mangan.

'Let's go, Philip. Let's get you out of here.'

He looked at her, that level look, and then down at his feet.

'Come on, Philip, everything's all right. Let's move.'

He began to walk shakily up the jetty. She took him by the elbow. He felt clammy and she could smell something fetid coming off him.

'Quick as you like, then you can rest.' She urged him forward.

Ahead of her, she could see Cliff, his hand still clamped on Rocky's arm, standing a short distance from the car, looking towards the road, in the direction of the town.

She followed his eyeline. Some distance away, two vehicles were moving at speed towards them. She shouted.

'Get him in the car.' She was dragging Mangan now. He was shaking his head, his face crumpling.

Rocky was gesturing towards the SUV, looking expectant. *Time for me to get in?* Cliff was nodding, smiling, seemed to be telling him to relax. Patterson propelled Mangan forward. Mac jogged towards them to help. He had one of the MP7s on a strap, snug against his chest. Together they manoeuvred Mangan into the back seat of the SUV. Patterson climbed in next to him. Mac was quickly around the car to the driver's seat.

The two vehicles were closing fast, no more than a quarter of a mile away now.

'Cliff,' Patterson shouted. 'Now.'

'Coming, boss.' But still he just stood there.

Rocky was starting to get frantic. He turned his body, tried to break for the car, but the New Zealander held him.

The first of the two cars was slowing, coming to a halt about thirty metres away. The driver and another man got out. Both of them appeared to be Chinese. Both wore sunglasses. They just stood by the car, left the doors open. The second car pulled in behind.

Cliff walked Rocky a few yards towards them, then let him go, gave him a shove that sent him a few steps towards the men in sunglasses, the cars. Rocky stumbled slightly, then stopped, looked back at Cliff, realisation dawning.

Cliff turned and started walking quickly towards the SUV. Rocky was running after him, shouting something. The New Zealander turned back to him and held a hand palm out.

'No,' he barked. 'Not you.'

Patterson was out of the SUV quickly.

'What the fuck!' she shouted. But Mac was in front of her, shaking his head. She pushed past him. He made to take her arm but she rounded on him with a snarled 'Don't.' He backed away, half-smiling. The men in sunglasses were still standing by their cars, waiting patiently.

Mangan had dragged himself from the SUV and was leaning against the driver's side. Rocky shouted to him, his voice quavering.

'Philip. Tell them. I have very much. I am request to defect. I have treasure, Philip. Tell them.'

Mangan mouthed something, but Patterson couldn't hear what it was. She was approaching Cliff, stood in front of him, hands on hips.

'Why?' she said.

He just shook his head.

'Orders.'

She could hear Rocky shouting about defecting, information.

'Why was I not told?'

He shrugged.

'Don't shrug at me. Who gave you these orders? Why?'

He leaned down and put his face close to hers, whispering.

'I don't know why. Do the calculation. Someone doesn't want him. And they couldn't depend on you.' He straightened, turned back to Rocky, made an *off-you-go* gesture, dismissive, offhand. Rocky just stood there, and Patterson saw him put one arm across his front in a protective gesture and then dig his fingernails into the other forearm. He looked as if he were about to cry. The men in sunglasses waited.

Mangan leaned on the bonnet of the SUV. The metal was warm beneath his hands. Rocky, his *joe*, stood alone in a no man's land between the two cars. The men in sunglasses stood very still, watching. Cliff was barring Rocky's way. Patterson stood behind him, hands on hips, raging.

His mouth was sticky and dry. He tried to raise his voice.

'They'll shoot him. If you do this.'

But no one seemed to be listening.

Rocky was appealing to him. *Philip, I have treasure! I wish to defect!* He raised a hand and pointed first at Mangan and then at himself. *You and me, Philip!* Mangan pictured him in the Paddington safe house, grinning his elastic grin, leaping from affect to affect – *See my wry humour! And now my gravitas! And here is intimate, confiding me!* – spilling secrets as the smoke from his cigarette curled in the afternoon light.

Cliff had turned and was walking back to the SUV. Time to go, he was saying. Patterson was rigid. He had never noticed her height before, how tall she was, how physically powerful. In her fury, all her physicality leaped out, her powerful arms, the cords in her neck, the way she held her space. But in her eyes, shock, vulnerability.

Rocky was shouting at him.

'Okay, Philip, okay. I come with you now, yes?'

And then he was rushing for the SUV, darting past Cliff, towards Mangan. But Mac was on him hard, wrestling him backwards, then with a short, fissile punch to the side of the neck. Rocky staggered, his face dissolving into pain, but kept his eyes on Mangan. The two men with sunglasses took a step forward. Mac, grunting, once again forced the colonel away from the SUV, back towards them. Rocky looked behind him, saw the two men advancing on him, looked back.

And then Philip Mangan made the move, the move that, much later, would validate all Hopko's faith in him, the move which would always shock Patterson in its operational clarity of mind, its calculation.

Mangan took several steps towards Rocky. He spoke in Mandarin.

'You can still hurt them,' he said, quietly.

Rocky was looking at him

'You can still hurt them. Give it to me,' said Mangan.

Rocky turned and looked once more at the two men in sunglasses, and when he turned back his expression was one of pure malice.

'Give it to me, Rocky. Give me the thread. The thread that will lead me to the networks.'

Rocky spoke, his Mandarin a furious, urgent rasp.

'I give you this. You use it. Suriname. Paramaribo. 76 Prins Hendrikstraat. Lawyer, surname Teng. Find him, Philip.'

'If I find him what will I find?'

Mac was shoving him away. Mangan shouted at him.

'What will I find?'

Rocky stood there in the heat, the insects, hair awry, dripping sweat, forsaken.

'You'll find the thread. Use it, Philip.'

The two men in sunglasses were still biding their time. But Mac and Cliff had Mangan by the elbows and he was suddenly face down on the back seat. Doors slammed. The engine started. Cliff put the window down, shouted at Patterson.

'Coming?' he said.

She looked at her feet for a moment, then went to the SUV, got in the back without saying anything.

'Right decision, boss,' said Cliff. And he jammed the stick into reverse and hurled the vehicle backwards and into a turn. Mac rounded on Mangan.

'What did he say, at the end, there?'

'I don't know.'

'What did he fucking say?'

Mangan looked away from him, back to where the colonel stood in the road.

The two men were on Rocky now, and as the SUV sped away, Mangan saw them taking him, forcing his arms behind him, his head down. His mouth was open and he seemed to be tensing up, resisting them, and then Mangan saw him go hard to his knees in the dust.

71

They drove hell for leather for Chiang Mai, did it in just over four hours, Mac wrestling the vehicle through sheets of rain, riding the shoulder at one point to get past traffic jams, Cliff watching the mirrors. Patterson signalled 'Clear' from her secure handheld, sat back, closed her eyes. No one spoke. Mangan slept. They stopped just once, next to a river. Cliff took Mangan's pistol and threw it into the water.

At the Banyan guest house, Patterson took the street, while Mac kept the vehicle running. Cliff walked Mangan quickly up the stairs. In the room, Mangan washed and changed quickly, took his luggage, retrieved the passport and money from behind the cistern, and the two of them were back in the vehicle in eight minutes. They ducked and dived through Chiang Mai, watched their back, headed for the airport.

Mac pulled in at Departures, let them out, stayed behind the wheel, wordless. Cliff got out, helped them with their bags, stood there, tall, his easy posture, running a hand through his long hair.

'It's been a pleasure,' he said.

'Wish I could say the same,' Patterson replied, turning away, the disappointment eating at her.

'It's just work,' he said, to her back.

She rounded on him, but Mangan put a hand on her arm, turned to Cliff.

'You've killed him. You know that,' he said.

Cliff shrugged.

'I haven't. They will. Anyway, he wasn't ours. He had his own agenda.'

Mangan nodded.

'And we had our own agenda, it seems.'

Mac was knocking on the window, gesturing to Cliff to get back in the car. Cliff nodded, held up a hand for him to wait a minute. He looked at the two of them.

'You two,' he said, pointing first at her, then Mangan, then back at her. 'You're doubters. You infect each other. Make each other weak.' He nodded, then turned abruptly and got in the car, put the window down as Mac started the engine, gave them a last look.

'Doubters,' he said, and he patted the outside of the car door. Mac pulled away, headed, Patterson assumed, to some safe house in a darkened Thai town somewhere, some tourist place where they'd blend in, the house squatting behind high walls, with its cheap furniture and window blinds, mattresses with plastic covers, its empty fridge and mismatched crockery, the weapons cache beneath the floorboards, the comms equipment in black flight cases. And there they'd sit, cleaning and oiling the MP7s in the lamplight, stowing the body armour, watching the football on satellite television, before flitting away to their next mission. She watched the car disappear in the afternoon light.

She booked herself onto a flight for Bangkok due to leave in an hour. She'd just make the overnight to London. Mangan wandered away, and she found him in the restaurant, sitting at the bar, drinking a beer. He seemed exhausted, a gaunt, collapsed look to his face.

'They want you back in London,' she said. 'They want you to come in.'

'Not yet,' he said.

'Soon, though.'

He just nodded. She sat on a stool next to him.

'What did you mean?' she said.

'When?'

'When you said to Cliff, we had our own agenda.'

He shifted on his seat.

'I'm so naive, you know.'

'Why?'

'I was labouring under the impression that I was doing a job, performing a function. But I wasn't, was I?'

He took a pull on his beer. Patterson waited.

'They knew it was a lure: Hopko, all of them. They just needed a warm body to go out and bite on Rocky's hook. A deniable warm body.'

Patterson shook her head.

'She intended you to run him. And she worked very, very hard to get you out.'

'Rocky got me out.'

They sat in silence for a few seconds.

'Who benefits?' he said.

'What do you mean?'

'From all this. Who benefits? *Cui bono?*'

She felt a wave of exhaustion.

'I don't know, Philip. You, me, the money men, Western civilisation. I don't know. Signal when you're coming in. And make it soon.'

She reached for her bag, made to go, but he took her arm, spoke quietly.

'He gave us a lead.'

'What lead?'

'Right at the end, just before we left him there. A lead into a network.'

429

'What fucking lead?'

He was gazing at her, the level look, the one that saw you and didn't miss things, the one that was curious and generous, that waited for a response in kind. She felt a pricking in her throat, behind her eyes.

'Philip, don't,' she said.

'I won't,' he said.

'Don't do anything.'

'I won't.'

'And don't be long.'

'I won't,' he said.

She reached out to him and he took her hand. She felt the pressure of his fingers, his skin, the intimacy of it.

'Doubters,' he said, 'the two of us.'

And then it was her turn to walk away, into the airport concourse, towards the gate.

Who benefits?

72

London

Charlotte Fan had been found, the detective inspector reported to Hopko. Chen's people had been holding her at one of their safe flats in Watford, but they'd done a runner. Madame Fan had climbed, half-naked, through a window, run down the street to a newsagent's babbling about a plot to destroy China. Someone had called the police.

Her captors were god-knows-where by now. The police had taken her to a doctor, who pronounced her tired but unharmed, and then to the Kensington apartment, where family retainers had fussed over her, and she made tearful calls to China. And when the detective inspector had been able to get a word in, her nephew, the boy Fan Kaikai, had woodenly repeated, as if from a script, that everything was fine and there was nothing for UK law enforcement to concern itself with and no charges would be brought, even if her kidnappers were found. And Madame Charlotte Fan would be leaving the country as soon as possible for rest and recuperation in Hong Kong and possibly Macau and, no, it was highly unlikely she would be able to appear in court should such an opportunity arise. And at this point a fresh gout of tears engulfed Madame as she ascertained that her beloved brother, a great titan of Chinese industry, had been found in the city of Kunming – locked in an upstairs room at a military guest house – and returned to the bosom of the family, and the well-being of his person was no longer in doubt, and Madame sat and sobbed and shrieked as the cook and the maid wrapped her in blankets and brought cups of ginseng tea.

And the boy just stood there, with this stunned look on his face. Like he couldn't believe what was happening to him. As if he were utterly disgusted with something.

The detective inspector paused, let his memory work.

There was, he said, another woman present. She stayed close to the boy, hovered behind him, watched him, made sure he stayed on script. Rather striking, youngish, beautifully turned out. The expensive sheen of a woman who knows her way around Knightsbridge, Manhattan, the first-class lounge.

Just a family friend, she'd said, no name.

But the detective inspector saw on her the knowingness of one who has the full measure of events. And when he'd tried to talk to her, she had flitted away. Disappeared.

When the police had gone, and Aunt Charlotte had been escorted wailing to bed, Kai put on a baseball cap and shades and slipped from the apartment and walked to Park Lane. It took him a little while to find a public telephone. He dialled.

'This is DC Busby.'

'It's me. You talked to me, in my college.'

There was a short silence.

'I remember, yes.'

'I couldn't talk freely.'

'I rather assumed that was the case.'

'The woman, with you.'

The detective hesitated.

'What about her?'

432

'Tell her I . . . I will talk to her. I'm ready.'

'What makes you think she would want to talk to you?'

'Tell her. Please,' said Kai. And he put the phone down.

Who benefits?

A question that Hopko, coiffed and steely, all in black today, tight black shirt open at the collar, a leaf of silver at her throat, black pencil skirt, black boots, was only too willing to address with her customary obliqueness.

'Mangan wants to know who benefits? Well, I suppose we all do, don't we? China is saved from itself, quietly, and is grateful. We are saved from the prospect of China's unravelling. The status quo benefits, wouldn't you say?' She forced a smile, but it did not spread to her eyes. 'I'm told there was considerable relief in the City of London and the major financial centres of Europe and the United States. Instability in China gives them the collywobbles.' She made a flourishing movement with her hand.

Patterson was muzzy-headed from the flight, lack of sleep.

'I'm not sure that answer would satisfy him.'

'Well, he shall have to remain unsatisfied. At least until we can talk to him directly. Where the hell is he, anyway? And when is he coming in?'

'He needed time.'

'Don't we all,' said Hopko. She reached for a file on her desk, pulled from it a printout, a newspaper article.

'He'll see this, I imagine,' she said.

It was from the *Bangkok Post*.

'Chinese Officer Dead in Laos Casino'

They'd found him in his room, sprawled on the bed, white foam at his mouth, skin bruising. Local police sources hinted at an overdose. The casino was a few miles upstream from where they'd left him head down, kneeling in the dust.

Patterson sat heavily, smoothed her hair.

'We could have brought him out,' she said.

Hopko didn't speak.

'You knew, didn't you?' Patterson said.

'Knew what?'

'That he wasn't coming out. You thought that he and Mangan . . . that neither was coming out.'

Hopko was silent, then pursed her lips and spoke.

'Trish, I'm sorry to say you are being taken off the China beat.'

Patterson felt a flush of heat in her face, the prickling of shock.

'You will leave the P section and you are to be posted.'

'Posted?'

'To Washington. It's a Requirements position. Not operational, I'm afraid. You'll assist in the conduct of liaison, intelligence sharing.'

Patterson looked down.

'It's not such a bad outcome,' said Hopko, slowly.

'Do I get to ask why?'

'Human Resources, in two words.' She smiled. 'She will be happy to explain, no doubt.'

'Could you not have stopped it?'

'Possibly. But I didn't.'

Hopko paused, then spoke, her tone understanding.

'Trish, an intelligence officer is not a soldier. Your agents are not the objects of your empathy, the way soldiers under your command might be.'

Patterson stood on shaking legs.

'Have I failed? How?'

Hopko sighed.

'Human Resources thinks that you are . . . unreliable. That you are a little too *singular*, was the word she used.'

'*Singular?* And do you share this opinion?'

'I think that you have yet to . . . to fully encompass this work. I think you have yet to understand fully what it is we *do*. And besides, we all have to live out a period or two of exile.'

434

Patterson held up a hand to stop her speaking, walked from the room.

She went back to her cubicle, through the silent corridors.

On her handheld, a voicemail, from the policeman in Oxford. DC Busby.

Our friend says he wants to talk. And you never heard it from me.

She picked up her bags, took the lift, swiped herself out of VX. She walked to the bridge, leaned on the railing. The Thames was full of chop, glittering in a stiff breeze, hard sunlight. She looked across to the other bank, up towards Westminster.

And for a moment Patterson saw not a country but something else. Something adorned with the trappings of country, for sure, the Union Flags billowing from the rooftops, the curve of the river, the grandiose architecture of the state. But, in that instant, these things seemed merely a surface, a patina, and she felt the movement of some deeper musculature running beneath, the pulse of power and intention, its horizons far beyond the Thames, beyond London, elusive, virtual.

Cui bono? Who benefits?

She felt childish, gullible.

She took a taxi back to Archway and once in the flat she dropped the bags, undressed, pulled on jeans and a baggy T-shirt. She opened a bottle of cheap red, sat on the sofa, drank and watched the light dim as the afternoon clouded over. She went to the silent bedroom, got beneath the covers, pulled her knees up to her chest and held herself.

What should she have done? What should she do now?

She should have told Hopko that Mangan had a lead.

She should have told her that the Fan boy wanted to talk.

But she hadn't.

After Patterson had made her shaky exit, Hopko had risen from her desk, crossed the room, and closed and locked the door to her sanctum. She went to one of three black safes that lined the wall behind her desk, kneeled, and on the safe furthest to the left entered a combination on a digital key pad. From inside she took a plastic envelope that held a secure handheld and an index card. Hopko placed the envelope on her desk, took out the handheld, turned it on, checked to see that the battery had some charge to it, and dialled a number written on the index card. The number had attached to it the prefix of a Caribbean country. She waited a moment. The number rang and was answered, not with a greeting, but with an accented male voice reciting a short list of numbers and letters. Hopko responded in kind.

'*Ja?*' came the voice.

'The situation is resolved,' she said.

'*Dankjewel.*' And then a digital *pip*, and silence.

Sumatra, Indonesia

Mangan was aware of the faint glimmer of dawn, a gentle persuasion of azure in the eastern dark. He listened to the waves on the beach. Far off in the night, he could see the lights of tankers in the Straits of Malacca, imagined the throb of engines over the black, churning water.

He had boarded a flight to Medan at the last minute, found a rattletrap taxi to drive hours through the night, stopping to eat at a roadside *warung*, nothing more than canvas stretched over a bamboo frame, plastic stools, a hurricane lantern reeking of kerosene. He ate *gulai* with his fingers, a scrawny chicken stewed in coconut milk, turmeric, garlic, caraway. The proprietor brought him an Anker beer, offered him a *kretek*, which he took and lit, the sugar on his tongue, clove-laced smoke hanging on the air.

It had been three in the morning when they reached the place, a speckling of splintered huts on a stony beach he knew, and he shamelessly roused the owners, pressed a wad of rupiah on them, and they gave him a mosquito net and water, waved him to a cabin in the darkness. His ribs ached, and his hands were discoloured and numb.

The silver flicker of lightning in cloud, high above the sea.

They want me to come in, he thought.

The hiss of water on shingle.

But I won't. Not yet.

He thought of Rocky, wild-eyed, sweating, hissing at him a name, a lead, a thread to pull on. He thought of an unravelling, an unblinding. He felt the draw of it, a taut wire in his veins.

I am present at the hatching of my choices.

He watched the lights of the ships across the relentless, heaving sea, watched them recede into the warm dark.

ACKNOWLEDGEMENTS

As ever, my profound thanks go to Catherine Clarke, Michele Topham, Caroline Wood and all at Felicity Bryan Associates. My thanks go in equal measure to Ed Wood and Iain Hunt and their colleagues at Little, Brown. I am very fortunate indeed to be working with all of them.

I was introduced to Ethiopia by two remarkable journalists, one who showed me Addis Ababa and its environs, and another who took me to Dire Dawa and Harer. Their insight, generosity and commitment to their craft made a very deep impression on me. They showed me their beautiful, haunting country as it teeters on the brink of change, and they introduced me to extraordinary people, thinkers who are charting Ethiopia's future and pondering China's role in it. They bought me coffee, too, the like of which I have never tasted. I wish I could name them, but recent events in Addis Ababa make that impossible. I am so very grateful to them. They reminded me that journalism as practised in many countries requires of its practitioners a kind of cold courage unfamiliar to most of us.

As I imagined a world of contemporary espionage, I took advice from a number of people, some of whom know the trade and also can't be named. They know who they are and my heartfelt thanks go to them. The book *Chinese Industrial Espionage: Technology Acquisition and Military Modernization* by William C. Hannas, James Mulvenon and Anna B. Puglisi has been an invaluable reference, as has the work of Peter Mattis. However, the world depicted in the novel is my creation and mine alone.

During the writing, help and support came from David Abramson and Kelly Hand, Robert Bickers, Warren Coleman, William Davison, Mike Forsythe and Leta Hong Fincher, Kim Ghattas, Paul Hayles, Ronen Palan, Jeff Wasserstrom, and the wondrous folk at Goldsboro Books in London. My warm thanks, too, to the staff of the public libraries in Takoma Park, Maryland, and Takoma, DC, especially Ellen Arnold-Robbins and Patti Mallin.

Finally, I am grateful for the generous portions of inspiration, advice, love, humour, perspective and solace provided daily by Susie, Anna and Ned.